Praise for Elaine Everest

'A warm tale of friendship and romance'
My Weekly

'Captures the spirit of wartime'
Woman's Weekly

'One of the most iconic stores comes back to
life in this heartwarming tale'
Woman's Own

'Elaine brings the heyday of the iconic high-street giant
to life in her charming novel'
S Magazine

Christmas with the Teashop Girls

~

Elaine Everest was born and brought up in north-west Kent, where her books are set, and has written widely for women's magazines – both short stories and features – as well as fiction and non-fiction books for the past twenty-three years. Successful in writing competitions, she was shortlisted for the Harry Bowling Prize and was BBC Radio Kent's short-story writer of the year in 2003.

A qualified tutor, she runs The Write Place's creative writing school in Hextable, Kent. Elaine lives with her husband, Michael, and their Polish Lowland Sheepdog, Henry, in Swanley, Kent.

You can say hello to Elaine on
Twitter: @ElaineEverest
Facebook: Elaine Everest Author
Instagram: @elaine.everest
Website and blog: www.elaineeverest.com

Elaine Everest

*Christmas with the
Teashop Girls*

PAN BOOKS

First published 2020 by Macmillan

This paperback edition first published 2020 by Pan Books
an imprint of Pan Macmillan
The Smithson, 6 Briset Street, London EC1M 5NR
Associated companies throughout the world
www.panmacmillan.com

ISBN 978-1-5290-1592-8

1 3 5 7 9 8 6 4 2

A CIP catalogue record for this book is available from the British Library.

Typeset by Palimpsest Book Production Ltd, Falkirk, Stirlingshire
Printed and bound by CPI Group (UK) Ltd, Croydon, CR0 4YY

MIX
Paper from
responsible sources
FSC® C116313

Visit www.panmacmillan.com to read more about all our books
and to buy them. You will also find features, author interviews and
news of any author events, and you can sign up for e-newsletters
so that you're always first to hear about our new releases.

For my saga author friends xx

Prologue

~

Christmas Eve 1940

Rose Neville felt extremely sick – so sick, in fact, that she couldn't lift her head from where she lay. It was if her whole body was trussed up like the chicken her mother, Flora, had prepared for their Christmas Eve meal at Sea View guesthouse. She wriggled, trying to free herself. Was Lily behind this? Her friend was always one to be over-generous with the sherry. No doubt someone had helped her to bed, and then tucked her in too tightly to stop her falling out.

Rose opened her eyes, but could see only darkness. Fear gripped her heart as, deep inside, she began to realize something wasn't right. She made an effort to breathe slowly and deeply until the sickness passed a little, then tried to wriggle free again, gradually finding that at least her fingers and toes were working. This reminded her of the times she'd been on board Mildred Dalrymple's fishing boat, out in the Channel beyond Ramsgate Harbour, when waves of sickness would flow over her until she found her sea legs. She stopped wriggling and sniffed; come to think of it, she could smell a mixture of engine oil and fish. And whatever she was lying on felt too hard to be her own comfortable bed.

A small groan from nearby prompted her to lean as best she could towards the sound. 'Who's there?' she called, fearful of who else might be in the room.

'Rose?' came Flora's voice in reply. 'Where are we? What has happened?'

'Mum!' Rose almost screamed, then thought better of it in case whoever had put them on the boat was still aboard. 'Are you hurt?'

'I don't think so. I feel rather wobbly, and more than a little sick. My head aches — it's as if I've been bumped against something hard. Can you reach me?'

'No . . . I seem to be trussed up and tied to something. I've moved as far as I can towards you,' Rose replied, doing her utmost not to sound frightened in case it worried Flora. She had no idea if her mum's injuries were serious.

'Then stay where you are; I'll shuffle towards you. My hands are tied behind my back and my ankles are tethered together. Keep talking, so I know where you are.'

Rose swallowed hard. Never had she wanted her mum by her side more than at this very minute. She pulled hard on the ropes that bound her, but could tell the ones around her hands were attached to the boat. Making good use of the time it would take for Flora to reach her across the few feet that divided them, she closed her eyes, trying to remember the layout of Mildred's small fishing boat. There was a wheelhouse towards the front, where Mildred steered and controlled the boat. It was just about large enough for a second person to stand alongside her while she worked. Rose knew they were most definitely not in that area. Even in the dark, everything seemed to be in the wrong place and out of reach.

It was late on Christmas Eve, and judging by the way this boat was being tossed about, they could not be moored in the relative safety of the harbour – they must be out in the open channel. She forced herself to concentrate on her mental image of Mildred's boat. Further back, it was open to the elements – that was where the fish were hauled in, along with the crab pots. The only other space was below deck, where Mildred kept her equipment along with a small, hard bed for long journeys, and a gas-ring stove. A door at one end led to the engine room.

Rose realized that they must be below deck, where they were unlikely to be seen or heard; not that anyone would be looking anyway, in the dark and out at sea. But why were they here?

'Ah, here you are,' Flora said as she wriggled alongside Rose. 'It's as dark as the night in here.'

'It's Mildred's boat,' Rose said, in case her mum wasn't aware. 'I'd know it anywhere.'

'I know, love. It even has the smell of Mildred about it.'

Despite their predicament and feeling afraid, both women laughed.

'We really need to get free of these ropes; then we won't be at a disadvantage if anyone comes back who wishes to do us harm,' Flora said. 'What I intend to do is wriggle down to where your feet are and see if I can unpick the knots in the rope around your ankles. It's going to be hard, as my wrists are bound tight and I just have my fingers to work with. Hold on,' she added as she shuffled along on her bottom until she was close to Rose's feet.

After what felt like an age, Flora gave a quiet but triumphant cheer and Rose felt the ropes fall slack around her ankles. She shook them loose and stretched her legs, enjoying the freedom. At least now, if anyone came back, she would be able to kick out at them. That's if this hadn't been part of an elaborate joke. 'I may be able to reciprocate and untie your feet,' she said to her mum.

'See if you can pick apart the knots at my wrists first,' Flora said, leaning as close as she could. 'Go slow and steady,' she instructed as Rose started to pick.

By the time Flora's hands were free, Rose's fingertips were swollen and sore. Gingerly, Flora pulled herself to her feet, feeling the low ceiling above her head. 'I'm going to find the hatch to see how far out at sea we are.'

'Be careful, Mum. There may be someone up on the deck,' Rose said fearfully, hoping Flora would hurry and release her wrists. With them bound, she knew she couldn't do much if anyone came below deck.

'There's no sign of anyone. It's pitch black out there, from the little I can see,' Flora called out. 'We could be anywhere. Why would anyone do this to us? Has something happened at Sea View, do you think?'

'I have no idea. My head is fuzzy, and I can't remember much,' Rose said, feeling her head spin. 'I really need to get up and move about before I'm sick. Lying here is not helping. Do you think you can release me, then I'll help you with the rope around your ankles? Be careful, though,' she added as Flora stumbled to her side.

'I could have untied my own feet if I'd been thinking straight. Silly me,' Flora tried to grin, fighting off a sob. 'Who would do such a thing?'

Rose could only shake her head. She had no idea.

Once the women had freed themselves, they stood up and rubbed their cold, aching limbs. Rose felt along the side of the boat until she came across a cupboard, and began to rummage about. 'I wouldn't be surprised if Mildred has a drop of something in here that we could drink to warm ourselves up. She always used to, although she told me it was medicinal,' she laughed, her tinkling voice echoing through the small boat. 'Here we are . . . although have no idea what it is,' she added as she tried to pull out the cork.

'Take it over to the hatch. There may be a label you can read. The last thing we want is for you to poison yourself.' Flora shivered. 'Perhaps we should be looking for a blanket. I don't know about you, but I'm frozen to the bone wearing just my best frock and no cardigan.'

'At least you have your best pinny on,' Rose smiled, although she too was shaking due to the cold. 'It's another layer of clothing.'

As they made their way to the open hatch, Flora slipped her hand into the pocket of her crossover pinny and gave a shout of delight. 'Ah! We won't starve,' she declared, waving a carrot above her head. 'I'd gone to the kitchen to find a carrot for young Pearl to leave out for Father Christmas's reindeer. I was returning to the front room, when . . .' She shook her head in confusion. 'I don't remember what happened after that.'

Rose slipped her arm around her mum's shoulder,

sensing her fear at not remembering. 'I went out to the kitchen to see where you'd got to, as Pearl was ready to post her letter up the chimney to Father Christmas. The light was off in the hall, and then . . . and then someone grabbed me and put something over my mouth and nose. I don't know what happened next,' she said with a sob. 'This isn't a game, is it? Thank goodness Pearl didn't follow me, or she could have been hurt.'

The women clung together, trying to comprehend what had happened to them. From outside the hatch they could hear the drone of planes approaching. 'Oh God, that's all we need. The Luftwaffe will spot our boat in the moonlight – we are a sitting target!' Flora cried. 'Perhaps we should dive into the sea and try to swim for it? Get away from the boat before it explodes?'

Rose cuddled her mum, trying to soothe Flora's ragged breathing. She could see, when the moon appeared from behind the scudding clouds, that they were far from shore. Even on a summer's day it would be a long swim, but today, Christmas Eve, they'd catch their death in the cold water before they got anywhere. 'Shh, listen. There's not been an air-raid warning. We'd hear it, even this far out at sea. Those planes must be our lads coming back to Manston. Don't lose hope yet. Come on, let's get up on deck – but we need to be careful as we have no idea what has happened to our abductors. They could still be nearby.'

Flora looked around her warily. 'No – whoever has done this is not on board. Someone will be in trouble,' she added as she looked towards Ramsgate, pointing her finger. 'There's a light showing. Probably one of the pubs' kicking-out time. The landlord's a bit tardy, letting the light show like that. I'll have to remember to tell the wardens at our next ARP meeting.'

Rose smiled to herself. Did Flora never stop thinking of her war work? 'I wonder if I can remember how to steer the boat. It's been a while, and I always had Mildred helping me,' she said, thinking back to her childhood days helping Mildred bring in a haul of fish. Whiting, cod and skate, she thought, as the lessons Mildred had taught her came flooding back. Heading to the front of the *Saucy Milly*, she stopped and quietly swore to herself. Someone had run a heavy chain around the wheelhouse and secured it with a hefty-looking lock. They didn't mean anyone to get inside and start up the engine. Perhaps, Rose thought, if she dropped anchor, the boat wouldn't head out any further into the Channel – and they could sit tight until they were spotted and rescued? But this plan was soon scuppered when she found the anchor missing. Someone had meant to make sure they would not return.

The two women sank down onto the deck and sat leaning against the wheelhouse. Rose squinted at her watch as the moon appeared for a few seconds. 'It's midnight. Happy Christmas, Mum,' she said, thinking of the busy day they'd had planned. There seemed to be no hope of that now, unless someone come to rescue them before their abductors returned.

1

September 2nd 1940

'Oh Miss Neville, I'm that thrilled for you,' the young Nippy exclaimed as Rose walked into the staffroom of the Lyons teashop she managed in Margate. 'Fancy being engaged to an army captain! Show us your engagement ring?'

Rose smiled at the girl standing in front of her. 'Thank you, Edie. I'm afraid I don't have the ring yet – my fiancé is having it altered. His grandmother's fingers were larger than mine,' she explained as she looked down at the slim fingers of her left hand, thinking back to the moment Ben had slipped the ring on after formally proposing.

'You mean it's second-hand, Miss? I'd have thought a posh bloke like him could have afforded to buy you something new,' Edie said, giving her a pitying look. 'When my sister got engaged to her chap, she had a new ring, and he's only a corporal.'

'You are a silly child,' a familiar voice said from behind Rose. 'Do you not know that Captain Benjamin is a man who comes from the landed gentry of England? What our

9

Miss Neville is to be wearing on her finger will be an ancient heirloom,' Anya Polinski reprimanded the girl. 'Show some respect to our manageress,' she added with a dismissive sniff, looking down her nose at the younger woman – something that was easily done, since Anya stood a head taller than most of the staff in the teashop.

The younger staff members were unsure of their Polish colleague, who always carried an air of authority even though she was just like them, albeit a 'Sally' who looked after the front counter of the Lyons teashop, where she served customers with all manner of goods. The older staff found her helpful and knowledgeable, although they too were in awe of the woman who'd left her homeland and come all the way to Thanet in search of her pilot husband, Henio. When the couple had been reunited, more than one Nippy had been heard to sigh at the romance of it, remarking that Anya's life was straight out of an edition of *The People's Friend*.

Rose clapped her hands together to gain the attention of the other Nippies and Sallys. 'Ladies, we have but fifteen minutes before the doors open to our customers,' she said with a smile, before taking a look at the notes in her hand. 'I would like to inspect your uniforms first, and then I will give you some news about a few staff changes that will affect our work here at the Margate teashop while I'm away in London. I trust you all to carry on your hard work while I'm absent.'

This was met with excited chatter and nods of agreement before a hush fell as Rose walked along the line of Nippies, checking their black uniform dresses, white cuffs and collars were clean. 'Annie, your hem is coming down.

You will find thread and needles in the drawer,' she instructed a newer Nippy, nodding towards the large table where the staff sat while taking breaks for their meals. 'There is also red thread, for any of you who have loose pearl buttons,' she added as many of the women ran their hands down the fronts of their dresses, where two neat rows of white pearl buttons ran from their collars to the waistbands of their crisp white aprons.

'Please, Miss Neville, I have a ladder in my stocking. If there is time, may I change it? I didn't notice until I was on my way to work,' an older Nippy asked.

'Most certainly you may.' Rose smiled, pleased that her team took such pride in their appearance. She'd not found one dirty fingernail, and each worker had clean, shiny hair underneath the white starched caps bearing the Lyons badge. Rose made a point of supplying soap, towels and brushes for them to scrub their nails and have a wash at the teashop, in case they hadn't been able to do so at home. Since the terrible bombings only weeks earlier, she had made it her mission for each member of her staff to be able to wash, wear a clean uniform and have a filling meal inside her, so that they could all go home to their families and face whatever the Germans next threw at them. She knew some of the staff had been made homeless and were relying on family and friends to put them up while they found alternative accommodation; others continued to live in their bomb-damaged homes.

Rose shuddered as she thought back to the day of the bombings. Most of the townsfolk in her hometown of Ramsgate had taken refuge below ground, in the tunnels, which had certainly saved many lives. In Margate, residents were not so lucky – they didn't have a warren of tunnels beneath their town. Fortunately, the bombing had not been so fierce these past couple of days.

'I need to supervise the delivery man,' Anya said, as banging was heard at the back door of the teashop. 'Yesterday he forgot my bloomers,' she muttered, looking surprised as all about her started to titter. 'You English, you act so strange; I will never understand you,' she huffed as she left them to their meeting.

Rose tried not to join in with the laughter, even though she found her friend's words as funny as her staff had. Anya seemed tetchy these past few days, she thought. She must try to find time to talk with her before heading off to London. At least there she would be free of the bombing that had ravaged Thanet in past weeks. With Ramsgate being one of the closest points to France, and Manston airport nearby, the seaside town was in more danger than the capital. Rose had spent many a long hour stuck, along with her friend Katie, in the tiny Anderson shelter in the garden of Captain's Cottage, their home in Broadstairs.

'All seems in order,' Rose smiled at her staff, before glancing up at the large round clock on the wall. 'Time to go to your workstations. But before you leave, may I remind you all that my office door is always open? I'm here to listen if you have a problem. We live in dangerous times, and we need to look out for each other. This teashop is not just a place of work but also, I like to think, a place where friends help each other and we can share our problems.' With that, she nodded for them all to go about their daily duties.

'Miss, would you like your tea tray now, or when Mr Grant gets here?' Edie asked.

'Perhaps when Mr Grant arrives. And can you put a little something on a plate for him? He is bound to be hungry,' Rose said. The area manager was always ready for a bite to eat, whatever the time of day. 'If we happen to have any iced buns in with today's delivery, I'm sure he would enjoy one of those too,' she added. Walking back to her small office, tucked away at the back of the teashop, she reflected that it would be a good idea to keep her boss happy. She had a special request to make, and wasn't sure how he would take it – especially what with there being so many disruptions to the teashops in Thanet owing to the constant bombing.

At least it was quiet today, she thought, as she sat down to make a list of jobs that required doing in the seafront teashop that day. Her first priority would be to show the new staff how to place the wooden shutters on the shop windows each night once the business closed for the evening. Since the shutters had been delivered, Rose was thankful they didn't arrive for work to find broken windows, which left looters able to steal from the premises. Thankfully they'd not been targeted so far, unlike some other shops in the same parade. Oh, and there was the issue of the Nippies not always wearing their gas masks while they worked, she recalled. It was easy enough for them to fix the masks to the belts at the back of their uniforms, but even so, some forgot. She sighed as she thought about how her daily duties had changed since Hitler had decided to target Thanet. For all their suffering, the people of Kent had kept smiles on their faces and gone about their day-to-day lives, not letting the enemy break their spirit; they were made of sterner stuff, of that she was sure. She liked to think that her Margate teashop brought a small measure of normality to everyone's life. As long as supplies could be transported across Kent from their London base, and as long as the rationing now imposed on households did not affect the teashops, there would be a cup of tea and a bite to eat for whoever came through her door.

'Excuse me, Miss Neville – could you spare me a minute?' the young Nippy said, poking her head round the office door.

'Of course, Edie; come in and close the door behind you,' Rose smiled, expecting that the girl, no more than a child, was about to ask for time off for her sister's wedding. 'Do you have a problem?' she asked, seeing how nervous she looked.

'It's not me, Miss; it's the new girl who started in the kitchen last week.'

Rose tried to think which girl she was referring to. Several of the kitchen staff had changed recently, with so many of them going off to do war work.

'Jennie, miss?' Edie prompted.

Rose nodded her head as she recalled a small, thin girl with a pinched expression who always seemed to be looking down at the floor rather than making eye contact. 'Yes, I know her. I didn't take her on myself, as I was off duty that day – Mrs Jones interviewed and hired her. Is there a problem?'

'I don't think she has anywhere to live. Twice I've seen her kipping on the seats by the seafront. I spotted a copper moving her on the other day. I called out to her, but she didn't hear me – or chose not to,' Edie added, looking sad. 'It's awful to think of her not having anywhere to sleep at night.'

'It's very good of you to think of your colleague,' Rose said as the Nippy got up to go. 'Leave it with me. I promise to see what I can do.'

'Thank you, Miss Neville. I hope you don't think I was poking my nose in where it's not wanted.'

'Not for one moment,' Rose said. 'I like to think of the staff here as one big happy family, and sometimes one of us just needs a little help. I do believe I can hear Mr Grant. Would you prepare that tea tray please, Edie?'

Edie stepped back as the door opened and their area manager, Mr Grant, walked in, followed by the area salesman, Tom White. 'Shall I make that tea for three?' she said as she smiled shyly at the younger of the two men. She was rewarded with a charming smile and a wink that had her giggling as she hurried away.

Rose took a deep breath. There was something about Tom White that she did not like. He was too charming by half, and she had a gut feeling that he wasn't all he seemed.

'Ah, Miss Neville,' Mr Grant said as he entered the room and shook her hand enthusiastically. 'I hear that congratulations are in order?'

'Thank you,' Rose murmured as she indicated the two chairs across the desk from where she was sitting. 'It has been a pleasant surprise to find colleagues so delighted by my engagement.'

'Who wouldn't be delighted by the news of a

forthcoming betrothal? And to a captain, no less. Most suitable – most suitable indeed,' he beamed. 'I hope we won't have to wait too long for the wedding. You must keep me updated on developments, as I am sure Lyons can be relied upon to present you with a wedding cake for the nuptials.'

Rose knew that her employers were always generous when it came to long-term staff marrying, but under the present circumstances she wasn't sure whether gifting cakes would be deemed proper; after all, the country was at war. Still, it would be churlish to do anything but make her thanks, which she did with a grateful smile.

'Will the wedding be here or in London, where I believe Captain Hargreaves' family are in business?' Mr Grant asked, settling back in his seat. 'Mrs Grant and I were married in London. My wife is one of the Smiths of Kensington,' he added, giving Rose a knowing look.

Rose had no idea what he was talking about, but it seemed clear that he was impressed by names and titles. 'My mother and I have been invited to visit my future mother-in-law to discuss wedding plans.' Rose suddenly blushed, worried she had spoken out of turn to her manager. 'That is if I can be spared from my work commitments?'

'Oh my dear, of course you must go,' Mr Grant said. 'Joe Lyons wouldn't like it if one of his valuable staff was unable to accept an invitation from someone as venerable as Lady Diana McDouglas. That would never do.'

The door opened, and they watched Edie hurry in with a laden tea tray. Mr Grant rubbed his hands together as he spied the ice buns. 'It's never too early in the morning to sample a Lyons cake,' he remarked, as Rose started to pour the tea.

'I thought we'd be served a cooked breakfast,' Tom White huffed, although he was quick to tuck a napkin into the stiff collar of his shirt and reach for a sandwich.

Rose had hardly stirred her tea when the wail of the air-raid sirens began, gradually building momentum through the town. She rose to her feet. 'I suggest we go down to the cellar immediately. If you will excuse me, I must see that the staff are carrying out their air-raid duties,' she explained as she quickly locked her desk drawer, checked the door of the safe was secure and tucked the keys into the pocket of the navy blue woollen jacket that matched her calf-length skirt. 'You do know your way to the cellars?'

Mr Grant piled his plate high with food and hurried from the room, closely followed by his colleague. As pleasant as the area manager was, Rose did not approve of the way the two men hurried past her female staff rather than stopping to help them to the cellars. Thank goodness there weren't many customers in the teashop just yet, she thought as she picked up her gas mask and went to supervise her workers. They needed to secure the premises, and then head down to shelter in the cellar. With luck this air raid would soon be over, and the town would be safe again until the next visit from the Luftwaffe.

Flora Neville concentrated on her knitting. This was a special little cardigan for a child who had stolen her heart. She had put the wool by to make something for Lily's

Mary for Christmas, but that could wait. She sighed and closed her eyes, still continuing to knit. If she tried hard enough, she could forget she was down in the tunnel below her home and imagine she was in her cosy kitchen, listening to the wireless set and her favourite programme, *Music While You Work*.

Further down the tunnel, she could hear the strains of a familiar tune being played on a piano; voices occasionally joined in with a chorus or two. They weren't a patch on her Rose's beautiful singing voice. Thinking of her daughter made her hope Rose was safe in a shelter, and not caught out in the air raid on her way to work. No one should be sitting underground contemplating their fate at this ungodly hour, she thought to herself, as the ground shook with another bomb hitting the harbourside town of Ramsgate. Why, she'd not even finished cooking the residents' breakfast when the siren went off. She prayed Sea View was faring well, and thanked her lucky stars they hadn't had time to open some of the wooden shutters that Rose's Ben had suggested would protect the larger windows. She loved to see the sunshine on the polished furniture in her best rooms, but not if the bloody Luftwaffe were going to drop bombs every five minutes and shatter the large panes of glass. The shutters, along with the anti-blast tape, would protect the windows from the brunt of any bomb dropped further from the house. Mind you, they wouldn't save anyone from a direct hit.

She stopped knitting for a moment, her fingers poised as the needles ceased their relentless click-clacking, while she thought of poor Ellen Davis and her family. During an air raid, only three nights before, Ellen had unwisely not gone down into the tunnels to shelter. Whatever reason the woman had had for staying above ground, God only knew.

Flora had been on ARP duty that night, and helped pull rubble from what had been the home Ellen was so proud of. She could see Ellen now, washing down the tiled path that led to her house; she would always wave across the square if she spotted Flora or her guests at the door of Sea View. Flora and her colleagues had stopped several times as they listened in the silence for something to give them hope that the Davis family had survived. A small cry had them fervently battling on, passing masonry and bricks back through the chain of people who hoped against hope that there would be a survivor.

It had been Flora who spotted the dusty brown lace-up shoe and knew the wearer was Mrs Davis. Hadn't she handed those very shoes to the woman not one week since, at the WVS clothes swap down the church hall? She'd coveted the almost-new shoes herself, but knew they should go to someone more in need; and Ellen's need was greater, what with her having to run about after her four girls and push that large pram up and down Madeira Walk to queue at the shops. Flora blew the whistle that hung around her neck to alert others that someone had been found, although she could see it was too late. As she stood up straight and raised her arm to beckon to her colleagues, she wiped the back of her hand across her face, smudging the dust and tears into a streaky mess. She no longer worried about how she looked. What was the point? A muffled cry came from close to Mrs Davis's body, and Flora leant in to see where it came from. Gently easing the body of the woman aside, she found her youngest child underneath its mother, tucked securely in a blanket and placed in a wooden box. Had Ellen's last thoughts been for her children? Flora carefully lifted the baby and carried it from the rubble, assisted by the helpful hands of her fellow workers.

A young woman from the Auxiliary Ambulance Service took the child to the back of her vehicle. 'It's a miracle, when you think about it,' she said after declaring the baby no worse for its experience. 'There's not a scratch on the poor mite.'

Flora looked back to where her colleagues had fallen silent as three small bodies were lifted from the rubble, followed by their mother, who'd been placed on a stretcher. 'Is it still a miracle when this little scrap of life is left alone in the world?'

'The father . . . ?'

'Lost on the beaches of Dunkirk,' Flora said, fighting back the urge to scream and curse against a war that could kill innocent children and leave others orphaned. 'Little Daisy Davis here has no one left in the world and will never know her mother or sisters. Hitler has a lot to answer for,' she added bitterly.

'Life can be bloody hard,' the ambulance woman said as she gave the baby an extra hug. 'Now, what are we going to do with you? I'd usually take the kiddies off to hospital and they'd take it from there. But she's not injured, and what with the bombings, the local places are full to bursting. I'm not sure what's to become of her, in the scheme of things.'

'I take it she will go to a children's home eventually?'

'That's right, until they've traced any family, but it seems so unfair when she's been ripped away from her mum. As good as those places are, this little mite needs mothering and cuddling right now.'

Flora's heart lurched as she looked at the little girl. Now the brick dust had been wiped from her face she looked like any other baby, with her perfect cupid's-bow lips and soft pink complexion. 'You're going to be a little stunner,' she whispered as she stroked one small chubby hand. At once the baby curled her fingers around Flora's, looked up into her eyes and beamed.

'I'll take her,' Flora said, snatching the baby from the surprised ambulance woman's arms. 'What I mean is, she can stay with me until a suitable place is found for her. I'm not about to kidnap her. Doctor Hewitt will vouch for me, and we already have one smaller baby about to move into Sea View when her mummy comes out of hospital.' She nodded across the square to her own home.

The woman let out a sigh of relief. 'I thought I recognized you, but it's hard with you wearing your uniform and a tin helmet, as well as being covered in so much brick dust. I'm Polly Bell – I used to work with your Rose, when we were both Nippies up at the teashop. Seeing as you are known to the authorities, I can't think of anyone better to take the poor little thing in until we sort things out. It would be a weight off my mind,' she added. 'It's going to be another busy night. Hopefully once the mother's family have been traced, this little one will be moved on . . .'

Shaking her head to pull herself back to the present, Flora put her knitting down on her lap and turned to her lodger, Joyce Hannigan, who had just finished feeding young Daisy. 'I'll take her for a while, if you want to stretch your legs?' she said, holding out her arms.

'Thank you. She took an age to get that bottle down her, and fell asleep halfway through. I was tempted to take the bottle away, but her eyes soon opened when she thought she was going to miss out on a full feed.'

Flora chuckled. Daisy had wrapped everyone around her little finger in the few days since she'd arrived. 'I'm surprised she even woke up. She's been flat out since we got down here,' she said, looking towards the large coach-built pram she'd purchased second-hand for when Lily came out of hospital with baby Mary. Thank goodness it was large enough for the two little ones to travel top to tail for a while. It would be a godsend down here in the tunnels.

'I want to hang onto that child and never let her go,' Joyce said as she handed Daisy to Flora. 'It seems like so long since my Pearl was that age. It was a joyous time in my life, and I'll go to my grave with the memories in my heart.' She placed one hand to her breast. 'I tell Pearl often about when she came into the world, and how special she is to me. It is such a shame this poor mite won't have anyone to tell her about her early days . . .' She shuddered as the ground shook with another explosion nearby. 'At least my Pearl is safe from all of this danger.'

Flora nodded her head in agreement. As much as they missed young Pearl, who had lighted up the residents' lives at Sea View with her constant chattering and lively spirit, it was better that she was staying with Joyce's sister in the Kent countryside, away from the constant bombing in Thanet. Without a husband, Joyce's sole concern in life was her daughter. Flora admired the way the woman had been both mother and father to the young girl.

'I suppose, in a way, it's good Daisy won't remember what happened,' Joyce said thoughtfully. 'But then, she'll have no memory of her mum or her big sisters.'

'I'm going to make sure she knows about them. I've been given a box of bits and pieces that weren't destroyed, and I'll make a scrapbook that I can read to her when she's older.'

Joyce frowned slightly as she looked sideways at Flora. Had she forgotten Daisy was only staying at Sea View until her family were found – or until she was put up for adoption?

Rose looked around her at the low-ceilinged cellar that ran the full length of the building underneath the Margate tearoom, and wondered how long it would be before the all-clear sounded. Some days it came quickly, while on one memorable day the air raid had lasted seven hours, and she had begun to think it would never sound.

'All present and correct, Miss Neville,' one of the older Nippies said, handing Rose a clipboard with a list of all the staff who were on duty that day. 'I took the liberty of adding Mr Grant and Mr White's names, as they'd not signed in when they came into the building.'

Rose pursed her lips, unseen by the staff member in the dull light of the two bare bulbs that hung from the ceiling of the cellar. How many times had she told the two men to sign in when they came into the building, in case there was an air raid? If the youngest members of her staff could manage this, why couldn't they? Far too busy eating the stock, she thought to herself, and had to suppress a laugh at the image that came into her head. She decided to try one more time to impress upon them the importance of following rules – even those imposed by a mere woman. Thanking the Nippy and taking the clipboard from her, she sought out Tom White. True to form, she found him sitting amongst the younger Nippies, basking in their admiration as he told them about the London head office.

'I expect to be promoted before too long. Then I'll be waving goodbye to Kent and heading to the bright lights of the capital . . .'

Rose was horrified to see how the young women hung on his every word. 'Hopefully you'll be able to find your way there in the blackout,' she remarked in a waspish tone. 'May I have a quick word, Mr White?'

The Nippies made a space on the bench for her and turned their backs, trying to be seen to give their manager-ess some privacy – although of course every word would be listened to carefully, and saved for discussion at a later date.

'I note you did not sign in when you arrived at the teashop this morning?' she said, tapping the clipboard with a sharpened pencil. 'It is a basic rule that I insist all staff follow during wartime.'

Tom shrugged his shoulders and gave a short laugh. 'Everyone knows when I'm in the building,' he smirked, checking the knot of his tie with one hand and looking round to see if he was being admired by the female staff. Several of the girls giggled at his words.

Rose gave a small cough to warn her staff she wasn't

impressed by their input, and silence quickly fell. 'I'm afraid I do not have time for vanity when lives are in danger,' she snapped at him.

'I say, that's a bit strong,' he objected. 'After all, I am senior to you, Miss Neville. In my position within the company, as well as by being a man.'

Rose made an effort to remain calm. The nagging doubt she'd had since the day, just two weeks ago, when her friend Lily gave birth to her darling daughter, Mary, surfaced. 'It was you, wasn't it?' she hissed, leaning in as close as she could so that no one else heard. 'It was you that got Lily Douglas pregnant, wasn't it? You were the one who put her in the desperate position of wanting to kill her child, as she had nowhere to turn.'

Tom White looked startled, then sneered. 'I've heard she's generous with her virtues. That child could be anyone's.'

Rose was outraged. Her friend had not had a good life, with her mother passing away and leaving her in the clutches of her odious stepfather. Lily had done her utmost to keep a roof over their heads, and had been thanked with his drunkenness and much worse. However, Lily was trustworthy, and she was kind – and she wasn't one to be overly friendly with men. At the moment, the identity of baby Mary's father was a mystery; but Rose would lay good money down that Tom White had something to do with it. In any case, she didn't like his attitude or the way he tended to be so familiar with her staff. She wagged her index finger close to his nose. 'Be very careful, Mr White. I'm watching you,' she hissed. 'If you put one foot out of line, I'll have your guts for garters – so watch you don't get too close to my girls.' Giving him a hard look, she turned away and joined her friend Katie, who was sitting with Mr Grant. Something would have to be done about Tom White, she huffed to herself. If only Lily would confirm he was the father of her baby, then Rose would do all she could to help Lily fight for financial support for the child.

Katie budged up and made room for Rose, so that she was sitting next to the area manager. 'I was telling Mr Grant about your mother taking in that poor baby that was orphaned, and how she'd rescued it from the rubble of the building. She's such a brave lady.'

Rose nodded in agreement, although she was still seething after her conversation with Tom White. Already she could see him with his head close to several Nippies as they laughed together. She had a feeling she was the butt of his joke. 'Mum sees it as doing her bit for the war effort. If she isn't doing her ARP work, she's down the WVS helping those who've suffered in the bombing.'

'Don't forget her waifs and strays,' Katie said. 'Flora Neville doesn't stop at babies. She will take anyone under her wing who she thinks needs a helping hand. I'm testament to that. I doubt I'd be a happily married woman right now, if it wasn't for Flora and Rose's help.'

'You intrigue me, Mrs Jones. Please tell me more,' Mr Grant said as he leant closer to listen to Katie explain about her life in the children's home, and how she had gone to school with her best friends Rose and Lily.

'You say your husband is in the navy?' he asked.

'Yes, he's on the . . . Oh dear, I really can't say where he is, can I? I hope you don't think me rude not being able to answer your question, Mr Grant.'

'Of course not, my dear. What is it they say about

keeping mum?' He tapped the side of his nose in a knowing way. 'You must miss him, though?'

'Yes, I'm hoping he will be home on leave soon. He hinted as much in his last letter. I'm so proud of him.'

Rose reached across and squeezed the younger woman's hand. She wasn't fooled by Katie's brittle smile. She could see behind the facade, and knew her friend was heart-broken to see Jack go off to fight the enemy.

She turned to tackle Mr Grant about signing in to the teashop when he visited. Mr Grant listened as Rose explained about the safety of everyone in her care whilst working in the Margate teashop. 'So you see, if you could remember to sign the sheet pinned up in the staffroom, it would be a huge weight off my mind.'

'I agree with what you are saying, Miss Neville, and I assure you that both Mr White and I will follow your request. Now, if you will excuse me, I will rescue Mr White from those young Nippies and see if we can spend our time down here going through some paperwork,' he said as he moved over to Tom White, who looked none too happy at having his boss join him.

Katie gave Rose a grim look. 'I think it's the Nippies who need rescuing from Tom White,' she said. 'I really feel uncomfortable around that man. I wonder what it was Lily saw in him that convinced her to go out to dinner, just the two of them?'

'Perhaps she was lonely,' Rose suggested. 'I don't think either of us knew what her life was really like after her mum died. I feel guilty that I didn't do enough to help her.'

'But now she has her gorgeous baby, and once she's out

27

of hospital we can all live together at Captain's Cottage and everything will fine.' Katie sighed.

Rose frowned. If only she could see the world as Katie did. Deep inside, she felt that regardless of the war, life might not be as straightforward as Katie imagined for Lily and her baby.

2

Rose sighed and snuggled closer to Ben as they sat on a wooden bench looking out over Ramsgate Harbour. There was a light breeze, and the harvest moon was hidden by clouds as they scudded across the evening sky. 'I can't believe that in a few weeks I'll be your wife,' she said as he tenderly kissed her forehead. 'I feel as though I'm the luckiest person in the whole world.'

'Only you could sit here in the blackout, just hours after the all-clear has sounded, and say that you're lucky. You've only just explained to me how you've been holed up in the cellar of the teashop falling out with Tom White for most of the day,' he laughed. 'I'll argue that *I'm* the luckiest person in the whole wide world, as I found you, my darling girl, and you agreed to be my wife. We will be like Darby and Joan, living out our days together surrounded by our children – and later, their children.'

With the arm he'd earlier draped around her shoulders, he pulled her closer. Rose could feel his heart beating close to hers, as he nuzzled her ear and left small delicious kisses on the side of her neck. She shivered with delight, feeling her cheeks start to burn, imagining how it would be once she was married to Ben and they'd be sharing a bed. Thoughts of the few fleeting hours they'd once spent together, alone in his mother's London home, made her heart beat faster. Could she wait? Running her hand across his shoulder, she encouraged his lips to meet hers. For a while, they were oblivious to the waves lapping against the harbour wall and the distant sounds of an air-raid siren, until its threatening insistence made them pull apart.

'I think we ought to get to the shelter,' she whispered breathlessly. 'I'd hate either of us to be injured and have to cancel the wedding. Although with there being so many air raids of late I fear our wedding will be held under-ground in the tunnels.'

'You've convinced me,' he said with a groan as he pulled her to her feet. They hurried, hand in hand, to the nearest entrance to the tunnels that ran under the town.

As Rose joined her mother and the other residents of Sea View in the now familiar tunnels, her mind went to the day, only a few weeks ago, when she'd accepted Ben's proposal of marriage. She sighed as she remembered how, before that, she'd almost lost him – all because of her refusal to listen. A simple misunderstanding could have torn them apart forever.

It was down here in these tunnels that they'd made their peace; and only hours later, back in the comfort of Sea View over cups of hot tea and slices of bread pudding Flora had magically produced from the pantry, Ben had gone down on one knee in front of all her friends and asked her to be his wife. Amongst the cheers, she'd replied,

'Yes please,' before bursting into tears of joy. Before she could catch her breath, Ben had been using the telephone at Sea View to put through a call to London, where his mother had been staying in the family apartment during one of her brief visits from her Scottish home. Rose wasn't sure what surprised her most – that the telephone was working, or that she was being introduced to Lady McDouglas by her exuberant son.

'My dear, I can't tell you how happy I am for you both. Between you and me, Ben's had a chequered romantic life, to say the least,' her future mother-in-law had declared. 'I know you will make my son extremely happy, and that's all a mother can hope for.'

Rose – who felt as though she ought to be curtseying, having never spoken to a Lady before – had been aware of Ben standing close beside her. 'I'll do my best to make him happy,' she'd said, hoping his mother would believe her.

'I'm sure you will,' Lady McDouglas had replied. 'Now, may I speak with your mother?'

Rose had been taken aback. Why would Ben's mother wish to speak to her mum? 'Of course, I'll go and fetch her. Here is Ben,' she'd said, carefully passing back the receiver. As she hurried through to the kitchen, where Flora was chatting with Miss Tibbs and Joyce, she'd thought about how casual Ben was while using the telephone. Even though Rose used the instrument in her small office at the Margate teashop, she was always relieved when it was placed back in the cradle on the desk.

Rose was snapped back to the present as Flora nudged her with an elbow. 'A penny for your thoughts?'

'I was thinking about the wedding and about meeting

Ben's family. Do you think we are rushing things, wanting to marry within weeks of him proposing? I so wanted the grand white wedding and for everyone to enjoy our special day; and I've yet to meet his daughters. What if they don't like me?' she said, then grabbed Flora's arm as they felt the thud of a distant bomb hitting its target, making them both jump. Even this far underground, they could still hear the hell above.

Flora patted Rose's hand and stood up. 'Come with me. I want to show you something,' she urged her daughter, leading her along their tunnel into a slightly wider one. 'Look at this,' she said, pointing to where many inhabitants of the town had set up camp.

'Oh my gosh,' Rose said, gazing about her. Even by the weak glow of overhead lights and candles, she could see clearly that families had started to move their entire lives underground. 'Of course, I've known that life went on down here – but people have actually made rooms!'

She gazed in wonder at the ingenious arrangements of the townsfolk, who'd strung up sacking and old curtains to create an element of privacy for themselves. She could smell cooking – and wasn't that Vera Lynn singing? Someone must have struggled all the way down here with a gramophone player. How clever. 'Perhaps we should do something like this ourselves? If we all muck in, we can soon have a cosy area for the residents of Sea View,' she said, warming to the idea.

'Well, yes – but that isn't why I showed you the encampment,' Flora said with a smile. 'My point is that life goes on. It may not always be how we planned it, and God knows if it will ever be the same again after this war.

However, the human race is resilient and will carry on, regardless of what is thrown at us. It is good to have dreams, and I do hope that those two children love you – there's no reason they shouldn't – but what I'm trying to say is that we have to live for today. It doesn't matter what you wear or where you marry, as long as you and Ben are together. Create your family as soon as you can, for goodness knows what we will face in the years ahead. I want to see my daughter happy and content. If that means you getting married in a Nippy uniform, then so be it.'

Rose kissed her mother's cheek. She only needed reminding that these things didn't matter. 'I was being silly,' she smiled. 'I'd rather be married to Ben now than wave him off without a wedding band on my left hand. It would have been nice to have waited and had Lily fit and well enough to be one of my bridesmaids, but I'm sure she will understand.'

'Well done!' Flora said, giving her a big hug. 'Why, we can always have a proper wedding later on. There's no reason why not.'

Rose agreed, and found she suddenly had to force back tears that threatened to fall. 'Although I won't be marrying in a Nippy uniform,' she laughed with a hoarse voice, 'or my manager's uniform, come to that.'

'That's my girl,' Flora said, linking her arm through Rose's. 'Now, why don't we go find that handsome fiancé of yours and make some plans? You know your future mother-in-law would like the wedding to be held in London, don't you? She mentioned some fancy registry office to me, and then suggested celebrating at the Ritz hotel. I couldn't help thinking that there wouldn't be many girls who work for Joe Lyons doing such things.'

Rose chuckled. 'I don't care where I marry, as long as I do marry. Lady McDouglas sounds delightful, doesn't she? And so down-to-earth, just like Ben. I can't wait to meet her.' A knot of excitement again caught her unawares. 'Mum, you do know that many Nippies who work at the London Corner Houses make very good marriages, don't you?'

Flora stopped and looked at Rose with a puzzled expression on her face. 'Then why was that Miss Butterworth so strict when it came to you Nippies chatting with the customers?'

'Because she was an old tyrant,' Katie said as she joined them. 'She even stopped me talking to my Jack, when he popped in once with news of his posting.'

'Hello, Katie love,' Flora said as they both gave the young woman a peck on the cheek and hugged her. 'I'm glad you are down here and safe with us.'

'I was on my way to Sea View when Moaning Minnie started wailing. Honestly, she never lets up for more than a few hours. Now, why were you talking about Miss Butterworth?'

'I was telling Mum that many Nippies who work in London make good marriages, but Miss Butterworth almost stood guard over us to make sure we remained as pure as the driven snow,' Rose giggled, thankful that in the gloom of the tunnel no one could see the blush spreading over her cheeks as she thought of the one night she'd spent with Ben. 'I do feel sorry for her, though – having to give up her job to care for her sister.'

'Don't be, because you'd never have become manager of the Margate branch otherwise and been such a wonderful boss,' Katie said generously.

'Crikey, you seem to be in a good mood,' Rose said, laughing off her friend's compliment.

'I should be,' Katie replied, reaching into the pocket of her coat. 'I've received a telegram from Jack. He has shore leave, and will be with me within a few days.'

'That's something to celebrate,' Flora said, clapping her hands together in delight. 'Come on – let's open up the flasks and toast your Jack with hot cocoa.'

'We certainly know how to live,' Rose grinned, as they followed Flora back to where the other Sea View residents had set up for the duration of the air raid.

'When are you going to visit Ben's daughters?' Katie asked as they fell a little behind.

'I was hoping we would be able to see them here in Kent, but it seems they're on a trip up to town to see their grandmother. Ben's sister, who cares for them, has some kind of appointment, so they're killing two birds with one stone.'

'Three birds, if you include meeting their future step-mother,' Katie grinned. 'Just fancy you having a ready-made family even before you are married.'

Rose laughed, but deep down inside she couldn't help but feel a little apprehensive about what lay ahead.

'Why don't you sing us a song, Rose?' Joyce Hannigan said. 'I'm sure it would cheer everyone up. It's the waiting down here that bothers me most. When I've something to keep me occupied, things don't seem as bad. A bit of a sing-song would be perfect.'

'What about singing "When You're Smiling"? That always has me feeling happy,' Miss Tibbs said as she passed a sleeping baby Daisy back to Flora. 'I've changed her nappy, Flora, so she should sleep through for a few hours. Not that much disturbs the little mite.'

Flora hugged Daisy close to her. 'When you think what the poor child's been through, it's enough to make you want to weep,' she said, gently kissing the baby's forehead. 'Nothing nasty will ever happen to you again,' she murmured, causing Katie to nudge Rose in the ribs.

'It looks like your mum's getting broody,' she hissed. 'What will happen when the authorities take the child away?'

Rose simply shook her head, looking worried. She knew her mum had taken to the child, and there would be tears when Daisy left Sea View. 'Let's start the sing-song, shall we?'

She kept the people in their part of the tunnel singing, while outside the Luftwaffe did their best to destroy their hometown. Miss Tibbs and Joyce even got to their feet at one point and gave a rousing rendition of 'The Lambeth Walk' complete with a little dance routine, which caused much laughter when everyone joined in, calling out 'Oi!' at the end of each verse.

'You seem quiet,' Ben said to Anya as they sat watching. 'I hope you aren't worrying too much about Henio? By all accounts, the lads are doing a sterling job up there protecting the airfields and the towns. You should be proud of him.'

'I am proud,' Anya replied, 'but I am also the wife who is worried for her husband. Men do silly things – they take chances. They do not think of the family down here, praying for their safety. When they get into those planes to fight, they turn back into little boys again; and I'm thinking that is not so good.' She reached for Ben's hand and held it tightly. 'You must promise me you will not play silly boy games when you go back to the fighting. You must think of Rose, your girls and your future. Stay safe, Captain Ben. There are many who will mourn if you lose your life.'

Ben liked the Polish woman. To some she appeared stern and had a sharp way about her, but to him she was the perfect example of how brave women could be in this war. Leaving Poland after the invasion, she had headed to England to find her Polish fighter pilot husband and made herself a new life here in Ramsgate. Anya was made of stern stuff, that was for sure; but she still had a soft, caring nature that he admired. 'I promise I'll be careful, but we do have a war to win. I know that Rose and my family will understand if something happens to me,' he said, giving her hand a squeeze. 'Will you promise me something?'

'If I can,' Anya said stiffly, holding her chin high.

'If . . . if anything should happen to me, will you look after my Rose? I know you will make her carry on, and not dwell on her loss.'

'It is a big thing you ask of me,' Anya replied seriously, looking him straight in the eye. 'I may not be here in Thanet for much longer. I cannot take care of someone if I only write the letters.'

Ben frowned. 'Where do you plan to go? You know it is far too dangerous for you to return to your homeland, even if it was possible to do so?'

'No, I fear I will never return home. This country is now my home – even if I do not like all these songs,' she sniffed, as a line of people danced past them doing the conga before they all collapsed with laughter. 'Sing a better song,' she called out to Rose. 'Sing about the lilac. That is a song I do like.'

Rose broke into 'We'll Gather Lilacs in the Spring Again'. They listened to her for a few moments before Ben tore his attention away from his fiancée and turned back to Anya. 'Where are you planning to go?'

Anya looked around to make sure no one was listening. 'My Henio tells me he is being moved to an airfield called Biggin. I plan to follow him there. He swore me to silence, as he would have the big trouble if he spoke about it. I cannot bear to lose him, Captain Ben. So I go to this place he called "the bump", and I do all I can to keep him close to me.'

'So you're sodding off to London while I'm stuck here in hospital,' Lily sniffed, before grinning when she saw Rose's sad expression. 'I'm pleased for you, I really am. I'm just sorry I'm missing out on all the fun.'

'You've not missed much so far. We celebrated with cocoa and bread pudding at Mum's, and apart from that I seem to either be at work or down the tunnels taking cover.'

'I've been wondering about Captain's Cottage and how it has been faring. I miss our little house,' Lily said. 'I hope it doesn't get hit – all the bits and pieces I've put aside for Mary are there. Mind you, by the time we both get out of here she'll have outgrown some of the stuff before she's even worn it.'

'There's no need to worry on that account. Katie and I decided to move as much as possible downstairs, and we packed up all our special things into a hamper and stored them in the cellar. Mary's clothing is safe as houses,' Rose said confidently.

Lily laughed out loud. 'With so many houses destroyed by the Luftwaffe, you may wish to think that comment through again. I just wish there was room in the cellar for us to shelter. That way we wouldn't have to trek down to the bottom of the garden to the Anderson shelter – I swear we take our life in our hands going down there in the dark, with just the thin beam of a torch. God knows how I'll manage when I have Mary to carry as well.'

'We'll all muck in. That's what friends are for,' Rose reassured her, although she really was rather worried about how Lily would cope with a small baby and no husband. 'I have some good news,' she added.

'So do I,' Lily beamed.

'Then you go first.' Rose settled back in the hard hospital seat that had been placed beside her friend's bed.

Lily gave the biggest grin. 'I've been told I can go home next week. Isn't that wonderful news? Of course, with my leg still not one hundred per cent, the doctor has told me I'll need some help at home until I'm more mobile. I assured him that with you and Katie living at Captain's Cottage, there would be plenty of people coming to and fro. Oh, and Mildred is sure to visit, being that the cottage was once hers and she likes to do repairs for us. Mind you, I'm not sure about her touching Mary, as I don't want her smelling of fish . . .' As Lily's excited chatter came to an end, there was silence for a moment. 'What's wrong?' she asked, a worried frown replacing her smile.

'Katie's heard from her Jack – he will be home on leave next week. She's talking of going somewhere with him, so they can be alone. They didn't really have a honeymoon after the wedding,' Rose said, knowing she sounded as though she was making excuses.

'That's all right. You'll be there, and perhaps Flora will visit me while you're at work,' Lily replied, although she still looked worried.

'I'm sorry, Lily. Mum is coming to London with me to stay with Ben's mother. Mr Grant kindly gave me a week's leave. I'm going the day after tomorrow. But I'll cancel,' she said, noticing how disappointed Lily looked. 'It's important that you and the baby are safe and secure at home. I can go to London another time.' Even as she spoke, she knew it was going to be nigh on impossible to change her plans to suit all the people she cared about.

'I'm sorry,' Lily said. 'I feel as though I've messed up all your plans. I'll tell the doctor I'm too poorly to leave just yet.'

'No, don't be daft. You're not to worry about a thing. Now, I need to get to work, or the staff will wonder what's happened to me – but we can make plans later. For now, I'll get the show on the road my end. And I promise that you will be home safe and sound next week.'

After kissing Lily's cheek and telling her again not to worry, Rose hurried from the hospital and headed to the bus stop to catch the next bus to Margate. However was she going to explain this to Ben? Would he be annoyed? It wouldn't look good to his mother, either . . .

The teashop was busy when Rose arrived, with Nippies dashing about serving late morning snacks to hungry customers. She nodded to a couple of the regulars, and hurried to her office. She'd just removed her coat and checked her appearance in a small mirror hanging behind the door, when there was a quiet knock and one of the senior Nippies appeared with a tea tray.

'I thought you could do with a cup of tea?' the woman said, placing a silver teapot on the table alongside a cup and saucer and a small jug of milk.

'Thank you, Phoebe,' Rose said, sitting behind the desk and picking up a pile of post. 'It always amazes me that even though we spend so much time in air-raid shelters, the post still arrives on time.'

'Life goes on,' the woman replied, smiling at her boss as she backed out of the room.

Life goes on, Rose thought to herself as she poured the amber liquid through a tea strainer into her cup before adding a dash of milk. Yes, it certainly does go on. And sometimes it can spoil carefully made plans, as well.

'Cheer up. You look as though you lost sixpence and found a penny,' Katie grinned as she stuck her head round the door. 'Can we chat for a few minutes?'

'Come on in,' Rose said. 'I'm next to useless today. I've hardly started on the post, and I've yet to check the kitchens or go through the stock lists.'

'That's not like you,' Katie said, closing the door behind her and sitting on a chair opposite her friend's desk. 'You put us all to shame as a rule. You're not going down with something, are you? Or perhaps you are pining for Ben. I take it you've not seen him since last night during the air raid?' she laughed as she ribbed her childhood friend.

Rose brightened up as Katie joked with her. 'You only have a smile on your face because your husband is due home next week.'

'I won't argue with that. Oh, Rose, I can't wait to see Jack again. It seems an age since our wedding. That's what I wanted to speak to you about. Would it be an awful cheek if we had Captain's Cottage to ourselves for a few days? I can't find a hotel to put us up, and it would be lovely to live as husband and wife properly, even if it's only until Jack has to go back to his ship.' Katie coloured slightly at the implication of her words.

Rose bit her lip. It felt as if the situation was getting completely out of control.

'Is there a problem?' Katie asked, looking concerned.

'No, not at all. I'm probably not going to London now, as Lily is due out of hospital next week and will require looking after. She can't be left on her own until she is back on her feet and fighting fit.'

Katie frowned as she thought about the situation. 'But you really must go to London to meet Ben's family and celebrate your engagement with them. It's a big occasion. You've yet to meet Ben's daughters. If you leave it too long, you won't meet them until your wedding day – and I don't think that would be a good idea. Those two little girls need to feel comfortable with you being their new mummy, and you turning up dressed like a Christmas cake might make that more difficult,' she grinned. 'You've told me how you want to do everything right. Then there's Ben's sister. You have no idea how she will react to a manageress from Lyons nipping in and taking over. If you don't do your utmost to meet your new family before the wedding, you could be causing all kinds of problems that would take years to resolve – if ever. Don't worry about Lily and the baby. We will care for them.' She smiled bravely. 'Jack and I have our whole lives to be alone.'

It was Rose's turn to argue. 'No, that wouldn't do at all. Why, who knows what will happen in this war – and if . . . if . . .' She stopped speaking, knowing that with every word she was digging a hole for herself. What she had almost said would upset her friend.

'If my Jack should perish at the hands of the enemy, do you mean?'

Rose felt ashamed. 'I'm sorry, I wasn't thinking straight. I do apologize.'

'Rose, how long have we been friends? If we can't say what we are thinking to each other, it doesn't say much for our friendship, does it? Look at the three of us. There's poor Lily, a single mother and no parents, stuck in hospital – and all she wants is to go home to Captain's Cottage and get on with bringing up her daughter. There's me, never having known who my parents are and wanting to live as a proper married couple with my new husband for just a few days. Then there's you . . .'

'Who is about to become engaged, has a mother, two

homes if you count Sea View – an inheritance from a man who I never knew was my father – and my share of Captain's Cottage . . .' Rose pointed out, looking ashamed.

'And don't forget, your mother-in-law has some fancy la-di-dah title,' Katie added, starting to giggle.

Rose was soon joining in with Katie's infectious laugh. 'We're a right trio, aren't we?' she chuckled. 'I'm sure we can sort this out between us. And before you say another word, I will not have you and Jack taking care of Lily and the baby while he is home on leave. We will just have to think about what else can be done.' Her tone was determined, making it clear to Katie that she wouldn't accept any argument. 'Now,' she added, checking the clock on the wall, 'I need to inspect the teashop. It could be falling down around us for all I know, hidden away in here. Will you help me?'

Katie stood up and straightened her Nippy cap as she gazed into the mirror. 'All set for action, Miss Neville,' she said as she put her hand on the door handle, just as the telephone rang.

'I'll catch you up,' Rose said, waving to her friend as she lifted the receiver and gave her name.

'Rose, it's me, your mum. I'm sorry to bother you at work, but we have a small problem here at Sea View. Would you and Katie be able to come over here after you finish work? Mildred said she would collect you in her van when she's finished her deliveries. Perhaps Anya could travel back with you?'

'Mum, what's happened?' Rose asked, as a feeling of foreboding started to creep over her.

'I don't want to explain on the telephone – you know

what they say about walls having ears? Besides, I'm uncomfortable using this thing, you know that.'

'Then I'll see you later. Take care, won't you, Mum?' Rose whispered as she put the receiver down.

She hurried to catch up with Katie, and found her showing a new Nippy how to lay a table correctly. Rose raised her eyebrows at her friend to intimate that there could be a problem. 'I'm sure you will remember how to do it next time?' she said to the girl, who quickly scuttled away once dismissed.

Rose and Katie moved over to a mahogany workstation that ran along one wall of the shop. This was where the Nippies collected trays of drinks, and where an impressive soda siphon was situated. Rose checked that the machine was clean and polished and her staff had not left a mess in their haste to serve customers.

'What's the problem?' Katie whispered as she picked up a cloth and buffed the soda siphon.

'It was Mum on the telephone. You know how she hates to make phone calls,' Rose said, looking around in case anyone had noticed they were chatting. It wouldn't do for the manageress to be seen breaking rules. She quickly explained what she'd been told.

Katie looked worried. 'Something must have happened. Do you think it's serious?'

'I don't know; but Mildred will collect us both. And I'm to tell Anya to come with us rather than take the bus.'

Katie rolled her eyes skywards. 'Rather you than me. You know how she hates that van, as it smells so much of fish.'

'Then she can sit up front with Mildred. I'd better tell

her right now. Would you check the kitchen supplies and complete the stock list for me, so I can place the order before I leave?'

'Of course. I suggest you speak to Anya now. She keeps looking over our way. I swear that woman doesn't miss a thing.'

Rose made a beeline for the counter close to the front door of the teashop, where Anya and another Sally were serving customers. Never had Rose been more thankful that Joe Lyons was still able to produce bread, cakes, pies and other food to supply the teashops. She did wonder how long it would last, with the constant bombing of the area. She'd decided a little while ago not to worry about future supplies and focus more on each day as it came. The tariff card that each Nippy offered her customers still carried a delicious array of meals and drinks at reasonable prices. If an item wasn't available then her customers, as a rule, were grateful for what was on offer. Back at Sea View, her mum was having to remind her paying guests to hand in their ration cards – and keep an eye on Miss Tibbs, who was known for being over-generous with their meagre butter allowance. Rose was reminded that she must have a word with Mildred about turning part of the garden at Captain's Cottage over to growing vegetables, to help ensure a steady supply of food. Although goodness knows when they'd all find time to tend to the veg – let alone learn how to grow it. Something else she'd have to have a chat about with her mum. That thought had her wondering again: what could it be that Flora so urgently needed to see her about?

'I would rather catch the bus,' Anya sniffed, when Rose

told her about Flora's request that they all return to Sea View after the teashop closed. 'I do not like to smell of the fish. It is not becoming on a lady.'

'Please, Anya, just this once, would you travel in Mildred's van? Mildred is such a dear agreeing to collect us. As you know, she isn't supposed to make special trips, because her limited supply of petrol is to be used only for delivering food.'

'Will she be in trouble for carrying us instead of the fish?' Anya asked.

'As Mildred is driving home from her deliveries, then I doubt she would be in any trouble,' Rose replied, wondering who would dare to reprimand Mildred.

Anya nodded thoughtfully. 'I would have to put the newspaper on my seat, and we drive with the windows opening. I will not have anyone saying Anya Polinski smells like a codfish. I still think the bus would be best; that way, I only smell of sweaty people.'

Rose pushed her pleas a little harder. 'Whatever Mum wants, it must be important for her to have used the telephone to contact me at work.'

Anya thought for a moment. She was taller than her colleagues, and her hair, as dark as night, was worn pulled back into a severe bun at the nape of her neck, giving her a haughty demeanour. Her friends knew, however, that the Polish woman had a heart of gold once she was comfortable in a person's company.

'Then I will go with you just this once. Now, if you excuse me, I have work to do. Joe Lyons will not be happy if I do not do my job properly. You may also think of that,' she said as she went back to serving the queue of customers.

3

Rose followed the grumbling Anya into Sea View. She could feel the tension in the air as she removed her coat and hung it on the stand in the hall. 'We're here,' she called out, as the women hurried down the few steps at the end of the hall that led to the kitchen.

Flora hurried to kiss her daughter and Katie, as Anya backed away in horror. 'Keep away from me, unless you too wish to stink of the fish,' she said as she opened the back door and stood in front of it.

'It's not that bad,' Flora said, trying not to laugh at the look on Anya's face. 'If you wish to change your clothes, I'll hang what you are wearing on the line to air.'

Anya nodded her head in agreement, at the same time glaring at Mildred. 'Now what is this thing that we had to rush home for, and why I now stink of the fish?'

Miss Tibbs, who'd been pouring boiling water into Flora's largest brown china teapot and lining up teacups on a tray, couldn't resist being the bearer of bad news. 'Thing? I'll have you know we are all in a fluster. There have been *two* pieces of news while you've all been

48

working. It's all I can do to hold myself together, I'm that upset.'

'Then let me take that tea tray,' Rose said, hurrying over to grab the tray as it wobbled in Miss Tibbs' hands. Katie helped the old woman to her seat at the large table in the middle of the room. This was where the inhabitants of the guesthouse always gathered to chat: the heart of the house, really.

Miss Tibbs took a handkerchief from the cuff of her cardigan and dabbed at her nose. 'Who'd have thought this war could change so many lives?' she sniffed.

Anya froze. 'Do you mean that there is bad news? Is this why you insist we are to come here in filthy fish van? What has happened to my Henio?' she all but shrieked.

Flora hurried to Anya's side and went to hug her, but Anya held up a hand to stop her in her tracks. 'Remember the smell.'

'Oh, Anya – we've not heard news of Henio. As far as we know, he is as fit as a fiddle and still at Manston. You have no need to fear.'

'I fear all the time,' Anya said quietly. The women could see her hand shaking as she held it to her chest and breathed deeply.

'Not my Jack?' Katie's voice cracked as she stood up quickly, causing the table laden with teacups to shake. 'Please don't let it be my Jack,' she begged.

'I've not heard news of Jack either. Or Ben, come to that,' Flora added quickly, noticing that Rose's usually pink cheeks had turned pale. 'Don't you all think if there had been news of your menfolk, I'd have come to the teashop to break the news to you myself – rather than telling you to hurry home after work?'

They all visibly relaxed at Flora's sharp, if reassuring words.

'Then what has happened?' Katie asked.

'I received the bad news,' Joyce Hannigan said from the doorway.

'Oh God, no, not little Pearl,' Rose cried out. They all missed the bright young child. 'Please tell me she's not been injured?'

'I'm here, Aunty Rose, and I'm not hurt. I've come home to Sea View to be with you all,' Pearl said as she appeared beside her mother, and then ran into Rose's arms. Rose swung her around with such joy that the child shrieked in delight, begging to be put down. 'Is Aunty Lily's baby here?'

'Not yet, darling.' Flora stroked the little girl's hair. 'I do have a photograph of the baby, though. If you go into the front room, you will find it on the sideboard. You may also find some sweeties in the top drawer. I was going to post them to you,' she smiled as the child beamed and ran from the kitchen. 'Perhaps you would let the girls know what has happened?' Flora said to Joyce as she started to pour the tea. 'I'll have to get our meal started before too long, and fill the thermos flasks in case the Luftwaffe pay us another visit this evening. I hope not – I for one could do with sleeping in my own bed, at least for one night.'

Joyce looked back towards the open door of the kitchen. 'Would you pull the door to, please, Rose? You know what little ears are like.'

Rose nodded, realizing that what Joyce was about to tell them was not suitable for Pearl to hear. She stood guard at the door, leaving it open a crack to watch in case the child returned and overheard whatever it was Joyce was about to impart. 'All clear,' she said.

'I collected Pearl this afternoon after identifying the body of my sister. As you all know, Pearl was staying with Phyllis, as I felt it would be safer for her in Tunbridge Wells than here. However, fate intervened and while Pearl was at school and sheltering safely, Phyllis was caught in a blast while out shopping, before she could reach a shelter. It seems she threw herself over a baby in a pram. The child survived, but my sister died instantly.'

The room fell silent as the inhabitants of Sea View absorbed what they'd been told. It was only broken when Mildred pulled a large, white handkerchief from the pocket of her dungarees and blew her nose noisily. Shaking her head in anger, she managed to say a few words before stopping to wipe her eyes. 'This bloody war. Let the men kill each other, but when an innocent woman is killed . . .'

The women nodded in agreement. Even Anya forgot about the smell of fish and gave Mildred a supportive hug.

'I'm so sorry for your loss, Joyce. Your sister did a very brave thing. I hope the baby is reminded of her sacrifice when she is old enough to understand,' Flora said, reaching over and squeezing her hand. 'It can't have been easy for you, having to identify her.'

'Couldn't someone else have done that instead of you?' Katie asked.

'I'm her next of kin. There were only the three of us

– and now there are just the two. I don't know what I've have done if I'd lost my Pearl as well as Phyllis. I want to keep her by my side all the time and never let her out of my sight, but I have to do my bit to stop this war. I have no idea what to do,' Joyce sighed.

'I have the answer,' Mildred said with a beam on her face. 'We will all care for Pearl. Surely between us there will always be someone here to care for the child when she's not at school. Why, we are like one big happy family at Sea View, so let us all pull together to care for our youngest member.'

'You forget,' Anya said. 'The youngest member of this family is the baby, Daisy. I am not sure I wish to care for such a young child. I do not have the experience.'

Flora sighed and pulled an envelope from the pocket of her crossover pinny. 'This is the second part of my news. The authorities have decided that Daisy should be taken to a children's home. They've been unable to find a living relative and they feel the best thing would be for her to be put up for adoption. She will be collected the day after tomorrow. Air raids permitting.'

Rose looked at her mum's drawn face and could see how much this news had affected her. In the short time the child had been cared for at Sea View, Flora had become like a second mother to Daisy. She'd had a passing acquaintance with the child's mother and sisters, which was something no adoptive family would be able to claim. If the baby lost contact with Flora, she would never know about her flesh-and-blood family.

'Mum, surely they could let her stay with us?'

'No, it seems they want a stable family for the child.

One where there will be a father and siblings. I agree with that,' Flora admitted.

'Well, I disagree!' Rose almost shouted. 'Why, I never had a proper father or siblings, and I didn't do so badly.'

The others agreed with her, quite vocally.

'You should write to the authorities and tell them that Daisy is staying with us,' Joyce said, getting into her stride. 'I've seen how good you are with her, so they can't argue that you wouldn't be a good mother. We will all vouch for you and I'm sure others would, too. Why, you know all the local councillors and police through your work with the WVS and the ARP.'

'There's no time,' Flora said as she slid the letter across the table to show Rose. 'They are coming the day after tomorrow – and that's when I'll be in London visiting Ben's family with you. Perhaps I should stay here,' she said, looking worried.

'You'll do no such thing,' Mildred said, thumping her fist on the table so that the tea left in their cups slopped into the saucers. 'You'll just have to take her with you. If she isn't here, they can't take her back. It makes sense.'

Rose wasn't so sure that her mum turning up in London with a baby would be such a good idea. Having stayed in Lady Diana's home, she knew it wasn't a suitable place for a youngster who'd just started crawling. Besides, Ben had mentioned they'd be going out to a nightclub and possibly the theatre. Who would look after the baby? Flora would be expected to accompany them to celebrate Rose's engagement. 'I'm not so sure, Mum,' she said, worried that it would look as though she didn't want young Daisy to join the family.

'I'll take her to Captain's Cottage,' Katie said with a grin. 'They won't think to look for her there.'

Anya snorted, showing her contempt for the idea. 'What will you do with the child while you are being the stand-in manageress for Joe Lyons? Also, your husband will be home from his ship. You have not thought this through.' She gave Katie a sharp look, shaking her head.

'Thank you, Anya.' Flora sent Katie a pitying smile. 'Katie was trying to be helpful.'

'We still have to think about Lily. She is expected to be home from hospital next week, as long as there is someone to be with her at the cottage. She can't be left alone with a baby, as there may well be an air raid. I've already told Katie that she must spend some time alone with Jack in the few days he will be on shore leave. She can't be expected to go to work as well as nurse Lily and two youngsters. Jack would take one look and run away,' Rose added with a smile, knowing that in fact Katie's husband was a gentle creature who would muck in and help everyone living at Captain's Cottage.

'Oh, for goodness' sake,' Joyce said before Mildred could open her mouth to add her two penn'orth. 'Lily should come here to Sea View. She's part of this big family we were talking about not ten minutes ago. We will just make sure that we arrange our work so that someone is always here. Surely that's not so hard to do?' She looked round the room at the women, who were surprised to see how outspoken she had become, as usually she went along with whatever was happening. 'And before you leave for London, you can write a few letters and tell those people in authority that Daisy is staying here with us, and we will care for her while you go to London. If anyone turns up we will say you are on air raid duty. With so many raids lately, it is unlikely we will be home when they visit anyway.'

'Here you are, darling. Let me give you an 'and.' A friendly soldier helped Flora and then Rose into an already busy train carriage, pushing a couple of sailors out of the way so they could sit down. 'Off to join up, are you?' he asked as he sat down opposite and started to roll a cigarette.

Rose grinned at her mum. Their luck was in when they chose this carriage; the soldiers and sailors were true gentlemen. 'No, we're off to London to meet my fiancé's family. We were lucky to get passes to use on the train. The last time I went to London I had a lift in an army truck, and we got well and truly stuck in the snow.' She laughed at the memory.

'I've done that trip a few times and I remember the snow back at the beginning of the year. Not that I recall any female company coming along – and I'd have remembered a young lady like you,' he grinned, holding his hand out. 'Corporal Morris.'

Flora shook his hand. 'I'm Flora Neville, and this is my daughter, Rose. We live in Ramsgate,' she added, then went on to explain about the guesthouse. However, the young man soon grew visibly uncomfortable.

'Mum,' Rose whispered, laying her hand on her mother's arm. 'Don't forget about keeping mum and all that . . .'

Flora slapped her hand to her mouth. 'Please forgive me. Whatever was I thinking?'

'You were being neighbourly, Mrs Neville, and nothing more,' a voice said from behind a copy of the *Daily Express*. As they turned towards it, its owner placed the newspaper onto his lap and nodded hello to the two women.

'Why, Reverend Dunlop, what a lovely surprise,' Flora said. 'What takes you out of Ramsgate?'

Rose and the corporal burst out laughing, while the vicar ran a finger across his moustache as his lips twitched. 'Oh, Mum, you take the biscuit,' Rose giggled.

'What have I done now?' Flora said, looking bemused. Then the penny dropped. 'Oh my goodness. The way I'm talking, I'll be locked up in the Tower of London before the day is out,' she said apologetically. 'I'm sorry, gentlemen. It's all this excitement about our Rose getting engaged, and me going to London after such a long time. I hope you can forgive me if I've put our country in danger?'

'Mrs Neville, I don't think for one moment you are a threat to national security. Am I right, ladies and gentlemen?' the vicar said, addressing the others in the carriage.

There was a muttering of agreement and a few lively comments from the servicemen, which pleased Flora no end. 'Thank you,' she said, looking relieved. 'It wouldn't do for me to get into trouble when my daughter is about to marry an army captain,' she said proudly.

The vicar tried to change the subject before Flora got carried away. 'So, tell me, how is young Daisy Davis? I was pleased to pen a letter in support of your quest to adopt her after Miss Dalrymple caught me in the vestry yesterday evening when she kindly dropped off a parcel of fish for me to pass to the parishioners. In fact, I posted the letter as I walked up to the station this very morning.'

Flora was lost for words until she remembered her manners. 'You did that for me? I . . . I don't know what to say,' she stammered. 'I just want to give the child a decent home, and Sea View is just across the way from where her own home stood until those basta . . . until the Luftwaffe bombed the hell out of the town, and she lost everything. Her mum, her sisters. There are no other relatives, and she's not even a year old yet.' Flora drew a deep breath as she felt tears threatening. 'Besides, she's taken hold of my heart, and if she is taken away from me now . . . well, I don't know what I'll do.'

'We are all prepared to help out,' Rose chipped in as Flora composed herself.

Reverend Dunlop raised his hands to stop Rose talking. 'Ladies, believe me, I know you will provide the perfect home for young Daisy. In fact, I said so in my letter. I also took it upon myself to speak to Mr Phillips, our mayor, and his dear wife and ask them to put in a good word for you. They promised to discuss it with a few of our hard-working councillors. I have no doubt Daisy will soon be a Neville.'

Rose nudged Flora not to say anything untoward. Flora wasn't enamoured with some of the current town councillors, having called them lazy good-for-nothings when they turned down requests by her fellow ARP wardens and the ladies from the WVS.

'Thank you, Vicar. I really don't know what to say.'

'There's no need, dear lady, no need at all. At times like these, we all need to keep an eye on the young people and make sure they get through this war in one piece.'

Flora nodded in agreement, thinking of young Pearl

and her lucky escape in Tunbridge Wells. If she had her way, she'd collect all her friends and keep them safe at Sea View until the war was over – that's if Sea View itself got through the war in one piece.

'Now, Rose,' the vicar continued, 'when do you intend to pay me a visit to arrange your wedding?'

Rose shifted uncomfortably in her seat. She'd been dreading this question. 'The thing is, with my fiancé being in the army and goodness knows when he will be shipped off, we thought a quiet registry office wedding would be better,' she said as he raised his eyebrows.

'I'm sure we can do just as well at St George's and just as quiet, unless you choose a rousing chorus of "Jerusalem" for the congregation to join in with?' he chuckled. 'You just tell that young man of yours I'll be expecting a visit before too long.'

'Yes, Vicar,' Rose mumbled, seeing her vision of having her photograph taken on the steps of Caxton Hall fade away. 'I'll have a word with Ben.'

'Do you help your mother run the guesthouse?' Corporal Morris asked Rose. 'Haven't you thought about joining the forces? Many women have.'

Rose gave a small grimace. She'd noticed of late how some people assumed that all women should be doing war work, when some already had perfectly good jobs at which they worked extremely hard. 'I'm the manageress of a Lyons teashop in Margate.'

Corporal Morris's reply surprised her. 'Then you work harder than many of us. I've been in those teashops, and you Nippies are run off your feet all the time. I take my hat off to you all.'

Rose thanked the man. 'You must come and make yourself known to me when you are next in the area,' she smiled.

'Rose and her staff were busy helping feed the men as they disembarked from the Little Ships, after being rescued from the beaches of Dunkirk. Those girls were on the seafront and at the railway station for days on end. I was very proud of them all,' Flora said with a broad grin.

'Blow me down – I was one of those that was rescued,' the corporal said. 'Who'd have thought it? We didn't expect that kind of welcome. Do you know, there were people lining the railway tracks all the way up to London? Treated us like heroes, they did. But I don't mind telling you, none of us felt like heroes. We'd been taken off those beaches and we felt we'd let our country down. We were running from the enemy,' he added glumly.

'My dear chap, don't think that for one moment,' Reverend Dunlop said, again lowering his newspaper. 'We live to fight another day, eh?'

Rose and Flora nodded in agreement. 'Goodness, yes, we are so proud of our lads in the forces, and the people who owned those Little Ships,' Flora said. 'One of my residents took her own fishing boat across the Channel. She did four trips.'

'A lady, you say?' the corporal said in amazement. 'Well, knock me down with a feather.'

'We women are capable of playing our part in this war,' Rose said, smiling at the astonishment on the army corporal's face.

'I don't doubt it for one moment – but to take a fishing boat back and forth across the Channel while under enemy fire would frighten even the bravest of men. I'd like to meet this lady.'

'Then you must visit us at Sea View when you are next in Ramsgate,' Flora said generously, reaching into her handbag for something to write on. 'Here you are.' She held out a scrap of paper. 'You'll have to take us as you find us, though . . .'

'Thank you. I'll make sure not to arrive unannounced,' he said, tucking the slip of paper into the breast pocket of his khaki uniform.

The rest of the journey passed in companionable conversation. Flora shared the Spam and pickle sandwiches she'd made, while the corporal passed round his cigarettes.

'We've had a reasonably good journey,' Reverend Dunlop said as he reached above his head to pull his briefcase and raincoat from the overhead rack. 'A few weeks back we sat for over two hours while there was an air raid in progress.'

'Weren't you frightened?' Rose asked, shuddering at the thought of either sitting it out or, as one of her customers had once reported, having to climb out and shelter underneath the carriage.

The vicar raised his eyes skyward and gave her a gentle smile. 'Never,' he said.

Reaching Charing Cross, they waved goodbye to Reverend Dunlop. Rose promised to pay him a visit, along with Ben, to arrange their wedding.

'Just smile and agree with the man,' Flora whispered as they waved him off. 'You can do as you please; it's your wedding day.'

'Now, where are you ladies heading?' Corporal Morris asked as he picked up their suitcases.

'We have to go to Cadogan Gardens,' Rose said. 'I'm going to hail a taxicab outside the station.'

Corporal Morris – Stan, as he'd asked them to call him – raised his eyebrows and whistled gently between his teeth. 'That's some address,' he said. 'Your captain must be doing well for himself?'

Rose chuckled, partly in embarrassment. 'It's my fiancé's mother's home. We've been invited for a few days, then we go back home to Ramsgate. Really, there's nothing posh about us.'

'She just happened to fall in love with a lovely man whose family had done well for themselves through hard work,' Flora explained. 'They are in flour,' she added, trying not to boast. Personally, she'd no idea what 'being in flour' actually meant, but she hoped to find out by the end of their visit. She'd first used the term after hearing Ben use it, when she was trying to impress a fellow ARP warden who'd sniffed down his nose when Flora mentioned her daughter worked for Joe Lyons. 'You're turning into a right snob,' she muttered to herself as she followed Stan and Rose out of the busy station.

Stan put the suitcases down on the pavement and placed two fingers in his mouth, giving out a piercing whistle. At once a taxicab pulled up, and the driver climbed out to take the cases. Rose gave the address, and they turned to thank Stan.

'Don't forget to come and visit us,' Flora called, as their cab joined the busy traffic leaving the station.

Rose settled back in her seat and thought for a moment.

'Are you trying to matchmake, by any chance?' she asked Flora.

'I've no idea what you mean,' Flora replied absently, trying to look at the sights through the dirty window.

'Inviting Stan back to Sea View just because he was interested in Mildred's adventure at Dunkirk. You do know she prefers the companionship of women these days?'

Flora shook her head in disbelief. 'We all need a companion. I'd like to see Mildred settle down with a decent man, and that Stan seems delightful. Perhaps when he visits us, Mildred too will see how nice he is.' She sighed with satisfaction, as if a plan was coming together nicely.

'Do I look all right?' Flora asked as she turned around in front of Rose. Her ivory silk gown fitted closed across the bodice with very little decoration before falling in gentle folds to her calves. 'It doesn't look too old-fashioned, does it?'

'Oh, Mum, you look beautiful,' Rose said, taking in her mother's shining curls that for once weren't pulled back into the severe bun she wore while working. A touch of rouge to her cheeks, a dab of powder and Rose's favourite Victory Red lipstick had Flora looking ten years younger. 'Here – you'll need this,' she added, taking a pale green wrap from where it lay on her bed. Rose didn't mention how embarrassed she'd been when last staying at Cadogan Gardens to only have her outdoor coat to put over her cocktail dress when going out with Ben to dine. Ben had lent her a mink stole belonging to his mother, and she could still feel the softness of it on her bare shoulders. She held her breath for a moment, thinking of that magical night and what had followed. 'Don't forget you have your matching evening bag,' she smiled. Flora took the accessories and twirled around again to show the full effect of her outfit. 'I feel like a queen,' she laughed before stopping to look at her daughter. 'Make that a queen's mother,' she said, sighing at the sight of her beautiful daughter. 'You've never looked lovelier, my darling – and to think today is your official engagement day. Ben is such a lucky man.'

Rose looked down at her rose-pink frock. Like her mum's, it was silk, but the bodice was held up by the lightest threads of fabric and the skirt flared out almost to her ankles. 'Is it vain of me to say I feel beautiful?' she asked shyly. 'This isn't the kind of dress I'd usually wear, but I felt that celebrating our engagement in London called for something really special. I was lucky to find this frock at such short notice. Thank goodness the war hasn't stopped shops still having a few nice pieces to sell, though we searched hard enough.'

'But for how long?' Flora said as she leant forward to shake out a crease in Rose's skirt. 'I'm just pleased Miss Tibbs could alter this for me. God bless her, she can be little tetchy at times, but she always seems to come up trumps with her needle and pins when we need help. When we left Ramsgate she was running up a couple of little dresses for Daisy on her sewing machine out of one of my summer skirts.'

'Come on – we'd best join the others, or they'll be telling us we're late,' Rose said, picking up a lightweight stole made from the same fabric as her dress.

'There you are,' Lady Diana said, coming forward to kiss Rose and then Flora on the cheek as they entered the drawing room.

'I hope we haven't kept you waiting,' Rose said, looking round the large drawing room for Ben.

'Not at all – in fact, we have time for a cocktail before we leave for dinner. Ben is just fetching the ice. It will be my daughter who will keep us waiting,' she smiled at Flora. 'Come and sit with me. We have much to talk about now we're almost family.' She led Flora to a large sofa covered in dark green velvet. 'I do believe we have something in common?'

Rose watched as the two women started to chat like old friends. Any worries her mother had had about not fitting in seemed to have been forgotten. She turned as she heard a sound from the doorway. Ben stood there, holding an ornate silver ice bucket. Rose had never seen him so handsome – he was out of uniform, wearing a formal black dinner jacket complete with bow tie. Her heart gave a lurch as he set the bucket down and hurried towards her, enfolding her in his arms. Kissing her gently, he then held her at arms' length.

'Good evening, wife-to-be,' he smiled.

'Good evening, my handsome husband-to-be,' she replied, her words no more than a whisper. It felt as though time stood still as they looked into each other's eyes.

'We have an exciting evening ahead of us,' he said. 'I hope you enjoy what I have planned.'

'I'm sure I will,' she smiled back, knowing that she'd follow Ben to the ends of the earth and never question where he took her.

He reached into his pocket and pulled out a small jewellery box. Carefully lifting the lid, he removed a delicate diamond-encrusted ring. 'I collected it just an hour ago,' he said as he slipped the ring onto her finger.

'A perfect fit,' she replied, as he lifted her hand and brushed her fingers with a kiss she would remember for the rest of her life.

Rose gazed at the ring with tears in her eyes. 'Words fail me,' she whispered. 'It is perfect.' She slipped her arms round his broad shoulders and almost had to stand on tiptoe to give him a kiss.

'Careful,' he whispered into her ear with a ragged breath, 'or I'll have to carry you away somewhere private.'

Rose sighed with delight. 'If only you could – but our mothers would have something to say about it.'

'Oh, how lovely, you have the ring,' Lady Diana said, beckoning Rose to where the women sat. She took Rose's slender hand. 'It suits you, my dear. This was Ben's grandmother's ring,' she explained to Flora.

'Darling, it is beautiful,' Flora said with a catch in her voice.

'But what is this?' Lady Diana said taking a closer look. 'Ben, one of the stones seems to be set at the wrong angle. You'd best take it back. Rose doesn't want to lose one of the diamonds before she's even married to you.'

Rose felt wretched as the ring was removed from her finger and put back into its box.

'Time to open the champagne, Ben. Come along now, we have much to celebrate, even if the ring cannot be worn yet,' Lady Diana declared. 'I too have a surprise. In fact, I have two,' she smiled as she went to the sideboard and picked up a flat box emblazoned with the name of a well-known West End jeweller. She gave it to Rose with a smile. Rose gasped as she pulled back the lid.

'Oh my!'

'A lady can never have enough jewellery,' Lady Diana remarked as Rose carefully lifted out a necklace made up of a triple row of pink pearls and what looked like a silver clasp encrusted with diamonds. Petite earrings nestled in the box at either side of the necklace.

'Thank you, oh, thank you,' she said as Ben draped the necklace around her throat and hooked the clasp together. She shivered as his fingers lightly stroked the back of her neck. 'I don't know what to say,' she added, kissing her future mother-in-law's cheek.

'It is I who should be thanking you, my dear, for putting a twinkle back in my son's eyes. We've had our tragedies, but they should be forgotten now,' Lady Diana whispered for Rose alone to hear. 'Now, where is that champagne?' she said out loud.

Rose showed her jewellery to Flora as Ben opened the bottle and started to pour. 'You are a lucky girl,' Flora smiled, although she felt a slight twinge of regret that the gifts she'd collected in her bottom drawer for her daughter were nothing compared to what Ben and his mother had given Rose. Who wants sheets and towels when you can have diamonds? she thought to herself.

'Is that a champagne cork I heard popping?' a female voice called from the hallway.

'You are just in time. Come along in and meet Rose and her delightful mother, Flora,' Lady Diana called.

Ahead of Ruth, two little girls ran into the room and

launched themselves at Ben. He scooped them up, one in each arm, and turned to Rose. 'Meet my daughters,' he said as he introduced first Annabelle, and then Marina.

Both girls smiled shyly, then leant over and hugged Rose. As she embraced them, Rose felt a rush of love unlike anything she had experienced before. This was a different kind of love from what she shared with Ben. If she felt like this about another woman's children, how would she feel when she had her own?

'I'm so pleased to meet you at long last,' she said, trying to forget the unfortunate circumstances in which she had seen them from afar for the first time – with the woman she now knew was Ben's sister, but who at the time she thought must be his wife. 'I hope we will become very good friends,' she added warmly, as Flora stepped forward to meet the children.

'So this is the blushing bride?' Ruth, blonde and smiling, gave Rose a hug. 'I must thank you for making my baby brother the happiest man in this war-torn country – and taking these little monkeys off my hands,' she said with mock horror, as the children screamed with laughter.

Ben set the girls back on their feet and poured the champagne. To the children's delight he also gave them a glass, although there was very little in each flute. 'Just this once,' he said with mock severity. 'I don't want our daughters turning into gin-swilling floozies.' Opting not to explain what a floozy was, he raised his glass and gave a toast. 'To all the women in my life – particularly this darling girl, who has been brave enough to accept my proposal in marriage even though she has no idea what the future holds or if I'll even be here this time next month.'

'There's no need to speak like that, Benjamin,' his mother said with a glance toward the two little girls, who were busy giggling over their champagne glasses. 'Winston says we can win this.'

'You know Winston Churchill?' Flora said, impressed that she knew someone who had met the man she admired so much.

Lady Diana shrugged her shoulders. 'He's as infuriating as any other man. Now, I do have that second surprise . . .' she went on, crossing over to a mahogany magazine rack and taking out a newspaper. 'I took the liberty of placing an engagement announcement in *The Times*. I have a copy for you to keep, Flora,' she smiled, as she opened the newspaper and passed it round to show the adults.

Rose shivered as she read the words. *Rose Neville, daughter of the late General Wilberforce Sykes and Mrs Flora Neville of Sea View, Ramsgate.* It was the first time she'd seen her parents' names together. A strange sense of foreboding engulfed her . . .

4

'Wake up, sleepyhead,' Ben said as he popped his head round Rose's bedroom door, after knocking several times. 'Breakfast won't be long, and we have a busy day ahead of us.'

'We do?' Rose yawned as she sat up, and silently patted herself on the back for wearing her best nightgown. Even so, she pulled the blankets up to her chin.

'I'll put this down here and leave you to whatever it is you women do to make yourselves look so adorable,' he said, placing a cup of tea on her bedside table.

'You mean I don't look adorable at the moment?' she teased him.

Ben groaned and leant close to kiss her lips. 'If only we were alone.'

Rose reached up to pull him closer. 'Surely you could spare ten minutes?' she whispered, feeling her body start to heat up.

'With our mothers just the other side of that wall, talking about our childhoods?' he laughed, taking her hands from his shoulders. 'It does somewhat dampen the ardour.' He smiled at her disappointed face. 'Soon, my darling, soon,' he said, placing a kiss on the tip of her pert nose and leaving the room, calling, 'Hurry, or we'll go without you,' over his shoulder.

Rose was out of bed in a flash, sipping the tea as she got herself ready for the day ahead. She was still in a state of excitement after the thrilling evening they'd had celebrating their engagement. She'd never forget how Ben had ushered their mothers, along with his sister, into the waiting taxi and said the words, 'The Ritz, please,' to the driver. She couldn't believe her ears.

'Are we really going to the Ritz?' she asked, as the taxi pulled away and joined the busy traffic.

'It's the best place to celebrate our engagement. But I hope you don't expect this treatment every day of the week,' he said with a smile, as her eyes shone with excitement.

'Only on days when I get engaged to the most handsome man in town,' she laughed back.

'Don't say things like that, or his head will get bigger than it already is,' Ruth said, giving her brother a playful punch.

Watching the friendly banter between the siblings, Rose wished she'd had a brother or sister of her own to share life's highs and lows. Granted, she had Lily and Katie, who were the next best thing to family; but even so, there was something about having a close relative that she felt she'd missed. If only she'd had contact with her half-sister from the General's marriage before he met her mum.

Ruth noticed Rose watching her. 'I'm thankful you've taken this brother of mine on. You'll have your hands full,' she said as she reached into a dainty silver clutch bag for her cigarettes and offered them round. She lit her own when everyone else refused. 'You know, we should meet up on our own and get to know each other better,' she went on, with a generous smile that was so much like her brother's. 'Although it would have to be up in town, as I'll be working at the War Office from next week. This damned war can be such a bore at times.'

'Who will have the children?' Flora asked.

'That's something that will have to be discussed. I've made a few decisions,' Lady Diana said, 'but now is neither the time nor the place for such things. Let us celebrate our family's news. Tomorrow we can talk about mundane things like the war. Ah – we are here,' she exclaimed as the taxi pulled up in front of the hotel. A commissionaire stepped forward and opened the door.

'Oh my gosh,' was all Rose could think to say as they were ushered inside and shown to their table.

The evening rushed past in a blur of champagne, delicious food and wonderful music from the resident orchestra. Fellow diners approached their table to give the happy couple their congratulations and good wishes for the future. Ben seemed to know many of the gentlemen there in uniform, while Lady Diana nodded and exchanged words with the older diners.

A beeline of young men made their way to the table, inviting Ruth to dance. Flora too was not short of attention, which somewhat tickled Rose, who had never had the occasion to think of her mother as attractive to men. She was simply Flora Neville, landlady of the Sea View guesthouse – and, most importantly, her mum.

Just when Rose didn't think the evening could get any

more exciting, Ben announced that they were moving on. He ushered the women out to another waiting taxicab, which whisked them away into the now dark night.

Rose was delighted when she recognized the nightclub where Ben had taken her when she'd visited London to do her manageress training at the Lyons training school.

'A nightclub?' Lady Diana looked none too impressed. 'I think perhaps I'll head home and leave you young things to enjoy yourselves.'

'No you don't, Mother.' Ben took her elbow and steered her through the blacked-out doors, down a flight of steps into the enormous room. Chandeliers hung from the ceiling, and waiters buzzed about between tables that were dotted around the large dance floor. The place was alive with noisy chatter, until the bandleader raised his arms to the musicians and the next dance began.

'It's the orchestra I sang with when we were here before,' Rose said to Ben. 'Fancy you remembering.'

'How could I forget?' he smiled, as he led her to the floor for a foxtrot. Rose closed her eyes for a moment as she allowed him to lead her around the floor to the strains of 'The Way You Look Tonight'.

'I feel as though this is all a dream, and I'll soon wake up and have to hurry to the teashop and open up for the early morning shift,' she said as she smiled up at him. 'Could anything be more perfect?'

'I want our life together to be as perfect as possible,' he smiled back, as they neared the stage and the music came to an end. Rose clapped politely and began to move back towards their table, but Ben held onto her hand.

'Wait just a moment,' he said, as Rose frowned in confusion.

The orchestra leader turned to the audience and once again raised his hands, this time for silence. 'Friends, we must give our congratulations tonight to a very special young lady – Miss Rose Neville, on the occasion of her engagement to Captain Benjamin Hargreaves.'

A spotlight that had been focused on the stage moved to where Rose and Ben stood. Although acutely embarrassed, Rose raised her hand to wave her thanks and nudged Ben to do the same.

'Miss Neville once graced this stage and sang for us. I wonder if she would do so again?'

A cheer went up from the audience and Ben leant forward to whisper in her ear. 'Would you sing for me?'

Rose nodded, and nervously went to the side of the stage, where the orchestra leader was waiting to assist her. After a quick exchange of words he went back to the microphone. 'The song Miss Neville is about to sing is a special arrangement made for that well-known singer Helen Forrest, which Captain Hargreaves was able to acquire as a surprise for his bride-to-be. Ladies and gentlemen: I give you Miss Rose Neville, singing "You Made Me Love You".'

Rose felt her heart soar as the opening bars of the song started to play before she stepped forward and started to sing. Ben was a darling, she thought; he had obtained the correct musical arrangement so that she was able to sing the song just like her favourite singer, Helen Forrest. She closed her eyes, thought of the man she loved, and let the words pour from her heart – just for Ben.

'That was beautiful, Rose,' Lady Diana declared afterwards, dabbing at her eyes. 'Ben told me you could sing, but I had no idea . . . Tell me, Flora, do you sing as well?'

Flora, who had leapt to her feet to hug her daughter, smiled in reply. 'I'd like to say she got it from me – but no. I can belt out a tune and dance a little, but that's as far as it goes.'

'Mum, don't be so modest,' Rose said, as she gratefully took the glass of champagne handed to her by Ruth, who first patted her on the back by way of congratulations. 'Mum used to perform on stage when she was younger. That's how she met my father,' she declared, determined that no one should forget General Sykes.

'Oh, what a coincidence. I too met my husband in the theatre,' Lady Diana exclaimed. 'I just knew that we would get along fine, Flora, and now we have something else in common.'

'What's the first?' Ben asked in amusement.

'Being the grandmothers of your child, of course,' Lady Diana declared, causing Rose to choke on her champagne.

'Hang on a moment, Mother,' Ben exclaimed as he thumped Rose on the back to help her stop coughing. 'We aren't even married yet.'

'That doesn't usually stop a couple. Not when they plan a hasty wedding,' she replied. 'Don't think for one minute that I disapprove. I know this is a match made in heaven. So what if the child is an early baby – or even a honeymoon baby? It will be loved just as much. I'm no fuddy-duddy, you know,' she finished as she raised her glass and toasted the couple.

'I tried to explain that you wanted a quick wedding

because of the war, and Ben possibly going away. But she wouldn't listen,' Flora said to Rose, as the band struck up a waltz and Lady Diana was escorted onto the dance floor by her son.

Rose giggled. 'I may be a little tipsy, but I'm finding this so funny. I honestly thought Lady Diana would be a right snob, and here she is shocking the pair of us.'

'I think she's delightful. We will get on like a house on fire. In fact, she has already said that she intends to visit us at Sea View and sample the delights of a seaside holiday.'

'Whatever next? No doubt she'll be wanting to go out on the *Saucy Milly* and fish for our supper alongside Mildred?' Rose suggested. Mother and daughter burst into laughter at the thought of the robust Mildred instructing Lady Diana on how to haul in the nets and give a hand gutting fish. Life, it seemed, was not going to be dull.

'There is something that I don't understand,' Flora said, turning to Ruth.

'I'll help if I can,' Ben's sister replied, moving closer to Flora so they could hear each other above the dance music. 'Fire away.'

'Why is it that both you and Ben have the surname Hargreaves, while your mother is Lady Diana McDouglas?'

Ruth chuckled. 'It's Daddy's fault. He went and got himself made a peer for services to something or other, and Mummy became a Lady. We still pull her leg about it, but she loves all the attention really, and of course it does mean we get the best tables in restaurants and are bumped up the waiting lists for theatre tickets. Daddy, on the other hand, carries on as if nothing has happened. He's always busy doing something with his flour mills, and when he isn't, he prefers the quiet life up in Scotland. The place in London is Mummy's – he only stays when he's here for some frightfully important meeting, or needs to be at the House of Lords.'

Flora nodded thoughtfully. 'Oh, I see. So, does that mean that you will be Lady Ruth some day – when your mother . . . ?'

'Pops her clogs? No, never. Titles are passed down through the male line. It's our Benjamin who will inherit the title, and Rose will be a Lady.'

Flora was lost for words. She looked at Rose, whose face had turned a ghostly white. Flora had always wanted the best for her daughter – but to be a Lady one day? Crikey! 'I'll be curtseying to you before too long,' she smiled, trying to alleviate the shocked expression on her daughter's face as Rose took in the information.

'But I manage a teashop for Joe Lyons. That's just a jumped-up Nippy, for heaven's sake. I'm not cut out for being posh . . . oops, sorry!' she quickly added, knowing her soon-to-be sister-in-law was as posh as a person could be.

Ruth guffawed loudly as she saw the consternation on the two women's faces.

'I thought Mummy had explained?' she said, turning to Flora. 'She too worked in the theatre. She will admit to being a third-rate actress, and if Daddy hadn't appeared on the scene and swept her off her feet, then she was destined to wait on tables and no doubt be a Nippy as well.' She laughed. 'Sorry, I didn't mean to make it sound like a demeaning job. I know it's bloody hard work.'

'There's no need to apologize. I know there are women of all social levels who work as Nippies. More so in the

London Corner Houses, though,' Rose smiled. She was beginning to like Ben's sister very much.

'And they were called Gladys at that time,' Flora added.

Ruth looked between Rose and her mother and started to laugh again. 'Believe me, there was nothing posh about Mummy. Or Daddy, come to that. Daddy worked hard taking on his father's almost bankrupt flour mill, and did such a marvellous job of it that he created many jobs. His business put bread on a lot of people's tables when the men came back from the last war. Mummy's family were shopkeepers, and they were horrified when she ran off to be an actress. Mummy loves to appear posh, but believe me, she makes no secret of her humble beginnings. She's proud of them.'

'Crikey, so you are the only really posh family member?' Flora said, before clamping her hand to her mouth and apologizing. 'Blame the champagne for my rudeness. I'd not normally come out with such blunt comments.'

Ruth laughed so much that she had to reach into her small clutch bag for a handkerchief to wipe her eyes. 'Lord love you both. Mummy bought my poshness with good schools. She expected me to marry well, but so far, no such luck. Not that I've not enjoyed myself.' She winked, seeing a slight frown on Flora's face. 'I love the men, but they don't love me enough to marry me.'

Flora leant over and patted her arm. 'You are still a young woman. Don't give up yet,' she consoled her. 'There are plenty of fish in the sea.'

Rose glanced at Ruth, and they both burst out laughing. 'Oh, Mum – a woman can be perfectly happy without marrying.'

Flora looked hurt. 'I was trying to help the situation. I don't think what I said is that funny,' she frowned, as the two girls continued to giggle.

'You all seem to be having a good time,' Lady Diana remarked as she returned to the table. Ben held out her chair for her. 'It's good to see you all getting along. What has made you so happy?'

'We were discussing marriage,' Ruth said as she held her glass out for Ben to top it up. 'And my lack of husband material.'

Ben looked at his mother and grinned. 'I take it the latest specimen hasn't come up to scratch – or has the spinster of the parish eaten him?'

'Oh, for heaven's sake, Ben, you make me out to be some kind of praying mantis. I swear I've never harmed one single hair on any man's head. If mother will produce such poor candidates, then of course I will send them packing,' Ruth said dramatically, before knocking back her champagne in a single gulp.

Rose watched in fascination. Ruth was like a breath of fresh air – she'd never met anyone like her. Life would never be dull with her around.

Ben sat down next to Rose and draped his arm around her shoulders. 'Are you enjoying yourself?'

'More than you'd ever know,' she replied, her eyes shining brightly. 'However did you manage to get your hands on the arrangement for "You Made Me Love You"?'

'Much easier than you give me credit for. When I came here to speak to the band leader and see if he would invite you to sing, I mentioned your great love for Helen Forrest, and he told me he knew someone who had worked with her. Before I knew it, he'd got his hands on the arrangement – and Bob's your uncle, as the saying goes.'

'This is like stepping into another world. I'm not sure I can live up to you and your family. I'm just a normal girl from a seaside town who runs a teashop,' Rose replied in amazement.

Ben took her hand and gave it a squeeze. 'I love you for what you are. Besides, you also have a wonderful talent. You sing like an angel, and I love you all the more because you have no inkling how good you are.'

'I sing because I enjoy doing so. I won't lie and say I didn't once dream of someday making singing my living, but it was a ridiculous dream – imagining myself fronting a big band, just like Helen Forrest. Did you know we're about the same age? Look at what she's done with her life,' Rose said wistfully. Then suddenly she brightened up. 'But Helen doesn't have a wonderful man like you who wants to marry her. That makes me so happy.'

Lady Diana clapped her hands for attention. 'Benjamin, have you informed Rose and Flora of the surprise you have for them tomorrow?'

Rose looked to her mum, whose eyes had already opened wide. After the wonderful dinner at the Ritz, and being able to sing here in the nightclub that already held such happy memories for her, what other surprises could Ben possibly have up his sleeve?

'I'd like to take you to see our business empire,' he said, keeping a straight face.

Ruth snorted. 'He's pulling your leg. The family owns a flour mill,' she said as she punched her brother's arm.

'Rather a big flour mill that's kept you in silk knickers

for many a year,' her mother reprimanded her. 'I do feel it is about time you stepped in and paid us back. A nice little job in one of our offices would suit you down to the ground. Didn't you learn to type at some point? I recall signing a cheque.'

Ruth laughed again. Nothing seemed to faze her. 'Don't forget, Mummy dear, I have an appointment tomorrow to see some top brass in Whitehall. Your daughter will soon be earning a wage.'

Lady Diana nodded in approval. 'Well done, my dear.'

Flora leant over to speak to Rose. 'What about the children? I thought Ruth cared for them somewhere in the countryside, so they were away from London?'

Rose shook her head, not knowing what to say. She'd yet to speak to Ben about the children and their future lives. She'd been swept along with his proposal, and there was still much to plan. She knew the girls were happy with the present arrangement, but in her heart she saw them all living together as one happy family once she'd married Ben. Perhaps they were to stay at Lady Diana's flat and be cared for by the staff who were looking after them this evening? She'd have quite liked to have the girls celebrate the engagement with them at the Ritz this evening, even if they'd been sent home afterwards while the adults went on to the nightclub.

She turned back to Ben with a smile. 'I'd very much like to look at your family business. It will be part of my life too, once we are married and you leave the army after the war. It interests me a lot,' she said truthfully, though she didn't yet know exactly what it entailed.

'Count me in,' Flora said. 'Do we have to travel far?'

'We can start at the docks in the East End,' Ben said. 'I'll show you how my father built the business almost from nothing.'

Rose could see the passion in his eyes. 'You must miss working for your father's business?'

He shrugged his shoulders. 'We need to win this war; then I'll go back to it. My father's still overseeing things, even though he's up in Scotland more these days. He'll never fully take his hand off the rudder.'

Rose looked at the man she loved and knew that he, too, would be a hard worker until his dying breath. 'I look forward to meeting your father,' she said.

'That will have to wait, I'm afraid. He's unlikely to come to London unless there's a problem with the business.'

'Or he's in the House of Lords,' Ruth butted in. 'Then he's on the next train north, unless he has to be in Canada for his work.'

Flora shook her head in surprise. Fancy Ben's father not wanting to be with his family. It was certainly another world for the wealthy, she thought.

'I am ready for my bed,' Lady Diana declared, standing up. 'I hate to cut things short when it is such an important evening, but I'm not one for late nights anymore. Please, you must stay,' she insisted, as Rose and Flora stood.

'As we have a busy day tomorrow, I'd quite like to leave as well,' Rose said, realizing it was already nearing midnight. Late enough, in her book. 'I'd like to say thank you to the band leader before we leave, if you don't mind?'

'I'll come with you,' Ben said, and they threaded their way through the dancers until they reached the side of the stage.

The band leader spotted them and came down to talk. Rose couldn't stop thanking him for making her evening so special. He was enthusiastic in his thanks to her and reached into his pocket, bringing out a gilt-edged card. It felt like déjà vu to Rose, as this kindly man had given her his business card once before.

'If at any time you wish to come and sing for me, whether it be one evening soon, or years later, I will be overjoyed to welcome you,' he said as he kissed her cheek and then shook Ben's hand, wishing them the very best for the future. Rose tucked the card into her bag, thinking as she did so that it would remind her of a special evening, but would lead to nothing more than that. Her future was to be Ben's wife.

'Oh, you're back in uniform,' Rose said as Ben joined them in the dining room the next morning. He looked so handsome that she could hardly take her eyes off him as he greeted Flora, and then crossed to room to kiss Rose. A look between them acknowledged their earlier embrace in her bedroom. She ached to be alone with him.

'I have to report to the powers that be. It's all rather sudden. Would you mind very much if I took you both to the office this afternoon? I did mean to treat you to lunch, but sadly the war has ruined my plans once again.'

'Oh, darling, we understand completely,' Rose said, although she was disappointed not to have his company for the full day. 'Mum – do you fancy a walk, and perhaps lunch at the Corner House down the Strand?' she suggested. 'How about you, Lady Diana?'

'Any other time I'd love to, but I have a meeting this morning. I wonder . . . ? No, it would be an imposition,' Ben's mother said, dismissing whatever she had been about to say.

'Please, if there's something you'd like us to do, I'm sure we'd agree,' Rose encouraged her, wanting more than anything to please her future mother-in-law.

'If it is something you want collected from the shops, we can do that for you,' Flora prompted with a smile. Not that she thought for one moment they'd be queuing at a corner shop. No doubt it would be Harrods, she thought, trying not to grin to herself.

'Oh dear, now I feel as though I'm imposing on your good nature,' Lady Diana said, looking flustered. 'I was about to ask if you might take the children out for the morning? Ruth has disappeared, and with Ben and myself tied up . . . No,' she declared. 'They can stay here with the housekeeper. They have their colouring books and crayons to keep them quiet.'

Rose knew that this could be her best chance to get to know Ben's children properly. With time so short before the wedding (not that they'd decided on an exact date yet), she wanted them to know her and to like her before they all lived together as one happy family. That's *if* they were to live together. In the last few days, Rose had come to realize just how little about their future life had been settled. She'd stepped into this relationship without thinking about a home, or their ready-made family. All she knew was that she loved Ben with all her heart and trusted him implicitly, whatever he had planned for their future life.

'Of course we can take them out for the morning. We can still see the sights and have lunch as planned. It will be fun,' she added, a tad too brightly. She wondered how the two girls would take the news about being offloaded onto two strangers – even if one of them was about to become their stepmother.

'That is extremely good of you,' Lady Diana said, as she rang a bell to fetch the maid. 'There's no need to hurry so, my dear,' she smiled at the red-faced woman who came scurrying in. 'This is not Buckingham Palace, and you won't be sent to the Tower if you don't arrive within three seconds. Now, would you inform my grand-daughters that they should really be here eating their breakfast by now? And to hurry, as Rose and Flora wish to take them out for the morning.'

The maid bobbed a curtsey and hurried out as fast as she'd entered.

'A delightful girl – but she's always in such a hurry. She makes me feel out of breath,' Lady Diana said.

Rose needn't have worried. When the two girls came bounding in, they chatted like they'd know her for years, hardly stopping to draw breath in between tucking into boiled eggs and soldiers with gusto. Within half an hour they found themselves on the pavement outside Cadogan Gardens, still undecided where to go, but with Ben's instructions to enjoy themselves – and his promise that he would try to meet them for lunch – still ringing in her ears.

Rose decided to leave it up to the children. 'What is your most favourite place in London?' she asked them.

'Harrods, to see the animals,' they answered in unison.

'I'd quite like to visit Harrods myself,' Flora said, as she took Marina's hand. 'I didn't know they sold pets?'

'Oh, yes. Even elephants,' the little girl said confidently, as the doorman hailed a taxi and held the door open.

Rose thanked the man and ushered everyone into the vehicle. 'I do hope you all have your gas masks?' she asked as the taxi pulled off. The girls waved the small boxes that hung over their shoulders, and Flora did the same. 'Oh, so I have three children to look after today?' Rose said primly, making them all laugh. A warm glow filled her as she realized that this would be her life from now on. A ready-made family, and a handsome husband she loved with all her heart. She started to dream about finding a cottage to rent close to the teashop in Margate. No doubt while Ben was away with his regiment, she would be alone with the girls, but she would look at it as a time to bond with them. And perhaps they could stretch to hiring a housekeeper part-time, to be there and keep an eye on the girls while she was working?

Throughout the morning, while they wandered through the well-known department store, her head filled with plans for her future life. Would this be where she shopped one day? Would she turn into a younger version of Lady Diana? Reaching the pet department, they spent some time looking at kittens and puppies and discussing whether, after the wedding, they might have a kitten to live with them.

Ben was already in the queue when they arrived at the Lyons Corner House not far from Trafalgar Square.

'I'm so sorry we're late,' Flora said, after he'd greeted them all. 'I insisted we used the bus so I could take in the views. When I spotted Trafalgar Square, I just had to get off and walk so that I could tell everyone back at Sea View I'd seen the lion statues. It made me so proud to be British – even though there were so many air-raid precautions in the area,' she sighed.

'Have you never seen Trafalgar Square before?' Annabelle asked in amazement as she held Flora's hand.

'It was such a long time ago that I'd almost forgotten.' She smiled down at the child. 'It was when you were a child and I had to visit London on important business,' she explained to Rose, who had looked at her in an enquiring manner. 'Mind you, I do remember this Corner House,' she added, as Ben led them inside and requested a table for five.

'Mum, you are full of secrets. What else have you kept from us – you worked for the War Office, perhaps?' Rose grinned.

'Sadly, nothing so exciting. However, it was the first time I'd met a Nippy and heard all about the name and how busy those girls were,' Flora said, just as a young Nippy arrived at their table with a tariff card that showed what food was on offer that day. Leaning closer to Rose, Flora whispered, 'I recalled thinking what a wonderful life you would have, and how no daughter of mine would wait on tables. I saw a bright future and a good marriage for you.'

Rose felt close to tears. 'I never thought I was a disappointment to you when I started working for Joe Lyons.'

Flora patted her hand. 'You've never been a disappointment to me, Rose. I was just a fanciful young mother with ideas above my station in life.'

'At least I'm about to make a good marriage, so your

fanciful ideas are coming true,' Rose said, making sure Ben couldn't hear them, as he'd be sure to pull her leg. 'Mind you, if Ben had been a fisherman working out of Ramsgate Harbour, I'd have been just as keen to walk down the aisle with him.'

Flora accepted the tariff card from the Nippy and leant over to add, 'But one day you will be a titled lady. No fisherman's wife can say that.' Her lips twitched slightly, and she tried not to laugh for fear of being asked what they were talking about.

'At least this way you can dine out on my future title,' Rose said, knowing she would never in a million years act like Lady Diana, as lovely as she was. 'Just think what the WI will think of that?'

'And the ARP, the Mothers' Union and the WVS,' Flora grinned, making Rose splutter into her handkerchief. 'Some of those women have looked down their noses at me for years for running a guesthouse.' Turning to the two children, she said, 'Did you know that Rose has been a Nippy, and now runs a teashop at the seaside?'

Annabelle and Marina's eyes were like saucers as they looked towards Rose to confirm Flora's words. 'You are a waitress?' the elder girl asked.

'I was a Nippy until I was promoted to running the teashop,' Rose said, not sure of the look that flitted across the child's face.

'All the staff who work for Lyons have to be trained, and they have to observe high standards,' Ben said. 'When our waitress returns for our order, we can ask her all about it. Now, what would you like to eat?' he asked, leaning over to help them choose a meal.

By the time the Nippy returned, Ben was able to request tea all round for the adults while the girls chose lime juice cordial and soda. 'We have a very mixed menu here,' Ben said as he slowly asked for curried meat and rice, meat pudding, sausage and mash, and fried fish cakes and chipped potatoes for the children. 'Perhaps we should have some baked beans and carrots as well?' he said as he passed back the tariff cards. 'If you have time, my children would like to ask you about being a Nippy.'

'Of course,' she smiled. 'Let me just put your order in so you don't have long to wait, and then I'll be back with your drinks.'

'I don't feel we should interrupt her duties. She may get in trouble for speaking to us,' Flora said. 'I remember you saying how that manager you had when you worked at the Ramsgate teashop was a right tyrant.'

'She was, but most of the manageresses are very pleasant. I had to attend this very branch when I came up for training, and I found all the staff to be very nice.'

'They had to teach you how to serve tea?' Annabelle asked incredulously. 'Even I can do that.'

'Pouring out one cup of tea for Grandmamma is not the same as being a waitress,' her younger sister replied. 'Besides, you managed to spill it in the saucer and made a terrible mess. She told you never to make her tea again,' Marina added, reaching out to hold Rose's hand. 'I think you would have been a very pretty Nippy.'

Ben winked at Rose as she made her thanks.

'If you watch the Nippies, you will see they have a certain way of presenting the food. They also have to know how to address the customers and know how to add up purchases,' Rose explained as she pointed out several of the waitresses working close to their table.

'Here you are, sir. Your meals won't be long,' their Nippy said as she returned with a tray laden with their refreshments. 'I take it these are yours?' She smiled as she placed the lime cordials in front of the two girls. 'I hope you enjoy them. Now, what was it you wanted to ask me?'

Annabelle sipped her drink before turning to the Nippy. 'Thank you, this is very tasty. May I ask if you have to be clever to be a manageress of a teashop? Not a big one like this,' she added, looking in Rose's direction. 'Perhaps a small one at the seaside.'

Rose heard Flora take a sharp intake of breath and prayed she'd say nothing to the child. At the moment she was Ben's responsibility. She could see that Ben was about to speak, but the Nippy answered first.

'Goodness me, Mr Joe Lyons only hires the most clever and intelligent women to run his teashops. You have to be someone very special to take on that job. Very few of us Nippies are promoted to manageress,' she added, giving a sly smile in Rose's direction. 'Now, if you will excuse me, I'll go and see if your food is ready.'

Annabelle fell silent during the meal, but Rose could see she was watching the staff very closely, as well as an older woman dressed in a stern uniform who walked back and forth through the ground-floor serving area.

'There are two floors to this restaurant, and they also have music to entertain the diners. Look, you can see the platform where they perform, over by the aspidistra plants,' Ben said as he noticed his eldest daughter looking around. 'Now, eat up, and we may just have time for some ginger pudding and custard. Flora tells me it is her favourite, and Rose often takes it home for her.'

'Ooh, yes please,' both girls chanted together, and quickly cleared their plates.

'We will have to be on our way soon,' Ben said as they all finished their puddings. 'Apart from giving you the grand tour of the family business, I have something we need to talk about – and we need to drop the girls back at Mother's first.'

'Oh, can't we come with you?' they both begged.

'No, not this time,' Ben said rather abruptly.

Flora was surprised at the way he spoke to his daughters. It crossed her mind that Ben had not been quite as animated as he normally was, falling silent several times during the meal. She hoped there wasn't a problem. Would he be able to talk privately with Rose if she was tagging along? 'If you don't mind, I think I'll go back with the children. I have a headache coming on.'

'Mum, we'll come with you. Ben can show me the business another time.'

'No, I'll be fine. I think it was the champagne from last night. Why don't we catch a bus back?' she said to the girls, who nodded in agreement.

'Take care, and if the air-raid sirens start, follow the conductor's instructions,' Ben said as he kissed them goodbye. Flora hurried to catch up with the children as they rushed to the door of the restaurant.

Rose went over to where the Nippy who'd served them was standing with several of her colleagues. 'Thank you for taking the time to answer the children's questions,' she smiled.

'That's all right, miss. We recognized you from when you were here as part of your training. To be honest, it was the handsome army captain we recognized first, and Tilly here had said as how you was taking on one of the seaside teashops. We thought as how lucky you were. I take it the kiddie is being a bit of a madam?'

'Nothing I can't handle. You certainly impressed her,' Rose grinned as she bid them good afternoon.

Outside the Lyons Corner House, Ben took her arm. Rose felt proud to be escorted by such a handsome man. At any time Ben looked tall and distinguished, but in his army uniform he stood out on the crowded London street. She'd noticed women looking his way and giving admiring glances as they walked by. 'Are the offices far from here?' she asked as he led her to the edge of the pavement and hailed a passing taxi.

Ben looked surprised. 'I thought I'd told you. The business is down at St Katharine Docks. It's a fair journey, and as we are running late, a taxi will get us there much more quickly than public transport.'

'The docks . . . by the River Thames?' she asked as he helped her into the vehicle, keeping hold of her hand. 'You have offices by the river? I thought they'd be here in the city.' She wondered whether she was dressed appropriately for a trip to the docks. Would her smart woollen suit be the right attire?

As if reading her thoughts, Ben squeezed her hand to reassure her. 'You look lovely,' he whispered, sending a shiver of delight down her spine.

'Tell me more about your family business. I'm ashamed that I haven't asked before now.'

'I wouldn't expect you to be interested. A flour mill business isn't exactly exciting.'

'Oh, but I am,' she said earnestly. 'After all, what can be made with flour plays a big part in my work. Without our baked goods, Lyons teashops would go down the pan. I'm surprised that your family's company mills in London, though.'

Ben laughed. 'We use warehouses at St Katharine Docks to import grain. What started as a small flour mill near Fife during my grandfather's lifetime has been turned into a multi-national business by my father. Some grain is transported to our mills in Scotland and Suffolk, and some is sold to other companies. The likelihood is that what we import is turned into products for Lyons, but by a third party.'

Rose wrinkled her nose as she thought of what he'd told her. 'There was me thinking your father grew the wheat and baked bread.'

'We did once . . . we still do to some extent, as my grandfather's original farm is still owned by the family. But the business has grown to the extent we have to ship in grain, and where better than from Canada? In fact, the reason I want to show you the warehouse today is that we have two grain ships docked and unloading. It will give you an idea of the size of the operation we run.'

'But what about the war? I've seen on Pathé News that our shipping is under threat all the time from U-boats. Has that affected your business?' she asked as Ben leant forward to have a word with the cab driver.

Leaning back in his seat, he nodded, his expression grave. 'It's a problem that is getting worse. Father is in Canada right now, but he's looking at ways to help the government work on increasing the potential of the farming industry back here. The more home-grown produce, and I don't mean just grain, the less reliant we are on shipping, and that means fewer lives will be lost at sea.'

Rose shook her head. 'This war is a horrid business, isn't it? To think men's lives are lost just trying to bring food into the country. There's word from head office that rationing will get worse before it gets better.'

Ben gave her a weak smile. 'We just need to do our best to make sure people are fed. It's going to be hard, but we won't go down without a fight.'

'I don't understand why you are in the army. I'd have thought you worked in a reserved occupation?'

'In a way it is. But there are others who can do my job, and the Hargreaves men have always served their country,' he explained.

Rose nodded and gazed from the window as the smart streets of London turned into a grimmer scenario of small streets of terraced houses, where children played in the roads and women stood at doorways chatting. The children seemed happy enough, but their clothes were worn hand-me-downs, and more than a few of them ran around barefoot. She had a lot to be grateful for, she thought, as the women turned to look at the taxi before returning to their conversations.

'I asked the driver to come this way to show you something,' he smiled as the cab continued to weave its way along until she spotted the ornate structure of Tower Bridge and drew in a sharp breath.

'Oh, I've always wanted to see this. The girls back in Thanet are going to be so jealous,' she sighed as she gazed in wonderment. 'Surely the Tower of London is close by? That's if I've not got my history lessons wrong.' She craned her neck, trying to see as much as possible.

'Over there,' Ben said and watched her face as she took in the famous building.

'It must be marvellous to live in London and see these well-known sights every day . . .' she said, before stopping as a thought crossed her mind. 'This may seem a daft thing, but I've given no thought to where we will live once we are married. I suppose with you in the army, life will go on much as before – with me at the teashop and you God knows where. But what about the girls? Surely they should come to live with us, which could cause a problem as I share a house with Lily and Katie . . .' Rose stopped talking to draw breath. 'I did wonder if we could rent a house near Margate for the four of us. But then, we've had so many air raids of late, I'm not sure it would be safe for the children.'

Ben took her hand again. 'That's what I need to talk to you about,' he said, looking serious. 'But later, when we are alone.'

5

'It's hard to imagine that there are men up there fighting for their lives,' Lily said as she lay on her back, her head resting on a cushion looking up into the clear blue sky. The early September sun shone down on them, and Lily did her best to ignore the anti-aircraft guns set out at regular intervals along the cliff and the barbed wire stopping people from getting onto the beach below them.

'They are fighting for us as well,' Katie said, shielding her eyes from the sun to gaze in the same direction as her friend. 'Can you tell which planes are ours?' she asked her husband Jack, who was sitting on a rug holding Lily's baby, Mary. The little thing was sleeping peacefully in his arms. As he started to explain the difference between British and German planes, Katie smiled and shook her head. 'I'm none the wiser. Some are no more than specks in the sky. I just pray that our lads are safe up there. Oh, my goodness,' she exclaimed as one of the planes emitted a cloud of black smoke before spiralling out of control into the sea. 'Did the pilot get out?' she asked, covering her eyes with one hand and then spreading her fingers wide to take a look.

'It's too far out to tell,' Mildred Dalrymple said, as she scrambled to her feet and peered out from their vantage point on the grassy area known as Westcliff. 'Hang on – I can see a parachute. At least, I think it is . . . I do wish I had my binoculars. I can't believe I've been told that civilians can't use them. They'd come in mighty handy right now. Our local coppers are far too officious, if you ask me,' she huffed.

Katie grinned at Lily. They both knew that Mildred had squirrelled away her binoculars, along with an ancient handgun, on her fishing boat, swearing to use them if there was an invasion. 'Mildred, we've already had one run-in with the law at Sea View, what with Mr Cardew being arrested as a spy. I think it best that we don't do anything else that would cause problems for Flora, don't you?'

Mildred shrugged her shoulders. 'I'd not want Flora to get into trouble. She has enough on her plate right now, what with running the guesthouse and her war duties. I'm surprised she had time to go off to London to meet that posh family Rose is marrying into.'

'You can't say Ben is posh,' Lily said as she took her daughter from Jack. 'He's like one of us, even if he does speak better than us lot.'

'His parents are still toffs. Lady this and Lord that. You don't see many of them to the pound down here in this part of Kent. I'll be surprised if our Rose wants to stay on at the teashop once she marries into the aristocracy,' Mildred added for good measure.

'Nothing will change our Rose,' Lily said as she saw the worried expression cross Katie's face. 'Don't you go worrying your head over anything that's not happened, Katie. If Rose goes all posh on us, we'll soon set her straight. You just enjoy the time you have with Jack here before he has to return to his ship. How long is it, Jack?'

'I've another two days, unless we get called back sooner,' he said politely. He was a quiet lad who was content to be with his bride, and not one to add his opinions or thoughts to a conversation. He knew his wife's friends ribbed her about him being her shadow, but he also knew it was all in good fun. The important thing was that Katie had people to look out for her while he was away . . . and if anything should happen to him.

'I don't know about you lot, but I need to get up and stretch my legs. Goodness knows where the afternoon has gone. It'll be teatime before we know it,' Katie said, allowing Jack to help her to her feet and brush blades of grass from the skirt of her summer frock. 'Are you coming back to Captain's Cottage?' she asked the other two women.

'I thought we'd walk back into the town and have a bite to eat,' Jack said to his wife. 'It's the last chance we have, as you are back at work tomorrow.'

Katie looked to her friends. 'Do you mind?'

Lily laughed out loud. 'Of course we don't mind; you two lovebirds should be enjoying each other's company as much as possible while Jack is home.' She didn't add what they were all thinking: there was a sad chance Katie might not see her young husband again. 'I do need to go to the cottage to collect some more clothes for myself, and the rest of Mary's bits and bobs. I love living at Sea View, as there's so much going on – and I'm getting used to being waited on hand and foot. I hardly see young Mary here when Joyce and Pearl arrive. I swear Pearl believes Mary is a doll she can dress and feed. As for Miss Tibbs, she seems to have taken over the cooking while Flora is away and is hell bent on fattening me up. She seems to think it'll help me produce milk,' she added. Jack turned bright red at this, which made them all laugh.

'Well, I'll have plenty of space in my van, as long as you don't mind me picking up some empty boxes on the way back and dropping them off at the boat. Then we can make a small detour so you can collect what you want from Captain's Cottage, if you like?'

'Mildred, you are a sweetheart.' Lily grinned at the older woman. 'We'll be long gone by the time you both get back,' she assured Katie and Jack, giving them a crafty wink. 'If one of you can give me a hand up, we can get cracking.' She passed the baby to Katie and held her hand out to Jack.

'Here, let me help,' Mildred said as she put both her arms around Lily and levered her onto her feet. 'I didn't hurt you, did I? It's hard to believe it's only been weeks since you were injured and this little one came along. I'm not even sure you should be out and about yet. Flora did say you were to take it easy.'

Lily brushed away Mildred's question, although her face had turned pale with the effort of getting up. 'Well, she's not here to boss me about, is she?' She winced as she took the walking stick that Jack handed to her and started to hobble towards the van. Mildred had parked close to a grassy area where they'd sat for the past couple of hours, enjoying some rare time together to cheer Lily up. She'd complained she'd hardly seen any sun since coming out of hospital and moving into Sea View.

Thank goodness there hadn't been an air raid, Mildred thought. She'd been mindful of where they stopped, so she'd be able to get Lily and the baby to an entrance to the tunnels and safety if Moaning Minnie should decide to announce the Hun were on the horizon. When Katie and Jack had strolled by arm in arm and decided to join them, she'd heaved a sigh of relief that she'd have help at hand if it was required.

'Do you think there's time for us to pop down to the teashop and show Mary off to the girls?' Lily asked as Mildred settled her in the front seat and handed the sleeping baby to her.

'What, go down to Margate?' Mildred asked in amazement.

'It's not the end of the world, and only a mile or so on from Captain's Cottage. The girls have been so kind, visiting me while I was in hospital and sending presents for Mary. I feel a bit embarrassed not having seen them to say thank you,' Lily said, looking beseechingly at Mildred.

'Oh, all right then. But you can stand me a bun and a cup of tea for my trouble,' Mildred huffed good-naturedly. She closed the door as quietly as possible, so as not to wake the baby, and started up the engine. As she pulled away from the kerb she started to think about where the closest air-raid shelter was to the teashop. With it facing out over the Margate sands, she was worried about them being a sitting target. Mildred had promised Flora she'd keep an eye on Lily until she was stronger and back on her feet properly. It would be a poor show if anything happened to the girl and her child on her watch. Hell, she'd look out for these girls until her dying breath, she thought to herself as she helped them into the teashop at their journey's end.

As the Nippies hurried to fuss over baby Mary, Phoebe, one of the senior Nippies who often assisted Rose, pulled Lily aside. 'I'm so pleased to see a friendly face.'

'Whatever's wrong?' Lily asked the normally efficient woman, who looked decidedly flustered.

'I've got that Tom White in the office and he's being quite obnoxious. He threatened to sack me,' Phoebe added, her eyes bright with unshed tears.

'Why ever would he do such a thing?' Lily asked, feeling herself bristle at the mention of the man's name.

'He said I've made a mess of the paperwork, and that no one bothered to bring him lunch in the office when he arrived. Just because I'm in charge today he is taking liberties, but I can't answer him back and put him in his place like Rose can. Honestly, Lily, the man is a bully. Rose has always told him that the Nippies are not his servants, and he is to eat in the staffroom like the rest of us.' Her chin started to wobble as she finished.

Lily rested her hand on Phoebe's shoulder. 'Look, love, you aren't to worry about this. I'll go and have a word with him. He doesn't frighten me, and he can't sack me as I'm not working for Lyons at the moment.'

Phoebe gave her a grateful nod. 'I hope that doesn't mean you're not coming back when Mary is older? We do miss you: especially at times like this.'

'Oh, I'll be back before you know it, don't you fret. I need to put food on the table for me and the baby. I'm not one for relying on friends for support, as I've always paid my way. Let me collect Mary from the Nippies – then I'll go in and have a word with Mr High and Mighty.'

'Thanks ever so, Lily. If it's any help, the staff have put a few bob in an envelope to help you out. We all know what it can be like. You're not the first Nippy not to have a man to support you, and the way this war's going there's likely to be a few more women on their own before too long.'

Lily gave the woman a quick hug and hurried to collect her daughter, who was holding court with the young Nippies as well as a few regular customers. She felt bad that her friends were dipping into their pay packets to help her out, but knew it would upset them if she were to protest or hand it back. She'd do her best to pay them all back in other ways.

'What do you want?' Tom White looked up from the sports page of his newspaper as Lily walked in holding her baby close to her breast. He wrinkled his nose in distaste as he noticed the child.

'I think it's about time we had a little word, don't you?' she said, sitting down on a hard wooden seat across the desk from where he'd taken over Rose's more comfortable place. 'I see you've made yourself at home quick enough. Miss Neville's only been gone a few days, and here you are going against her words and upsetting her staff.'

Tom White sneered at her. 'What concern is it of yours? You aren't even on the payroll anymore since you ran off to have your by-blow.' He swatted away a fly that was persistently trying to land on his half-eaten pork pie.

Lily felt herself shrink inside. She'd heard the term used before for women who'd conceived out of wedlock and fallen foul of respectable people's opinions. She might have made mistakes in her life, but she wouldn't have anyone say a nasty word about her beautiful daughter – especially this man. Mustering as much strength as possible, she squared her shoulders and looked him in the eye.

'I must have been an idiot to go with you that night and give in to your demands. I'm just thankful I saw sense even though, in some ways, it was too late,' she added, running a hand over the baby's head and following it with a kiss. 'So, I'm taking this opportunity to thank you for giving me the most precious thing I've ever had, even though you don't deserve the right to be her father.'

A look of shock gradually filtered onto Tom White's face as his cheeks turned an angry shade of pink. 'I hope you aren't telling people I fathered that . . . that . . .'

'This by-blow?' Lily said, thankful that she was holding her child; otherwise she'd most likely have smashed Rose's paperweight into Tom's astonished face.

Tom stood up suddenly, slamming his chair back against the wall, causing the baby to jerk awake and begin crying. He neither seemed to notice or care. 'You aren't going to blame your – your indiscretions on me, are you? Why, I'll have you dismissed from Lyons and make sure everyone knows how you picked on me as an excuse for you acting like a streetwalker. Plying your trade then catching some unfortunate guy, expecting him to pay for your problems!'

Lily sat silent, watching the man she'd briefly found attractive, and who she had even imagined might be her ticket out of Ramsgate and the life she'd felt, at that time, had her trapped. She'd thought long and hard while in hospital and realized that what mattered was her little girl, and the friends who had made her life worth living. To think that if Rose hadn't stepped in to stop her, she would have got rid of her baby after conception. At the time she had been so ashamed of what people might say – and fearful that the baby might have been her step-father's, after his brutal attack on her. Gazing down now into little Mary's face as she soothed her back to sleep, she could see that the father was in fact standing there in front of her – if she'd ever needed more evidence, it was there to see in the likeness between father and daughter. Evidence she'd been told before her stepfather's violent death proved he could never have fathered a child, which had cleared the mist from her eyes and made her accept that one mistake – one night with Tom White – had created this sweet child.

Turning the baby towards Tom White, she gave a thin smile, all the while holding in her anger. 'Say hello to your daughter.'

Tom slowly raised his hand to point a finger between Mary and Lily. Over Lily's shoulder, there was a small mirror hanging on the wall; Rose had placed it there so that she could check her appearance before venturing into the teashop to greet customers. His mouth was half open, ready to put Lily in her place and deny any part in fathering her child; but what he saw silenced him. He looked at his own angry features, then glanced at the baby, red-faced from being awoken so suddenly. It could have been his own late mother's image; and didn't people always say how much he resembled the woman who had more than once beaten him half unconscious when he'd brought trouble to their door? Hadn't she tried to beat him into being a good kid? Perhaps if he hadn't left home as soon as he could, things might have worked out as his mother hoped. Instead he'd hopped from job to job and bed to bed until arriving in the employ of Joe Lyons and staying put. He'd hoped that a job in catering would mean he wouldn't be called upon to fight for his country, and could see out the war in a reasonably safe job. If it became known to his bosses that he had fathered a child out of wedlock – and with one of the female staff, no less – he could end up losing his position and having to enlist. And then what?

Silence stretched between them as Tom tried to put his thoughts into some kind of comprehensible order. Lily held her breath. She'd expected angry retorts and for him to call her even more nasty names. She could cope with that, as in some ways she was to blame for her indiscretions. She should have said no when he'd encouraged her to stay the night, but she hadn't. At that point she was keen to be with him, not thinking beyond him making her his girl in time. That didn't happen, and instead she was left with a child on the way. She'd come into this office only to tell him what she thought of him, expecting nothing in return.

'Have you told anyone who her father is?' he asked in faltering words.

Lily shook her head slowly. Whatever was he thinking?

'No, I'd be too ashamed to label you as being Mary's father.'

'Mary?'

'That's her name,' she said proudly.

'It was my mother's name,' he said, not showing any form of emotion to Lily, although his stomach had lurched at her words. Was his mother still punishing him for ruining her life? 'What is it you want from me?'

Lily thought for a moment. Half a crown a week would come in handy while she wasn't working. It would be a buffer between using her meagre savings and worrying about the future. Then again, Tom would have a kind of hold over her, and it would tie him to her more than she was really comfortable with.

'I don't have much money to spare, if that's what you're after,' he added as he watched her. Anger was starting to stir inside him again, but he knew he had to walk with care or Lily Douglas could make his life hell. If only the child didn't resemble him so much . . .

Lily bit her lip as she thought, then came to her decision. 'I want a promise from you.'

'I told you, I don't have much money,' he interrupted, and she frowned.

'I don't want your money.'

Tom felt cheered for a moment before considering the alternative. 'I'm not about to marry you, if that's what you're thinking,' he said bluntly. 'I've no inclination to marry.'

Lily sneered. 'I'd not touch you with a bargepole, once was enough. You're no big catch, so don't go thinking women are falling at your feet to have a gold band on their finger.' She thought of the ring she'd purchased from Woolworths to make herself look respectable, and to protect her child from cruel taunts, and tucked her fingers under the finely knitted shawl that was wrapped around Mary to keep her snug. 'No, I want you to make me a promise.'

Tom frowned. 'What kind of promise?'

'I want you to promise that you will leave the girls who work in this teashop alone. You are not to make life hard for Rose, either.'

Tom shrugged his shoulders. Lily couldn't watch him all the time, so he'd make the promise and not stand by it. 'I can do that,' he said, trying hard not to smirk. The woman is a fool, he thought to himself.

Lily eyed him closely. She noticed a small smile on his lips. Did he think he was getting off lightly? 'I want you to sit down and write your promise twice, along with the acceptance that Mary is your daughter. You will sign and date it. I will also countersign to show that I have witnessed your promise. Oh, and I'll have a person witness the signatures.'

Tom bristled at her words. 'I'll not have any Nippy see what I have written,' he snarled.

'Don't worry about that. I know someone who will sign and keep our little secret.'

Tom sat back down and visibly relaxed. 'Then it can wait until another day when this person is available.'

'Oh no. She is here now. I'll go and call her while you get writing.' Lily nodded towards the vellum notepad and pen on Rose's desk. 'I won't be long.'

Lily could hear Tom muttering under his breath as she

left the room. Looking back, though, she saw that he'd already picked up a pen and was dipping it into the inkwell. Smiling to herself, she hurried to where Mildred was tucking into an iced bun while pouring herself a cup of tea.

'Want to join me?' Mildred grinned as she wiped crumbs from her chin.

'I'll have a cup of tea, if there's one left in the pot?' Lily sat down opposite the older woman and leant in close. 'Mildred, I have something I want you to do for me. But you must promise to keep it to yourself unless I say otherwise,' she added, and went on to explain the situation. Mildred listened intently whilst finishing her bun.

'I can't see a problem with that; but are you sure you can live on what money you have? You do know I'll always help you out. You, Rose and Katie are like the children I never had – that's why I gave Captain's Cottage to the three of you. I have no intention of ending up an old maid, living out my days there with a dozen cats and a budgie.' She shook her head in horror.

Lily giggled at the thought before becoming serious. 'I've chatted about this with Rose and Katie. We wanted you to know that if you do meet someone you want to share your life with, rather than a load of cats, we will move out straight away. First and foremost, it's your home.'

Mildred finished her tea and wiped her mouth with a napkin before giving Lily a smile. 'Rest assured that will never happen. You know my life there with my father was never happy. I much prefer living at Sea View, where I can look out over the harbour and be with my friends. Now, shall we go and sort out this chap before he scarpers?'

Lily handed Mary back to one of the doting Nippies and led the way to Rose's office. As she entered the room, Tom was blotting the second of the statements. He looked up at Mildred with distaste.

'There's no need to look like that, lad. Lily has told me everything – and I mean everything,' she said, sitting down opposite him and picking up the two sheets of notepaper. The room was silent as she studied his words, before tearing them into small pieces and throwing them into a convenient wastepaper bin. 'Let's start again, shall we? Lily, I feel that you should begin by stating you will have no call on Mr White's money in respect of the child, unless Mr White breaks any of the conditions listed below. Then, Mr White will write that he promises not to bother any Nippy working in one of the Thanet teashops, and will act in the manner befitting a . . . what is your position?'

'Salesman,' Lily said, before Tom could open his mouth.

'Salesman. You will also state that you will not be bothersome to Miss Rose Neville while she works in the employ of Lyons teashops. I also suggest that we add a clause to say that if Mr White should in any way break his promise, he will bestow the sum of five hundred pounds on Miss Mary Douglas.'

Tom blanched at the suggestions, but picked up the pen and reached for the notepaper. 'I would like it mentioned that I will not allow the child to use my surname,' he said, glaring at Mildred.

'That seems reasonable under the circumstances. Shall we have another cup of tea while Mr White finishes his writing?' Mildred said to Lily as she opened the door of the office.

Lily followed Mildred into the teashop, where they both burst into laughter before sitting down at a vacant table. 'Is any of that legally binding?'

'I doubt it – but isn't it wonderful to have him squirm a little? It hardly makes up for what you've been through, but it's a start,' Mildred smiled, before nodding to a Nippy and ordering tea for two and another bun. 'The threat of having to pay you five hundred pounds ought to make him behave at least for a while.'

'It also means no other young Nippy will fall foul of his antics,' Lily said with a bitter smile.

At that moment, her attention was caught by a developing scene behind Mildred. 'Whatever is going on?' Mildred said, noticing her friend's expression change. She spun round in her chair to see staff and customers looking out the windows of the teashop, pointing in alarm. One older woman started to cry, and a young Nippy screamed, earning a reprimand from Anya, who was behind the counter serving a customer.

'Mary? Where is my Mary?' Lily said, getting to her feet and hurrying to the door, where two Nippies were holding the child and looking up at the sky. 'What is happening, Elsie, Irene?'

'Look, Miss. The sky is full of planes. I've never seen anything like it,' Elsie said as she handed over a now sleeping Mary.

'What does it mean?' asked a trembling Irene, looking around urgently as if the answer might be found in the teashop.

Anya joined them, pushing past the worried staff and stepping out onto the pavement. 'It means that England is about to be obliterated, just like my homeland,' she said, jutting her chin out as she glared up into the sky.

Mildred noticed the Polish woman's hands were shaking, and wrapped an arm around her shoulders. 'Chin up, love. It ain't over until the fat lady sings – and I'm not about to burst into song anytime soon.'

Anya frowned. 'I have no idea what you say, Mildred, but I think it is good. We fight on, eh?'

'We certainly do, my love, we certainly do. And no German's going to be putting his feet under my table anytime soon, you mark my words. Winston will soon be seeing them off. I have complete faith in him.'

'Winston and my Henio,' Anya said proudly, cuffing away a tear that had dared fall onto her cheek. 'We fight together until the end.'

Lily watched silently as the planes passed overhead, up the Thames estuary towards London. She couldn't begin to understand what this meant to her beloved country.

'There are hundreds of them,' someone cried.

'Over a thousand, I'd say. Look, some of our guys are attacking, but it's like putting out a bonfire with a thimble-ful of cold tea.'

'Please, my Henio, stay safe,' Anya said, not taking her eyes from the sky.

'We should go down into the cellar,' Elsie declared. 'I know the siren's not gone off yet, but they might bomb us all at any minute.'

Mildred shook her head. 'No, Goering's saving them for London. The poor sods up there are in for a bad time,' she said, looking both worried and angry.

'But Flora and Rose are in London. What if something happens to them?' Lily grabbed Mildred's hand without thinking. 'What can we do to help them?'

'We can only pray,' Mildred said, her voice rising above the thunder of planes up above. By now, the air-raid sirens had started to wail, echoing up the Kent coastline towards London as a warning to the vulnerable residents living on each side of the river Thames.

6

'Thank you,' Rose said with a smile, as an elderly secretary placed a small tray containing tea and biscuits on a side table and hurried from the room. Perhaps now Ben would tell her what was on his mind.

'I didn't know what to expect,' she went on, turning to him, 'but not once did I think your family business would be so . . . so *huge*. Ships moored out in the dock, and all of this. Crikey!'

Ben, seated behind a large oak desk, roared with laughter. 'The ships aren't ours. They bring grain for us to process. It isn't often we have two in the dock at the same time.'

Rose nodded thoughtfully as she kicked off her shoes. It had taken two hours for Ben to show her round, and her head was still buzzing. She'd had the idea in her head that their tour of the business would be a quick trip to the Thames, to look around a small office and peer down into the murky water. Nothing could have been further from the truth. The river was as busy as the roads of London, but with ships and smaller boats instead of lorries and cars. There must have been a hundred workers in the offices and warehouse, before you even began counting the sailors on the ships as they prepared to offload the grain from Canada.

Ben looked up at the clock. 'I'd hoped to have been done by now and treat you to dinner and possibly a show, but I've so much to sign off before . . .'

'Before what?' Rose asked. Ben, although animated as he talked about the business, had turned quiet at times. She'd watched him look out over Victoria Dock, clearly deep in thought. He'd seemed very far away from her for a moment, and it had made her uneasy. 'Is there something on your mind?'

Ben gave her a smile that lit up his face. It was something she'd noticed when she'd first known him: his smile could wash away her fears. But this time she thought he was hiding something. 'Now's not the time. Let's enjoy our engagement, shall we? Drink your tea while I finish this, and then who knows – we might just be able to do something later this evening, if only for an hour or two. Perhaps we could go dancing? I know I'd like a few hours away from all this to be with my favourite girl.'

'Don't try to sway me with your promises of food and dancing, Ben Hargreaves,' Rose laughed. 'I'm happy to sit here and watch you work. However, I have a feeling you're keeping something from me,' she added, the smile slipping from her face. 'You will tell me what's troubling you – won't you? Let's never have secrets from each other. You know I want to be a proper mother to the children. We need to make plans.'

'Later, my love. I promise you'll have my undivided attention once we're away from here.'

Rose was happy with his answer, and sipped her tea thoughtfully before walking over to a large window that overlooked the docks. 'There's something so soothing about water. A few minutes just standing and watching, and I feel so calm,' she sighed. 'We should always live close to the sea, or at least a river . . .'

She halted mid-sentence as air-raid sirens started to wail. Being used to the sirens in Thanet and knowing that she could reach an air-raid shelter comparatively quickly, she knew it would be the same in London. There would be time for them to get to safety. Craning her neck to look to the skies, she cried out in horror. 'Oh my God – no . . .'

Ben was out of his seat within seconds. Rushing to her side, he pulled her from the window, but not before he saw the full horror of what had made her cry out. The sky was almost black, as hundreds of planes blocked out the afternoon sun. 'What the hell?' he swore out loud as he threw Rose to the ground, pushing her under the solid wooden desk for safety. A massive explosion shattered the windows even through the criss-crossed tape.

'We're going to die,' Rose sobbed as she clung to Ben. 'We're going to die before we get married and spend any time together. I hate this war!'

Ben soothed her as the building shook around them. 'We need to get out of here and to the shelter. I don't feel we should attempt the cellar here, but we should try to get to the public one a few streets away from the docks. It will be much safer there.'

'What about your staff?' Rose asked as she wiped her eyes on the cuff of her jacket and slipped her feet back into her shoes. 'Do you think they are safe?'

'We can check as we go downstairs,' Ben said, avoiding her imploring look. He doubted many had reached safety in time, although he prayed that he was wrong. 'Come on, let's get cracking,' he said as he helped Rose to her feet and held her hand. They headed to a door that was now hanging from its hinges. 'Stay close and try not to let go,' he advised as she pulled back at the sight of the staircase. Much of the balustrade was missing and the air was filled with dust, making them both cough until they were gasping for breath.

'Is it safe?' she asked as he tentatively tested the first step.

'If it takes my weight, it'll take yours,' he said encouragingly.

Gradually they took the steps one at a time, leaning against the outside wall. The sound of dripping water could be heard, and they were bathed in a strange light filled with dust motes: part of the roof had gone. Ben stopped suddenly and turned to Rose as he let go of her hand to pull off his army jacket. 'I want you to be brave and trust me,' he said, looking her straight in the eye. 'I'm afraid Miss Fortescue didn't make it to safety, and is lying at the foot of this staircase. I will cover her as best I can to protect her modesty, and we can alert the services when we are able to make a report. Will you be all right?'

Rose bit her lip and nodded. Hadn't she seen countless injured men being brought ashore from the Little Ships when they'd docked at Ramsgate and Margate? Death is nothing to be feared, she told herself as she stepped past the covered body of the elderly secretary who only moments ago had brought tea and biscuits to them. The woman's arms and legs lay at grotesque angles, but Ben had covered her head and torso as best he could. Rose tried to tell herself that this was much more of an ordeal for Ben, who must have known the woman for a long time. 'God bless you,' she murmured as they continued across the small landing and down another flight of stairs. This time there wasn't so much damage, but even so Ben tested each step.

'Only one more floor and we'll be at ground level,' he said, looking back with a smile that didn't quite reach his eyes.

'Be careful,' she whispered as she saw that more doors along the passage had been blown away. Typists and administrative clerks had worked there; she had seen them during their tour. She forced herself not to look, keeping her eyes on Ben's back as he reached the last flight of stairs.

'These are concrete steps, though some have been damaged,' he said as they spotted the jagged remains of metal supports and lumps of concrete. 'The banister seems to have held up . . .' He gave the metal bars a good shake. 'We can do this.'

'We can, Ben, we can,' she agreed, although her voice was weak. 'But please don't do anything silly.'

Ben put a foot onto the first step, then grabbed the banister as the concrete crumbled beneath him. Letting go of Rose's hand in case he pulled her down, he held tightly onto the banister as another step failed. 'It looks as though we won't be able to use this staircase,' he said as he pulled himself back up beside her.

'Are we trapped?' she asked. More explosions could be

heard, not far away; the bombs were continuing to rain down on the East End of London. A sudden anger engulfed her. She'd be blowed if the enemy was going to kill her when she had so much to look forward to. 'There must be another way out of here, surely?'

'There's a fire escape on the outside of the building, but it may have perished,' Ben said as he wiped dust and sweat from his face.

'There's no use talking about it. Let's go and look,' she urged him.

'Yes, Miss Neville,' he said, giving her a mock salute as he again took her hand and guided her to a metal door on the other side of the landing. Sliding back the bars that held it closed, he hung onto the door frame.

'They are still there,' Rose exclaimed as she peered over his shoulder before freezing in horror. 'Oh my God!'

It was as if the world had come to an end.

Flora kept her arms around the two young children. 'Shh – we are safe. No one can hurt you,' she soothed them.

'But Daddy is out there with Rose,' the youngest girl, Marina, hiccuped as she did her best to stop crying. 'The bombs may have hurt them.'

Flora thought the same as the child, and was praying that her daughter was keeping safe wherever she was. Close to tears herself, she knew she needed to stay strong for the youngsters – and also Lady Diana, who was being cared for by Ruth. She'd tripped as they went down into the cellar underneath the building, twisting her ankle.

The cellar was just like a smaller version of Lady Diana's apartment.

Flora's thoughts strayed back to Ramsgate and Sea View. What was it like for her friends and residents on the Kent coast? She hoped with all her might that they were safe and had reached the shelters in time. She closed her eyes, trying to imagine life below ground in the Ramsgate tunnels. Mildred had worked hard creating a small space for them to stay in together. She'd even joked that it was like camping, but without a view. A rough framework had been built, and covered in sacking to create walls. There was room for four beds, although six of them had huddled together during the last raid before Flora left for London with Rose. Miss Tibbs had brought a picture of the king and queen to hang on the wall, and a vase that she said would look nice filled with flowers and placed on the upturned orange box they used as a table. Each time they went underground, they took items to make their 'home from home' as attractive as possible. Mildred had provided a hurricane lamp and a small paraffin stove as well as two deck chairs, declaring that if they had to rough it at least they would do so in comfort.

Pearl had promised to care for baby Daisy. Flora's heart lurched, thinking of the possibility that the young child would be taken from them. In the weeks Daisy had lived at Sea View, she had become part of the motley band of people who called the guesthouse home. Flora hoped the support of the vicar and the mayor would mean the child could stay with them. Who knows, perhaps in time she could adopt the child – that's if they all survived this relentless bombing. She ached to be at home again in

Ramsgate, carrying out her air-raid warden duties and looking after her brood. But she'd not leave London until she knew Rose and her Ben were safe.

In a side room of the shelter, one of the building staff was preparing hot drinks. Flora left the girls cuddled up to each other and went to see if she could help in some way.

'Thank you, madam, but we have everything in hand,' the man said. Flora knew him only as 'Porter', and wasn't sure if that was his actual name or his job title. 'However, if you'd like to wind up the gramophone, it would be pleasant to have some music. It would help to block out the sounds from outside.'

Flora shook her head in disbelief as she went to find the gramophone and turn the brass handle to wind it up. Wait until the residents back at Sea View heard about this shelter complete with a servant, she smiled to herself. Now, what record should she select? She spotted a favourite song, and placed the needle on the 78-rpm record before rejoining the two children sitting between them. They'd perked up as they saw what Flora was doing.

'*Daisy, Daisy, give me your answer do . . .*' she started to sing, as the crackly music came from the large horn above the gramophone.

'Oh my, I've not heard this in many a long year,' Lady Diana exclaimed. All thoughts of her aching ankle were forgotten as she too joined in with the song.

Everyone applauded as the song came to an end and Flora rose to curtsey, much to the children's amusement.

'Why, Flora, I can see where Rose has inherited her talent from,' Lady Diana said as she too applauded.

'You're not so bad yourself,' Flora grinned. 'Do I detect a trained voice?'

Lady Diana brushed away the comment. 'That was another life and a long time ago,' she smiled, as her grand-children rushed to the toy box kept in the shelter. 'You and I aren't so very different, Flora Neville,' she added. 'Why don't we sing another song? I'm partial to Vesta Tilly, or perhaps Marie Lloyd. I take it you know their songs?'

'I do,' Flora said, trying not to look surprised. Marie Lloyd's songs were considered by some people to be a little risqué. 'I prefer Florrie Forde myself. I take it you have attended some of London's variety theatres?'

'Don't get Mother started on her theatrical memories,' Ruth grinned as she went to join her two nieces, who had settled on the floor with a jigsaw puzzle.

Lady Diana gave her daughter a knowing nod as if she was used to being ribbed about her early years. 'I more than visited them. I was a star turn at one time, along with my siblings. We were the Desmond Sisters. You may have come across us? Actually, I do recollect you in your heyday,' she said, giving Flora a wink.

Flora couldn't believe her ears. 'Why, we followed you on many a bill. I was hardly more than a chorus girl, but you and your sisters were . . . why, you were stars!' she exclaimed. She could clearly recall the four sisters – Doris, Deirdre, Dorothy and Diana – who sang and danced their way to the top of the variety circuit. They had all married well apart from Doris, who as far as Flora could remember had left the troupe early, fading from the scene.

Lady Diana dismissed Flora's compliment with a flick

of her hand. 'Those days seem so long ago now. How I wish . . .' she started to say with a big sigh.

'You wish we could return to them?' Flora asked. 'I do confess to feeling the same way. They were such gay times, and we were so young. How are your sisters?'

Lady Diana looked to where the children were playing and patted the seat next to her, encouraging Flora to sit closer. 'We lost Deirdre three years ago. Her heart was never good, not even in our performing years. It was one of the reasons we gave up touring. I do miss her,' she sighed. 'Dorothy – we call her Dolly – settled in Canada and is doing wonderfully well. Her husband is a theatre impresario. Dolly still has her finger in the show-business pie, lucky thing. She wants me to go out there until this horrid war is over, but I'm loath to leave the family. I'd feel like a failure. However, what use am I here? I do nothing for the war effort, and try as I might, I cannot think of a way to help.'

'How is Doris?' Flora asked, wondering as she always had what had happened to the sister who vanished.

A shadow crossed Lady Diana's face. She hesitated, then shrugged her shoulders. 'I've never told a soul what happened to the fourth Desmond Girl. But as you are almost family, Flora, I shouldn't keep it a secret any longer . . . Doris went to prison. There, I've said it.' She exhaled slowly, as if a great weight had been lifted from her shoulders.

'Oh,' was all Flora could think of to say. She thought to herself that it had been kept very quiet. The whole of the entertainment circuit had wondered what had happened to Doris, although many had been quick to give their opinions. 'I'm sorry, Lady Diana – that must have been a big disappointment to you. I hope it didn't split the family apart. I know these things can.'

'You must call me Diana,' she replied, patting Flora's hand. 'We are almost family, after all. As for Doris – there was no saving her,' she said rather dramatically. 'Unbeknown to us, she'd married into a family of crooks and thieves and quickly fell under their spell. When she was caught stealing jewels from a well-to-do family, who were close to the royals no less, she was sent down for quite a few years. Fortunately for us, she was arrested and charged under her married name, so the mud didn't stick to the Desmond Sisters. If, as did happen occasionally, a reporter enquired about Doris's whereabouts, we let it be known that she was poorly; and gradually she was forgotten. Then, of course, time moved on, and the rest of the sisters married and stopped performing together. I have written to Doris on occasion, as part of me would like to heal the rift. However, I've yet to receive a reply.'

Flora nodded. However much money someone had, they could still be haunted by family troubles. 'I'm sorry to hear of your problems. If it is any consolation, I never heard a whisper about Doris. Your secret is safe with me, Lady . . . I mean, Diana,' she corrected herself – although it felt strange to be calling this woman by her Christian name.

Rose reached out to hold onto Ben, feeling giddy with the shock of what she could see from the open doorway of the fire exit. They were twenty feet from the ground.

The metal staircase that clung desperately to the side of the bombed warehouse was buckled in places, but still secure. The whole dock area was on fire; the tall warehouses had either been demolished by the relentless bombing, or were now burning. Even the ships in the docks had not escaped. She gasped as she saw the two large ships that had brought grain to Ben's family's warehouse – one had sunk, while the other was in flames and sat low in the water, gradually slipping deeper as she watched. Above them, the enemy planes she recognized as Stukas were screeching as they targeted ships and buildings, while more planes moved on up the Thames to the city of London to do their worst.

Despite the crashing of damaged buildings as they collapsed and the onslaught of the enemy planes, Rose could hear the cries of the injured and dying; some of them in the river, fighting to stay afloat, while others were trapped inside burning buildings. 'We've got to help them,' she said, turning to Ben. 'Please, Ben, we can't stand here watching people die.'

'We need to save ourselves first, then we can help others. And if we aren't careful getting down these stairs, we'll be of no use to anyone,' he said as he checked the small platform before taking a few tentative steps. 'Stay close, and if I tell you to turn back or jump, do as I say and don't question me,' he shouted over his shoulder as another plane dropped a string of bombs along the dock. They were suddenly drenched from head to foot in dirty water, mixed with fuel leaked from the damaged ships as bombs exploded underwater. Ben ran a hand over his face and hair. 'Are you all right?'

'I'm fine. Let's get going before I change my mind,' she shouted, giving him a gentle push on his back. 'Hurry, before another plane attacks the warehouse.' She would never forget this day as long as she lived – that's if she survived today.

Eventually reaching the ground, Ben turned and lifted Rose down from the last of the steps. For a brief moment they clung together before pulling apart.

'I'll take you to safety, then I'm coming back to help,' he said, not expecting her to disagree.

'You'll do no such thing. I can be of assistance here. I know a little first aid, which could help. I'd never forgive myself if I ran and hid when I'm able to aid the injured until proper help arrives.'

Ben took her by the shoulders and looked into her eyes. 'You do realize you will see some distressing sights? I want to protect you as much as possible, my love,' he said.

'We're a team, Ben Hargreaves, and I'm going with you whether you like it or not,' she replied. 'Now, come on, let's get cracking.'

Although still under fire from enemy aircraft, Rose was soon helping uninjured staff from businesses surrounding the docks to tend to the walking wounded. Sadly, there was very little that could be done for many people. As the fire service arrived along with ambulance staff, Rose eventually found she was surplus to requirements.

Gratefully accepting a mug of tea from a woman in a WVS uniform, she took a deep gulp, only then realizing how dry she was. It seemed a lifetime ago that she'd sat in Ben's office drinking tea brought in by his secretary, who was now lying dead inside the building. She shook her head to remove the image. Now was not the time to think of such things.

'I've been watching you,' a young woman said as she took her own mug and joined Rose. 'Are you in the services?'

'No, I was caught up in the air raid while in that warehouse over there,' Rose said, pointing to what was left of Ben's family business. 'I stayed to help out.'

'You've done well. I thought perhaps you was an off-duty nurse or something?'

'Goodness no, I'm nothing so grand. I'm a manageress of the Lyons teashop in Margate. I picked up a bit of first aid while in the Girl Guides, and my mum dragged me along to learn about bandaging and suchlike. She's an ARP warden and also helps out on the WVS. She puts me to shame.' Rose smiled ruefully.

'You should think about joining up. We can always do with girls like you in the ambulance service. Even better if you can drive, as we always want more drivers who can keep a clear head about them in situations like this. You seem to be made of stern stuff.'

'I don't know about that,' Rose said, suddenly feeling quite light-headed. She reached out to hold onto the counter of the WVS canteen truck.

'Steady on,' the girl said, taking her arm. 'Here, sit down on this wall. I bet you've not eaten for hours, have you?'

'I'm fine; I had a big lunch,' Rose said, feeling rather silly.

'Then no wonder you feel as you do after working so hard. You've missed your dinner. Eat this,' she said, reaching for a cheese sandwich that was being passed out through the serving hatch of the canteen by one of the women in the van. 'It's that National Bread, but it doesn't taste too bad. And in the twilight, who can tell it's not as white as it should be? You're probably used to better food in your teashop,' she grinned.

'I'm not fussy,' Rose said as she took a large bite, and sighed as she chewed the bread and cheese. 'Caviar couldn't taste any better – not that I've tasted caviar,' she grinned at the girl. 'I'm Rose Neville, by the way,' she added, holding out her hand. Her fellow diner shook it vigorously.

'Pleased to meet you. I'm Janet Sullivan. You know, you really should think about joining up. I know you'd do well. You are wasted working in a teashop.'

Rose smiled and explained how, along with fellow Nippies, she'd helped as the troops from Dunkirk came back to the Kent shores, and how they were always busy keeping customers fed and the teashops open for business. Even so, as she spoke, she felt rather guilty that she wasn't directly doing her bit for the war effort. She promised herself she would do more to help out. Perhaps she could join her mum with the WVS, and anything else that came up. Mind you, she'd soon be married, and then there would be children to consider . . .

'You seem miles away,' Janet said as she brushed crumbs from the blue full-length uniform coat she wore as an ambulance driver, before reaching for a fresh mug of tea.

'I was just thinking that I'll be married before too long, and then who knows where I'll be.'

'Isn't your chap in the services?'

'Yes, Ben is a captain in the West Kents. He's here somewhere helping out,' Rose said, glancing round to see if she could spot him in the fast-descending gloom.

'Then best you rush him up the aisle before he disappears off to fight. There's no knowing when he'll be back. Come to that, he may not come back,' Janet said.

Rose was taken aback at her abrupt words. There again, hadn't she said the same to Katie when she'd thought about waiting to marry her Jack? They really should set a date. Although they both said it should be soon, nothing had been decided. 'Yes, you are right,' she agreed, still deep in thought.

'Well, I'm off. There's no peace for the wicked,' Janet said as she slapped Rose on the arm. 'It was good to meet you, Rose. I'll maybe get down to Margate and visit your teashop before too long. I'm due a bit of leave.'

'Please do that. I'll stand you a slap-up meal,' Rose called out as she watched the girl depart, before heading out to where she'd last seen Ben. Staying away from the dockside, where fires were still raging on the ships, she picked her way towards the family warehouse and soon spotted Ben deep in conversation with a group of men. As she got closer, she could hear what he was saying.

'I'll not be around much longer, so I'll leave this with you,' he said, shaking hands and turning to see her. 'Rose – I was about to come and find you.' They both jumped as an explosion came from across the dock. 'There's not much more we can do to help here. Come on, let's get you somewhere safe. The family will be wondering what has happened to us.'

'I'm concerned for their safety,' Rose said, allowing him

to take her arm as they walked further from the dock area as the all-clear sounded. But for how long? she wondered. The people she'd worked with tending the injured seemed to think this was not the only attack on the capital; and what had Ben meant when he told those men he wouldn't be around much longer? She stopped walking and turned to look at him. 'I refuse to walk another step until you tell me what is on your mind,' she said stubbornly. 'Are you going away?'

Ben pulled her into his arms and kissed her oil-streaked forehead. 'I'm sorry. I should have said something earlier, before we were caught up in this air raid. I've been recalled for duty earlier than expected. I'm afraid it means us putting a hold on our wedding plans.'

'Oh, Ben,' Rose sobbed into his jacket. 'This bloody war seems hell-bent on keeping us apart. I'm not worried about a wedding; I just want to know you are here with me, and not off somewhere putting yourself in danger.'

He stroked her face before raising her chin and claiming her lips, silencing her distress. 'I promise you I'll be back with you as soon as I can. Perhaps by Christmas we will be man and wife?' he said, giving her a tender look.

'Just come back to me. That's all I ask.'

7

'My dears, we've been so worried about you,' Lady Diana said as she hurried to hug Rose and Ben before gesturing for them to sit beside her on a sofa. 'I tried to use the telephone to contact the office, but the wretched line was out of action.'

Rose gave Flora a kiss before joining Ben. 'How has it been for you here?' she asked, trying to put off the moment when they would have to break the news of the destruction of the warehouses. 'Where did you take shelter?'

'We managed to reach the cellar very quickly, even going down by the staircase,' Flora said, giving Rose a small smile to reassure her. 'It's nothing like the air-raid shelters we've used. Why, it's a smaller version of these rooms. I could easily move down there permanently.'

'So could the children, after the fun they've had,' said Ruth, walking into the drawing room and throwing herself down into an armchair, leaving one leg draped over the arm. 'If I have to sing another chorus of "I do like to be beside the seaside", I swear I'll scream. You two have opened a can of worms with your singing and reminiscing,' she said, aiming a grin at Rose and Lady Diana. 'They will never stop singing that line from "Burlington Bertie", *I had a banana with Lady Diana* . . . I must admit it's a bit of a hoot. Why did she never tell us more about this, Ben? I swear our mother was a different person in her youth.'

'Because dear Mother made a point of not mentioning her past life,' Ben smiled indulgently towards Lady Diana. 'It wouldn't have been seemly for a family moving up in the world and mixing with royalty to have had a member who kicked up her heels on stage.'

'Oh, I don't know,' Ruth said as she teased her mother. 'I heard from Tilly Hartdyke that the young princesses like nothing more than to put on shows at Buck House for family and friends, and their mother knows many of the words to the songs.'

'But it wouldn't have been seemly for your father to be known to have married an entertainer. He moved in such influential circles, and it was important to be seen as a responsible businessman. I kept my head down and learnt the ropes as the wife of someone moving up in the world. Before too long, my past was forgotten – although it is a period of my life I look back on fondly. Times were so different back then,' Lady Diana sighed. 'I know I am older than you, Flora dear, but I'm sure you found it very much the same?'

'You are right, Diana,' Flora agreed. 'My romance with General Sykes was kept quiet for the benefit of his children. At that time, he was separated from his first wife and lived alone, but to be seen with a girl from the chorus line was still frowned upon. However, like you I look back with a smile, because without those days I'd not have had my darling Rose. Despite the hours spent in the shelter, today's reminiscing has been enjoyable; and it took the children's thoughts away from the constant bombing.' She smiled. 'To think we moved in the same circles so many years ago, Diana – and you knew Rose's father.'

Rose raised her eyebrows as her mum called Lady Diana by her first name alone. 'You knew the General? Please do tell me, and don't leave out a single thing. I wasn't made aware he was my father until long after he passed away,' she explained to Ruth and Ben.

'There will be time for that,' Lady Diana said, 'but first, you must tell me what happened at the docks – and to our staff. Your father will be expecting a report sent to him in Canada.'

'It's not good news, Mother. Both grain ships were hit in the dock and much of the warehouse and offices all but demolished. We stayed to help, but there was very little to be done,' Ben said in a serious voice. 'I fear, like many other businesses set around the docks, that this will be a serious setback to the food industry. Father needs to be made aware of what has happened. I've already sent a telegram requesting his return as soon as possible. I've also spoken to the ministry. There's not much more I can do, apart from speaking to the families of our employees and making sure they do not suffer financially for the loss of their loved ones. We will provide for the funerals of our employees, just as Grandfather did in his time.'

Lady Diana gasped. 'There were lives lost? Please don't say it was many . . .' she cried, reaching for her handkerchief.

'That's a bugger,' Ruth swore and sat up straight in her armchair. 'Do we know them, Ben?'

He stood up and paced up and down, trying to compose himself before nodding, a grim look on his face. 'Some will be known to you. Miss Fortescue, Dad's secretary, was working late in the office, as were some of the women in the typing pool. Six men down in the warehouse, and God knows how many went down with the two ships . . . I've done as much as I can for now, and have told everyone how they can reach me while I'm away and before Father gets back – which could be a couple of weeks yet. Ruth, I'll need you to step into the breach, old thing.'

'As much as I'd love to, sweetie, I'm not going to be around much. That's the reason I came up to London, that and to meet Rose and Flora. Bertie Johnson wants me to join him at the War Office. It seems he feels I have skills he can use to fight the Hun.'

'So many lives lost . . .' Lady Diana moaned, unable to take in her daughter's words.

Rose looked round the room at the assembled people, taking in Lady Diana's unhappiness, Ruth's determination to do her bit, and Flora's sadness at what the war had brought to these people who were soon to be part of her family. Most of all, she looked at her beloved Ben, with his firm jaw and steel-grey eyes. He'd seen some horrifying sights today, and not faltered in what he had to do – all the time knowing he was off again to fight the war, and leaving the women he held close to his heart to fend for themselves. Rose's heart ached for him, and also for herself. When would the wedding be, and would he survive to make her his wife?

'Oh Ben,' she said, rushing into his arms, where he held

her close as she cried. 'Stay safe, my love, and come back to us as quickly as you can.'

Rose couldn't keep her eyes from the large clock hanging from the ceiling of the busy Lyons Corner House. Had it really only been a few days since they'd enjoyed lunch here with Flora and the girls? Now, in a few hours Ben was leaving to join his regiment.

He looked so smart in his uniform, the polished buckles and buttons catching the light as he moved. She sipped her tea, hoping it would dislodge the dry bread of her sandwich, which wouldn't move despite her swallowing. Grimacing, she dropped another sugar lump into her cup and stirred.

'You'll wear out that spoon if you keep stirring like that,' Ben said, trying hard to make her smile.

Rose put down the silver teaspoon, trying desperately hard not to break down in front of him. The last thing he needed was the memory of her tear-stained face. 'Oh, Ben, this is so wretched. Why, now of all times, do they want you back with your regiment?' she said, looking dejected.

'My love, the enemy has no interest in those of us wishing to marry and live quietly. I promise you that when the time is right, we will walk down the aisle with dozens of bridesmaids and a ton of cake. Our mothers will be resplendent in their best outfits, weeping all the while, and church bells will ring out to tell the world you are my wife . . .'

'Oh, please stop,' Rose begged, pulling her handkerchief

from the cuff of her cardigan. 'I promised myself I'd not let you see me cry, and here I am doing just that,' she sniffed, although she was smiling at the thought of what he'd said. 'I'd be happy with Annabelle and Marina, as well as Lily and Katie, your sister as well. I shouldn't leave out young Pearl, either,' she added as an afterthought. 'Oh, and Mary may well be toddling by then, so I must include her. Then there's Daisy . . .'

Ben laughed. 'That sounds like more than half a dozen to me. What about a few Nippies outside the church, holding teapots on high as they form a guard of honour?'

'Now you are teasing me,' Rose said, pretending to slap his arm before joining in with his laughter.

'That's more like it,' Ben said as he watched the smile return to her face. 'That's how I want to remember you, my love. You must write every day with all of your wedding ideas. I want to be able to imagine the day as it gets closer and closer.' He threw his napkin onto the table. 'Shall we get out of here, while we still have time? I want to be alone with you, if that's at all possible.'

'That's a great idea, and I have the ideal place,' she replied. They quickly paid the bill, and stepped out onto the busy London street.

'Follow me.' Rose took his hand and hurried along to a cinema. 'Here you are.'

'*Old Mother Riley Joins Up?*' he laughed, looking up at the sign above the main doors of the cinema. 'How will we be alone in a packed picture house?'

Rose just giggled and led him inside to the ticket booth. 'Two in the stalls, please,' she said, reaching for her purse.

Ben gently brushed her aside and paid for the tickets.

'A gentleman always pays,' he said as he accepted the tickets and change, and they walked across the plush carpet, stepping through two swinging doors into the silence of the cinema.

'Can we sit at the back, please?' Rose asked the usherette, who gave her a wink and shone her torch to where a long stretch of empty seats was caught in the beam of light.

'Take yer pick, love,' she said, before moving away to check the tickets of newcomers.

'Let's hope there won't be many people wanting to watch Old Mother Riley in the middle of the afternoon,' Rose murmured, as they removed their coats and settled down.

Ben draped his arm round her shoulders. 'Why, Miss Neville, I do wonder how often you've done this before?' he said, nuzzling her ear as the lights dimmed even more and the latest report from Pathé News started.

'Oh my God,' Rose exclaimed. 'Look, it's the docks! Isn't that one of the ships that was delivering to your warehouse?'

'It's hard to comprehend,' Ben said as he squeezed her shoulder. 'We were lucky to get away from there with our lives.'

They watched in horror as the film showed parts of London completely annihilated by the blitzkrieg.

'You're going back to Ramsgate on the next train. Just collect your suitcase and your mum, and go,' Ben said, his eyes never leaving the screen.

'But I was going to stay on for a few days and help look after the girls while Mum and Diana went shopping and had a few more days to get to know each other. With Ruth starting work, someone needs to care for the children.'

'I'm getting the girls out of London as soon as possible. They can't stay here. They'll be killed – I just know it,' he said in despair, as the film continued to show the devastation of London. 'I just need to think of the safest place to send them,' he added before being hushed by a couple in the seats in front, and giving his apologies.

'Let them come with me,' Rose whispered as she clung to his arm. 'I know we've had a lot of bombing, but it must be safer in Ramsgate right now – it's nowhere near as bad as here.'

'I don't know. I gave up the lease on the farmhouse because it was too close to an airfield in Kent. Surely Thanet is just as bad?'

'We have the tunnels under the town, and there are so many people who will care for the girls while I'm working,' she assured him. 'Where else can they go?'

He shrugged. 'Back to Scotland would be ideal, but it depends on what Mother has planned. The house there is mainly closed at the moment with her being down here. The plan was for her to join Father in Canada, and the girls to stay with Ruth in your home county. But that's neither here nor there, now all this has happened,' he said, nodding to the screen, where a family of Cockneys was grinning at the camera while pushing their worldly belongings heaped on top of an old pram.

'Please consider sending them down to stay with us while you decide,' Rose begged. 'It will also give them time to get to know me better.'

'I'll speak to Mother and Ruth, but you must leave for Ramsgate tomorrow. Promise me you will? I couldn't rest knowing you were here and in danger.'

Rose chuckled. 'There's me worrying about you, and you worrying about me. What a fine pair we are.'

'We are a pair, married or not, and I hope we will remain a pair for many years to come,' he said, leaning closer, seeking her lips as the B picture started.

Rose returned his kisses, closing her eyes, enjoying being as near as possible and alone with the man she hoped to marry. She sighed suddenly and leant forward, looking at the large screen.

'What's wrong?'

'It's Johnny Johnson . . .'

'Who the hell is Johnny Johnson?'

'For goodness' sake, Ben. Johnny plays secret agent Clive Danvers. We never miss one of his films. The girls will be green with envy knowing I've seen his latest.'

Ben leant back in his seat and did his damnedest not to laugh out loud. 'Here I am going off to war, and all that's required is an actor to win the war for us.'

At that moment an air-raid siren started to wail, and a notice appeared on the screen advising customers to go to the nearest shelter.

'Where's Johnny Johnson when you need him?' Ben laughed as they grabbed their coats and hurried out of the building.

'I am pleased that Flora and Rose are safe,' Anya said as she piled the few loaves of bread that had been delivered onto the shelves behind the counter. 'Did you know we all cheered when she made a telephone call to Sea View?'

Katie nodded, lost in her own thoughts. Her red-rimmed eyes showed she had spent most of the night crying, and had continued to do so as her husband kissed her goodbye before returning to his ship.

'You will be no good to Joe Lyons if you look like the limp lettuce,' Anya admonished her. 'Go to the staffroom and tidy yourself – and put a smile on your face. We are here to cheer up our customers as well as feed them,' she commanded. 'Not that we have had as much delivered as usual,' she muttered as Katie obeyed, forgetting for the moment that it was she who was in charge of the tearoom that day and not Anya.

Heading into the staffroom, she heard a chair scrape across the floor, followed by the rustle of paper. Puzzled, as it wasn't time for staff tea breaks, she called out, 'Who is here? Why are you not working?'

There was silence before one of the kitchen staff made herself known. 'It's only me, miss. I was changing my apron, as there was a tea stain down the front of it.'

'Then why do you have crumbs around your mouth and down your front?' Katie snapped. She was in no mood to mess about with Nippies who were shirking their work – but she didn't expect the girl to collapse into one of the wooden seats and burst into tears.

'I'm sorry, Miss, I was ever so hungry. It was only a stale bun someone had left on top of the bin, ready to take to the pig bin. I wasn't stealing anything, honest I wasn't.'

Katie's heart melted just a little. Telling herself she shouldn't be so sharp with the staff, she took a seat beside the girl, who was no more than a child really. In fact, there was something about her . . . but Katie couldn't quite put her finger on it. 'Didn't you have time for your breakfast?' she asked gently as she passed over one of the clean hand-kerchiefs that were always kept in the drawer of the table. It had been Rose's idea to keep a stock of clean white linen handkerchiefs, as there were times when the girls would have a problem to share or need a shoulder to cry on. There was a similar supply of them in the manageress's office.

'There wasn't anything to eat, Miss,' the girl snivelled, 'and I was late getting to work so missed out on having a bite here.'

Katie thought for a moment. The girl's excuse was plaus-ible, but something at the back of her mind was nagging to her that there was more to this than a young girl missing a meal. Raiding a bin for food wasn't the usual way to act when you'd missed breakfast – was it? 'What's your name, child, and how long have you worked here?'

'I'm Jennie, Miss. I've only worked here a couple of weeks. I'm grateful for the job,' she added before blowing her nose and giving Katie a weak smile.

'Well, Jennie, I want you to wash your face and put on that clean apron. Before you set to work, you are to go to the kitchen and tell cook I said to give you a breakfast. You will sit here and eat it before starting work. Is that clear?'

'Yes, Miss,' she beamed.

'And mind you don't rush your food. I don't want to see you having a fit of the hiccups and causing mayhem in the kitchen, do you hear?'

'Yes, Miss,' the girl giggled before hurrying to the washroom.

Katie smiled to herself as she cleared the table of crumbs and put their chairs straight. It wasn't so long ago that, along with Lily and Rose, she'd started work at Lyons and had been as timid as Jennie. Not that she'd ever needed to steal food. Something just didn't add up, and the young woman was not telling her everything.

Once she'd seen the girl go back to her duties, she hurriedly washed her own face and went to the office to check that day's post. Although Rose had told her and Phoebe, the other Nippy helping out in the office, to leave everything until her return, Katie felt she could at least open the post and pull out anything of importance, in case it couldn't wait for the manageress's planned return to work at the end of the week.

Refusing a tray of tea from one of the Nippies, she quickly set to work. Rose had taken to putting all important paperwork into a safe that Lyons had fitted in the office. Not only did it keep the takings safe before they were taken to the bank, but Rose had realized there was room to store important letters and stock sheets in case the teashop took a hit from the Luftwaffe during a raid. Life would be difficult enough with having to worry about missing paperwork that was important to the tearoom. She'd not imparted this news to the area manager, but her two assistants knew of her decision and continued to do the same while Rose was in London.

As Katie carefully opened each envelope, using the silver paperknife that had been gifted to her friend upon her promotion to manageress, there was a quiet knock on the door.

'Enter,' Katie called out, thinking how important she

felt giving such an instruction, although she had to try hard not to smile at the thought.

'Excuse me, Miss, there's been a telegram delivered for you. The lad's waiting in case you wish to send a reply.'

Katie's heart missed a beat. Jack would be back on his ship by now. Had something happened to him? Taking the envelope and indicating to the Nippy to wait, she tore open the missive and scanned the few words inside.

Will be home on the 3 p.m. train. Wedding postponed. Will explain to you and Lily upon my return. Have the kettle on. Rose.

Giving a sigh of relief that her husband was safe, but at the same time feeling sad that there wasn't going to be a wedding soon for her friend, Katie told the waiting Nippy to inform the boy there was no reply and handed her tuppence to give to him for his trouble. Looking at the large clock on the wall, she calculated that it would be five hours until Rose's arrival. As she was working a long shift, she decided to ask Lily to come to the teashop to meet Rose and find out what was happening. Hopefully Mildred would be able to bring her in the van to save Lily having to catch a bus, as her leg was not yet strong enough to support her for long.

Thankful that Flora had had the foresight to have a telephone installed at Sea View, she lifted the receiver and dialled the number. Rose would no doubt need all the support her friends could give her, if the impending nuptials were not to go ahead.

*

'Good grief,' was all Lily could say, once Rose had explained her experiences of being caught up in the bombing of the London docks.

'I couldn't have coped like you did,' Katie said, looking fearful, her face having turned pale as Rose described how they'd escaped the damaged building. 'Did you see any . . . any bodies?'

'There were many killed. You won't always get the truth from the newspapers as the government want the Germans to see happy smiling Cockneys, while we are all as miserable as sin at what is happening,' Anya butted in.

Rose's face twitched at the way Anya spoke. Always truthful, she wasn't one to embroider the facts. 'It's a clever ploy to fool the enemy. I hope it annoys Hitler to see our smiling faces.'

'Clever, yes, but then he sends even more bombs and has the last laugh,' Anya spat back. 'I think he laughs very much at the moment, while we have little to laugh about.'

'He who laughs last laughs longest,' Rose pointed out before explaining, 'It means we will bide our time, and then we will laugh when we win this war.'

Anya continued to scowl. 'You English, you have such funny sayings. And while you say them, my Henio and his comrades put their lives at risk up in the skies, fighting the enemy.'

'Oh, Anya, we aren't trivializing the war. Far from it,' Katie said, looking sad. 'My Jack and Rose's Ben are also putting their lives on the line.'

'Do you still have a Ben?' Anya asked, as Rose had yet to explain why her wedding was cancelled.

Rose sighed. It was hard to answer her friends' questions and also give her news. While travelling home on the train she had planned what she was going to tell them, and it had seemed quite simple. Now, being bombarded with questions by the concerned girls, everything was becoming complicated. She didn't wish to forget a thing in her rush to explain before they had to get back to work. 'There will be a wedding. You'll be pleased to know that it has just been postponed, as Ben had to go away with his regiment.'

'You all told me and Jack to marry sooner rather than later, as we didn't know what the future would bring,' Katie said, looking sad. 'I do hope you get your wedding . . . Is there no chance?'

'No; everything is so complicated right now and with the business taking such a battering, along with the terrible loss of life, it didn't seem the right time to be having a happy family event. Also, Ben's father has to travel back from Canada, and that could take a couple of weeks. He doesn't want to be sipping sherry and making small talk when he has war work to do. As much as I would love to be married to Ben this very minute, it will just have to wait . . . However, we had the most marvellous engagement announcement in the newspaper,' she added, pulling a copy of *The Times* from her handbag and spreading it out on the desk for them to see.

Lily whistled through her teeth. 'Blimey, you're almost marrying into royalty,' she laughed as they passed the newspaper round.

'If there ever is a wedding,' Anya said, looking sad. 'I feel for you,' she added as she patted Rose's arm. 'We are now all distanced from our menfolk – apart from you, as you do not have one.' She nodded towards Lily, who mouthed 'Thank goodness' to Rose.

Lily cocked her head to one side, thinking about Anya's words. 'But isn't your old man only based at Manston, Anya? I know he does a dangerous job, but you can still see him from time to time. God knows when Rose and Katie will see their loved ones.'

'My Henio has been moved. I see him no more . . .'

'Moved? What do you mean?' Rose said, looking worried. Anya had come to England to look for her husband after she escaped from Poland. Did this mean she would follow him again?

'He goes to a place called Biggin Hill. Do you know of it?'

'It's in Kent,' Rose said as she glanced at Lily, who she knew followed the war news avidly. 'He will be in the thick of things, Anya.'

Anya took her words stoically and simply nodded her head. 'It is what he wants to do. He fights for the freedom of many and for the people of my homeland who die at the hands of the Nazis. My Henio is a brave man.'

'Hear, hear.' Lily said, raising her empty cup. 'Oh, I think we need more tea.'

'Not for me. I have to get back to work.' Katie stood up, followed by Anya. 'I'm so sorry your wedding has been put on hold. At least this way we can plan a bigger affair.' She grinned, hoping to put a smile on Rose's face too. 'Keep that newspaper notice in a safe place – it will be something to show the grandchildren one day. You are the only person I know to have had an engagement notice in *The Times*. Why, they've even mentioned Sea View! That could be good for business.'

'It would, if the residents could only sleep in their beds for one night,' Lily scoffed. 'Why, since you went up to London, we've been down the tunnels almost every night – it's our home from home since Mildred and Miss Tibbs did up our area. Katie didn't fare much better, as she was in the Anderson shelter at Captain's Cottage with her Jack.'

'Oh, I don't know. We were cosy enough.' Katie blushed. 'I did wonder if you and Mary would be moving back, now that I'm on my own. It was good of you to give me and Jack some peace and quiet. It was just like we had our own home, with me cooking his dinner and doing the washing. With Rose home, we can be the three musketeers again. All for one and one for all.'

'What does that make Mary here? Sancho Panza?'

The girls roared with laughter as it was explained to Lily that she had the wrong book.

'Oh, you know me. I'm not one for reading. I much prefer to listen to music – which reminds me. Did you know that there's a dance tomorrow evening at Dreamland, and the band is none other than our old mate, Silvano Caprice? Do you fancy it, if I can get someone to look after milady here? I may not be able to dance much with my leg the way it is but I can still enjoy myself.'

'I will care for the baby,' Anya said from the doorway, as the three friends smiled at the thought of a night out. 'Now come along, Katie, we have work to do. Joe Lyons will have our guts for garters if we do not work hard.'

'I don't think she'd know Joe Lyons if he walked past

her in the tearoom,' Lily laughed as she closed the door behind them. 'But she means well, in a funny kind of way.'

'It must be awful to be alone with just your husband in a strange country. I do admire Anya,' Rose said, feeling quite choked. 'I pray that nothing happens to Henio.'

'You do need a night out,' Lily said, looking at Rose's pale face and the shadows around her eyes. 'Was it that bad in London?'

Rose nodded, not making eye contact with Lily as she felt so close to tears. 'Ben's family are marvellous, and Mum got along like a house on fire with Lady Diana. I simply adore Annabelle and Marina, and they seemed to like me – which as you know was a bit of a worry. But that bombing at the docks has really brought it home to me how awful war is. I know we've seen a few sights down here, but what went on and what is still going on in London is so horrible. Helping out the other day, and seeing the dead and dying, made me realize I'm not doing enough for the war effort. Now I don't have a wedding to think about, I must do more to help bring this war to an end.'

Lily gave her a worried look. 'You're not thinking of giving up working for Lyons and joining up for something, are you?'

'I don't know what I'll do. But I saw how hard those ambulance girls were working, and also the ladies in the WVS canteen. All the time we are hearing of women starting to do war work. Why, they're even working in factories making bombs.'

'Women did that and so much more during the last war. My mum worked in a munitions factory and said it was a right laugh.'

'I'm not wanting to do war work for a laugh,' Rose sniffed. 'I want to make a difference, just like the men are.'

Lily shook her head and looked sad. 'You do make a difference. You are keeping people's lives on track and giving them something to look forward to. Imagine what it would be like if we weren't here to give a smile and serve a decent cuppa when people came in with all the worries of the world on their shoulders. I can't wait to get back to work and earn a few bob, as well as put a smile on customers' faces.'

Rose was surprised at Lily's words. 'But you've not long had a baby. Mary is the future of our country – she is what we are fighting for. You have no need to work.'

Lily stuck out her chin defiantly. 'I didn't have my child to get off going to work.'

'I'm sorry – I didn't mean that. Why don't we see if you can do a few hours a week? I'm sure Mum and Joyce would look after Mary. She's such a good baby.'

Lily nodded her head in agreement. 'Thank you. I'll not say no to your suggestion, although I don't want to be a burden to anyone.'

Rose gave a sigh of exasperation. 'For goodness' sake, you are not a burden. We all wanted you to have this baby rather than . . . Rather than not have her,' she said, pushing away the thought of the awful house Lily had visited to get rid of her unborn child, before Rose talked her out of it. 'We all want to help bring up little Mary. She has an army of aunties looking out for her.'

Lily felt the tickle of tears in her eyes, and cleared her throat. 'Then there's something I want to tell you, Rose: Tom White is Mary's father. Mildred knows, and she helped me to confront him while you were in London. I don't want anything from him, although I've made him promise he's not to mess about with the Nippies anymore, or we will report him to head office.'

Rose was relieved that Lily had confirmed her suspicions. 'I had a feeling that was the case – but how will you stop him? Promises are like pie crusts: easily broken, in the case of people like Tom.'

Lily gave Rose a crafty wink. 'Mildred sorted him out. You might just find a signed piece of paper in the office safe. Mildred has my copy for safekeeping, in case he tries to get his hands on it.'

'Woe betide anyone who crosses our Mildred,' Rose nodded.

'You can say that again. Why, she was like a dragon when she sorted him out. He almost got away with it as we went outside to watch the enemy planes going up the Thames. Then of course we hurried the customers down to the cellar for protection as the sirens went off. Mildred caught him trying to slide off. She took him by the collar and back to this office, then stood over him until the paperwork was completed. By then it was getting pretty hairy outside, and even I was prepared to say forget it and let's get to safety.'

Rose shuddered. 'As if we don't have enough to put up with, without Tom White messing up your life.'

Lily gave her a gentle smile and reached out to squeeze her hand. 'It was six of one and half a dozen of the other. It's not as if he pinned me down and forced himself on me – not like . . .' She shuddered as she thought of her late stepfather before giving herself a shake. 'That's all done and dusted now, and at least I have my little Mary to care for. I can't think of life without her. It's as if she is the missing bit of a puzzle, with us all being part of the whole picture.'

Rose laughed. Lily had a funny way of putting things at times, but she knew exactly what she meant – and knew that the baby would have a good life, with all her adopted aunties there to guide her way.

'Who knows? She may well have a few little cousins coming along before too long.'

Lily gasped. 'You're not . . . ?'

'No, I'm not! Go wash your mouth out with soap and water, Lily Douglas. The wedding comes first, then the babies. Oh, sorry,' Rose added, thinking of how Mary had arrived.

Lily snorted with laughter. 'You and your big mouth. Well, I didn't follow the normal path to having children, and no doubt I'll bear the brunt of the gossips' tongues for a while to come, before they pick on some other unsuspecting woman. But the way you spoke, I thought perhaps you and Ben had managed to have some time to yourselves – like you did before,' she said, with a glint of amusement in her eyes.

Rose chose to ignore Lily's inference about the one night she'd spent with Ben. 'I was thinking more of our Katie. Wouldn't it be lovely if she and Jack had a family? If anyone deserves such a thing, they do.'

'Fingers crossed Jack's few days of shore leave did the trick, even if they did spend a lot of time down the air-raid shelter at Captain's Cottage. With me staying at Sea View and you in London . . .'

Rose felt her cheeks start to burn. Why did such talk always embarrass her? 'Now, I must get some work done, and also sort out my staff rota now that you are coming back to help me out. Will you hang about for a while so we can go back to Sea View together? I told Mum I'd go back for my dinner. It will be nice to see everyone again. It feels an age, when it's really only a week since I went away.'

8

Flora yawned as she placed her key in the front door of Sea View. It was good to be back home amongst friends, in familiar surroundings. Placing her suitcase down, she kicked off her best brown brogues and opened a small cupboard to retrieve her well-worn slippers, breathing a sigh of relief as she did so. Once her coat had been removed, she reached for her faded cotton crossover apron and pulled it tight round her small frame, tying the belt securely. 'Now for a nice cup of tea before everyone gets home,' she said to herself as she headed to the kitchen. Before she'd reached the door it swung open and Joyce hurried out, closing it behind her.

'Thank goodness I caught you in time,' she said, slightly out of breath. 'We have a visitor.'

'Not that nice man who came calling the other day to escort you to the talk at the church hall about pig-keeping?' Flora asked as she tried to squeeze past her lodger. 'It's such a shame I couldn't make it. Not that we have any room for a pig at Sea View,' she smiled, before noticing Joyce's concerned expression. 'Whatever is wrong?'

'No, I doubt I'll see Gerald again. He didn't make a good impression on Pearl,' Joyce said, looking sad.

'Oh dear,' Flora replied. She'd had high hopes for Joyce's romance with the pleasant man from the Observer Corps. 'Let's chat about it later when we're on our own, shall we? Now, who is this visitor?'

'It's Councillor Mould. She says she's here on official business. I pointed out that you were still travelling back from London, and if there was a hold-up with the trains it could be hours before you reached home. She said she would wait. I'm so relieved you're here now,' Joyce sighed.

Flora knew Councillor Wendy Mould by reputation – and also from a few times they'd had run-ins on the committees they both belonged to. She was known locally as 'Wet and Mouldy', owing to the fact she wasn't good for the town and had a very negative disposition. It was only her husband's position on the board of an engineering company, and the fact that they could throw money around, that meant she was held in high esteem by some on the town council – not something to be proud of, in Flora's book. Flora supported the locals, while Wendy Mould supported anything that benefited her own interests.

Looking down at her old apron and comfy slippers, Flora turned back to the hall cupboard. Kicking off the slippers, she pushed her feet back into her best shoes. Removing her pinny, she pulled on her smart coat and placed the matching hat on her head.

'Please don't go out and leave me alone with her again,' Joyce wailed.

'No, I wouldn't do that. I'm simply fighting fire with fire. It will not do any good for her to see me in my work clothes. I do have a good idea why she is here. She wants to take over the hall I use for the WVS and our women's groups. No doubt she's got something nasty up her sleeve, as I refused point blank to move my ladies to the Methodist Hall. We've fallen out a few times in committee over this.'

'What, that old wooden building outside of town? It only needs a puff of wind and it will fall down. That's if the Luftwaffe don't flatten it first,' Joyce grimaced.

Flora squared her shoulders and led the way to the kitchen, which was the only room they kept for communal use. The other downstairs rooms were now used as bedrooms, so the residents could escape quickly during an air raid. Flora had the foresight to realize that elderly Miss Tibbs would find it hard to get down two flights of stairs when Moaning Minnie went off in the middle of the night. Although 'her ladies' had to share, she knew they were safer. 'That's the one. Come on, let's sort this out while I'm in the mood,' she said. Her disappointment for Rose and her postponed wedding meant she was spoiling for a fight with someone, and Wet and Mouldy would be the ideal person.

'Good afternoon, Councillor Mould. I'm sorry I seem to have kept you waiting, although I had no idea you'd made an appointment to visit. I do apologize. As you can see, I'm just back from my trip to London, where I've been staying with my daughter's future mother-in-law. Do you know Lord and Lady McDouglas?'

For just a moment, Councillor Mould's eyes widened in surprise. 'Our paths may have crossed at social events,' she murmured.

'Really? Lady Diana informed me she had never socialized with anyone from Thanet. Perhaps you are thinking of someone else?' Flora said as she checked the teapot. 'Be a dear and make a fresh pot, Joyce, that's if you have time. Councillor Mould, another for you? I appreciate you are a busy woman, and I too have a lot of work to catch up on since my foray into London society.' Flora noticed Joyce's mouth twitch into a smile as she took the teapot to the sink and emptied the cold grouts into the dish, ready to go out to the pig bin. Sea View might not have room for a pig of its own, but the residents did their bit, collecting scraps that would feed the nation's pigs.

'Not for me,' Wendy Mould replied. 'I came to see you about the outstanding problem vis-à-vis the clash of dates, and your groups taking the time slots I require for my charity fundraising committees. I would prefer to discuss this when your, er . . . staff aren't present; but needs must, if your drawing room is not available.'

'My drawing room is out of commission due to the war.' Flora smiled sweetly as she sat opposite the councillor and removed the pins from her hat. She'd have liked nothing more than to kick off her shoes, but thought better of it. 'Joyce is a valued friend, and friends do not have secrets from one another. Shall we consult our diaries to see how we can solve the problem of you wanting the hall, when I have a prior booking arrangement?' She reached for a well-worn diary that lay next to a pile of unopened letters. 'I could perhaps move my Wednesday WVS clothes exchange and make it an hour earlier. I usually spend that time talking to the ladies who help out before we open the doors to the public. I'm sure we can be out on time. However, just sometimes we need to help latecomers find something for their children. I'm sure your committee would understand, what with there being a war on?' She smiled sweetly.

The councillor sat stony-faced. 'You don't understand, Mrs Neville. I wish you to take your meetings and get-togethers elsewhere.' She dipped into her handbag and pulled out a letter. 'I've received complaints from some of the ladies who sit on my committee. It seems one of them picked up . . . picked up something distasteful from clothing left after your last jumble sale.'

A clattering noise came from the sink as Joyce dropped the lid of the brown earthenware teapot; it was followed by a muffled snort that had Flora not trying to laugh. 'My goodness,' she exclaimed, taking the letter from the councillor's hand before she could snatch it back.

'Hmm,' Flora said dramatically as she passed back the letter, holding it between two fingers and at arms' length, as if it were contaminated. 'I do believe this is the lady whose little boy was sent home from school with his head full of nits. Do you know the lad?' she said to Joyce as she called out his name to her.

'I certainly do. My Pearl couldn't stop crying as I scrubbed her head with carbolic soap to ward off the wretched things. You wouldn't expect it from a family who think their you-know-what doesn't stink. Are you sure you'd not like another cup of tea, Councillor?' Joyce asked as she scratched her head, intimating that there was something unwelcome in her hair.

Councillor Mould snapped her handbag closed, her expression grim. 'Mrs Neville, I insist that you give up the hall. My committee work is much more important. You and your friends can meet elsewhere. I hear you've set up quite a little community in the tunnels. Could you not meet down there?'

Flora felt her blood start to boil, but did her best to remain calm. She thought about everything the ladies who worked with her did out of the goodness of their hearts: collecting and sorting clothes for those in need, as well as taking shifts in the mobile canteen after air raids. Many were knitting for the troops and teaching others how to make do and mend so that their growing families had clothes on their backs. Why, they were even rolling up their sleeves and getting stuck in collecting pots, pans and iron to donate to the Thanet 'Build a Spitfire' campaign, after putting in God knows how many hours of work and bringing up their families. Many of the women were now alone as their husbands were in the services, while Councillor Mould and her cronies did nothing but drink tea and make lists. 'Do you have any idea how much essential work my ladies do?'

'We all do our best, Mrs Neville. If it weren't for my committee members and their organizational skills, the women of Thanet would be at a loss to know how to cope. That is why we need the hall most days each week.'

Joyce snorted loudly as she placed the tea tray on the table, jolting the crockery. 'Everyone relies on Mrs Neville. If it wasn't for her, many families would go without. Why, if our council had half a brain, they'd make her the next mayor. I've heard that her name has been put forward. When she's not running this place and organizing everyone, she's out doing her ARP duties. She puts us all to shame, there's no mistake.'

Flora had never heard Joyce speak out in such a way before. She felt quite humbled by her words. 'Thank you,

Joyce. I'm fortunate to have hard-working supporters. Between us, we'll do all we can to shorten this war.'

Joyce fell silent after speaking out, and started to pour tea for Flora. 'I'll take mine up to my room. I left baby Daisy sleeping. When she wakes up, I'll bring her through to you,' she said, before leaving the room.

'Ah, yes – the child you decided to take in without consulting the authorities. I was coming to that next, once we'd sorted out the problem of you using the hall . . .' the councillor said, as she again opened her handbag and pulled out a sealed envelope.

Flora's jaw dropped, but she couldn't think of one word to say in reply. She'd got the letters of support from the vicar and the mayor and was sure Daisy would be allowed to stay with her. She was only waiting for the official letter approving her as Daisy's official foster mother. In time, she had great hopes of adopting the child and bringing her up as her second daughter.

'You may wish to read this once I've gone, so you have time to digest the contents. Needless to say, as someone with influence on the adoption board, I was able to contribute to the decision on the child's future.' Councillor Mould placed the sealed letter on the kitchen table. 'I'm sure you will be in touch once you've considered your position about the use of the hall. Good day,' she concluded through thin lips before taking her leave.

Flora stood up to let her out, but the letter lying there, almost calling out to her, was too hard to resist for long . . .

*

'Anyone at home?' Rose called out as she headed to the kitchen of Sea View followed by Katie, and Lily with Mary in her arms.

'Perhaps there was an air-raid warning and we missed it?' Lily suggested.

'I don't think we'd have missed such a din,' Katie said in a serious voice before realizing Lily was joking. 'I fall for it every time,' she said with a theatrical sigh.

'We're in here, and I have dinner ready,' Joyce called out as they all piled into the cosy room.

Rose looked about her. 'Not everyone. There are a few familiar faces missing.'

Joyce cracked another egg into an already full frying pan, being careful that the golden yolks didn't break. 'Miss Tibbs isn't back from her bridge club yet and my Pearl is still at Brownies. Brown Owl is dropping her and a few other children home, but will take them to the shelters if the siren goes off. Mildred's in the outhouse having a quick wash. I told her she was to take off those stinking overalls so I could fire up the boiler and give them a good wash. Honestly, as much as I love Mildred, I could smell her five minutes before she arrived and it wasn't pleasant.'

The girls all chuckled. 'Oh, Mildred's a darling,' Lily said. 'I don't know what we'd do without her, although I agree it would be good to see her out of her overalls once in a while and wearing a nice dress.' She sat down at the table and rocked Mary in her arms as the baby started to whimper. 'I think this one needs changing . . .' She sniffed. 'She smells as bad as her auntie Mildred after a long shift at sea.' This made the girls laugh even more.

'Who mentioned my name?' Mildred said, coming into

the kitchen wearing a long winceyette nightdress that enveloped her large frame as she rubbed her damp grey hair with a towel. 'Why are you looking at me like that? It's nigh on seven o'clock and as I'm not likely to be going out again this evening, I may as well put on my nightclothes.'

'But what if there's an air raid?' Joyce asked.

'Then I'll pull on my overalls over the top,' Mildred looked at Joyce as if she'd said something daft. 'What's for dinner? I'm famished!'

'The hens have been laying well, and I've made bubble and squeak as Miss Tibbs cooked too many potatoes and too much cabbage last night. She thought you were coming home yesterday,' she explained to Rose. 'The poor dear seems to be getting more forgetful by the day.'

'Sounds delicious. You can't beat home cooking. Here, let me help,' Rose said as she reached for Flora's apron, which was hanging behind the door. She frowned. 'But where's Mum? Has she been called out, or something?' Her mum was always at someone's beck and call.

Joyce shook her head, looking sad. 'She decided to go for a little walk. Something was bothering her, and I suggested she get some fresh air for a while. She promised to be back for her dinner.'

'But she was fine when we parted at the railway station this afternoon. What's happened to make her act like this?' Rose asked, looking at Mildred and Joyce.

'Don't look at me. She wasn't here when I got in,' Mildred said, looking concerned. 'I never thought to ask where she'd gone.'

'She had a visitor waiting when she arrived home, and then there was a letter . . . I'd have followed her, but there was no one to leave Daisy with and to be honest, I thought she needed the time alone.'

'Who was it?' Rose asked.

'Councillor Wet and Mouldy.'

They all groaned, knowing that the woman never made a call to be pleasant to someone.

Rose reached for the coat she had only just laid over the back of a chair. 'I'll go and look for Mum. Don't worry about my food,' she said, as Joyce started to object. 'I'm sure we won't be long.'

'I'll come with you,' Katie and Mildred said at the same time.

'No, I'll be fine. She's no doubt taken her favourite walk down to the harbourside. I'll be down there in five minutes if I walk briskly.'

'Take the torch. It'll be sunset before too long. The nights have started coming in quickly. You don't want to be bumping into something, or tripping over the pavement,' Joyce said as she took the hefty torch Flora used for her ARP duties from the dresser.

'If you aren't back within half an hour, I'm coming to look for you,' Mildred said, giving her a stern look. 'We get some dodgy-looking people hanging about down the harbour these days. They're always after something or other. I can send them packing, but a young slip of a thing like you is a completely different matter.'

'Promise me one thing, Mildred,' Rose said as she accepted the torch from Joyce after buttoning up her coat. 'Put some clothes on first, please.'

Rose pulled the front door of Sea View behind her with the sound of her friends still ribbing Mildred about her fancy night attire. Smiling to herself, she crossed the road and set off down Madeira Walk. She loved this part of Ramsgate; there were so many memories of when she was a child and she would accompany General Sykes for his constitutionals, as he called them. That was before he became weak and frail, and took to his room until he passed away. If only she'd known he was her real father, she sighed to herself; but then, she couldn't have loved him more than she had done. As the road bent slightly towards the sea, the harbour came into view up ahead. Sitting on the wooden bench she now thought of as hers and Ben's, she could see the huddled figure of her mother.

Sitting down as close as she could to Flora, she tried to make light of her mum not being at Sea View when she'd arrived. 'There you are. If you don't make a move back home, your bubble and squeak will have squarked and given up the ghost. You know how Joyce cooks everything until its crisp at the best of times.' She laughed.

'You didn't need to come out looking for me, love. I just needed to get my thoughts in order, and it's not easily done at Sea View when we have a full house. Not that I'd wish any of our guests not to be there.'

Rose knew that to be true. 'You know this is the bench where I sit with Ben, don't you? I come here when I want to think about him, and pray he is safe.'

'It's a good place to be,' Flora said, reaching for Rose's hand and giving it a squeeze. 'I've done a lot of thinking over the years, looking out over this harbour when I have questions that need careful thought.'

'But do you get the answers you are seeking?'

'Not always. There are times when I simply come to understand that life is not quite straightforward, and we have to take on the chin whatever is thrown at us.'

'What's been thrown at you, Mum? Does it have something to do with that odious Councillor Mould, who visited this afternoon? Joyce told us she had been round.'

'Yes, love. She wants me to give up running my groups at the church hall, as she needs it for her own committee work.'

'She can't do that! Why, the first-aid group, the WVS, as well as the ARP have meetings there, and all organized by you,' Rose cried. 'Tell her to go jump in the harbour, and take her stuffy committee members with her. All they do is cause problems in this town. I've heard . . .' She broke off in midstream as Flora patted her hand to stop her.

'She can, and she will,' Flora said as she reached into the pocket of her coat and pulled out a crumpled letter. 'Read this before you say another word.'

Rose gasped as she spotted the heading at the top of the typed letter. It was from the adoption society. She glanced at her mum's face before starting to read. Even in the dusk, she could see there were tears glistening in Flora's eyes.

She scanned the words quickly, holding the page close to her face, then went back and re-read it more slowly, making sure she hadn't misunderstood. 'But why have they decided that you're not a fit person to care for Daisy? She's thrived in the weeks since she's been with us. Who would do this to you – and to Daisy, for that matter? I cannot believe they are coming to collect her so soon.

Who is behind all of this? And why would they be so horrid?'

Flora straightened the creased letter and pointed to the top left of the page, where the names of the panel who oversaw the adoption society were printed. 'Do you recognize any names there?'

Rose needed to use her torch to check the small typeface, turning it off again quickly in case she was told off by a warden for showing a light. 'Oh, Mum. I could swear, I really could. Why has that despicable Councillor Mould got it in for you? Surely this has nothing to do with her wanting to use the hall, and you standing your ground? It doesn't make sense at all.'

'People can be strange, my love. I was once told that Councillor Mould can bear a grudge for life and makes a bad enemy. I just wish I knew what had angered her, so that I could make amends.'

Rose couldn't believe what she was hearing. Her mum wasn't someone to back down in a fight when she was up against a bad sort. 'You'd try to be friends with her? Why?'

'I'd invite Hitler to dinner and knit him a woolly hat if it meant Daisy could stay with us,' Flora said as she lifted her handkerchief to her face and started to sob. 'I'm sorry, love. You shouldn't have to see me like this,' she sniffed between sobs.

Rose could only put her arms around Flora and hold her until the tears subsided. 'I would miss her too. I've come to think of Daisy as a little sister, even though I'm old enough to be her mother. Where would they take her?'

'To the children's home,' Flora said, as she did her best to stop her tears.

All Rose could think about was Katie, who had been brought up in a home. Her friend never spoke much about her childhood, apart from saying that she had always been fed and always had clean clothes on her back. In a small way, her friendship with Lily and Rose at school had been the thing that kept her going until she was old enough to leave the institution. 'Daisy can't have the same life as Katie did. It's an unbearable thought, especially when she would have a wonderful home with us. Don't worry, Mum – we'll get to the bottom of this. You have my word.'

Flora blew her nose and composed herself. 'We will all do our best, love, but I fear we have the wrath of Councillor Mould to overcome first. Right,' she said, standing up and holding out her hand to Rose. 'I refuse to let that wretched woman spoil my life – or Daisy's, come to that. And I won't have her spoil my dinner. Come on; let's get back home and make a plan. With a bit of luck it will be a quiet night and we won't have to head down the tunnels. I'm not on ARP duty until tomorrow, so there's nothing to stop us all putting our heads together and seeing what we come up with. Why don't you and the girls stay the night, rather than go back to Captain's Cottage? I can fit you all in. It'll be like the old days with you all under the same roof.'

'That sound like a plan,' Rose said, slipping her arm through Flora's as they started to walk back towards the guesthouse. She smiled for her mum, although deep inside she knew they'd have an uphill struggle to keep Daisy as part of their family.

Back at Sea View, they found everyone tucking in to dinner. Joyce hurried to the stove and put the large frying pan back over the heat. 'It won't take two ticks to fry you both an egg, and your bubble and squeak is keeping warm along with a portion for Miss Tibbs and Pearl.' She looked up at the clock. 'Pearl is due home any minute, but goodness knows where Miss Tibbs has got to. No doubt she's been chatting and lost track of the time.' She poured cups of tea from the large brown earthenware teapot keeping warm on the side of the stove, and put them in front of the two women. 'Now, will you tell us all what the problem is, or have we got to wheedle it out of you?'

Flora looked at Rose, who nodded for her to go ahead. The women listened in horror as Flora brought them up to date about her conversation with the councillor and then passed the letter to Lily to read out – knowing she'd be the strongest amongst them, and least likely to break down halfway through the reading. When she had finished there was silence before they all spoke at once, voicing their opinions of the woman and what should be done to her. Mildred favoured dumping her in the harbour, while Lily mentioned knowing a chap who would help make her disappear for a very long time. It took Anya to bring them to their senses.

'Flora, this woman is dangerous. You must not jest about drowning her or making her vanish,' she admonished them. 'Even to make idle threats could mean trouble if someone overheard. We need to be like the poster in the pub. We need to keep mum. I learnt whilst fleeing Poland that I should not speak to anyone in case it caused me a problem later on. Now, you all need to do the same.'

'We need to find out all we can about this woman,' Lily

said. 'The more we know, the more ammunition we have to fight her.'

'What if there isn't anything?' Katie said, looking fearful.

'Everyone has a skeleton of some kind in their wardrobe. We just need to find hers,' Lily said. 'Flora, do you have a piece of paper and a pencil? We should make a plan.'

'First you eat,' Joyce said, as she placed plates in front of Flora and Rose. 'We can plan while you two have your meal.'

Pearl came bouncing into the room just as Mildred was reading out the list they'd cobbled together.

'Are you doing homework? I didn't know grown-ups had to do homework too,' she said, leaning over Mildred's shoulder.

Joyce grinned at her Brown Owl friend, Patricia, who'd walked in behind the child. 'Pearl is full of having to do homework when she moves to her new school,' she explained. 'I'm not so sure she'll be as thrilled after a few months, though.'

'My two were the same. The novelty soon wore off when they found out they had to do homework week in, week out. I'd love one.' She smiled at Katie, who was pointing towards the teapot. 'I must say you all look very industrious.'

'We are starting a campaign to make Flora the next town mayor. If not that, we will put her forward for saint-hood,' Lily laughed, only half joking.

'That is intriguing,' Phyllis said, sitting at the table alongside Mildred. 'I would think it might be easier to apply for sainthood, knowing what I know about some of our councillors.'

'Please do tell,' Rose said. Joyce hastily shooed Pearl

away to change out of her uniform in case she overheard a morsel of gossip and squirrelled it away to use at an inopportune moment – as she often did, to the embarrassment of her mother.

'You really should stand for councillor in the next local election, Mum,' Rose said, looking serious. 'You do so much for people as it is – I can't see why you don't have an official title. Then you really could be made mayor in time.'

Flora shrugged. 'Only if you think it would help the town. I'd not take on the job to feather my own nest, like some do.'

'That Councillor Mould is feathering her whole house and more,' Patricia sniffed disapprovingly. 'There's talk her husband has picked up a good few lucrative contracts by using the council's name.'

'That's illegal, isn't it?' Lily asked as she put baby Mary over her shoulder to wind her. 'I don't know how they've got the nerve, I really don't.'

Mildred was drumming the table with a pencil she'd used to write notes, and looked deep in thought. 'Patricia, would you mind very much writing down what you know? I promise you won't get into trouble, and at no time will I say I've spoken to you.'

Flora frowned. 'What are you up to, Mildred? I don't want anyone getting on the wrong side of that woman. It's bad enough she has the clout to stop me keeping Daisy.'

Patricia, who'd looked rather worried after Mildred's request, was shocked at what Flora said. 'Give me that notepad at once. I've got a lot of things to write down about that woman. She's no friend of mine, I can assure you,' she added, with anger flashing in her eyes. 'Perhaps you would put the kettle on again? This could take a while.'

'Why don't you take Patricia into my room, Mildred? There's a comfy sofa, and Joyce lit the fire earlier. I'll bring in the tea.'

Rose delved into her bag. 'I almost forgot. We had some buns left over at the teashop. There's enough to go round if we cut them in half.'

Anya, who'd been quiet while the women chatted, looked up and sniffed disapprovingly. 'Too much under-hand work goes on around here. There will be trouble. Mark my words.'

9

'Excuse me, Miss, can't a gal get some service round here?'

Rose spun on her heel as she hurried across the busy Margate teashop. She'd just been informed about a poorly staff member and was on her way to check the situation. To have a customer complain was unusual, but needed attention.

'I'm sorry, madam, I'll have someone . . . Why Ruth, how lovely to see you. You too, Annabelle and Marina,' she said as she recognized her soon-to-be sister-in-law and stepchildren, giving them all a hug before sitting down in the one empty chair at the table set by the window. 'Have you been served yet?'

'Yes. We're having jelly and ice cream,' Marina said with a grin.

'Without having to eat proper food first,' her sister added. 'It's always fun going out with Aunt Ruth.'

Ruth winked at Rose as she placed a cigarette into an ornate holder and lit it with a gold lighter. 'Keep the kiddies happy, eh?'

Rose wasn't sure it was really the right attitude, but

with their daddy being away and the constant bombing in London, it couldn't hurt for the children to enjoy a treat or two. 'It's such a joy to see you. Is this a day trip?'

Ruth laughed out loud, causing nearby diners to glance and smile at the family group. 'We are reconnoitring the area, my dear.'

'My goodness, that does sound serious,' Rose said, looking at the giggling children. 'Are you planning to invade Thanet just like the enemy?' She feigned surprise. 'Am I marrying into a family of spies?'

'Oh, Rose, you are funny,' Annabelle said. 'We are moving here. It was your idea, remember?'

'I do recall it was mentioned,' Rose said, cocking her head to one side as if in deep thought, still teasing the children. Looking up, she spotted Anya leaving her counter and waved for her to join them. 'I want you to meet a very interesting lady. She comes from Poland and lives with my mum at her guesthouse.'

'Did you want something? I was going out to queue in my lunch break,' Anya said, ignoring Ruth and the children.

'What are you queuing for?' Marina asked, looking the woman up and down. 'You are very tall.'

'Then I sit down – then I'm not so tall.' Anya smiled gently, taking a chair from the next table and joining them.

'Anya, this is Ben's sister, Ruth – and these are his two daughters,' Rose said as they all shook hands.

'But you haven't told us what you are queueing for?' Marina said insistently.

'Pigs' hearts,' Anya said. 'The butcher may even have some liver.'

'Yuck,' both the girls said, screwing up their faces. 'I'd not want to queue for that.'

'Then there would be nothing for tea, unless Mildred has caught more of her smelly fish,' Anya answered, mirroring the children's expressions by screwing up her face in distaste. 'War should not interfere with our food, should it?'

Marina gave her a shy smile. 'I like you. You speak funny.'

'Darling, that is rather a rude thing to say,' Ruth reprimanded her as she stubbed out her cigarette in a silver ashtray placed there by a Nippy, who then served the meal.

'I do speak funny, but in my country you would be the one speaking funny,' Anya fired back at the child, who convulsed into giggles, causing her to join in. 'We should leave you to your food,' she said, getting to her feet. 'I hope to meet you all again soon. When you next visit, perhaps?'

'We are going to live here when we find a house,' Annabelle said, gazing longingly out of the window towards the beach. 'I do hope it is by the sea.'

'Why look, when you can all live at Sea View?' Anya said as she buttoned up her coat. 'It is simple to me. Flora, she takes in all the waifs and the strays. It is by the sea as well,' she added, giving Annabelle a wink.

'We wouldn't have to eat liver or smelly fish, would we?' she asked.

'We are at war. You eat if you are hungry enough. I wish you good day,' Anya said, nodding to Ruth.

'Anya, hold on a minute. Can you post a letter for me?' Rose quickly made her apologies to Ruth, caught Anya by the sleeve and indicated for her to follow her to the office.

'I like your new family,' Anya said as Rose closed the door behind them. 'That Ruth did watch me quite a lot. Why is that? Do I have a blot on my nose?'

Rose had noticed Ruth's interest. 'She's just being friendly,' she said. 'However, I'm not sure Mum can take in any more lodgers right now. Ruth has a job in London, so it would be two young children to care for.' She knew the subject had been mooted before but, being realistic, she wasn't sure it would work. 'Mum has Daisy to care for, and with all the upset of the child possibly being taken away and us fighting Councillor Mould . . . well, Sea View may not be the best place for the girls just now.'

Anya gave Rose a scathing look. 'You may be Miss Neville at work, but you are still the silly person who is not thinking straight. You say this Ruth had job in London, but children say they are moving here? Something does not add up. Start to think like that man in the movies you all drool over. Clive Danvers would see through this at once. Someone is not telling you everything, Miss Neville. Now give me that letter – I am losing my queueing time.'

Rose was lost in thought as she stuck a stamp on the envelope and passed it to Anya. Was Anya right?

'Oh, that girl who works in the kitchen was being sick when I went to fetch my coat. You may need a mop and bucket. Too much sleeping in the doorways and benches by the sea, I think. Too many times I see her.' Anya left the room, calling back, 'You need to do something before she is sick all over the customers.'

Rose shook her head and tried not to smile. Anya was

a tonic and never failed to amuse her. The telephone rang as she was about to head to the staffroom. Muttering to herself that she would get there at some point in the day, she lifted the receiver.

'Hello, darling,' a familiar voice said.

'Ben,' she shrieked in delight before apologizing for shouting into the receiver. 'Where are you? How are you?'

'I'm well, and you know I can't tell you where I am. Keep mum, and all that.'

'Of course. I'm a fool for asking. So, you've called me at my workplace to tell me you can't say anything?' she teased.

He laughed. 'Just to hear your voice is enough reason to make a call. I too am working, but wanted to let you know about Mother.'

'She is well, I hope?'

'You'll be able to find out before I do. Were you planning to visit Sea View anytime soon?'

'Don't say she's visiting my mum? It was only days ago that we were with you all in London,' Rose replied, rather confused.

'Darling, our mothers have been plotting. In a way I blame Flora, as it was her idea.'

'Her idea for what?' Rose asked in exasperation. 'Are you going to keep me on tenterhooks?'

'If it means I can keep hearing your voice, then yes. It feels as though you are a million miles away.'

'Ben . . . !'

'Oh well,' he sighed. 'Their plan is for Mother and the girls to move into Sea View.'

Rose smiled to herself. 'This could be Mum's secret

weapon against Councillor Wet and Mouldy. How absolutely perfect.'

'Whatever are you talking about, woman?'

Rose explained about the problems with the interfering councillor, and how worried she was that Daisy would be taken away from them.

'Then Mother's the ideal person. She loves to get stuck in when there's trouble. Have no fears there.'

'I thought perhaps the girls would continue to live in the house in the countryside. It would be safer than Ramsgate.'

'The lease came to an end, and with Ruth now doing her bit for the ministry, it would mean hiring a stranger to care for the children. You'd not get Mother living in the sticks.'

'I wish I could care for them myself, but . . .'

'My dearest love, you have a job to do and it isn't to care for my children, even though one day – and I hope it is soon – you will be their stepmother. And I know you will be an admirable parent.'

'Thank you,' was all Rose could say as she thought of bringing up the two adorable girls and shaping their future lives.

'Look, I'm not sure I'll be able to use the telephone to speak to you again anytime soon. Will you write and let me know when Mother and the girls arrive? The address I gave you will reach me.'

Rose nodded, even though Ben could not see. 'Would you like to speak to Annabelle and Marina now? I saw them not ten minutes since, eating jelly in the tearoom. They're with Ruth.'

'Wouldn't I just!'

'It's funny, Ruth not saying anything about them moving to Sea View.'

'It's best in case anything goes wrong – they'd be so disappointed.'

'You didn't inform me either . . .'

Ben laughed. 'Mother was going to tell you. She's the one organizing everything. It's pure coincidence that Ruth planned to take them to your tearoom today. Now, can I have a quick word with them before I have to rush off and do something terribly important to save our country?'

Rose laughed. She loved the way Ben made light of his war work and did his best not to worry her. 'I'll be two ticks. Talk to yourself or sign a few important documents until I get back to you.'

On hearing that their father was on the line, the children screamed with delight and ran ahead to Rose's office. By the time she reached the room, along with Ruth, they were both holding the receiver and chattering excitedly.

'That's a lovely picture,' Rose said, her words catching in her throat. 'I can't wait for when we are a proper family.'

'Don't wait too long,' Ruth said, laying a hand on her arm. 'I'm not sure this war will end anytime soon.'

Rose thought of Katie. 'You know, I said the same to a friend. Her intended was going off to join his ship and was going to wait. We all mucked in to help and they had a wonderful day. He was recently home on leave for a few days. They are such a lovely couple.'

'If anything should happen, at least she will have her memories, and so will his family.'

'Katie and Jack are both orphans. They met in an orphanage in Ramsgate. She only has her friends.'

'God, it makes you think, doesn't it?' Ruth said, reaching into her handbag for a cigarette. 'Now come on, you two – let Rose have a last word with your daddy. We won't win the war if he chats with you all day,' she called to the girls, who were regaling Ben with the story of their visit to the seaside.

The children made their excited goodbyes before handing the telephone back to Rose. 'We haven't finished our jelly,' Marina said.

'Then let's get back to the table before the Nippies clear it all away,' Ruth said as she ushered them from the office.

Rose picked up the receiver, and was just about to speak when she heard the air-raid siren from further down the coast. Even as she shuddered and began to bid a quick goodbye, a closer siren took up the cudgel; then the one closest to the teashop. 'Can you hear that? I have to go,' she said before whispering, 'I love you.'

'Take care, my darling. Now, hurry and do what you have to do. I'll be praying for you.'

Rose checked the safe was locked and grabbed the staff rota before hurrying into the teashop, encouraging customers to go down to the cellar and assuring them that they would be given hot tea while they waited for the all-clear. She like to be the last to enter the cellar, having made sure that the doors were locked so the teashop would not be looted while they were taking shelter. Rumour in the town had it that a number of shops had already been looted during raids.

'Miss, I don't think I can go down there. I still feel ever so poorly,' a timid voice said, as Rose went to close the door to the staffroom.

'It's Jennie, isn't it?' Rose asked, crossing over to where the young girl was slumped in a chair. 'You do look unwell.' She felt the girl's forehead and found it very hot. 'What have you had to eat?'

'Not much,' Jennie sniffed. 'I had a bit of fish last night, but nothing today. I'm too sick to keep anything down.'

Rose looked at the girl. She was all skin and bones, with mousey hair hanging to her shoulders. The dark shadows around her eyes and her thin, pale lips belonged to an old woman, not the young girl she was. She seemed to carry the world on her shoulders. 'Where do you live? We should see you home once this air raid is over.'

Jennie shrugged her shoulders before bursting into a fit of coughing. 'Round and about, Miss,' she said, trying hard to breathe evenly. 'But I'll be all right in a while – just please don't ask me to go down into that cellar. It gets so stuffy.'

Rose frowned, trying to recall what it was she had been told about Jennie. Sitting opposite her, she tried to make her see sense. 'You know we really ought to go down to the cellar. What if you sat on the steps by the door? There's a draught that comes in, so it wouldn't be so stuffy.' Overhead, she heard the rumbling of plane engines as they approached the town from the Channel. 'They sound pretty close,' she said, trying not to show her fear.

Jennie shrank back in her seat, shaking her head. 'I feel sick,' she said as she started to heave, clapping a hand to her mouth.

Rose hurried her to the staff toilet and closed the door. She couldn't leave the girl, but she needed to make herself as safe as possible before the bombs fell – and chances were they would, if not in Margate then at least nearby. She prayed that her mum and everyone at Sea View had reached the tunnels in time. At least Annabelle and Marina were safe in the large cellar here, with Ruth to care for them.

Deep in thought, she didn't at first hear the banging on the shop door. A short break in the aircraft noise alerted her to the rattling of the handle and frantic calling. Hurrying from the staffroom, she spotted Anya and let her in. 'Why didn't you go to the public shelter?'

'I wanted to get back here to help you, but then I tripped and cut my knee. These stockings are ruined,' Anya grumbled as she limped towards the cellar. 'Are you not coming? Do you wish to be blown to smithereens?'

'I can't . . .' Rose stammered as the building shook. The door to the toilet flew open, and Jennie came rushing out.

'We are going to die!' she screamed.

Anya froze and stared at Jennie. 'Why are you putting the life of our Miss Neville in danger? You should be in the cellar.'

'She's not well,' Rose tried to explain. 'Once the all-clear sounds we can have someone take her home. The cellar is too st . . .' She faltered as Anya butted in.

'The girl has no home,' Anya declared, pointing her finger at Jennie. 'She has lied to get this job. Joe Lyons would not have employed someone who sleeps on benches and in doorways.'

Rose turned to look at Jennie, who had, if possible, turned even paler. 'Is this true?'

The girl nodded miserably, before falling into a dead faint at Rose's feet.

Rose felt dreadful as she recalled being informed about the girl and not doing enough to help her. With so much going on both at work and with her personal life, she'd forgotten. She prayed it wasn't too late.

'I'd hoped that your first night in Ramsgate would not have been spent in the tunnels,' Flora said as she passed an enamel mug of hot cocoa from Miss Tibbs, who was sitting closest to the one-ring paraffin stove, to Lady Diana. 'Now, are you warm enough?' she asked, looking at the old rug wrapped around the older woman's knees.

'You must stop fussing so,' Lady Diana scolded. 'I've not had so much fun since . . . well, since I don't know when. I know the children will be safe with Ruth and Rose, so you must stop fretting and put the time down here to good use. What do you say, ladies?' she said, beaming at Miss Tibbs and Joyce.

'We could spend the time carrying on with our plans to sort out this business with Councillor Mould,' Joyce suggested, looking over her shoulder in case the woman materialized.

'There's no need to worry,' Flora said, noticing Joyce's worried look. 'I happen to know she is in Canterbury today on council business. I heard when I was at the ARP hut this morning.'

'You must tell Lady Diana all about the councillor, Flora dear, or she won't have any idea what we are talking about,' Miss Tibbs said, making a polite bow to their guest.

'Flora brought me up to speed on this gorgon, so say what you want – I'll keep up. My, this is tasty cocoa. You must tell me how you make it, Thomasina. Mine is invariably lumpy, and my granddaughters both refuse to drink it. My daughter, Ruth, tells me it looks like mud,' she chuckled.

Joyce gave Flora a puzzled look and mouthed the word 'Thomasina?'

'I had no idea that was your Christian name, Miss Tibbs.'

'You never asked,' the older woman replied, before explaining at great length to Lady Diana how best to make a mug of cocoa.

'Isn't she wonderful?' Flora whispered to Joyce.

'She doesn't seem to have any airs and graces at all.'

'I don't know about that. She does use her position to her own advantage – but in a good way,' Flora quickly added. 'And you'd be surprised at her past history.'

'Really?' Joyce asked. 'It's like meeting royalty, isn't it?'

'I must say, you've made this space extremely cosy,' Lady Diana said as she looked around the small area in the tunnel the residents of Sea View had made their own.

'It's mainly down to our Mildred. You'll meet her later. She was out working when the air-raid warning started, so would have taken shelter elsewhere.'

'Would she still be out at sea catching fish?' Lady Diana asked. 'It must be so dangerous. I don't envy her one little bit.'

'She thrives on it. There's no one like our Mildred.' Flora smiled. 'She's one in a million.'

'Excuse me, Flora . . .' A short, grey-haired man was pretending to knock on the sackcloth that covered the doorway to their little space.

'Hello there, Ron – come along in and meet my latest

guest. Diana, this is Ron Dickens. He plays the organ at our church and also the piano down at the Crown. Ron, this is Lady Diana – she's Ben's mother. You remember Ben, don't you?'

'Of course I do. He's a decent chap, is Ben,' Ron said, wiping his hands on his jumper before bowing and taking Lady Diana's hand. 'I'm honoured to meet you, ma'am.'

'I'm pleased to meet you too, Ron. But please, don't stand on ceremony for me. I'm no one special,' she replied, pumping his hand up and down in a good old-fashioned handshake. 'Now, can we offer you some of this delicious cocoa? Thomasina makes the best I've ever tasted,' she said, reaching for an empty mug.

'No, not for me, love – I mean, ma'am – I mean Lady . . .' Ron trailed off, looking flustered. 'I just wondered if your Rose was round and about, Flora? It looks like we'll be down here a fair while, going by what the lads up above ground are saying. I thought we could 'ave a bit of a sing-song, like?'

'I'm sorry, Ron, she's at work. Although I would think she's down in the cellar of the teashop right now, if she has any sense. Is someone else able to lead the singing?' Flora asked.

He scratched his head and looked confused. 'Why, I'd not rightly thought about it. I was 'oping Rose would sing. She has such a sweet voice,' he explained to Lady Diana.

'I agree with you, she has,' Diana nodded, and then thought for a few seconds. 'Why don't we help out?' she said, pulling Flora to her feet from where she sat in a deck chair that Mildred had borrowed from a pile roped together near the beach.

'Ma'am, it's just a sing-song around an old Joanna. It's not some posh opera malarkey,' Ron said anxiously, as the two women stepped out of their makeshift living quarters.

'Lead on, Macduff,' Diana declared, giving him a poke in the back to hurry him up. 'Let's get this show on the road.'

'I'll watch Daisy,' Joyce called after Flora. 'If you see my Pearl, tell her not to go too far down the tunnel or she might get lost.'

'Will do,' Flora laughed back.

After a rousing chorus or two of 'Down at the Old Bull and Bush' to get the neighbours going, Lady Diana whispered to Ron, and he made an announcement. 'For one night only, we 'ave one of the Desmond Sisters to entertain us. Blimey, what a treat,' he said, running his fingers over the piano keys.

Lady Diana struck a pose before announcing in a theatrical voice: '*I'm Bert* . . .'

The crowd cheered, recognizing the popular song 'Burlington Bertie from Bow'. However, it was the ladies from Sea View who laughed the most when she reached the line '*I had a banana with Lady Diana* . . .'

Flora, who had heard the song just days before, still couldn't help thinking what a true sport the woman was. Even with all her wealth, she was still the same Diana Desmond Flora had admired all those years ago when they both trod the boards of the variety theatres.

An hour later, as they walked back arm in arm to their little home underground, Flora gave Diana's arm a squeeze. 'I'm going to enjoy having you live at Sea View,' she said.

'I'll enjoy living there. However, I must pull my weight. You must tell me what I can sign up for.'

'Oh my goodness, where to start? I have a list a mile long. There's the Spitfire Fund, the clothes bank as well as the ARP and the WVS ... But down here isn't the right place to discuss such things. Not while the world is going mad above ground,' Flora sighed.

'You are right, my dear. However, I have the inkling of an idea that will not only raise funds for the locality, but will put you head and shoulders above that Councillor Mouldy in the eyes of this town. People will see you in a new light.'

'Whatever do you mean?' Flora asked as they reached their haven in the tunnels.

'I mean, my dear, that we are going to put on a variety show that will not only entertain, but bring in quite a few bob,' Diana replied with a tinkling laugh as she put on her best Cockney voice. 'Better still, it will be your name across the top of every poster and programme. *Flora's Follies* has a nice ring to it, don't you think?'

'It does,' Flora said, cocking her head to one side as she thought about the suggestion. 'But don't you think that might infuriate the councillor even more?'

'Just you let me handle her. If I can rub shoulders with royalty and the like and get away with it, then Councillor Wendy Mould will be a piece of cake.'

Flora gave Lady Diana one of her best smiles, although deep inside she was afraid that they were biting off more than they could chew.

'Now, how about you teach me how to make some more of that cocoa?' Lady Diana beamed at Miss Tibbs. 'And

I think it may be time to crack open those sandwiches. Kicking up my heels has made me rather peckish.'

Deep underground in the Ramsgate tunnels it could have been any time of day or night, but Flora, checking her watch, realized it was teatime. 'Yes, let's have something to eat – and then perhaps Pearl should be trying to get some shut-eye. You still have school tomorrow, young lady. Once Annabelle and Marina move into Sea View, you will have to be like a big sister to them and show them around. They may even be attending your school.'

Pearl's eyes lit up. 'That would be fun. Will I have to share my clothes and toys with them, if they are evacuees? I've heard they don't wash, and have nits too,' she added, absent-mindedly scratching her head.

'Lord, no!' Lady Diana laughed. 'The girls will have their own toys shipped down, and they will have a tutor.'

Flora shook her head as Joyce pulled a disbelieving face in her direction. Wherever was she to fit all these people and their belongings? She loved a full house, but . . .

'What a mess,' Mildred declared as she entered the Margate teashop. 'Would you like a hand?'

'We need more than one hand,' Anya said, but smiled to show she was joking. 'I get used to the English way of speaking. Please will you lend both hands?'

Mildred roared with laughter and slapped Anya on the back, sending the woman staggering forward. 'I'll just give this to Rose, and then I'll be back to help with that window,' she said, nodding to where a couple of Nippies were carefully picking up broken glass. 'Tell those girls to leave that glass alone before they cut themselves. Luckily, I have my work gloves in my pocket. Always prepared – that's me.' She slapped her leg with her one free hand. 'I'll be back in a tick.'

Anya shook her head. 'Pah, what is this tick?' she muttered before continuing to check the bread and buns that had been on a shelf beside the shattered window. A fine layer of dust and plaster was also visible. She carefully wiped the loaves and put them to one side. 'Bread and butter pudding, I think,' she smiled, licking her lips.

'If we have any currants,' Katie said as she joined her. 'You're not really going to use them, are you? There may be thin pieces of glass inside. That window was hit with some force. Perhaps we should put them in the pig bin instead,' she added with a deep sigh.

'Why the unhappy face? Be happy we are alive,' Anya said, waving her hand towards the space where the largest window had been until the air raid. 'As one of my customers said only this morning, "Damn Fritz, but he won't win." Not unless we starve,' she added, examining another loaf of bread.

'Oh, it seems such a shame. We were due to open the Ramsgate tearooms tomorrow, and it looks as though Margate is now out of commission. It's like building a sandcastle as the tide comes in.'

'Stop that miserable talk. Joe Lyons would not like it one little bit. We Brits are made of stern stuff,' Anya said as she picked up a couple of buns. Seeing Katie's surprised look, she added, 'I am honorary Brit while I live and work here. If my Henio fights with the RAF, then I fight with the women of Thanet. One day, who knows – our children will be proper British people.'

Katie burst into tears, picking up the hem of her apron to hide her face.

'What is this crying for? I will have my children one day. I know they will be British, but deep inside they will be Polish,' Anya said. 'Do not cry for me.'

Katie shook her head and in a muffled voice said, 'I'm not crying for you. I'm crying for me; not that I don't think you are brave to look to the future, despite what we are putting up with at the moment.'

'Then why, little Katie?' Anya said, as she put down the buns and went to the other side of the counter to give the girl a consoling hug. 'We are here. We survived. We will have bread pudding.' She smiled.

Katie straightened her tear-stained pinny and looked round to make sure no one was listening. 'I had a visitor come this morning.'

Anya frowned. 'A visitor? But you have been here working on the early shift. Who was it came to visit you?'

'I mean, I have my monthly visitor. I was so hoping that with Jack having been home for a few days, I might be pregnant.'

Anya's quizzical look softened. 'Oh, my dear child. I too have been hoping the same. I do not see my Henio very often, but you know . . .' She gave a crafty wink. 'We try our best. One day, you and me, we will be surrounded by little babies and sit together in the sun as we watch them play. Our husbands, they will have jobs that keep them home and safe, and this war will be a distant memory.'

Katie smiled. 'Can you promise me that?'

Anya shook her head and looked away. 'I wish I could promise you, my little friend, but for now we just have to hold onto those dreams and keep fighting. Will you fight with me?'

'I will, and I do hope your dream comes true,' Katie answered.

'Now, you help me check this bread. I refuse to give good food to the pigs,' Anya smiled, handing a loaf to Katie.

'Knock, knock,' Mildred said loudly as she stood at the open door to Rose's office.

'Come on in,' Rose said as she spotted the friendly face. 'As you can see, we are up against it a bit. Thank goodness no one was hurt, but I doubt we will be open for a few days. The telephone isn't working, so I'm not able to get hold of anyone at head office to arrange for a builder to come and make repairs. What a mess!' She leant her elbows on the desk, putting her face in her hands, then froze for a moment before looking up at Mildred. 'Please don't say you've come with bad news?' she begged.

Mildred shook her head. 'No, as far as I know your mum and the inhabitants of Sea View were all safe in the tunnels. I stayed on the boat. I know, there's no need to look at me like that, I should have taken cover – but I was busy. Nine times out of ten these raids amount to nothing,' she mumbled, knowing she wasn't exactly telling the truth. 'You know me; I'd rather be able to see and smell the sea than be shut up underground.'

Rose knew that to be true. Mildred would often spend

the night under the stars, such was her love of the open air.

'Anyway, when the all-clear sounded I popped up to Sea View and left something in the pantry for supper, as I'd originally planned. I saw this letter on the hall stand addressed to you and thought I might as well kill two birds with one stone and bring it here, after I'd checked that Captain's Cottage was still standing. It was,' she added, seeing a worried look cross Rose's face. 'I thought it might be from your Ben,' she said as she put the envelope in front of Rose. 'I'll leave you alone to read it.' She turned to leave the room.

'There's no need, Mildred – this isn't from Ben. I'd know his handwriting anywhere. Besides, he spoke to me on the telephone just before the air raid. I have no idea who this could be from,' Rose said in puzzlement, reaching for her letter opener. 'Take a seat while I have a quick read.'

'I'll stand, if it's all the same. I'm a bit on the mucky side and don't want to mess up your furniture.'

Rose looked up from where she was straightening out a single sheet of notepaper. 'Have you seen the mess?'

Mildred glanced around. Every surface had a covering of dust and what looked like sand, no doubt blown in from the beach across the road by the force of the explosion where the land mine had come down close to the shoreline. Through the open door and what remained of the teashop windows, she could see the army already collecting what was left of the debris. Nearby, young lads were scavenging for shrapnel. If that land mine had dropped a few feet closer, Mildred thought, they'd be digging Nippies and customers out of the cellar right now. She looked at the smartly dressed manageress, remembering her as a little girl who always seemed to have scraped knees and a ribbon missing from her hair. Rose didn't appear to realize what a close call she'd had; the shock might well come later. Mildred decided then to take the girls back to Sea View, for Flora to care for them. Everyone was safe at Sea View.

'My gosh, just look at this,' Rose said, looking excited. 'It's a letter from my half-sister, Eileen. Fancy her finally getting in touch with me!'

Mildred took the letter and slowly read it. 'It says here that she read about your engagement to Ben in *The Times*. Is that right?'

'Yes, Ben's mother placed the announcement as a surprise. Mum has a copy back at home. It looks really posh. It mentions Mum, and my late father. You've seen this kind of thing, surely? They are always so formal, and being in *The Times*, it looked very important.'

'So that's how she'd have known about you, and found you,' Mildred said thoughtfully, turning the page over to see if there was anything written on the reverse side.

'Yes. Isn't it wonderful to think that the announcement of my engagement to Ben was seen by a relative I've never known, and that she was able to write to me?' Rose's eyes were bright with excitement as she spoke, and she did not notice the concerned expression on Mildred's face.

10

Mildred looked at Rose's excited face, thinking about how to put her doubts into words without upsetting the younger woman. Having been an only child herself, she could appreciate how it must feel to suddenly have a half-sibling get in touch; but she had a strong instinct that something wasn't quite right here. 'I wonder why your sister has never made contact before.'

'From what I understand, there was some ill feeling when the General and Mum fell in love – and then I came along. He did have a wife and children, after all, although he lived apart from them. Mum was well provided for; you know that he purchased Sea View so Mum would always have an income?'

Mildred nodded. 'Very generous of him, under the circumstances. I saw him at a distance a few times when he took his constitutionals, but that was in the days before your mum took in lodgers, so I lived elsewhere. I'd like to have known him. He was an interesting chap, by all accounts.'

'I wish I'd known he was my dad,' Rose said, with a distant look in her eyes. 'We were close, and he did teach me about books and the like – but I was still a young child when he died. And then Mum kept that secret to herself, to protect everyone.'

'It was a rum do,' Mildred said, thinking back. Flora and her daughter had not spoken to one another for months after Rose had discovered the secret. 'And now your half-sister decides to write to you. What do you feel about all of this – that's if you don't mind me asking?'

Rose looked at Mildred, her eyes shining brightly. 'I think it's wonderful. You can see from her words that she holds no grudges against Mum, and that everything that happened should be placed firmly in the past. It's jolly good of her to say that, considering she must have missed out on growing up with her dad, don't you think?'

Mildred nodded. 'She sounds keen to get to know you. What will you do next?'

'Well, first I need to sort out the mess here. We are going to be closed for a while, until the Lyons building department can get some men over here to do repairs on the teashop. But I can't even report to head office until the telephone is fixed. Then I'll sit down and write to my half-sister and her husband, inviting them to come down here for a visit. She's been bombed out, so now seems like a good time.'

'I suppose that's why there's only a post office address,' Mildred said, looking thoughtful, before slapping her leg. 'Now put that letter somewhere safe, and show me around so I can make a list of the damage. I may just be able to help you out.' She rubbed her hands together with glee. Mildred loved nothing more than getting her hands dirty on a building project around the house; both

Sea View and Captain's Cottage had benefited from her handiwork.

'I would think there's more damage here than you can fix with your trusty toolbox, but thanks for the offer.'

'Good grief, girl – I may be able to do a few small jobs, but I was thinking of asking some of me mates off the boats to give a hand with the rest. We can patch the shop up so you won't have to close. There's a lot of people in Thanet who rely on you and your Nippies to provide a bite to eat and give a ready smile. If we can keep you open, there will be some happy customers.'

Rose gave Mildred a big grin, but then a shadow crossed her face. 'I don't have the authority to spend any money, though. And I can't take it out of the shop's takings, because that money has to be accounted for. Let's go and see what needs doing, but to be honest, we should really close down for the foreseeable future. The Ramsgate teashop opens in a couple of days – and from what Katie said when she visited, you would hardly know they'd had bomb damage there at all.'

Mildred shook her head. 'I'm sorry to be the bearer of bad news, but the other teashop looks worse than this one after today's raid.'

'Oh no!' Rose wailed. 'There was me thinking I could send some of the staff to the Ramsgate branch, so that they wouldn't have to manage with lower wages while we get this place fixed up.'

'Then let's see what can be done, eh?'

'Oh Mildred, whatever would I do without you? You are just like the good witch in *The Wizard of Oz*. One wave of your magical wand, and everything is fine.'

'Oh, I don't know about that,' Mildred blushed. 'I just like to help you girls out when I can.' She smiled, thinking that there was no one less like Glinda the Good Witch than she. 'It was a good film, though.'

'Perhaps you could wave your magic wand and make the sickly girl in the staffroom disappear?' Anya said, appearing at the door of the office.

'Oh my goodness, I'd forgotten the poor child,' Rose said, clapping her hand to her forehead. 'We have a poorly young worker in the staffroom,' she added by way of explanation to Mildred, who was looking puzzled. 'One of the kitchen girls was taken sick, and we sat with her in the staffroom during the air raid. I am concerned about her.'

'So you should be. She has nowhere to live,' Anya said. 'I interrogated her, and she broke down and told me everything.'

'You mean you didn't take cover during the air raid?' Mildred growled at the same time Anya spoke.

Rose raised her hand to stop them. 'Please, I can't think straight with you both speaking at the same time. Mildred, it wasn't intentional to stay in the teashop during the air raid, but this girl – Jennie – was too ill to cope with being shut in the cellar. Then Anya arrived. It's as simple as that.'

'Then the world exploded all around us,' Anya added dramatically. 'I was sure we would all die, along with those in the cellar. It did not matter where we were.'

Mildred listened carefully. 'So where is this girl now?'

'I have made her comfortable in the staffroom on a stretcher bed,' said Anya. 'There has not been any more sick for a while, but she is very poorly. But you can't forget her forever – and she cannot sleep here when we all go home tonight.'

Rose thought for a moment before making a decision. 'Right, Anya; you are to go back to Jennie and make sure she rests and tries to drink something. Ask the kitchen staff to make some toast; that should settle her stomach.'

'The gas has been turned off down the street. We can't cook.'

'Then give her some dry bread,' Rose said, before ushering Anya out of the office with instructions not to ask Jennie any further questions. 'She will tell us all in good time. We don't want her deciding to run away – then we'll just have to go looking for her. I'll be with you in a moment, Mildred,' she added as she waved to one of the Nippies. 'Phoebe, I understand there is no gas supply to the kitchen to make hot drinks. Would you please check our milk and cold drink supplies, and make sure everyone has something to quench their thirst?'

'Miss, we do have the large water boiler that plugs into the electricity supply. But it's covered in plaster where the ceiling came down in the corner of the restaurant.'

'Then hand out cold drinks until we've sorted it out. Are there still customers in the cellar?'

'There's a few, Miss. Katie thought it best to keep them there until we knew it was safe for them to leave. Goodness knows what it's like out in the street.'

'The army are cordoning off the part of the road that was damaged, and there's broken glass and masonry everywhere,' Mildred reported. 'They only let me through because I said I was a workman, as they have yet to check if some of the buildings are safe. It's best your customers stay here; but you can't make them, of course.'

'I want to put you in charge of looking after them, Phoebe. Food and drink – at least, whatever we can manage without gas for cooking – is on the house. Tell the kitchen I said so, and I'll be in to speak with them shortly. Thank you.'

'I'm impressed with your organizational skills,' Mildred said. 'I've not seen you in action before.'

Rose shrugged. It felt strange to receive a compliment from one of her oldest friends. 'I'm just doing my job,' she said. 'May I ask if you really think we could keep the teashop going?'

'Grab hold of your notebook and let's go and look. Would your staff agree to help out with cleaning?'

Rose looked up at the clock on her office wall. It was hanging at an angle, but still working. 'We do have a cleaner, but she doesn't come to work until we've closed. That's hours away.'

'If you want the teashop open by tomorrow, we may all have to roll up our sleeves and get stuck in. That's as long as there's no structural damage.'

'Then we should stop standing here chatting and get cracking,' Rose said, waving her notebook in the air.

Staff stood by and watched as Mildred inspected the large windows at the front of the shop. Taking a broom from one of the Nippies, she told everyone to stand back as she pushed any remaining glass from the frame of the two main windows. 'There's no structural damage, which is good. We could do with a couple of men who would be able to lift and move this furniture while we clean this area.'

'I could ask the male customers in the cellar if they would help,' one of the two cooks suggested. 'We only had a bit of dust and sand blow into the kitchen and storeroom, so apart from having no gas we're nearly back to normal.' She waved to her fellow cook and an older woman who was a general help. 'We'd all like to help clean up. We like working here and wouldn't want to be out of work if the teashop doesn't open for a while. Cooking or cleaning: it's all the same to us.'

A group of Nippies standing nearby agreed, and with the help of three men who'd been taking shelter in the cellar with their families, the area near the windows was soon clear and tables and chairs were stacked against one wall. Being the tallest member of staff, Anya was called away from watching Jennie and given a broom with a cleaning cloth tied around the bristles. Balancing on a wooden chair with two Nippies holding her legs so she didn't fall, she waved the broom back and forth, cleaning the brass light fittings with their fancy glass shades until they looked as good as new.

'Well done, Anya,' Rose said as she helped her from the chair. 'Sit down, you look a little dizzy.'

Anya agreed and sat down, taking over the supervision of the cleaning of her counter from where she was seated.

For three solid hours the staff of the teashop dusted and polished, until there was hardly any evidence of the damage created by the air raid – apart from the two large missing panes of window glass. Smaller windows that had been cracked were fixed temporarily with blast tape, which formed a criss-cross pattern that made the windows safe. It would hold until the Lyons builders could be contacted and booked to come down to Margate to replace them.

'Excuse me,' an army corporal called through one of the windows. 'Is anyone in charge here?'

Rose hurried over, hoping there wasn't any bad news. They were so close to getting the teashop ship-shape again. 'I'm the manageress,' she said with a worried look.

'Just to let you know, Miss, that the gas will be on again shortly. We've capped off the pipes that were fractured, so you should be brewing your tea again before too long.'

'Oh, that's marvellous news. Thank you so much, corporal. Can I invite you and your fellow soldiers in for some refreshments?'

'No, ta, Miss. We'll be on our way shortly, but thanks for the offer. You could tell your ladies who work in the kitchen to make sure everything's turned off. There's no knowing what was left on before the air raid. We don't want you gassing yourselves now, do we?'

Rose promised to do just that, and went back to her staff to issue fresh instructions.

'Once the gas is back on and running properly, I suggest we all sit down together for a meal and a hot drink. Something on toast would go down a treat, don't you think?'

A cheer ran through the staff, and the customers who had stayed to help.

'I shall go to the shelter and inform those who are still down there,' Anya said. 'They will turn into mushrooms if they stay below ground much longer.'

'Blimey, was that Anya's attempt at a joke? I swear she is turning more English by the day,' Katie said, as she joined Rose and slipped her arm through her friend's. 'It's been a bit of a strange day, all in all.'

'You can say that again,' Rose agreed, thinking of the letter from her half-sister that she'd slipped into her handbag earlier. 'My biggest problem right now is what to do about those windows. I can't go home and leave the teashop open to the elements, and to any petty pilferer who may be wandering the streets.'

'Won't the wooden boards still fit over the window frames?' Katie asked.

'Oh, I'm an idiot,' Rose said. 'I suppose it wouldn't hurt to check. After all, it's only the glass that's missing. I'd been thinking I'd have to sleep here to protect the teashop! Let's go and get the boards from the stockroom now.'

The two women hurried to the room where the tall wooden window covers were kept. Each evening the Nippies were tasked with hooking the boards up at the windows of the teashop and securing them with padlocks. The idea was to save the shop if there were air raids overnight, and to protect the premises from looters.

'Here, let me help,' Mildred said as she lifted the shutters into place and stepped back to look at the protected windows. 'They fit a treat. You can leave the ones on the damaged windows in place until the glazier and builders have been.'

Rose nodded, but was unhappy that the shutters had been in the storeroom all along. 'If only we'd used them when the siren went off, the windows wouldn't have been damaged,' she sighed.

Mildred was not amused. 'You can't think like that. Besides, stopping to fix shutters to the windows when there's an air raid is dangerous. You could be killed. You know you should go straight to the shelter as soon as Minnie starts her moaning.'

'Just like you didn't today,' Katie said to Rose.

'I couldn't go and leave Jennie in the staffroom on her own . . . Oh my goodness, I've been that busy, I've not looked in on the poor child.'

'It's all right,' said Katie reassuringly. 'I've checked her. She's sleeping, and managed a few cups of water and nibbled on some bread. She's over her sickness, but still very weak. Our main problem is working out where she's going to stay tonight. I'd suggest putting her up at Captain's Cottage, although there is little enough room; but having a sick person in the house and baby Mary possibly catching whatever she has would be dangerous.'

'I'll take her back to Sea View. Flora can always squeeze another person in there.'

'It's not just one night, though. From what Anya has said, the girl is homeless.'

'Let's worry about that when she's better, eh?' Mildred said. 'If you want to fetch her coat, Katie, I'll take her back there when I leave. I don't think there's much more I can help you with here. We can get Jennie settled in a warm bed, and she will be feeling much better before too long.'

Katie agreed, and hurried away to prepare Jennie for the short journey to Ramsgate.

'That was exciting,' a familiar voice said from behind Rose. 'I'd have surfaced earlier but the children fell asleep with their heads on my lap, so it was hard to move. I'm dying for a cigarette.'

'Ruth!' Rose exclaimed. 'You must forgive me. I've been so busy with all this mess, I'd forgotten the three of you were here. We are just about to prepare some hot food if you'd like to stay?'

Ruth gave them all a charming smile. 'There's nothing to forgive. We've been kept safe and looked after. If you don't mind, I'm going to get the girls to Sea View before their grandmother worries too much.'

'You're going to Sea View?' Mildred asked. 'I could take you in my van.'

Rose made the introductions as Anya appeared. 'The van stinks of fish,' she warned. 'You will also stink of fish if you get into it. Sit on newspapers, and keep the window open.'

'I simply adore this woman. The children are going to love living with Mother at Sea View along with you all.'

Mildred raised her eyebrows and looked towards Rose. 'Will there be enough room?'

Flora answered the knock on the door with trepidation. It had been a week since Councillor Mould's visit, and she'd become wary of visitors in case it was someone arriving to take Daisy away. Instead, standing in front of her was a middle-aged man in the livery of a chauffeur, holding a large wicker basket. Behind him, she could see the front of a highly polished Bentley motor vehicle. 'Mrs Neville?' he asked, and made to step over the threshold when Flora nodded without saying a word.

'I have a delivery courtesy of Lady Diana. She is staying here at the moment, is she not?'

'Gosh, yes, please do come in. Di– I mean, Lady Diana has taken her grandchildren out for a walk. She should be back within the hour. Would you like to wait?'

'If I could leave this somewhere?' he enquired, giving a gentle smile.

'Of course. Perhaps it could be taken to her room?' she said, glancing towards the stairs, knowing there were a fair few steps up to the second floor.

'I'm sorry, I didn't make myself clear. Lady Diana has ordered these goods for you, Mrs Neville. You will find they are provisions.'

'Goodness, you must think me such an idiot. Would you be able to carry them to the kitchen for me? The kettle is on the hob, if you have time . . . ?'

'I always have time for tea,' he smiled as she pointed the way down a short flight of stairs to the welcoming warmth of the room, which was the heart of the guesthouse.

'I'm sorry, I've not told you who I am,' he said, removing his cap so she could see his well-groomed dark brown hair more clearly. 'My name is John Bentley. Lady Diana uses my services when she is in London.'

Flora tried her best not to laugh. 'John Bentley drives a Bentley?'

He grinned. 'You are not the first to have made that comment. If it helps at all, I also have a Rolls-Royce in the garage, as well as three lorries and a motorbike and sidecar.'

'I prefer the Bentley; at least I won't forget your name if I think of the vehicle,' she said, before realizing it was rather a forward comment. Why would she want to see him again? 'Please take a seat. I do have some coffee, and also cocoa if you prefer?'

'Tea will be fine. You have a very nice home,' he said as he placed his cap on the table next to the wicker hamper. 'Do you have a large family?' he asked, seeing all the chairs placed around the large scrubbed pine table.

Flora looked up from where she was warming the smaller of her teapots. 'Goodness, no, although I've always wanted a large family. I have one daughter, Rose. She is engaged to marry Lady Diana's son, Ben. That is how we know each other. Everyone else is a long-term guest here – apart from this little lady.' She smiled to where Daisy was sleeping in a crib made by Mildred, covered in a pretty daisy-strewn cover sewn by Miss Tibbs. 'This is Daisy. She's alone in the world since her family perished in an air raid. If you look across the road when you leave, you will see what remains of her family home.'

John stood up and went to look into the crib where Daisy slept contentedly, sucking on her thumb. 'War is a terrible thing. At least she has you,' he said. 'My one regret is not having children or grandchildren.'

Flora concentrated on preparing the tea tray, not trusting herself to speak until she had her emotions under control. 'Daisy may not be with us for very long. I've been deemed unsuitable to foster or adopt her.'

John frowned as he took the tea tray from her and placed it on the table before moving the wicker chest to a chair. 'Why, I've only known you for a matter of minutes, and I can tell you are a caring woman. Do you have a dark past?' he smiled, trying to make Flora smile too.

'I fell foul of a local councillor who has her finger in

too many pies. She doesn't like me, and this is a way she can get back at me. I assure you, my past is no darker than many others, and not half as interesting. You mentioned you don't have any children? I'm sorry that you and your wife were not blessed.'

'I lost the love of my life in the influenza epidemic of 1918,' he said.

'I'm so sorry, I shouldn't have asked,' Flora said, feeling as though she had imposed.

'It was a long time ago. No one knows how our lives will pan out, and now I have my business. I'm happy enough,' he said as Flora handed him his tea. 'I take it your trade was looking after holidaymakers before the war?'

Flora's eyes shone as she talked about Sea View and how gradually she had acquired her long-term lodgers, Mildred, Miss Tibbs, and later Joyce and Pearl. 'It was a regular income, which I was glad of with a daughter to bring up. Since then, the house is fit to burst, but I'd not have it any other way,' she smiled. 'My goodness, I've never opened my heart like this before to a stranger. Whatever must you think of me?'

'I think you are a remarkable woman.'

'Oh, I wouldn't say that,' Flora dismissed his comment with a wave of her hand. 'I managed, very much like any other woman.'

'But your uniform . . .'

Flora looked down, having forgotten she was still wearing her green WVS outfit. 'It was my shift on the canteen van this morning,' she explained. 'I'm on duty with the ARP later, but first I'll need to go out and see what's available at the butcher's for my lodgers. You're lucky to have caught me at home to take in Lady Diana's hamper,' she said.

'Remember, it's not for Lady D,' he said. 'If you don't believe me, read the label.' He leant over and untied a string attached to the basket, passing the brown card label to Flora.

Flora put her hand to her mouth before reading aloud the words. *'Dearest Flora, I hope this gift goes some way to recompense you for the disruption my granddaughters and I have brought to your household. Your generosity shows no bounds, and I intend to do my best to continue to contribute to the stocking of the pantry at Sea View . . .* There was no need for her to do this! I have their ration books, and Lady Diana has been more than generous in helping out around the house since she arrived. Why, she's even arranged for the visiting tutor to include Pearl in the lessons. In the few days they've lived here, the girls have become firm friends,' she finished, looking at the large hamper.

'Shall I open it for you?' John asked.

Flora nodded her head, holding her breath in anticipation as the lid was thrown back and he removed a layer of straw. 'Why don't you unpack the rest, while I pour us another cup of tea?' he suggested.

'This is like Christmas,' she exclaimed as canned goods, jars of fruit, a leg of lamb and a small ham joint were placed on the table. 'Where would she have found such things?' she asked, as in her mind she was already working out how best to use the provisions for meals, and what to store away for Christmas.

'Lady Diana has many contacts,' he said as he too looked

through the cans and jars. 'There's chocolate here, as well as boiled sweets.'

'Those are definitely being put away for Christmas. In fact, I'll hide them away right now, while the children aren't around. Once seen they will wheedle away at me until I weaken, and soon there'll be none left to wrap up for Father Christmas to deliver.'

'You're a hard woman,' he laughed as he watched her place the sweets into a tin and put it on the top shelf of the large dresser that ran the length of one wall. 'I must be making my way back to London,' he said, getting to his feet and reaching for his cap.

'London? You came all this way to deliver a hamper?' Flora asked, sorry to see him preparing to leave.

'No doubt you will see me again soon. Lady Diana will be requiring my services before too long. She puts a lot of business my way.'

'I'm pleased to hear it . . . I mean, I'm pleased you have work, not . . .'

John laughed as she tried to correct her words. 'I'm pleased too, and it's not about the work. I wonder . . .'

'Yes?'

'If you think it's not too forward of me, I was wondering if perhaps next time I called I could take you for a drive. We could find somewhere to have tea – that's if you'd like to?'

'That would be delightful. Thank you for inviting me.'

'I'll do my best to give you more notice next time,' he said as he held out his hand.

Flora offered hers and he shook it firmly. She enjoyed the physical contact, warmth and strength of his grip. 'Let me give you my telephone number,' she said, looking round for a piece of paper and pencil.

'Don't worry, I have it,' he reminded her, pulling out his wallet and showing her one of Lady Diana's visiting cards, with the telephone number of Sea View written in her distinctive handwriting.

'As long as we aren't cut off during another air raid,' she said, trying to think of problems.

'I'll send a postcard as well, and if I have to drive around the streets to find you, I'll do that too.'

Flora laughed, trying not to look too excited at the thought of spending more time with John.

'You are a charming woman, Flora Neville,' he said as he bid her farewell.

Flora sat back down at the table and sipped what remained of her tea before shuddering; it was cold, and tasteless without sugar as she was trying to cut back due to shortages and rations. She couldn't recall the last time she had been attracted to a man in such a short time. In fact, at any time at all. She'd warmed to Rose's father, the General, and love had blossomed, but with John Bentley the attraction was almost instantaneous. 'You'll have to be careful, Flora Neville,' she said to herself, 'or you could end up acting like a lovestruck young girl and make a terrible mistake. Goodness knows what Councillor Mould would do then.'

'Mum, are you home?' Rose called as she let herself in through the front door of Sea View.

'Down here, love. Come and look at all of this.'

Rose came into the room, removing her coat and throwing it over the back of a chair before checking the teapot. 'I'll make a fresh pot, shall I? By the way, I spotted a rather posh Bentley driving off down the road. One of our neighbours must know someone with a few bob – those cars don't come cheap.'

'It was a visitor for me,' Flora said, feeling her cheeks burn at the thought of John Bentley. 'Look what he left.' She pointed towards the hamper.

'Crikey! I take it Lady Diana had a hand in this, or have you lodged our ration books with Fortnum and Mason?' Rose joked, bending down to check the contents.

'You guessed right. Diana has been rather generous, but I will have to have a word with her. She can't keep doing things like this.'

'Why not? The woman spends money like water, and she means well. You could offend her by refusing her help. She's near enough family, Mum.'

'All the same, I'll be having a few words. She pays her rent like anyone else, and there's no need for her to spoil us. Perhaps I should offer her my bedroom? It is the largest in the house, and it's not as if I need a large room,' Flora said thoughtfully.

'Don't be daft. She's more than happy to use the front bedroom, and the girls are enjoying sleeping in the bunk beds next door to her.'

'I do worry that I've had to open up the top floors again. It will take longer to get downstairs and out the front door if there should be an air raid.'

'Don't you mean when there is an air raid? Look, Mum, I think you are worrying too much. Either Anya or Mildred will always be home and can hurry Lady D down the stairs, and it's not as if she's wobbly on her pins, is it?

Everyone else is muddling in together on the lower floors. Where have you put Jennie?'

Flora's face softened. 'Would you believe she's in with Miss Tibbs? The girl was so poorly when Mildred brought her back the other evening that Miss Tibbs said she'd care for her. There's still the single bed in the downstairs room where we moved Miss Tibbs when the raids started. Anya refused to sleep in the same room because Miss Tibbs snores so much – I was so fed up with their arguing, I moved Anya back upstairs.'

Rose chuckled. 'Nothing ever changes. I do miss living here. Captain's Cottage is quiet in comparison, even though Mary can keep us awake occasionally.'

'Bless her. She's a bonnie baby,' Flora said, then looked at Rose and frowned. 'Why are you here mid-afternoon? Shouldn't you be at work?'

'I wanted to have a word with you while it was quiet. This house can be like Charing Cross Station with everyone here in the evenings. I needed to go to the Ramsgate teashop to see if we could borrow a few tables and chairs while they are still closed down. A few of ours were damaged in the blast the other day. I caught the bus over, and thought I'd pop in and see you and have a chat on the way back.'

'There's nothing wrong, is there? It's not Ben – have you changed your mind about the wedding?'

Rose raised her hand to stop Flora firing questions. 'There's nothing wrong between me and Ben. As for the wedding – I'd like to know about that myself, but at the moment he has no idea when he will have leave, so we can't plan ahead. No; it's this letter from Eileen. I've written a reply, but I want you to read it before I pop it in the post box. I don't want to do anything that would upset you.'

Flora hurried to the stove where the kettle was starting to boil, tipped some water into the teapot to rinse and warm it through before discarding, then added tea leaves from the caddy. After pouring in the boiling water, she covered the pot with a knitted cosy. 'Why would it upset me?'

Rose was thoughtful as she refilled the milk jug and collected a cup and saucer from the dresser, placing them on the table before sitting down. Reaching for her bag, she pulled out an envelope and removed the letter. 'I feel as though I'm raking up the past, and it must be painful for you.'

'Oh, darling; I have only good memories of the past. I can't stop you wanting to make the acquaintance of your half-sister. When I read Eileen's letter, I couldn't see that she bore a grudge about her father's romance with me. There's been so much water under the bridge since those days. It's time for you to know your family.'

Rose nodded thoughtfully. 'Because I've just taken time off to go to London, I can't really go gallivanting off to meet her. I thought I'd invite her to Ramsgate for a few days.'

'Now, that is a good idea,' Flora beamed. 'She will be able to meet your friends – and with luck, meet me too, if she wishes.'

'The thing is, Mum, there's no room to put her up at Captain's Cottage, so I wondered . . .'

Flora chuckled. She could read her daughter like a book. 'You wondered if I could put her up here?'

'Could you?' Rose said, almost holding her breath as she watched her mother's face.

'I'll have to open up and air the attic rooms Mr Cardew used to rent,' Flora said, raising her eyebrows at the mention of the former lodger who had turned out to be an enemy spy. 'At least we won't have any problems with family using them – I'm sure they wouldn't be here to spy for the enemy, or do anything underhand.'

11

November 1st 1940

'My God – I reckon I'll die down here, and they'll find me in a hundred years' time, and my hair will still be a mess,' Lily sighed as she rubbed at her head with a towel. 'That was the wrong time for the air-raid siren to go off. I'll never be ready for the dance this evening.'

Katie shuddered as they heard the sound of Stukas dive-bombing over the estuary. 'Honestly, Lily, people are no doubt dying out there and all you care about is your hair,' she said as she dug around in the bag she kept ready for hurried escapes to the Anderson shelter. 'I may just have . . . aha! Here they are,' she said, pulling out a tangle of pipe cleaners she used to put a curl in her hair. 'Let me brush your hair out, and then I can use these to create some curls, since you forgot your hairpins.'

Lily turned so that Katie could do her best to sort out her hair. 'Did you happen to pick up the post before the siren went off? I heard the letterbox rattle while I had my head in the sink.'

'There was a letter,' Katie said as she tugged the brush

through a stubborn knot, causing Lily to swear. 'It's from my Jack.'

'And?'

'I've not opened it yet. There wasn't time,' she replied, rolling a length of hair around one of the pipe cleaners and bending the ends over to secure the curl. 'I had to make the cocoa and lock up the house.'

Lily felt guilty, as she'd only wrapped her hair in a towel and grabbed her coat. 'I'm sorry, I should have helped more. Usually I have Mary to sort out, but with her being with Rose at Sea View, everything else kind of slipped my mind.'

Kate laughed. She wasn't one to bear grudges, and Lily had always been known as the scatterhead amongst the three friends. 'It can wait. Let me finish your hair, and we can have a mug of cocoa, and then I'll read out what he has to say.'

'Wouldn't you rather read it when you are alone? After all, you are married and will have private things to say to one another . . .'

Katie chuckled. 'You know darn well that my Jack isn't one for lovey-dovey words. His letters are more about our future, and what he's been up to since he was last home. We save personal stuff for when we are together. Who knows who censors what he writes?' She turned Lily to face her and checked her handiwork. 'That's the best I can do. If you sit close to the paraffin stove, it'll help dry your hair. It's about time we lit it, as it's very cold down here – mind you, it's cold above ground as well. Mildred reckons we're in for a hard winter, not that it can be any worse than the snow we had at the beginning of the year.

I wonder if we will have snow for Christmas? That would be lovely.'

Lily shivered and reached for her coat. She was already wearing a thick jumper over her siren suit, and two pairs of socks. 'Bloody Christmas. It's going to a miserable one this year, what with the beating we've taken here in Thanet. Someone ought to ban it until the war's over.'

'Oh, you are a grouchy one. I'm looking forward to it this year, even though my husband is unlikely to be home to share in the celebrations,' Katie sighed.

'You're too romantic by half,' Lily scoffed. 'With so many of the Lyons staff going off to do war work, we'll no doubt be working double shifts – and then there are the shortages . . .'

'But it's Mary's first Christmas. We've got to make it as magical as possible for her. I spotted a few paper decorations in the loft that Mildred's last tenant left behind. Paper chains and Chinese lanterns. We can decorate our front room, and Flora is sure to invite us to Sea View for our Christmas meal. If we muck in together, it will be fun.'

Lily smiled at the infectious excitement on Katie's face. She reminded herself guiltily that her friend had been brought up in an orphanage, and knew how to make the most of what she had. If it hadn't been for the other girls' mums inviting her to join their family occasions, Katie would have led a very bleak life. 'You're right. I'm being grumpy, and I shouldn't. Mary's not likely to remember her first Christmas, but we will, and we can look back on the season with fondness.'

Katie gave her a quick hug. 'That's the spirit. I'm making

a teddy bear out of an old coat I picked up at the church jumble sale. It wasn't fit to be worn, but it will make an excellent toy. And I may be able to use the odd scraps to shape into a ball.'

'I wish I was as good with my hands as you are,' Lily said. 'I have no idea yet what to give you all.'

Katie shrugged off the compliment. 'I'm all right with toys and silly stuff, but useless at making frocks. But you gave us Mary, and what a joy she is,' she said, shrugging off the thought that Lily had conceived out of wedlock and had no intention of marrying the father. Unless people's views changed, Lily might find it hard to find a man to take her on. At least she would have her friends. 'Now, why don't you pour out the cocoa, and I'll read Jack's letter.'

'She is a joy, isn't she?' Lily said as she placed two tin mugs on the upturned wooden box they used as a table and carefully poured out the cocoa. 'Do you want a sandwich as well? We have the fish paste sandwiches I brought home from work. I never thought, when I was in the Girl Guides and we used to chant "be prepared", that it could mean always having something ready to eat in case bloody Goering was sending over his Luftwaffe to try and blow us to smithereens. There's been no letting up lately. I just hope our lads can do their best to hold them back. It's bad enough down here, let alone in London – I'm glad I never went up there to work in one of the big Corner Houses.'

'Perhaps things would have been different if you'd followed your dream, but you'd not have had Mary . . .'

'I could have perished in the Blitz instead. So yeah, I'm grateful for what I've got. But I still don't like sitting in this Anderson shelter with damp hair that will end up smelling of paraffin. I'm not likely to find some handsome prince to whisk me away looking like this, am I?' she guffawed, before jumping as a plane screeched overhead. 'That was a bit on the close side. Read us Jack's letter to take our minds off what's going on out there.'

Kate took a sip of her cocoa before unfolding the single sheet of paper. 'He says he is well and working hard, and is still with the lads he was with before. He was worried about being posted elsewhere,' she explained to Lily.

Lily nodded. 'That makes sense; I'd feel the same in his position. What else does he say?'

'There's a lot crossed out by the censor, so I can't make sense of it, but then he says to send his love to everyone, and that he will write again soon.' She smiled, folding the letter and placing it back in the envelope. 'At least he is safe and well.'

Lily agreed, and kept her thoughts to herself. Jack could be at the bottom of the sea by now, but it didn't do to worry the girl. 'What the hell?' she exclaimed as a crashing sound came from the garden, followed by the sound of a man swearing. 'Someone's in our garden.'

'What are you doing?' Katie asked in alarm, as Lily pulled open the entrance to their shelter and started to climb out. 'The all-clear hasn't sounded yet; you could be injured.'

'Someone needs our help.'

'It could be a German,' Katie said, following close behind.

'Not swearing in English, it isn't. Look, over there in the apple tree. He seems to be entangled in the branches.'

'Are you having trouble?' Katie called up to him.

'I am, my love. Any chance you can help me down?' a polite voice answered back.

'At least we know he's one of ours,' Lily said as she hurried to the back of the house where Mildred kept a ladder, ignoring all thought of the all-clear not yet sounding.

'I'm not convinced. He could be a spy who knows our language, putting on an accent,' Katie replied as she took the end of the ladder and helped carry it back to where the man was dangling by his parachute. His feet were a full six feet above the ground.

'He's wearing RAF flying gear,' Lily snorted as she leant the ladder against the tree and looked up at the pilot. 'Can you cut yourself loose?'

'I will now there's something to climb onto,' he replied, waving a penknife in the air.

'Be careful,' Katie said, holding her hands out to grab his ankles and guide them to the top of the ladder.

'Can you pull the parachute down as well?' Lily asked as he started to carefully manoeuvre himself to the ground.

The pilot laughed out loud and reached up to tug the parachute from the tree. 'If anyone asks, I have no idea what you did with this,' he said, while Lily bundled up the silk as quickly as she could. Looking at Katie's puzzled expression, she grinned. 'Think of how many pairs of knickers we can ask Miss Tibbs to make with this!'

'Honestly,' Katie huffed. 'Whatever must you think of us? Can we offer you a cup of tea?'

'Thanks all the same, but do you have a telephone? I should let the airfield know where I am. Then I'd love a cuppa.'

Katie ran ahead to the cottage to put the kettle on, hoping that nothing would happen while they were out of the shelter. There again, this brave man deserved a drink, surely?

'So who are you?' the pilot asked as he walked alongside Lily. 'I've not been rescued by two pretty women before.'

'How often have you been rescued?' Lily asked coyly, wishing she wasn't wearing her hair in pipe cleaners and her oldest clothes.

'I've not counted, but this has been the most pleasant so far.'

Lily grinned and explained that she shared the house with Rose and Katie, and that they all worked for Joe Lyons. She mentioned that she was hoping to go dancing later on at the Coronation Ballroom, if only the all-clear sounded in time; but then it struck her that she must sound shallow, considering this man had been up in the sky fighting the enemy only minutes ago.

Leaving him in the hall to make his telephone call, Lily hurried to the kitchen, pulling the pipe cleaners from her hair as quickly as she could. 'Thank goodness my hair is almost dry,' she said, running her finger through the loose curls.

Katie raised her eyebrows at Lily. 'Surely you should be saying, thank goodness the telephone is working, and we still have gas to boil a kettle? That poor man drops out of the sky during an air raid, and all you can think about is your hair.'

Lily laughed as she rummaged in a drawer. 'Thank goodness I left an old lipstick in here somewhere . . . oh, here it is,' she exclaimed, quickly dabbing the stump of red onto her pursed lips as she looked into a small mirror on the windowsill. 'That'll have to do.' She nodded at her reflection.

'I'm Peter Pershore,' their new friend said as he removed his flying jacket and sat in an armchair, where he could see out over the front garden to the road. 'I can wait in the front garden, if you want to return to your Anderson shelter?' he added, noticing how Katie was nervously looking up to the sky. 'It's all but over for this time. We had them well on the run before I copped it. You know what they say: "Beware the Hun coming out of the sun",' he grinned.

'I've never heard that before – but then my husband is in the Royal Navy, so I wouldn't know flying terms, only naval ones,' she said proudly.

'How about you?' he asked Lily.

'I don't have a husband,' she smiled.

'I think he meant, have you heard the saying before,' Katie hissed as Lily fluttered her eyes at the pilot. 'Where are you based . . . are you allowed to say?' she asked, deciding to ignore Lily, who seemed to have lost the ability to speak sensibly.

'I suppose I can tell you, what with me dropping unceremoniously into your garden like I did. I'm based at Manston. Do you know it?'

'We do,' Katie exclaimed. 'Our friend Anya's husband is a pilot based there. He's Polish,' she added proudly, knowing how much her friend had suffered in order to reach England to find her pilot husband after the invasion of Poland. 'You may know him, Henio . . . Henio Polinski?'

A cloud passed over Peter's face for a moment before he grinned and shrugged. 'There are so many of us, it is hard to remember just one,' he said.

They chatted on companionably until the toot of a vehicle horn alerted Peter, and he jumped to his feet. 'There's my ride. I'll thank you for the tea and the use of your telephone – and perhaps I'll pop into your teashop and say hello one of these days,' he said, picking up his jacket and heading out the front door just as the all-clear sounded.

'That was exciting, wasn't it?' Lily said as she stretched out on the sofa.

Katie, who had followed Peter to the door, wasn't so sure. He did know Henio – his face had given it away – but why not say so? she wondered, as she slowly closed the door. Outside, Peter jumped into the waiting truck amid cheers from his fellow officers. Has something happened, Katie thought, and Anya doesn't know?

'Whenever will this all end?' Lady Diana asked as the inhabitants of Sea View trudged up Madeira Walk to the guesthouse.

'I have no idea,' Flora said with some relief as she saw that her beloved home was still standing, and in one piece. 'I'm just glad our home hasn't been destroyed while we took cover in the tunnels.'

'But you were out in this for some considerable time doing your ARP work,' Diana said with admiration. 'How do you do it and also carry on with your guesthouse, and caring for the children?'

'I don't think too much, and I try not to look back and dwell on the devastation. I'm there to help dig people out if need be, or just be a shoulder to cry on. Whatever's needed, I'll do my best to be a helping hand. As for these little loves, I'll protect them with my last breath,' she said as she gazed into the pram she was pushing, where Daisy and Mary were sleeping soundly.

'I must do more,' Diana said with a resolute expression. 'Both my children are doing war work, and my husband works with the government in ensuring food supplies. I'm the one letting the side down. That has to stop.'

'Don't feel so badly,' Rose said as she caught them up while holding the hands of Annabelle and Marina. 'You have started to help Mum at the WVS.'

'What does your daughter do?' Joyce asked, her arm around young Pearl, who was grumbling about walking when she felt tired. 'I know she works in London, but little more than that.'

Diana stopped and tapped the side of her nose. 'Top secret, my dear, top secret.'

Joyce smiled, and saw Flora do the same. 'Oh, I wish I did something important too.'

'We are all important in this war. If it wasn't for the women at home, the war would soon be lost,' Flora said with determination.

Further up the road they could see firemen putting out flames at a terraced house, with the residents standing about watching; meanwhile, others collected their possessions from amongst the rubble.

Flora stopped for a moment. 'My heart aches for those

poor people. Thank goodness we have support in the town to help anyone who loses their home.'

'How do people recover from such things?' Miss Tibbs said as she sniffed into her handkerchief.

Flora put her arm around the old woman and gave her a hug. 'We put the kettle on, of course. Come on, everyone, we'll soon be home if we put a spurt on. Why not run on ahead and open the front door, girls?' Flora said, holding out the key to Pearl, who whooped with delight and raced Annabelle and Marina up the road. Opposite Sea View, they ground to a halt and looked back at the women following them.

Flora frowned. 'Why have they stopped?'

'There's a couple of people on the doorstep,' Rose said. 'I don't recognize them.' She quickened her pace a little to catch up with the girls.

'If they think I have a room to let, then they will be disappointed,' Flora said. 'I'm not even sure I know a landlady I can recommend. The time has long gone when we could recommend each other to the holidaymakers.'

'My dear, I doubt anyone would want to take a holiday during the war, what with our country taking such a battering. Myself, I'd die for a trip to the South of France; or possibly back to see my sister in Toronto.'

'Wouldn't we all,' Joyce muttered with a grin. 'For now I'd settle on Pegwell Bay without an air raid, and barbed wire removed from the beach.'

They all liked Lady Diana immensely, but often smiled at her comments. As Anya had once remarked, they lived in different worlds.

'Can I help you?' Rose asked their visitors as she walked

up the short path to Sea View. She stole a furtive look at the couple as she took the key from Pearl and opened the door.

The woman had a round face with pink cheeks. Her hair was pinned up under a black felt hat with an oversized peacock feather. As she was of a similar age to Rose, this seemed rather old-fashioned, but her clothes were of good quality. A slightly older man stood behind her, wearing a bowler hat and trench coat belted tightly at the waist. If it were any tighter, Rose thought, he'd break into two pieces.

'We are here to see a Miss Rose Neville,' the man said without smiling, although the woman nodded and smiled.

Rose felt a shiver run through her. Was this about Ben? Had he been injured?

'I'm Rose Neville. How may I help you?' she said as the other women arrived to hear the exchange.

'I suggest you take these people into the small lounge,' Flora said with a worried expression. 'I'll bring tea in as soon as I can. We've just returned from the air-raid shelter,' she explained, trying to excuse their dishevelled appearance.

'If you will follow me,' Rose said, taking the couple into the hall and opening the door of a small room that looked out to the front of the house. Until recently, Flora had used it as a bedroom for Joyce and Pearl; but it had soon become clear that a reception room was needed for visitors and the children's tutor, so the mother and daughter had moved back to an empty upstairs room. They had assured Flora they would be able to get downstairs very quickly if an air-raid warning sounded. Lady

Diana had decorated the newly vacated lounge with some of her favourite ornaments from the London flat.

As Rose took the couple's coats, it struck her again that they both dressed older than their years. Once settled, she sat opposite them with her hands in her lap, bracing herself to hear bad news of some kind. 'May I ask why you wish to see me?'

'I received your reply to my letter,' the woman said. 'I am your half-sister, Eileen. This is my husband, Gerald – Mr Gerald Roper,' she said.

Rose had always imagined that when two long-lost siblings finally met they would fall into each other's arms, crying and apologizing for not having found each other sooner. Instead she found herself shaking hands with Eileen and Gerald, and commenting on their journey to Ramsgate.

'It was hell,' Gerald grumbled. 'Charing Cross Station is still not functioning properly. You'd think by now they'd have sorted out travel from that station. The bomb damage was done weeks ago.'

'I'm sure they're doing their best,' Rose smiled.

'I agree,' Eileen said.

'If we'd notified Rose of our intended journey, she would have been able to arrange a supply of petrol,' he sniffed.

'I'm not sure I understand what you mean.' Rose frowned in puzzlement.

'Your fiancé must have contacts. His father does hold an important position in the army.'

Rose chuckled, thinking he must be joking. 'You are mistaken. I have yet to meet my future father-in-law, and wouldn't dare to ask for favours. Now, if you will excuse me for a moment, I will see how the tea is coming along,' she said, hurrying from the room.

'Mum, it's Eileen and her husband. Rather than write again, she seems to have decided to turn up – and in the middle of an air raid! She must really want to meet me. Isn't that wonderful? Why don't you come and meet her?'

'I don't know, my love. You may be her sister, but I'm the woman her father lived with out of wedlock during his final years,' Flora said, looking troubled. 'To be honest, I don't understand why she has come here to the house he gave you, when she received nothing. Her memories are of her mother and siblings passing away while she was brought up by relatives. The family never wanted anything to do with him after . . . after he met me.'

Lady Diana took Flora's arm and gave Rose a pointed look. 'My dear, perhaps it is best that for the moment your mother doesn't meet . . .'

'Eileen,' Rose said, looking at Flora and seeing how upset she was becoming. 'Her name is Eileen.'

'I will bring the tea things through to your guests,' Lady Diana said with a smile. 'Perhaps, given time, your mother will be able to sit and talk with Eileen.'

'I understand,' Rose said. 'I didn't mean to distress you, Mum. That was the last thing on my mind.'

'Of course, and you haven't, my love. It was just a bit of a shock, that's all. To begin with, I could only think how nice it would be for you to meet your relative. Now, I worry it could cause upset, bringing up so much of the past. However, I'm sure we will all get along famously once we get used to each other.' Flora patted Rose's arm. 'Let me prepare the tray for your guests.'

'I'll bring it in to you shortly,' Lady Diana said, using one of her best smiles that warned Rose not to argue.

'Thank you for your help,' she said, before heading back to her guests.

'You have some beautiful things,' Eileen said as Rose entered the room. She was standing by a sideboard that displayed a few pieces of fine porcelain. 'Very nice indeed.'

'I had no idea you owned such a large property,' Gerald remarked. 'We'd not have booked rooms if we'd been aware. It wasn't mentioned in your correspondence with my wife – your sister.'

Rose frowned. She'd hate to think they thought she'd taken advantage of the General in any way. Her mother had always kept from her that the General had purchased the house for Flora, to pass on to Rose when the time was right. As for the figurines . . . well, they weren't hers, of course. But she didn't have to justify why they were here. Gerald certainly seemed nosy, considering they'd not long met. She felt uncomfortable as she turned to him with the smile she reserved for unreasonable customers in the teashop. 'All our rooms are full for the duration with our long-term lodgers. We gave up renting out rooms to holidaymakers a while ago now. In fact, I don't live here myself, as I share a house with my friends closer to the teashop I manage. This is my mother's business.'

'Oh, I thought . . .' Eileen started to say as there was a tap at the door.

'Excuse me, Miss Rose, I have refreshments for your guests,' Lady Diana said as she entered the room wearing one of Rose's Nippy aprons and caps that she'd left at Sea View.

Rose watched open-mouthed as Diana placed the tea tray down and poured out three cups. Taking the figurine from Eileen's hands, she checked it carefully and replaced it on the sideboard. 'Will that be all, Miss?'

Rose tried not to laugh. Whatever was Diana up to? 'Thank you, er . . .'

'Perkins, Miss,' she said, giving Rose a deep curtsey before leaving the room.

Eileen seemed impressed by the maid. 'I suppose you get used to having servants in your position,' she said.

'Not really,' Rose smiled back, not sure what to say. 'Now, let's have that tea, shall we, and then get to know each other. Look, there's cake as well,' she said, placing a slice of the Bakewell tart she'd brought home from the teashop onto one of her mum's best tea plates and passing it to her half-sister. 'Are you staying in the town long?'

'It depends very much on how things pan out. I am a busy man,' Gerald said before taking a bite of cake.

'I'm pleased you could come to meet me. What is your business?' Rose enquired, wondering what he meant but feeling it would be impolite to ask.

'Gerald has his finger in many pies. He is a businessman,' Eileen said as she gazed with pride at her husband.

'If your time is limited, I can take you to see the grave tomorrow.'

'The grave?' Eileen said, looking at her husband for support.

'Our father's grave – I take it you'd like to pay your respects?'

'We'd not like to put you out,' Gerald said. 'We prefer to get on with what we came down here to do. It was hard enough getting passes to enter Thanet. As it was, I had to mention your fiancé's name in order to get things rolling.'

Rose again felt uncomfortable at the man's assumption that Ben's name could be used for his benefit. But then, as Eileen had come to meet her at long last, she could excuse them being a little pushy. 'At least let me treat you to lunch at my teashop, and then we can go on to the churchyard afterwards,' she smiled. 'As long as there isn't an air raid, you may be able to come back here afterwards and meet my mum.'

At this suggestion Gerald's eyes lit up, and Eileen smiled. 'We'd like that,' he said.

Downstairs, Diana demonstrated her serving techniques to Flora and the lodgers until there wasn't a dry eye amongst them. 'Poor Rose didn't know where to look,' she chuckled.

'You are terrible,' Flora said as she wiped her eyes.

'I just wanted to cheer you up, Flora. I know it will be hard for you to face the General's child after he's been gone for so long. Let Rose get to know her sister and decide when the time is right to welcome the woman and her husband into the bosom of this wonderful family. Why, Christmas may be just the right time. It would give Rose a good few weeks to get accustomed to not being the General's only child.'

'You could be right, Diana. We should start to plan our Christmas right now. War or no war, we all need to have a little fun.'

'First, there is something else we need to plan,' Diana said, pulling off the white cap and apron and delving into her bag. 'I've made some notes for you to impress the people who matter in this town. We, my dear Flora, are going to put on a show not only for the local citizens and the troops billeted in the town, but also for the town council – so that they see you as a lady upon whom they can rely. After *Flora's Follies*, you will be the toast of the town – and that Councillor Mould will leave you well and truly alone.'

'I don't know what to say,' Flora murmured as she looked at the detailed notes. She passed them to Joyce and Miss Tibbs, who nodded in agreement.

'I could help with the costumes,' Miss Tibbs offered.

'I'll do all I can, but I'm not getting onto the stage. You know I can't hold a note to save my life,' Joyce joined in.

'If this doesn't show the mayor and his council that my heart is in the right place and I'm worthy of adopting Daisy, I don't know what will. But . . . can't we call the concert by another name?'

'No, *Flora's Follies* it will be,' Diana said firmly.

Flora soon agreed. 'We really should have my Rose sing a few songs. I wonder if her half-sister can sing as well as Rose? We must find out. It would be wonderful to have them both on stage performing together. Not quite the Desmond sisters, as there are only half the number of gals; but it could be just as interesting, don't you think?'

Diana nodded. She thought of her sisters, and of past times. To see Rose sing with her half-sister could certainly be entertaining. However, she couldn't shake off the thought she'd seen Eileen somewhere before.

*

'It feels an age since we had a night out together,' Lily said as she pushed her way across the dance floor of the Coronation Ballroom, carrying a tray of drinks back to the table where Rose was sitting alongside Anya, Flora and Joyce. 'It's packed in here, but I'll be blowed if I can see anyone worth dancing with. The place is full of old folk.'

'Don't be daft,' Katie said as she followed in her friend's wake, trying to avoid bumping into the dancers. 'I've seen lads from the army and the RAF, and look who the bandleader is,' she giggled. 'That'll please Rose.'

Lily groaned. 'If she keeps her head down, he may not see her and ask her to sing.'

'Too late. Silvano popped into the teashop the other day and caught her. If you remember, Rose was due to sing with him a couple of weeks back, but the air raids put paid to all of that. He asked her to sing a few old favourites to get the crowd on their feet.'

'Considering they are already on their feet, she may not have to bother singing,' Lily laughed as she reached their table and placed the tray where everyone could reach their drinks. 'Three port and lemons, a half of bitter and two gin and oranges,' she said. 'We've still got some money left in the kitty for later.'

'What is this kitty you speak of?' Anya asked as she picked up the glass of beer. 'We do not have any cats.'

Lily snorted and explained that it was what they called the collection they'd made to pay for their drinks. 'Don't even ask me why they call it a kitty. It's bound to be something clever, and I ain't that clever. Cheers,' she added, sipping her gin. 'When will you be giving us a song, Rose?'

'In a few minutes. He did ask for something different, as well, but I don't know what to sing.'

'How about "The White Cliffs of Dover"? I like that song,' Joyce said as she started to hum the popular tune.

'That's on the list for later,' Rose smiled. 'I love singing it too, as it's so full of hope.'

'I know,' Lily said with a grin. 'What about "Ma! He's Making Eyes at Me"? That'll get 'em all singing along. You could join Rose on the stage, Flora?'

'What, me? I've not been on the stage in years. No, you can forget that,' Flora said with a shudder. 'I'll join in with a sing-song, but I'll not be treading the boards again in a hurry. I'll leave that to the youngsters,' she said. A part of her, though, was wondering whether Diana expected her to perform in *Flora's Follies*, and she couldn't help feeling a small thrill at the thought of the concert. She had all kinds of ideas, but would need her daughter to help her. 'While we are all together, I must tell you about Lady Diana's idea,' she said, encouraging the women to sit closer and listen to what she had to tell them.

'I think that sounds wonderful,' Katie said, clasping her hands together in delight. 'It will do so much good for morale, and the mayor and council will be so impressed that they'll surely put in a good word for you to keep Daisy.'

'That's what Diana reckons, but I'm not so sure. I know it will be an uphill task to have enough acts.'

'You are right,' Anya nodded seriously. 'It may be easier to kidnap the child and hide her away.'

'Or perhaps have Councillor Damp and Mouldy bumped off,' Lily added mischievously.

Flora dismissed their suggestions, trying not to grin.

'No, it will have to be a concert, or Lady D will have something to say about it. Rose, you will help, won't you?'

'Of course I will – but I must get up on stage now and sing a few songs. Silvano keeps looking over this way, and he seems to be getting rather twitchy. I do have an idea,' she said as she hurried over to where her friend from her schooldays, Sam Coggins (known these days as bandmaster Silvano Caprice) was standing at the side of the stage. She chatted to him for a couple of minutes before he went back to the microphone and announced her name. Locals erupted in cheers as their favourite songstress joined him, and the band struck up the opening chords of 'A Nightingale Sang in Berkeley Square'.

Rose soon found herself lost in the words of the well-known song. It reminded her so much of being in London with Ben. They might not have visited Berkeley Square, but the sentiments were not lost on her. She closed her eyes and imagined the first time she had met her fiancé, when he was in the dance hall where she sang. Above anything else, she remembered his eyes as he gazed up at her. It had only been earlier this year, but Rose felt as though she'd known him all her life. With a smile on her face as she sang, she slowly opened her eyes, searching the dancing couples and dreaming he would be there smiling back at her. But it wasn't to be.

The song came to an end and as the dancers applauded, she went straight into 'Moonlight Serenade' and the lights gradually dimmed, with couples shuffling slowly to the tune.

'*A love song, my darling, a moonlight serenade,*' she sang from the heart, as the song finished with a flourish of notes from the saxophonist.

Silvano stepped forward to thank Rose and make an announcement. He placed his hand on her back as he did so, but for the first time ever, she didn't feel he was imposing himself on her as he had so many times before. Had he grown up at last and realized he had to respect women? 'Ladies and gentlemen, we have a real treat for you this evening. Along with our ever-popular Rose Neville we have her talented mother, Flora, accompanied by Miss Lily Douglas, singing "I'm Gonna Sit Right Down and Write Myself a Letter". Over to you, ladies.'

Flora was horrified at the announcement but didn't feel she could embarrass Rose by refusing to perform. She stood between the two younger women and put her arms around their waists as they crooned the plaintive words. Lily tripped over her words a little, but a small, encouraging squeeze from Flora soon had her confidently singing into the microphone again. The audience swayed along to the song and some joined in with the words, filling the ballroom with joy and happiness. Rose whispered to Flora and Lily, then nodded to Silvano, who raised his baton, and they started to sing a rousing rendition of 'Alexander's Ragtime Band'. While some clapped, others danced a quickstep around the room until the song came to an end. Making deep curtseys, the three women left the stage, hugging each other with excitement as they did so.

'You know what? I think we can do this,' Lily said, gasping for breath. 'Put my name down for anything you want to do to make the concert work. Let's show Councillor Wet and Mouldy we mean business.'

They were still laughing excitedly as the lights lowered

and a waltz was announced. Lily jumped as someone tapped her on the shoulder.

'Hello, Curly – or should I call you Vera Lynn?'

Lily spun on her heel and came face to face with the airman they'd rescued earlier in the day.

'I see you aren't the worse for wear after your crash landing?' she grinned, looking up into his ruddy cheeks and twinkling blue eyes.

'And I see the pipe cleaners did their work,' he said, taking one of the curls between his fingers, giving it a gentle tug and letting it fall back into place. 'Do you care to dance?'

'I care,' she smiled as he took her in his arms and swept her away.

'Who is the handsome pilot?' Joyce asked as they watched Lily disappear into the crowd.

'We found him in our apple tree this afternoon,' Katie sighed as she watched her friend dancing close to Peter, hoping this could just be Lily's happy ever after. The girl definitely needed some good luck.

'Oh for heaven's sake,' Rose said as Anya jabbed her in the ribs and pointed to a familiar figure at the side of the dance floor. 'Look – it's Tom White, and he's going over to speak to Lily. The man looks half drunk.'

'Half? The man is so completely drunk, he can hardly stand up,' Anya snarled. 'That man, he is trouble where our Lily is concerned. Someone should go over there before he does something.'

Katie grabbed Rose's arm. 'Come on, we can dance together like the old dears do,' she grinned, dragging her onto the dance floor and through the throng to where

Tom White was facing Lily and throwing his weight about.

'Now look here, mate: I have no idea who you are, but you are disturbing me dancing with this young lady. It's none too polite to interrupt us like this and use such language. Move on, please.'

'Young lady? You have no idea what this young lady is like, do you?' Tom snarled. 'It's not enough that she lures me into bed as she does other men, but she then blames me when she is carrying a baby. Told you about the kid, has she? I doubt it. I'd keep clear if you've got any sense, before you get caught up in her web like I did.'

Peter stood his ground, looking down steadily at Tom – who, being some six inches shorter and unable to control his actions owing to the excessive consumption of alcohol, was clearly at a disadvantage. Lifting his fist, the airman hit Tom fair and square on the jaw, knocking him backwards onto the ground. Leaning over him, he pointed one finger. 'Never, ever say such things about a woman, especially in her company. Now get yourself out of here before I really hurt you,' he snarled.

Lily spotted her friends and ran to their side. 'Oh, God. Why did he have to turn up and spoil things like this? Will I never be rid of him?'

Rose put her arm round her distraught friend. 'Look – I do believe Tom has met his comeuppance,' she said. Lily and Katie followed her gaze and saw none other than their boss, Mr Grant, with his wife on his arm. He was standing over Tom White, berating him for his conduct.

'I don't care,' Lily sobbed – and before they could reply, she turned and ran from the dance hall without looking back.

12

'Sit down, Miss Douglas,' Mr Grant said, indicating a chair opposite the desk where he sat with Rose beside him.

Outside the small office, there was the general hubbub of the busy teashop as the Nippies served lunchtime diners. For Rose it was a comfort as she waited to see what Mr Grant had decided after the unfortunate incident at the Coronation Ballroom the evening before. She gave Lily a gentle smile to show that, even if she was sitting on the management side of the desk, she was firmly on her friend's side.

'Now, Miss Douglas, I wonder if you could give us your version of what happened at the Coronation Ballroom last night? I wouldn't normally ask about anything that happened away from the workplace – but with so many people knowing who you and Mr White work for, it is prudent for me to speak to you both. It is such an unfortunate incident to have happened with you having only just returned to work on a part-time basis.'

Rose hadn't seen Tom White in the teashop that day, so could only assume he would be arriving soon. She hoped he would be in a better frame of mind than he had been last night. It had taken many hours to calm down their friend; Rose and Katie had sat up late into the night with her, drinking cocoa and talking over Lily's future. She was adamant she would leave the area, as she couldn't bring up her daughter in a town where she would always be labelled as an unmarried mother. Coming into work this morning and being informed by Mr Grant that he would be interviewing her about the incident had been no help whatsoever. Rose had only had time to go to the staffroom and beg Lily not to do anything rash. Katie had offered to accompany her friend into the office, but Rose had refused the request. This was something that Lily would have to do alone. Having made it clear to her friend that she was not to be outspoken or run off, and that Rose was on her side, they had gone into the office and taken their seats.

'Well, sir, it was like this. I had accepted an offer to dance with the pilot who me and Katie, that's Mrs Jones, had met in our garden that afternoon. He's a nice bloke, so I thought no harm would come of having a dance.'

Mr Grant raised his hand to stop her talking. 'There was an RAF pilot in your garden?'

'He was in the apple tree, actually,' Lily said politely.

'From what I was told,' Rose explained, 'the pilot bailed out of his plane, and unfortunately his parachute became entangled in our tree. I wasn't there at the time, as I was visiting my mother in Ramsgate.' She omitted to mention that she had been taking baby Mary to Sea View to be cared for so the girls could all go dancing; it could have sounded rather frivolous of Lily to leave a young child so she could enjoy herself. 'Lily and Katie saved him during the air raid,' she added, beaming.

Lily listened as Rose spoke. 'Yes, sir, that's about it. So I kind of knew him, although I didn't expect him to appear at the dance that evening. It would have been rude to turn down his invitation for a waltz.'

Mr Grant smiled benignly. 'Ladies, it is not for me to say with whom you should dance. After all, we are all strangers until we've been introduced. You are to be commended for rescuing one of our brave lads. I shall make sure that head office is aware of your courageous act.'

'There's no need, sir. We only did what anyone else would have done.'

Mr Grant nodded thoughtfully. 'Even so, your dance came to an unhappy ending. Why do you feel Mr White was so antagonistic towards you?'

Rose held her breath. What would Lily say?

Lily looked into her lap, where her fingers were tightly entwined. Taking a deep breath, she looked Mr Grant in the eye. 'I don't want to lie to you, sir, as I have too much respect for you. You've always seemed to me to be a fair-minded chap – er, man. The thing is . . . I have a daughter, and Tom White is the father. And until recently, he wouldn't accept responsibility.'

Mr Grant's cheeks turned slightly red. 'I had no idea. I take it the two of you are not married?'

'No, sir; I was a silly girl, and it was the one time, if you get my drift? Rose and Katie, they helped me through the worst time in my life – but now I have a beautiful daughter. Rose let me come back part-time, and I've not let my baby get in the way of me working hard for Joe Lyons – and my child has been well cared for, too, before anyone thinks otherwise,' she finished, jutting out her chin defiantly as if she expected to be criticized.

The room fell silent as Mr Grant absorbed what Lily had told him. 'Miss Neville, have you had cause to question Mr White's treatment of your staff in the past?'

Rose cleared her throat. 'To be honest, I've been less than impressed with Mr White's work ethic and his attitude to my Nippies. He treats them as his personal servants, and despite my asking him not to use this office for his meals and relaxation, he doesn't take much notice of what I have to say. He is also – how can I put it? – he is also overly familiar with the female staff. Sadly, some of the women take it as a compliment, and I've heard of two who, just before my time here, left under embarrassing circumstances and moved away from the area. I would say that Tom White has a kind of magnetism that attracts certain women. Not that he interests me,' she added quickly.

Mr Grant again went quiet for a moment. 'I spoke with Mr White this morning in his hotel room. I wanted to know his side of what happened yesterday evening. I'm afraid what he told me was the opposite to what you have both said.' Rose and Lily started to protest, but he put a hand up to silence them. 'I did not say that I believed his version of events. As you know, I was nearby at the time of last night's incident, and with my good lady wife I witnessed much of what occurred. Of course, I had no knowledge of what had gone on before yesterday, and it was that with which I felt I needed to familiarize myself.'

Lily looked him straight in the eye. 'So, you believe whatever it was he told you?' she said. 'I may as well get my coat right now.'

'Please don't do anything rash,' Rose reminded her friend.

'Ladies, please hear me out. Did I say I believed Tom White? I simply wanted to know what he had to say.'

'May I ask what he said to you?' Rose asked.

'He denied fathering your child, and as much as told me that you have blackened his name by intimating to others that he is the father of your daughter.'

'That's a lie,' Lily blurted out. 'As I said before, I did have a moment of weakness, but he was the only man I've ever been to bed with – and it was just the once. My mother would turn in her grave if she could hear this discussion. Don't you think I despise myself for what I did in that moment of weakness?' Her voice trembled as she started to sob. 'Am I to bear this guilt for the rest of my life? There are women hanging about the streets who earn good money for what I did. If I'd enjoyed what happened to me, I'd be doing the same by now, rather than scraping by and relying on my friends for help.'

'Please, Miss Douglas, do not distress yourself. I will tell you both something that must never leave this room,' Mr Grant said, taking a large handkerchief from his pocket and mopping his brow. 'My only daughter was led up the garden path by someone we assumed was a gentleman, and he left her with child. We are bringing the boy up as our own. Mrs Grant has told her friends that he is a late baby. He is loved as much as any other child in our family, and it is only for the sake of our daughter's reputation that we made up this story. You have had a similar experience, and should not blame yourself. A moment of weakness can happen to anybody. These awful bounders exist and will always prey on unsuspecting females. You have nothing to be ashamed of.'

Rose smiled to herself at Mr Grant's old-fashioned language. It was clear that he was a decent man at heart. Perhaps having experienced his daughter's problem, he would be more likely to make the right decision for Lily.

'I'm sorry to hear of your daughter's difficulties,' she said. 'She is lucky to have a family to support her. Lily only has us, as she lost her mother not long ago. Her stepfather perished in the first of the big air raids last August. Whatever you decide, please don't dismiss Lily. She's not a bad person, by any stretch of the imagination.'

'If only you could prove Tom White was the father of your child, it would put an end to his career with Lyons. I'd not be able to keep him on after last night's sorry business.'

Lily's eyes lit up. 'You'd dismiss a man because he fathered a child?'

'Well, Miss Douglas, it would be more to do with his having abused his position in the company and made us a public disgrace, acting like a drunken lout in public. Some people might sympathize if they thought you had wronged him, but . . .'

'But if I could give you proof, then all would be well?' Rose asked, getting to her feet and crossing to the safe in the corner of the office.

'If only you could, Miss Neville, it would put the whole situation in a new light. As much as I believe and support

Miss Douglas, we need hard proof. Otherwise I could be putting my own career in jeopardy by dismissing Mr White from the company.'

Lily watched as Rose rummaged through the pile of papers in the safe before pulling out an envelope, which had been sealed and dated. 'If you'd like to break the seal and read the contents, you might just find the proof you've been looking for,' she said as she placed the envelope in front of her area manager. 'Every page has been signed and witnessed. You will see that Lily states she does not want money from Tom White – and in return, Mr White has accepted Mary as his child and promised not to fraternize with my staff. We also happen to know that in Mr White's personnel record, which was left in my desk when you were last here, he states he is exempt from military service due to a heart problem. Although we cannot prove this, he did brag to Lily that his exemption is a forgery. In any case, Mr White accepted that if he caused problems for either Lily or Mary, these papers would be handed to someone within the company to do with as they pleased. I think you'll find that last night's little episode gives us the right to hand over the documents,' she concluded, as Mr Grant silently read the papers.

'It certainly does, Miss Neville,' he said at last. 'May I ask who Miss Mildred Dalrymple is? She seems to feature in these documents.' He glanced up enquiringly, indicating Mildred's signature.

'She is a family friend who came upon the situation with Tom White and wanted to help,' Lily said, hoping fervently that there was enough information to save her bacon.

They watched in silence as Mr Grant tapped his fingers on the desk while he read through the paperwork a second time. 'Ladies, if you wouldn't mind leaving the office for a while, I would like to make several telephone calls. I don't expect you to work,' he said, giving them both a hard stare. 'Sit down and have a cup of tea. These meetings can take their toll. I wouldn't mind something myself,' he added.

Rose ushered Lily from the room. 'I'll have some tea sent in,' she said before closing the door. Turning, she was surprised to see Lily rooted to the spot.

'Look over there. We have visitors.'

Rose grinned as, sitting at a window table, they saw Lady Diana in her finest fur coat alongside Flora in her best hat, bouncing Daisy on her knee. Miss Tibbs, Joyce and the three children were there too. The inhabitants of Sea View were sipping tea and looking at the menu as Anya stood close by, chatting to a handsome-looking pilot.

'It's Peter,' Lily whispered. 'Why is he here – and with our friends and family?'

'I should think they've come to support you,' Rose said, as she nudged Lily forward towards the table. It was abuzz with cheerful chatter.

'We are all here for you,' Anya announced, 'but I must go back to selling the bread, or I too will be given this "sack" they all talk about. Spending the morning in the air-raid tunnels means I'm all behind myself.'

'Oh, Anya. Giving someone the sack means to be dismissed from their job. Hopefully it will not be the case for Lily.'

'You English say the most ridiculous things,' Anya huffed as she returned to her counter.

'We are here as character witnesses,' Lady Diana said. 'May I speak with this Grant person?'

'Would you leave it a little while, please? If we need to call in the troops, we will do so after he has made his decision – that's if it is not acceptable,' Rose said. 'Can you excuse me for a little while? I need to arrange a tray for Mr Grant. Lily, why don't you sit over there and chat to Peter in private?'

Lily nodded, and moved to where Peter had been shown to a table. 'What are you doing here? Is it a simple co-incidence that you decided to dine here where I work?'

'It's not a coincidence. Mrs Neville spoke with me after you left the dance hall in such a hurry last night. She told me a lot of things.'

'So you've come to say goodbye?' Lily looked him in the eye. 'You could have left a note, or just walked away. There was no need for the personal touch.'

'Oh, Lily, do you think so little of me that you think I would judge someone harshly after she came to my rescue so bravely during an air raid? I'm here for the duration, if you think you can put up with me. A chat yesterday and one dance last night, and I'm smitten.'

Lily shrugged her shoulders and grinned. 'Flora told you about Mary?'

'Told me? I've met her already. I was given orders to appear at Sea View on the dot of eleven hundred hours. I'm not one to ignore orders when they are given.'

'What do you think of my daughter?'

'She is just like you. A real stunner. Any guy who takes you on will be getting two for the price of one. This war has changed so many lives, and for me that means seizing the moment, not reflecting on what went on before a couple met. As I've said, I'm here for the duration, if you want me to hang around? I'm serious, Lily,' he said as he reached across the table and took her hand. 'I'm trust-worthy. Not all men are scoundrels.'

'I know that,' she said, enjoying the touch of his hand. 'All the same . . . I'd like to take things slow. That's if you can, too?'

'As slow as it takes,' he grinned.

'Blimey,' Katie said, as Rose joined her and they watched the little scene unfold. 'It looks as though we're set up with parachute silk for life.'

'I pray that Lily finds love and contentment. She certainly deserves it,' Rose said. 'Come on, let's join the family for a little while until Mr Grant summons us back to the office.'

'You know, I thought Mildred would be here,' Flora said, once Rose had brought her up to date with what had happened in the office. 'She promised she would do her best to join us.'

'The tides rule life on a fishing boat. I'm sure she will get here if she can.'

'Mildred can be a rule unto herself,' Flora said.

'I'm glad she is, because without her help pinning Tom White down to signing those papers, Lily could have lost her job. Mind you – she did tell me that by the time he finally signed, the Luftwaffe were overhead, so that may have speeded up his decision.'

'Perhaps it's the one time we can thank the Germans,' Flora said thoughtfully.

'I'd rather thank Mildred, as she wouldn't have let Tom

White off the hook regardless of what was happening. She's a true friend to us all,' Rose said with feeling.

'A strange bunch of bedfellows,' Flora mused as she looked round the table. 'But I wouldn't change them for the world.'

A polite cough from the office door alerted Rose to Mr Grant standing there. 'Lily, it's time,' she said to her friend as she passed the table where she was deep in conversation with Peter. 'Why not sit with Mum and the others, Peter? We won't be long.'

With whispered good-luck wishes from their friends, the two women headed into the office and closed the door behind them.

'Sit down, ladies,' Mr Grant said, indicating the two seats now placed in front of the desk as he finished the last of his tea and brushed cake crumbs from his jacket. 'I've made a few telephone calls. First to head office, where I consulted our legal team, and then to Tom White, who is currently at his hotel.'

Rose felt Lily grip her hand. She was shaking so much, it took all Rose's strength to hang onto the trembling girl.

'Our legal team at head office feel that the documents are binding, and we have a clear-cut case against Mr White.'

'What does that mean?' Lily asked.

'It means, Miss Douglas, that I put through a telephone call to Mr White's hotel and informed him that not only was he out of work, but we would be notifying the draft board that he was a draft dodger if he did not join the services at once. You and many other women in this town are free from that man.'

Rose let out a long sigh of relief. 'I cannot thank you enough for what you've done, Mr Grant.'

'What about me?' Lily asked. 'Do I still have a job, or will Lyons be rid of me as quickly as they sacked Tom White?'

'You job is safe, Miss Douglas, and head office wish me to apologize for what you have gone through at the hands of one of our employees. There will be a generous cheque in the post by way of compensation.'

Lily looked shocked. 'I have no wish for money. I just want to be accepted and not have to face him when he comes into the teashop. You have done that by dismissing him, so I am happy to leave it there. Thank you very much,' she said, getting to her feet and heading out of the office. Rose stood up, ready to follow her.

'Let her be, Miss Neville. She has much to think about. There was one other telephone conversation. You may wish to sit down for this news.'

Rose took her seat, worrying that now it was her turn to be reprimanded. She couldn't help but worry that Lyons would hold her responsible for what had happened to Lily.

'There's no need to look so worried. This, I hope, is good news. There was a telephone call from Captain Benjamin Hargreaves, who I understand is your fiancé?'

'Ben – yes, he is my fiancé. Is there something wrong?'

'Not at all. He asked me to inform you that you were to start arranging the wedding, as he will have seventy-two hours' leave at Christmas, if you wish to have a white wedding on Christmas Day? I take it you do?' he said, looking at the wide grin that appeared on her face.

'Captain Hargreaves said he would place a telephone call through to you this evening at your mother's home, as he assumed you would be there making plans.'

'Oh, I would like that. I most certainly would. Thank you so much, Mr Grant. I wonder . . . ? No, it is too cheeky of me to ask,' she said, losing the confidence to continue with her request.

'Please continue. I cannot answer until I hear what you have to say,' he said gently, smiling at Rose's joyful face.

'I wonder. Would you give me away – if it doesn't interfere too much with your plans for Christmas Day?'

'I would be delighted,' he said, hurrying round the desk to give her a fatherly hug. 'I would be honoured. Now, I understand it is your afternoon off, and you must have plans?'

'Plans? Oh my goodness, my half-sister and her husband are supposed to be having lunch with me. How could I have forgotten?' Rose exclaimed, as she thanked her boss again and hurried from the room.

'This is nice,' Rose said as she passed a menu to Eileen and Gerald. 'I can recommend the meat pudding, but I suppose I shall have to watch my waistline now my wedding is getting closer.' A thrill of excitement ran through her as she thought that soon she would be Ben's wife.

'What will happen to your inheritance once you have a husband? I suppose he will handle your affairs?' Gerald asked before ordering veal and ham pie, apple turnover and coffee from the Nippy who was waiting with her pen and pad poised.

'How about you, Eileen?' Rose asked, aware that Gerald had been most impolite in ordering first, ignoring the women.

'Farmhouse pie, baked currant pudding and a cup of tea, please,' Eileen said, handing back the menu.

'And I'll have the meat pudding with an individual fruit pie for dessert, thank you, Elsie,' Rose smiled. 'If my wedding gown needs to be made larger, so be it.'

'Will that be mashed potato and cabbage with the meals, Miss Neville?'

Rose looked to her guests, who simply nodded. 'Yes, thank you, and I'll have a pot of tea, please. Now, where were we?'

'You were about to tell us how your inheritance would be handled once you were married,' Gerald said as he shook out his napkin and placed it onto his lap.

Rose was irritated by his question, but knowing he was family, she felt she shouldn't snap at him. 'I don't have an inheritance, and my husband is not really concerned with the few pounds I have in my post office savings account.'

Eileen laughed, but there was a sharp edge to the sound. 'Gerald meant the ownership of Sea View.'

Rose laughed at the question, although she wondered how they'd found out. It wasn't a secret that the General had left the house to Rose, but it irked her that her new-found relatives were so interested. 'I only found out recently that General Sykes had left the house to me, to be passed on when I reached adulthood. However, I refused the gift and gave it to my mother. I have a home with Katie and Lily, and once I am married and this war is over, I will live with my husband. Sea View is in good hands with Mum. It is her home more than mine now.'

They fell silent as the beverages were served. Gerald stirred his coffee angrily before turning to his wife. 'Do you not have anything to say, Eileen?'

His wife nodded. 'I do, Gerald. As the oldest surviving child, I feel that the house should come to me. Or, at least, a fifty per cent share.'

Rose frowned. Was this why they had sought her out? Eileen had admitted seeing the engagement announcement in *The Times* had made her aware their father had another child. 'I'm sorry you feel this way. I thought you had come here to meet me so we could be a family and remember our father. I had no idea it was purely a business transaction – and one that would upset my mother, who loved the General very much,' she said, doing her utmost not to show anger. 'The house is not mine to share or to give away, as it now belongs to my mother. We have documents to that effect. Ah, our meals are here. I hope you enjoy them,' she said, forcing herself to smile.

She'd just told a lie, and that was something she was not proud of. There was no official paperwork, and Sea View still belonged to her. As soon as she could, she would have Ben help her sign the guesthouse over to her mother. One day – and hopefully it was still a long way in the future – it would come back to her, when her mum had passed away. Hopefully Daisy too would have a share, if Councillor Mould did not interfere in their business. 'Eat up, as we will have to catch the two o'clock bus to get to the graveyard before we lose the light. There's not another bus for three quarters of an hour, and I really have to be back at Sea View promptly – Ben is going to speak to me on the telephone about the wedding,' she smiled, forgetting that she had been feeling angry just minutes before.

Eileen sniffed and continued eating for a short while before looking up. 'I'm not bothered either way. It looks rather miserable out there.'

Rose frowned. One minute the woman was asking about the inheritance, and the next she seemed uninterested in paying her respects. 'Well, I'm going. I like to visit at least once a month and leave flowers on the grave. It may sound silly, but I like to sit and chat and tell him what's been happening in my life.'

'We are going.' Gerald glared at his wife before tucking into his pudding.

'All right, but don't think I'm going to be chatting to him,' Eileen snarled back.

Rose couldn't make head nor tail of their strange attitude. Neither one had asked about her father or shown any sympathy; come to that, they'd not asked much about her either. Granted, Eileen would have little memory of her father, as he had walked away from the family when she was still young. But having made the effort to come down to Thanet, it seemed as though the only interest she and Gerald were showing was in the ownership of Sea View.

'While you finish your puddings, I'll pop over and pay the bill and see if Joyce is ready to leave,' she said.

'Joyce?' Gerald looked none too happy. 'I thought it was a family trip?'

'Joyce usually accompanies me, as her husband is buried

in the same graveyard,' Rose smiled, making an effort to keep her tone civil.

'Be careful, won't you, love?' Flora said, as Rose joined the family group at their table in the tearoom. 'It was mayhem out there this morning.'

'You should have stayed home, close to the tunnels. I know I'd rather be in Ramsgate than here if the sirens start going off,' Rose scolded her.

'We can't let the Germans win – and they will, if we are afraid to go out.'

'And you're a long time dead as well,' Rose tutted. 'Anyway, I don't have time to stand and argue about the war. I wondered if you still wanted to come to the grave-yard with me, Joyce?'

'Are you sure you want me to accompany you this time? I don't want to impose on your time with your family.'

'Don't be daft. You are more than welcome. Besides, I'm finding it hard to talk to them. She seems rather bitter, and he is downright nosy about my finances. Do you know, he . . .'

'I'm sorry to impose, Miss Neville,' Mr Grant said as he joined them. 'I'm setting off back to head office. If there's anything you require, you have my telephone numbers.'

'Thank you, Mr Grant. You've taken a big worry from our shoulders. May I introduce my family? You've met my mother before, but this is my soon-to-be mother-in-law, Lady Diana McDouglas.'

'I'm pleased to meet you,' Mr Grant said as he shook her hand. 'I hope you don't mind me asking; I see your son's surname is Hargreaves, but yours is McDouglas. Do the gentry have more than one name?'

Lady Diana hooted with laughter. 'My dear, I'm not gentry. My husband was given a peerage for his work in the food industry. I was plain old Mrs Hargreaves before that.'

Flora joined in the laughter. 'I'm so glad you asked, Mr Grant. I had wondered the same.'

Mr Grant smiled. 'I do hope you don't think I was being nosy. It's just that, having the honour of walking Rose down the aisle, I didn't wish to make a social faux pas.'

'That's lovely news,' Lady Diana said as she shook his hand for a second time. 'You will be the ideal person to look after our Rose and bring her safely to our Benjamin. You will find us all quite normal and easy-going.'

'But . . . your coat. Isn't it . . . mink?'

'Oh, this old thing? I only wear it when I wish to impress people,' she said, giving him a flirtatious smile.

'Impress – you mean me?'

'I have to make sure that if Rose and her friends need help, I arrive with all guns blazing,' she said, before bursting into infectious laughter that caused them all to join in.

'I see I shall have to watch myself with you around,' he said, as he bid them good day and left the teashop.

'We are ready,' Gerald said as he tapped Rose on the arm.

'I'm just about ready as well,' Joyce said, reaching for her handbag.

'I'll see you at the door. I just need to pay our bill,' Rose replied as she left the table.

Gerald looked at the women still sitting there, and did a double take at Lady Diana. 'Do I know you?' he enquired.

Diana looked him straight in the eye and shook her head. 'Perhaps from the society pages,' she smiled, using an extremely posh voice. 'One's photograph does tend to appear often.'

Gerald frowned. 'I don't think so,' he said, turning away.

Diana watched them leave. 'There's something about those two I'm not sure about.'

'Four to the cemetery, please,' Rose said as she handed over coins to the conductor.

'The number of bombs that have dropped on Ramsgate this morning, that place will soon be full,' the conductress said as she handed back the long strip of paper tickets. 'Did you hear that Dreamland's taken a hit as well? At this rate there'll be nothing left standing around here. God knows how many lives were lost today,' she muttered before moving on to other travellers where she shared the same news.

'She's a cheerful soul,' Joyce grimaced. She looked out of the window as they passed house after house that was damaged or destroyed. Her face fell as she spotted rescue services still digging for people buried in rubble hours after the last air raid. Other people were being stretchered into ambulances, while blankets on the ground showed the shapes of those who hadn't made it. The closer to Ramsgate they got, the worse it was. 'Thank goodness we have the tunnels,' she whispered, as tears fell unchecked down her cheeks.

Rose, who'd been doing her best not to look from the

windows, reached out and took Joyce's hand. The woman was older than her by a good ten years, but in many ways she was more innocent and naive. 'We've got to keep fighting back, if only for the children,' she said. 'I suggest we pay our respects, and then get back to Sea View. I know Mum has a bottle of whisky stashed away. Now might be the moment for a tot or two.'

Joyce nodded and wiped her eyes. 'You are right. We have to think about our children and their future. Hitler will not take that from us,' she said, although her chin still wobbled with unshed tears. Turning to where Eileen and Gerald sat behind them, she tried to strike up a conversation. 'Are you in the services, Gerald?'

'No, my husband does essential war work,' Eileen said before Gerald could open his mouth. 'How long before we are there? I'm not good on buses.'

'Here, I have a paper bag,' Joyce said, digging into her handbag. 'My daughter is the same,' she said as she passed the bag behind her. Eileen took it without a word of thanks, although it wasn't put into use.

Walking up the road towards the cemetery, the four were silent. Hardly any of the terraced houses in the area had escaped damage. Homeowners were already boarding up windows and sweeping away the debris. 'It doesn't seem right that we are going to visit those who have passed away when the living are the ones needing our help right now,' Joyce said.

'You are right, but we need to do this,' Rose replied, watching as her newfound family members charged ahead, ignoring all around them. 'They don't seem touched by any of this,' she said sadly.

'Then they're no family of yours,' Joyce observed. 'You and your mum are decent people who are affected by all this, and always want to help. There's definitely something not right about those two,' she added.

Entering through an opening in the wall where a large set of iron gates had once stood, Rose stopped and looked around her, lost for words.

'They've taken the gates away to make Spitfires,' Joyce said as she stood slightly behind Rose.

'No, look,' Rose said, hardly able to speak. 'Everything's been wrecked. I don't think there's one gravestone left standing.' She looked up, feeling as though she wanted to raise her fists to the sky. 'Why have they done this?'

With a cry, Joyce ran through the damaged graves to where her husband lay at rest. Sobbing, she started to pick up the pieces of marble, trying to fit them together like a jigsaw. 'Thank goodness Pearl never came with us,' she said as Rose reached her. 'This would have upset her so much.' She sighed. 'We will soon have you as right as rain, my love,' she said to the earth as she started to tidy what was left of the few plants that were always tended with such love.

'Can I help?' Rose said as she knelt beside her.

'I'll be fine. There's not much I can do here, apart from tidy up the plants. The headstone will have to be replaced. Goodness knows how much that will cost. Have you seen your dad's grave yet?'

'No; I wanted to check you were all right first. You will be all right, won't you?'

Joyce gave her a watery smile. 'Things could be worse. Nothing can hurt him anymore,' she said, laying a hand on the soil. 'I can soon have this fixed. Go to your family and see that they aren't too upset.'

Rose gave her a hug before looking around for Eileen and Gerald. She spotted them standing by the entrance, looking as though they were leaving. Hurrying over, she called out, 'You are going in the wrong direction. Dad's grave is over there.'

'My wife doesn't wish to go any further. She's seen things she should never have to look at,' Gerald said, looking to where there was a crater in the ground.

'You don't need to walk that way. The General's grave is in the opposite direction. If it's damaged, I may need your help to put it straight,' she pleaded as she hurried towards them, to stop them leaving the cemetery. Reaching their side, she tugged on the sleeve of Eileen's coat to encourage her to turn around.

'Oi! Get away from that wall,' an angry voice called out. 'Didn't you see the sign? You shouldn't be in there.'

Rose was confused. She'd not seen a sign telling them to stay away from the cemetery. Staggering backwards as Eileen pushed her away, she hit her shoulder on the high wall that surrounded what had once been a peaceful resting place. Trying to right herself, she leant against the wall, feeling dizzy. Why was everything moving?

An ominous crash was the last thing she heard as the wall toppled and came crashing down, covering her with rubble and dust.

'Rose!' Joyce screamed as she started to run across the damaged graves to reach the girl. 'Rose, please say something – are you hurt?'

She stopped ten feet from what was left of the long

expanse of wall, fearing to go further in case she stepped on Rose and hurt her. The man who had shouted out to them appeared by her side. 'Shh – we need to listen, so we know where she is.'

Joyce listened as hard as she could, but there was silence. 'No . . . please God, no . . .' she cried.

13

~

'Mrs Neville, where have you been? I thought you'd perished and put the child in danger.'

'Hello, Councillor Mould. I've been out for lunch, and "the child" was with me. Would you like to come in?' Flora asked as she squeezed past the red-faced woman and put the key in the door. 'Perhaps you could make yourself useful and bounce the pram up the steps, please?'

'Well, I don't think . . .' the councillor blustered as Marina and Annabelle took charge of the pram and Lady Diana carried the sleeping child in her arms.

'We're home, Lily. Stick the kettle on,' Flora called towards the kitchen, while they removed their coats and shoes and found the right slippers to slip their cold feet into. 'Come on, everyone, let's go and have some tea and toast,' she said, ushering the children ahead of her. 'You'd best follow me,' she added to the councillor, who was standing in the middle of the hall, not sure what to do with herself.

'I'll bring a tray in, shall I?' Lady Diana said, with a wink that only Flora noticed.

'That would be delightful, Diana, thank you,' she

replied as she headed into the small reception room, closing the curtains against the late afternoon gloom and turning on a lamp that stood on an occasional table in a corner. 'Please take a seat,' she said formally to their visitor.

'Are we all sitting in here?' a voice asked from the doorway. 'It's a bit on the cold side. Shall I light the fire?'

'Ah, Miss Tibbs, I think you would be cosier down in the kitchen, don't you?' Flora smiled at the elderly lady, who was growing more confused by the day.

'I'll just light this fire,' Miss Tibbs said, going to the where the fireplace was surrounded by a grand oak surround and reaching for a box of matches. 'Oh dear, the kindling is rather damp. Let me see . . .' she said, looking around until she spotted a piece of paper tucked behind an ornament on the mantelpiece. 'This'll do.' She folded the paper several times until it resembled a taper, and slowly bent until she was close to the fireplace. Striking a match, she lit the end of the taper and poked it into the fire, gently blowing on the small flame until it ignited the rolled-up newspaper underneath the kindling. 'That'll do it,' she said, rubbing her hands together. 'I've always been able to make a good fire. Anyone will tell you that,' she announced to no one in particular before disappearing in the direction of the kitchen.

'Mrs Neville, I do wonder if some of the inhabitants of this establishment should really be living here. Perhaps arrangements should be made . . .'

'To put her in the workhouse? While you're at it, you can place our Daisy in a children's home. Oh, and perhaps we could stick our Lily in the asylum, as that's where they used to put unmarried mothers, wasn't it?'

'Really, Mrs Neville, there's no need to be so hostile. Anyone will tell you I'm always on the side of the unfortunate people in this town, and you seem to have a few living under your roof. I came here today in good faith to inform you that I have found a family willing to take on Daisy and give her a good home. These people are Christians and feel it is their duty to care for a child who has lost everything due to the war.'

'Daisy is settled here, and we are happy to have her as part of the family. We all love her,' Flora said in an even tone. 'I couldn't love her more if I'd given birth to her myself.'

Councillor Mould looked down her nose and sniffed. 'There's no need for that kind of talk,' she said. 'I came here to tell you the good news. You should be grateful you have one less mouth to feed. It can't be easy running a boarding house with the kind of people who you take in.'

Flora held her breath for a moment. She was all for grabbing the woman and throwing her into the street – but that would not help her to keep Daisy, and that was what mattered right now. 'Councillor Mould, every person in this guesthouse pays the going rate and on time. I never have cause to complain about anyone under my roof.'

'I beg to differ, and this is the reason I'm against the child staying with you. Unmarried mothers, for a start, do not set a good example.'

Flora frowned. 'I'd like to know what you are up to. Pray explain,' she said, doing her utmost to protect Lily, who she knew to be a perfectly lovely young woman.

'For a start, there is Miss Lily Douglas, carrying on with a fellow employee at the Margate teashop.'

'Lily is not carrying on, and if you snoop . . . if you investigate a little more, you will find that Mr White is no longer in the employ of Joe Lyons. Also,' Flora continued as the councillor opened her mouth to speak, 'Lily does not live here. She owns a third of that delightful cottage on the road to Margate. You may know it – Captain's Cottage? I did my Christian duty and cared for the girl for a while when she came out of hospital. Any decent person would have done the same. I'm sure you would, too, under the circumstances,' she finished, raising her eyebrows and giving the councillor a hard stare. 'Oh, good – it sounds like tea is here.' She rose to open the door, trying not to look surprised when Diana entered carrying a laden tray and wearing a pinny.

'Here we are, my dear. I hope you don't mind, but I brought along a cup and saucer for myself.' She didn't wait for an answer, but sat down beside the councillor. 'Now, what were you chatting about?' she asked.

'Councillor Mould was informing me that Sea View is not the right place to bring up a child, and that she has found a Christian couple to take Daisy in,' Flora said, wondering what Lady D was up to. 'She feels the women living under this roof are not the right type of people to have near a child.'

'I agree, in a way,' Lady Diana smiled sweetly. 'One never knows who will turn up on the doorstep. Why, look at me. I was taken in along with my motherless grandchildren at a moment's notice. Who in their right mind would do such a thing? I pay my way, of course,' she said, smoothing out the pinny. 'Thankfully that dreadful

Cardew man has gone. Who'd have thought a man like him would be a spy? But then, you knew him, didn't you, Councillor?'

Flora and the councillor gasped at the same time.

'Yes, Flora dear. It seems Mr Cardew is a cousin of the councillor's dear husband.'

Councillor Mould opened and closed her mouth like a goldfish. 'How did you . . . Who told . . . I deny it all!' she exclaimed, once she could catch her breath.

'Calm down, my dear, and drink your tea,' Diana said as she poured out the tea and passed a cup to Flora and her guest. 'I talk to people. It's one of my failings, I'm afraid. My husband says I can get information out of people as easily as a winkle out of a shell. I like to think it's a compliment, don't you? Would you like a biscuit? We brought them back from the teashop today. We paid for them, as well,' she added with a sly wink.

'Mrs Neville, I came here to speak to you, not your staff,' the councillor said as she stirred her tea. 'Perhaps you could dismiss her. I'm sure there must be cleaning to be done in an establishment like this.'

'Oh, Diana is not staff, she's almost family. Her son will soon be marrying my daughter,' Flora said proudly. 'They've just named the day. We are looking forward to a Christmas wedding, aren't we, Diana?'

'We are, and I'll be mighty glad to hand over those two children to Rose to bring up. I supposed they will be adding to the brood before too long. As long as I don't get called upon to care for them. I'm not really what you'd call the maternal type. I hear you aren't either, Councillor?'

'Whatever do you mean? I sit on many committees

concerning children's welfare,' she replied, looking down her nose at Diana.

'But never had any yourself, ducks?'

Flora knew that when Lady Diana put on her fake cockney voice, she was trying to wind someone up. Yes, she was up to something, all right. This could be interesting, she thought, as she sat back in her seat ready to observe Diana in action.

The councillor put her cup down upon a side table and took a handkerchief from her handbag. Delicately dabbing at her nose, she put on the air of a wounded animal. 'My husband and I were never blessed,' she sniffed. 'That is why I do my best for all the unfortunate youngsters in this town.'

'Was it because of something that happened to you before you married?' Diana said, dropping the cockney accent as quickly as she'd put it on, and instead using her plummy voice. She leant forward and smiled. 'Pray tell us about the days while you were climbing the social ladder and had to visit one of those people who give women like you a helping hand. I hear the father of the child you got rid of was married? A man of some influence in this county, so the rumours go.'

The councillor sprang to her feet, knocking the side table over as she did so; one of Flora's best teacups shattered as it hit the nearby hearth. 'How dare someone who is no more than a skivvy tell such lies about my past? I have a reputation to uphold, and I'll see you are never accepted in social circles in this town – not that anyone would invite you into their home,' she snarled at Diana. 'I came for the paperwork. I take it you have signed to say you accept us taking the child?' she asked, turning to Flora.

'I placed it on the mantelpiece,' Flora said, and they all looked to where Miss Tibbs had taken a piece of paper to light the fire.

Councillor Mould's mouth dropped open as she realized that she'd watched the paperwork turn to ashes in the fireplace.

Flora too got to her feet. 'Before you leave, Councillor, I feel it would be rude of me not to formally introduce you to my guest.'

'I have no wish to meet your common friends,' the councillor sniffed as she tried to walk past Flora. 'Please allow me to pass.'

Ignoring the woman's request, Flora held her hand out towards Diana. 'May I introduce you to Lady Diana McDouglas.' She smiled. As she would later tell anyone who would listen, Flora would remember the look on Councillor Mould's face as long as she lived. She'd also remember the great weight that lifted from her shoulders.

'Let me see you to the door, ducks,' Diana said as she took the woman by the arm and assisted her outside.

Flora sank back into her armchair and finished her tea. In a moment, she'd have to clear up the mess made by the shattered cup and saucer. But for now, she intended to enjoy the feeling of happiness that was sweeping through her body.

Joyce hurried towards the spot where the brick wall had collapsed onto Rose. The elderly man who had joined them followed more cautiously.

'Can't you do something?' she screamed to Gerald, who was watching rather than moving a finger. As she approached them, she overheard Eileen say, 'This is a gift we didn't expect. We just need to know . . .' Joyce shook her head – perhaps she'd heard wrong, in her panic to help Rose. 'Come on! We have to get Rose free of the rubble. Can you see where she was?'

Gerald seemed reluctant to help, and stayed rooted to the spot. 'A brick must have hit me. I feel dizzy,' he said, clutching his head.

'Here, let me help you, my dear,' Eileen said as she led him away from the pile of rubble, fussing over him as she did so.

'Please – you've got to help me find Rose,' Joyce implored. 'Can you see where she was standing when it happened?'

'Down there somewhere,' Eileen said, pointing vaguely. 'It all happened far too quickly for me to notice. I was more concerned for my own safety.'

'No, it's more that way,' the old man said breathlessly. 'You there – you go and call some of those men from down the street to help. Don't just stand there, hurry – or it may be too late,' he shouted at Eileen, before turning to Gerald. 'If you are injured, keep out of the way – you're no use to man nor beast right now,' he barked. 'Do you think you can help me until others arrive, Miss?' he asked Joyce, who was grateful that someone was here who intended to help Rose.

'Whatever you tell me, I'll do,' she said.

'What's the lady's name?'

'Rose Neville. Why do you want to know?'

'So I know what to call out as we look for her. Now,

my feeling is she was standing around the middle part of the wall, where it butted against the side of that house. We will start there. Pick your steps carefully, over the graves or grass rather than rubble, in case your friend is underneath. Do you understand?'

Joyce swallowed and nodded. 'Yes, I can do that. Do you think she's dead? There's so much fallen,' she said, looking at the bricks from the wall and the rubble and timber from the derelict house.

'While there's life there's hope,' he said, as he led the way to where he wanted to start the search.

But is there life? Joyce asked herself. What if Rose was dead? How would Flora cope without her daughter, and Ben . . . what about Ben? She shook her thoughts aside as she picked up bricks and pieces of wood and started to move them to one side. A few more people were approaching to help.

'Stick it over there,' the man shouted. 'It'll give us all room to work.'

'But the graves . . . ?' Joyce shuddered.

'The dead won't be bothered. And if we don't act quick, there could be another one to bury before too long.'

So he does believe Rose has been killed, Joyce thought miserably. Then, as if a great strength washed over her, she set to. She'd be damned if she was going to let Rose die. This bloody war had done enough to destroy families; it wasn't going to destroy the group of friends – who were more like a family – that she'd come to know and love since she and Pearl arrived at Sea View. Everyone had welcome them with open arms, and now it was time she repaid their kindness by helping to find Rose.

'Step back a bit, Miss,' said a tall man with strong, broad shoulders as, along with three others, he joined the search.

'Stop!' someone shouted, and they all stood still.

'Rose, can you hear us? Rose?' they started to shout, until the same man raised his hand for silence. 'Carry on,' he called to the men.

Joyce stepped over to where Eileen had joined Gerald. 'Are you sure you can't remember where she was standing?'

'No, it's all a blur. I think I'm in shock,' Eileen replied. 'Gerald isn't well. I feel I should take him back to our hotel. I couldn't bear to see my half-sister's body pulled from the rubble.'

Gerald put his arm over his wife's shoulder and leant heavily on her small frame. His face held the look of someone attending a funeral.

'Please let us know the outcome,' Eileen said before the couple walked away.

'Well, I never,' Joyce said out loud to herself. 'There's something not right there.' She shuddered as she hurried back to help look for Rose. Anyone in their right mind would hang about to help. Especially if they were long-lost family. 'It's all very strange,' she muttered as she started to take bricks from a man in front of her and pass them to someone further back, efficiently clearing a space. This meant that the man who had taken charge could get closer to where they thought Rose was buried.

'Quiet, everyone,' the man called out as yet again they stopped and listened. 'Rose?' he shouted. 'Can you hear us, Rose?' He raised his hand for silence before shouting, 'Over here – I swear I heard something.'

The men, along with Joyce, worked with renewed

vigour until they reached a large marble headstone. 'Is that you, Rose?' the lead man called. They all cheered as a muffled voice could be heard in reply. 'Don't move, Rose. We'll have you out as soon as we possibly can. You are in a dangerous position at the moment, so we want you to remain calm until we make the area safer.'

More people had arrived by now, and a woman took Joyce's arm and led her away. 'You've done a grand job, love, but let the men take over now. It's best you don't see your friend until they know she's all right.'

Joyce suddenly felt her legs give way beneath her and stumbled against the woman, who helped her over to where she could sit down on a relatively undamaged bench.

'Here, take a few deep breaths; it's been a big shock to you. Let's get you a drink,' the woman said kindly, as someone passed a cup of water. 'I bet you could drink something stronger, eh?'

'I'm not one for drinking. I could kill a cup of tea, though,' Joyce said as she sipped the water gratefully. 'Rose – my friend who is buried – is manageress of Lyons teashop in Margate. She's going to be married at Christmas,' she said, before collapsing against the woman and sobbing. 'Why do these things happen to the sweetest people?'

'Don't fret, love. My Alf will have her out of there. He's done a fair bit of rescue work, what with being one of our ARP wardens. Your friend is in safe hands,' the woman said, patting Joyce's back to console her. 'Here, look – someone's made you a cuppa. A nice strong one at that.'

'I put a spoonful of sugar in it for you,' the woman carrying the mug of tea said.

'You shouldn't have done that, but thank you,' Joyce said. 'I'll pay you back.'

'Don't talk so soft. You'd do the same for any of us if the boot was on the other foot.'

Joyce nodded. She knew she'd do just that. 'You said your husband's in the ARP?' she asked Alf's wife. 'I wonder if he knows Rose's mum. Her name is Flora Neville, and she owns Sea View guesthouse down near the harbour.'

'I should say he does. I do, too. It's a close community here in Ramsgate.'

'Do you think someone could put a call through to her; that's if the lines aren't down? Flora should be home by now. If not, someone will be there. She should know.'

'The overhead cables are down, but I'll get our Cyril to shoot down there on his bike. It'll only take a few minutes.'

'Please tell him to say that I'm here – my name is Joyce,' Joyce added, as she started to shiver.

'Here, love, let me put this blanket round you or you'll catch a chill.' The woman took a blanket that had seen better days and draped it over Joyce's shoulders. 'It's not much to look at, but it's clean and that's the main thing. Would you like to come and sit in my house while they get your friend out?'

'I'd rather stay here, if you don't mind. Rose will want to see a familiar face when she's pulled out. I hope she's not too frightened.'

The women standing around Joyce exchanged glances that conveyed their fear of how badly injured Rose might be, but Joyce missed the look that passed between them. As she sipped the hot tea, she watched the men carefully continuing to peel back the debris. They were talking out loud to Rose, although Joyce could not hear any response.

'Bugger me,' one of the women beside Joyce said as she looked towards the horizon. 'Get the kids down the shelter, and make it quick. Why hasn't the air-raid siren gone off?'

'Those are Messerschmitts, and dozens of 'em,' called out one of the children hanging around the entrance to the cemetery. 'Look – our lot are attacking them.'

Joyce tore her eyes from the rescue to see that the children were right. 'But if they start bombing us, Rose could be killed,' she cried out. 'What shall we do?'

'Don't fret, love. We've seen worse, and our menfolk are working flat out to rescue Rose. Look, here comes a fire engine, so we've got extra pairs of helping hands.' She didn't add that there was also an ambulance coming up the road behind it.

The women gazed in wonder as the RAF fought off the Messerschmitts, the Spitfires weaving around the German planes and picking out several that went spiralling out of sight over the sea, leaving smoke trails in their wake. Each time, there was a cheer from the crowd of residents who had all come out of their shelters to watch. Joyce shuddered as one plane came low over the town, trailing black smoke with its engine spluttering, before crashing further inland.

As the crowds cheered again, Joyce said, 'That was someone's son.'

'And there are other women's sons up there defending our country,' someone added in a sad voice. 'It's a cruel war.'

'Look, someone's bailed out,' a man shouted, pointing

to where a parachute could be seen floating down towards the harbour.

Joyce thought of Anya's husband Henio, one of many brave Polish pilots who had escaped and come to England to continue fighting with the RAF. He could be up there now, defending them. Then she remembered Anya mentioning that he had gone to another airfield over the other side of Kent. She must remember to ask how he was when next they spoke. Anya wouldn't say much – she most likely didn't know much, as Henio wouldn't say. But at least she could let Anya know she was thinking of her husband, and was grateful for what he was doing.

'Some of the bombers are dropping their loads,' a woman screeched, just as the air-raid warning started to wail.

'I'm staying here,' Joyce said firmly, as someone tried to help her to her feet. 'Rose needs to know I'm close by. Besides, Flora will be here soon, so I need to look out for her.'

'I'll stay with her,' an older woman said. 'The rest of you, get yourselves down into the shelter. We will be fine. To me it looks as though the fight is over the sea, but you never know. We can shelter against the wall of this house.' She nodded to an empty property at the side of the cemetery.

Joyce agreed. From that spot she could see how the rescue was going, and also the road from where Flora would appear. 'I just pray Rose can be saved before something awful happens,' she whispered, looking skyward.

*

'Oh my goodness, you pulled a blinder there, Diana,' Flora exclaimed as she sank into the one armchair in the kitchen usually occupied by Miss Tibbs. 'I'm not so sure she will take the comments about her former life without fighting back. Whatever made you make them up?'

'My dear, they were not made up at all. When I take my constitutional each day, I pop in to chat with people who will know these things. There's the ex-mayor who runs a newsagent shop, who loves a little chat if the shop is empty. Then there's a retired policeman who sits on the same bench each day and seems rather lovely. The man who I use when I need a taxi-cab is rather chatty too. He knows a lot about the councillor's husband having ripped off people who use his motor services . . .'

'You mean it's all true?'

'Every single word, my dear. However, if she were to challenge me in court I'd have a problem, as I couldn't prove a word of what I've said. I promised the people I spoke to that what they told me would be kept between us.'

'I'll not say a word,' Flora promised.

'Feel free to tell anyone you wish here at Sea View,' Diana grinned. 'Just tell them not to gossip outside the house. I'd hate our friends to get into trouble. She wouldn't dare question me, as she's in awe of my title. People like her are easily impressed. That's why I do not include her ilk as my friends.'

Flora shook her head in amazement. 'Well, I know I'm impressed, but I must say I'd not like to cross you. You are a good friend, Diana Desmond. Thank you.'

'Oh for those days when life was less complicated, and

the only people I fell out with were my three sisters,' Diana sighed.

'You must miss them.'

'It's complicated. As you know, one is in Canada, and I do see her at least once a year. The years fall away, and we are young once more. Rather like when you and I start to chat about the old days when we danced for our living. I miss my other sister terribly since she passed away, and of course Doris vanished from our lives when she fell in with a bad crowd. Perhaps I've been unlucky with my family. But there was a short time when we were close. However, I'm happy with my lot and couldn't be prouder of my husband, children and grandchildren, as well as my friends; I'm a very lucky woman.'

'I must say I feel the same, although my family is made up more of friends. And much of that is thanks to living here at Sea View.'

'But Eileen is a relative, being Rose's half-sister, isn't she?'

'Not a blood relative for me, but I'll accept her with open arms once I get to know her better.'

'Hmm, yes, I know what you mean. There's something about her . . . but I don't know that I can put my finger on it. I feel as though I've seen her somewhere. Gerald seemed to recognize me, too. Oh well, it'll come to me in time. Now, why don't we look at our plans for this concert? Christmas is creeping up so quickly, and I do want to have everything just perfect for the day.'

Flora moved to sit at the table beside Diana so she could look at the detailed notes her friend had made. 'I'm extremely impressed.'

'It's amazing what one can obtain with a visiting card, especially while wearing one's best mink. You should try it some time.'

'If I had a mink coat, I'd be wearing it down the tunnels during the air raids to keep me warm. I'm not sure anyone would be fooled by Flora Neville and a posh coat, although I may just send you queueing for our rations if you keep obtaining such results.'

'Any time, my dear. In fact, I can take on that daily task for you. I feel quite useless at times, when you are all so busy. I'll take Miss Tibbs with me for guidance around the town. She knows her way better than I do.'

Flora was horrified. 'No, I can't ask you to do that. You are a guest here and pay for your board.'

Diana raised her hand and stopped Flora before she could say any more. 'I've decided, and I'll not listen to another word. You make a list and I'll get cracking. Perhaps when that young girl Jennie isn't working, I can get her involved in helping with some of the housework. She's more than fit since her illness passed, and seems to have been adopted by Miss Tibbs.'

'I'm not sure she will be staying that long. I can't expect Miss Tibbs to keep sharing a room with her. It was only supposed to be temporary while she needed caring for during the night.'

Diana thought for a moment. 'Anya has a larger room. Would she share, do you think?'

'I share with no one,' an indignant voice boomed from the doorway. 'If you insist, I shall leave at once. I will follow to wherever my Henio has gone to.'

Flora groaned to herself. 'Anya, dear, please don't upset

yourself. We would not think of you leaving us. Don't even say such things. Come and sit down and tell us what is wrong. You look exhausted.'

'I didn't mean to offend. Please accept my apologies,' Diana said.

'There is no need. I am just a little grumpy and upset. I hear today that my Henio is missing.'

'Oh, my dear,' Flora said leaping to her feet to take Anya's arm and lead her to a seat. 'How did you hear? I didn't know there'd been a visitor from the RAF.'

'That nice pilot friend of Lily's who fell into her apple tree. He told me when he came to the teashop.'

'That doesn't sound right to me,' Lady Diana said with a frown. 'News like that would normally be delivered by an officer or a special letter. They would not leave it for someone to tell you in a teashop.'

A bleak look crossed Anya's face. 'I lose him once and come to England. I find him and we are happy. Although he is on duty saving the English, I see him from time to time, so it feels like we are still the married couple. Then he is sent from Manston to this Biggin place, and I lose him again. He didn't even say goodbye.'

It was Flora's turn to feel confused. 'Anya dear, are you saying Henio is lost in action or are you saying he has moved from Manston to another airfield? I know we are not supposed to talk about such things, but you do need to know if he has . . . if he has . . .'

'Popped his clogs?' Anya said, shrugging her shoulders as she used words she'd picked up from working in the teashop.

'I'll make the tea,' Lady Diana said. 'She looks chilled to the bone.'

Flora took Anya's cold hands and rubbed them in her own. 'We need to warm you up. I don't know if it is shock or the nasty weather. Diana, would you be a dear and put a shovel of coal into the stove? Perhaps that hot water should be for a hot-water bottle. There are a couple under the sink. Do you mind?'

'Not at all. I told you, I want to pull my weight more, so how better than to warm up our Anya?' Diana said, getting onto her hands and knees to rummage behind a curtain under the sink and pulling out a stone bottle. 'This will have you warm in no time,' she said, wiping off the dust and placing it onto the draining board ready for when the kettle boiled. 'I'll just be a minute.' She hurried from the kitchen.

'I do not wish to be any trouble to you,' Anya said quietly.

'Anya, you are never any trouble to me. In the time you have been here, you have become a dear friend. I don't know what I would do without you here at Sea View.'

'What if it was me and a little one?' Anya suggested.

'You mean . . .'

'Yes, I am with child. Henio doesn't know. It was my wish to surprise him and we would share the joy together. Now, I do not know how we will cope. Flora Neville, you know what it is like not to have a husband around when you have a child. Tell me how it is I will cope?'

Flora was still trying to choose the right words to say to Anya, when Lady Diana hurried back in with her mink coat. She draped it round the woman's shoulders. 'This'll keep you warm, my dear.'

'It is beautiful,' Anya murmured as she ran her hands

276

down the sleeves. 'I had furs when I lived in Poland,' she said, 'but that was a different time. I must forget that life and think of my Henio.'

'And your baby,' Flora insisted as she went to help Diana with the tea.

'A baby? Oh, that is something to rejoice about.' Diana beamed as she poured hot water into the stone bottle and screwed the stopper as tight as she could. Wrapping it in a tea towel, she placed it on Anya's lap.

'With no husband?' Anya said scathingly, sounding more like her old self.

'Perhaps we should wait for official news of what has happened to Henio?' Flora said as she straightened the tablecloth before carrying the tea tray over and sitting down.

Diana followed with the cake tin. 'That is a good idea. I feel a small slice of cake lifts one's spirits, don't you? I must do some baking,' she sighed as she looked inside at the remains of a seed cake.

'Anya, would you mind very much letting us both know exactly what you were told about Henio? Perhaps between us, we can make sense of it?'

'There is little to tell. This Peter said that he understood that my husband was a pilot, just as he was. I told him that my husband knew better than to lose an airplane and fall from the sky into a tree. My husband is a good pilot who came here to fight Hitler.'

Flora did her utmost not to smile at the way Anya spoke. She could be outspoken and, not having a complete grasp of the language, could come across as blunt and sometimes rude. 'What did he say to that?'

'Would you believe he laughed?' Anya huffed. 'He told me that many pilots landed in the drink, and he'd seen my Henio do just that only recently. I asked if he had seen him since, and he said that he hadn't,' she finished, looking at Flora through unshed tears.

'I reckon you got the wrong end of the stick,' Flora said, looking to Diana for support.

'Flora could be right. Why weep just yet, when we don't know for sure what has happened to your husband? I know just the person who could look into this for you,' she smiled. 'Let me make a telephone call to my daughter. Why have family working in the War Office when one can't make use of them from time to time?'

'Thank you, but I do not think you should be making use of this War Office place for such things. Your daughter has her work to do and will not know about my husband. I did make the telephone call to the airfield, but no one would speak to me.'

'Anya's right, Diana. You may get her in trouble,' Flora said, looking worried. 'Besides, someone untrustworthy may overhear that a pilot is missing, and it will get back to the enemy. Why, anything could happen. Only the other week we watched one of those short information films at the cinema where a waitress overheard a sailor talking to his lady friend about his ship leaving port. Before you knew it, word had got to the enemy and the ship was torpedoed and the sailor perished – careless talk costs lives.'

'Stuff and nonsense. My daughter works for someone who can ask a colleague to make enquiries. As long as we don't talk to waitresses, we will be all right,' Diana said, dismissing Flora's words.

'It is rather hard to do when I work for Joe Lyons and talk to waitresses many times each day,' Anya said seriously before a rare smile appeared and she started to laugh. 'Please speak to Ruth, but do not cause her any trouble. Me, I intend to visit this place called Biggin and enquire as to what has happened to my husband. They may not wish to speak on the telephone, but they cannot ignore me when we are face to face.'

'That might not be a bad idea,' Diana said, nodding thoughtfully. 'I'll speak to Ruth, and she can tell me who we know socially who is based at Biggin Hill. There may be an unofficial way to find out what has happened to your husband.'

'Oh, for goodness' sake. I can't believe what I am hearing,' Flora said. 'Do you honestly think you will be able to walk into an airfield and ask after someone?'

'I have faith in Lady Diana,' Anya said. 'What else is there, if I don't have faith?'

'In that case, I'll accompany you to make sure you aren't arrested and locked in the Tower of London,' Flora huffed. 'Please don't go dashing off until we've made plans. As if I don't have enough on my plate right now. I shall have to make a list – then the children will need caring for. I wonder if Joyce and Miss Tibbs will look after them . . . ? I take it this will be a day trip?'

'It depends if we are locked up in the Tower you speak of,' Anya said, biting into a slice of cake. 'This cake is stale.'

'That sounds like Joyce coming in,' Flora said as they heard the front door open, followed by voices in the hall. 'She must have brought Rose back with her. I wonder what I can give them for their tea?' She got to her feet and hurried to the stone pantry to check provisions.

'Flora, are you home?' Mildred shouted ahead before she rushed into the kitchen.

'Gosh, whatever's wrong? You look all a-fluster, my dear. Have you had a busy day out on your fishing boat?' Lady Diana said, noticing her red face. 'Are you feeling unwell?'

Mildred ignored Lady Diana. 'Flora, I found a young lad out on the street. He's been looking for you. Come in here, son,' she shouted towards the hall. 'We won't bite you.'

A young boy entered the room, with a dirty face peering out of a balaclava. 'I 'ave a message for Mrs Neville,' he said shyly.

'I'm Mrs Neville,' Flora said, wiping her hands on her apron. 'What's the message? I hope I've not been called out for fire-watching. I've just done three nights on the trot.'

'I've not been told anything like that,' the lad said, looking fearful. 'Me mum said to tell you there's been an accident up at the cemetery. Someone called Rose is trapped and it doesn't sound good. There's a ton of bricks on top of her,' he added, getting engrossed in his story. 'There's a fire engine and lots of people 'elping.'

'Oh no,' Flora said, reaching to hold onto the back of Anya's chair. 'I must get to Rose right now,' she said, looking round, her expression vacant with shock.

Mildred reached into the pocket of her overalls and handed the lad tuppence. 'That's for your trouble. Now get yourself back home, and if there's an air raid, take shelter. You know where to go?'

'Yes missus, and ta,' he said, cuffing his nose with the

back of his hand. 'I'm sorry for yer troubles,' he called to
Flora before running out the front door, which remained
open.

As Flora tore off her apron and pulled her everyday
coat from a hook behind the door, the sound of air-raid
sirens could be heard out towards the estuary.

'I'm surprised they've only just sounded off,' Mildred
said. 'I've been watching the dogfights for the past hour
while I was coming back into harbour and sorting out
my catch. You'd best get yourselves down the tunnels,'
she instructed Lady Diana and Anya. 'If you take care of
Daisy I'll drive Flora up to the cemetery to see what's
happening.' She turned away so that Flora couldn't see
the look of consternation on her face.

14

Flora stared ahead, deep in thought, as Mildred drove as quickly as her old vehicle could manage through the empty streets of Ramsgate. Up above, enemy aircraft still filled the sky.

'We'll be there in a few minutes,' Mildred said as she swerved an ARP warden who jumped from the pavement, waving his arms. 'Get out the way, you silly bugger,' she snarled. Turning into a sharp bend, they were faced with a closed road. A house had crumbled into the street beside a large crater. 'I'll get us there, don't you worry,' she said, giving a quick sideways glance at a white-faced Flora before bouncing up a pavement to reverse the way they'd come and take the next road.

'It's as if the devil is stopping me reaching my daughter in time to say goodbye,' Flora mumbled.

'Rose is going nowhere – and if that devil of yours gets in my way, I'll run him over,' Mildred muttered. The gears of the van crunched in agreement as black smoke came from the back of the vehicle. The acrid emissions mixed with the familiar smell of fish would, under normal cir-cumstances, have had Flora gagging and asking Mildred to let her out before she was sick. Instead she gritted her teeth and continued to stare ahead, wishing the minutes away until she was with her Rose.

'I blame myself for not being with her,' Mildred said in her gruff voice. 'I knew Rose was going up to see the General, and I had said I'd try to finish earlier and give her and Joyce a lift. Those two should be commended for their devotion to keeping the graves tidy with what they have to put up with day and in and day out. I shouldn't have stopped to give the lads a hand, watching that mine until the Navy appeared.'

Flora reached over and patted Mildred's knee. 'You shouldn't blame yourself, you do more than enough for all of us as it is. Besides, Rose wanted to take Eileen and Gerald along to pay their respects as the General was, after all, her father too.'

'That's a rum do, with Eileen never having got in touch until now,' Mildred said, trying to get Flora to talk rather than sit thinking about Rose's fate. 'I'd have thought she would have tried to track you both down before all this?'

Flora shrugged her shoulders. 'To be fair, I didn't think to get in touch with Eileen after the General passed away, and by then her mother and siblings had died during the 'flu epidemic. She told us that she spotted the engagement announcement that was placed in *The Times* by Diana, and decided to make herself known to us. I'm pleased she has done so, although I can't help thinking there's nothing of the General in her. She must have taken after her mother.'

Mildred slowed down to allow an army truck to

overtake them. 'She seems quite prickly . . . and as for that husband of hers . . .'

'I've not been alone with them yet, but Rose says he seems to assume there is some kind of inheritance due to his wife from the General.'

'There's only Sea View, isn't there?'

'Yes, he purchased it as his home, however it was put in trust for Rose once she came of age. She gave it to me, as you have been so generous to her by giving the girls Captain's Cottage. I didn't want to take the property, but when all is said and done it will go back to Rose one day. There are a few pieces of jewellery. Perhaps Rose would feel inclined to pass a piece to Eileen? I'll speak to her when I know she is all right . . . if she is all right,' she finished, with a small sob.

'Rose is a strong girl, never you fear. I wonder if Gerald and Eileen are with her. Perhaps they've been injured too?'

'Yes, they all went by bus along with Joyce. Gosh, I do hope she hasn't been hurt as well. Young Pearl only has her mother.'

'She has us. We are one big happy family at Sea View. Cut one, and we all bleed. Still, I can't find myself taking to that Gerald and his wife. I'll be generous and give him the benefit of the doubt for now. I must learn not to be too quick to judge.'

'Then we are all guilty of that. Diana feels the same as we do. We must try to be more charitable. After all, they are here with our Rose, so let's hope they are well and helping with the rescue. Is this as far as we can go?' Flora said, as Mildred pulled up behind where firemen were standing around their vehicle. Up ahead, she could see an ambulance.

'It looks like it. It won't take more than a tick to walk up the road. Are you fit?' she asked, turning off the engine.

'Yes,' Flora replied, taking a deep breath, ready to brave whatever had happened. 'Stay close to me please, Mildred. If anything has gone badly wrong . . .'

Mildred took her friend's small hand in her large one and gave it a squeeze. 'I'll not be letting go until we know,' she said as they hurried up the road as fast as their legs would carry them, Flora having to hurry to keep up with her tall friend.

'Stand back, ladies. There's nothing to see here,' a policewoman said as she put an arm out to stop the two going through the entrance to the cemetery.

'It's my daughter, Rose Neville, who is trapped. Someone was sent to get me,' Flora said, looking beseechingly at the woman.

'Then let me call someone,' she replied, waving to one of her colleagues and stepping aside to speak with him.

'Will you follow me?' he asked as he helped them through the crowd of people milling around who seemed to be helping in numerous ways. 'Please be assured everyone is here to help,' he said, seeing Flora look around with a puzzled expression.

'I'm sure they are, and I'm truly grateful. It's just – there were three other people with Rose. Do you know if they survived – I mean, if they were hurt?' she asked, not wanting to wish harm to anyone.

'I only know of one lady, and you will find her over there,' he said, pointing to where they could see Joyce being tended to by a group of women. 'Perhaps it would be best for you to sit with her while I find out the latest news of your daughter. Please, don't be alarmed,' he said, placing a hand on her arm as her face took on a fearful look. 'She is conscious and speaking to the rescue team, which bodes well.'

'Thank God,' Flora said, as Mildred led her to where Joyce was sitting.

'Flora!' Joyce exclaimed, throwing off the blanket wrapped round her shoulders and hurrying over to greet her friends. 'Oh, Flora, I've never been so pleased to see you. You too,' she added, smiling at Mildred. 'Everything happened so quickly. The cemetery was a wreck when we arrived, and it seems there should have been a sign to say the wall was unstable. Rose went to talk to her relatives, and that's when it happened. One minute it was there beside that house, and the next there was a pile of rubble and Rose had disappeared. I should have been with her, but I was over there, trying to put my husband's grave straight. His headstone is in a dozen pieces, just like the stone for General Sykes.'

'Gravestones can be replaced, Joyce. Please don't upset yourself,' Flora said as she took her friend's shaking hands, hoping to reassure her. 'Oh my goodness, look at your poor fingers,' she said, staring in disbelief at the broken nails and abrasions.

'I was trying to look for Rose before all the help arrived,' Joyce explained, 'but there was far too much to move on my own.'

'What about Eileen and Gerald?' Mildred asked. 'Surely they could have helped.'

'They'd gone. Eileen wanted to get Gerald away from here as she was frightened he'd been hurt.'

'Frightened?' Flora screamed in outrage. 'They left my girl here, not knowing if she was dead, because Eileen was frightened? That is no way to treat family. Wait until I lay my hands on them,' she fumed.

'Don't you worry about them now. There's time for that later on,' Mildred said, although she hoped to lay her hands on the man herself long before Flora found him. She thought for just a moment about what she would do to him. Throwing him into the harbour without a life jacket came to mind.

There was a shout from near where Rose lay buried, and the three women hurried over to see what was happening.

'Careful now, careful,' a man wearing an ARP helmet shouted. 'We don't know what injuries have been sustained.'

'Rose, Rose,' Flora called out, elbowing her way through the group of rescuers to where her daughter was being placed onto a stretcher and throwing herself down on her knees beside her. 'Speak to me, my love,' she cried, trying to wipe the grime from Rose's face.

'Let me do that,' a woman in a St John's uniform said as she stepped forward with an enamel bowl and a piece of cloth. 'Rose, can you hear me? I am going to wipe your eyes so you can see, and then we will take you to hospital so we can check you over. Your mother is here beside you, and I will make sure she is in the ambulance with you, too. Now, keep still for a moment while I make you look beautiful again,' she said kindly as she carefully bathed Rose's face. She was passed a cup of water, which Flora held to her daughter's lips.

'Take a sip . . . careful,' she added, as Rose greedily gulped the water. 'We don't want you choking, do we?' she said, gazing into her daughter's frightened face. 'Oh Rose, we thought we'd lost you,' she added, resisting the urge to break down and cry in front of her brave daughter, or to hug her until she'd been checked for injuries.

'Let's get going, shall we?' an ambulance driver said. Along with a colleague, he lifted the stretcher and walked carefully towards a waiting ambulance. Flora hurried behind them as Mildred waved, indicating she would take Joyce home with her.

'It could have been a lot worse,' one of the men who been digging through the rubble said to Mildred and Joyce, as they stopped to thank everyone. 'She was found behind a large headstone, and that protected most of her body. Had it been one foot either side, she'd have been killed.'

Mildred shuddered as she looked to where the man was pointing. The stone that had protected Rose was her own father's headstone, which she'd never visited in the many years since he died. She hadn't even chosen his monument herself, having washed her hands of him years earlier. Perhaps she should visit with some flowers each week, along with the other women, she thought as she walked over to read the inscription: BELOVED FATHER OF MILDRED ALICE. She'd had no hand in the wording – or the funeral, come to that. She'd arrived late at the church and stood at the back, slipping away halfway through the final hymn. Was this his way of making things up to her by protecting her friend? she wondered, before dismissing her fanciful thoughts.

'Blimey – I thought we'd never get away from work today,' Lily said as she helped Katie check that the wooden boards were securely fixed to the windows of the Margate teashop. 'If I spend much more time in that cellar, I swear I'll be on first-name terms with the spiders. Have you noticed how we always seem to have the same customers down there with us?'

Katie smiled. It was a relief to see Lily in such good spirits. After Mr Grant's visit to the teashop that morning and having to endure explaining her private life to the area manager, Katie feared Lily would either have been given the sack or, more worrying, she'd have given the man a right mouthful and walked out. Instead everything had gone Lily's way, and she'd also received a visit from the handsome pilot they'd recently rescued. 'Perhaps it's because they are our regular diners, so it stands to reason they will be in the teashop when Moaning Minnie goes off. I'm glad they are safe with us, aren't you?'

'Yes, especially the older customers and the women whose husbands have gone off to fight. I like to see the servicemen come in for a meal or a cuppa and a sandwich. Do you know, one squaddie told me that we remind him of home, so that's why he comes in so often? It seems his sisters work in one of the Corner Houses in London,' Lily said as they went back into the teashop to check everything was in order before locking up for the day.

'And there was me thinking it was Anya's scintillating conversation that drew them in,' Katie chuckled.

'Talking of Anya, why was she deep in conversation with Peter?'

'Why do you ask? Do you think he fancies her more than you?'

'Don't be daft,' Lily shrieked with laughter. 'He's only friendly because we rescued him. That, and the fact he's far from home. Hell, why should I worry? I have my daughter and I have my friends. Come on, let's get our coats. The bus is due in five minutes and it feels as though I've not seen Mary for days. I hope she's behaved herself for Mrs Nichols. Which reminds me, I have some buns put by to take back for her as a thank you,' she laughed, not wishing to say too much about her feelings for Peter.

'That's good of you,' Katie said as she started to turn out the lights in the teashop. 'Mildred's idea to employ a part-time housekeeper who would look after Mary as well must be a weight off your mind?'

'It is, especially as she also cleans the house. I wouldn't have been able to afford to pay her on my own. It is decent of you and Rose to chip in with her wages.'

'Think nothing of it – I'm more than happy to do it, particularly if it means we don't have to worry about keeping Captain's Cottage clean when we get home from work.'

'She does the ironing, too,' Lily grinned.

'The woman is a saint,' Katie said as they checked the doors were secure before hurrying over the road as the bus came into view. They never looked back at the teashop. If they had, they'd have seen two characters lurking in the shadows.

The girls chatted as the bus trundled along towards Broadstairs and Ramsgate. A few stops before the town, Katie rang the bell and they hopped off, hurrying up the road towards their cottage. Already Mrs Nichols had drawn the blackout curtains, and they walked into a warm welcome with the coal fire lit in their small living room.

'The kettle's on and baby has had her bath,' Mrs Nichols said without her usual warm welcome.

'Is there something wrong?' Katie asked as she started to take off her coat.

'A message came just now – Rose has had an accident. She's at the hospital, and her mother is with her.'

'Oh no,' Katie exclaimed. 'I'd best get over there straight away. Lily!' she called out, explaining what had happened as Lily appeared with Mary in her arms.

'I will stay here and care for Mary,' Mrs Nichols offered. 'She's no trouble, bless her. I have my knitting and the wireless.'

'You have buns as well,' Lily said, nodding to Katie to fetch them from her bag. 'There are enough of them for you take back to Mr Nichols if you wish.' The girls knew how partial the lady was to a bun. 'Shall we knock on your door and let Mr Nichols know you are helping us out and will be late?' she added, knowing there was no telephone at the Nichols' cottage. 'We could invite your husband to come over here and enjoy this lovely fire, if he wishes? It will be company for you.' She felt happier that if there should be an air raid, Mrs Nichols would have help getting Mary into the Anderson shelter at the end of the garden and both would be safe much sooner. It was easy in daylight, but the darkness was another matter, having to push the pram and carry a torch down the narrow path.

'That would be nice, thank you,' the woman smiled. 'Give my best wishes for a speedy recovery to Rose – and don't worry about Mary. She is a delightful baby. I feel blessed that you entrust her to me.'

'I'm grateful to have you to rely on,' Lily said, as she handed over her child and kissed the older woman on the cheek. 'Enjoy the buns.'

'Oh, I will. You girls certainly know how to treat an old lady,' she chuckled.

The two girls hurried from the cottage, hoping they'd not have to wait too long for the bus that would take them to the hospital.

'What do you think could have happened?' Katie asked anxiously. 'Mrs Nichols told me the message said nothing about Rose being hurt in the air raid. Could it have been a traffic accident, or perhaps someone accosted her?'

Lily pulled out her purse as they spotted a bus turn at the end of the road, its shadowy shape obscured by the blackout but still recognizable by the sound of its engine. She'd be glad to be on board and away from the sharp wind blowing in off the sea. 'You must stop fretting, Katie. There's time enough for that, once we know what's happened to Rose and can do something,' she said firmly, nudging her friend to climb aboard quickly in case the conductor rang the bell and it set off without them.

'You think someone hurt her?' Katie asked in horror, before absorbing what her friend had said. 'Sorry, I'll keep quiet until we know what has happened. Let's talk about Christmas instead, shall we?'

Lily snorted with laughter. Ever since she'd known Katie when they met at school, her friend had always enjoyed the season of goodwill. 'Honestly, Katie, haven't you grown up yet? Christmas is for children.'

'How can you say such a thing, Lily Douglas? You know you love everything about Christmas, so don't be such a grouch. Come the day you are usually out of bed before anyone else and enjoying a sherry while still wearing your nightdress.'

'I'm not saying Christmas won't be fun for the children and we have to make it extra special for Daisy, but it will be the second Christmas spent at war. And with Rose's Ben, your Jack and so many men away fighting, it doesn't seem right for us to be celebrating, does it? Especially now Rose is in hospital. I hope she will be home by then,' she added sadly.

'Haven't you just told me not to have miserable thoughts about Rose until we know what has happened and whether she is injured?' Katie chided her.

'But she must have been injured or she wouldn't have been taken to the hospital,' Lily replied. 'However, we will find out shortly: only three stops to go.'

The two girls walked in through the main entrance of the hospital, passing a wall of sandbags and signs giving directions to the underground operating theatres and emergency wards.

Lily shuddered. 'It doesn't seem five minutes since I was down there, and now it's our Rose's turn.'

'Look on the bright side. You are fit and healthy now,

and so is Mary. There's no reason to think our Rose won't be too.'

Lily agreed, not wanting to remind Katie of the scars on her limbs, or her leg, which seemed to ache after a day on her feet. But yes, she was lucky, and things could have been much worse. 'Come on, let's ask over there at that desk. They should know where we can find Rose.'

The pair were sent through a labyrinth of corridors until they reached a ward where they could see, through a window in the door, familiar faces sitting around a bed. Hurrying into the ward, hoping they wouldn't be turfed out for having too many visitors around one patient, they quickly hugged Flora and Mildred and shared a wooden bench pulled from below the empty bed next door. The long ward was painted a mix of pale green and cream, with twelve neatly made beds on each side. Nurses hurried from patient to patient tending to their needs, their shoes making small squeaking noises on the linoleum floor. Lily wrinkled her nose at the familiar odour of disinfectant. 'What happened?' she asked, looking at her friend's bandaged head and pale complexion.

'A wall collapsed on her up at the cemetery,' Flora said, not taking her eyes from Rose. As she spoke she continued to stroke Rose's hand, which lay on top of the white sheet. 'She was trapped, and had to be dug out during that last air raid.'

'Bloody hell,' Lily said. 'Is she badly hurt?'

Rose's eyes fluttered, then opened. 'I thought I heard a familiar voice,' she murmured, trying to smile through dry lips.

'They say she has mild concussion and cuts and bruises,

but the doctor wants to keep her in for a couple of days for observation to be on the safe side,' Flora said, looking relieved. 'I feel Rose should come back to Sea View so we can look after her until she is fighting fit. I don't like the idea of leaving her alone at Captain's Cottage while you girls are working.'

'But Mrs Nichols will be there,' Katie said. 'She's a darling lady who will fuss over Rose, so you've no need to worry.'

'I prefer that Rose is in the family home. It doesn't seem right to give even more responsibilities to the lady caring for Mary. Babies can be a handful, and it isn't fair to expect her to look after Rose as well. What do you say, Rose – will you come home to Sea View?' Flora asked.

Rose gave a small nod. 'Yes, please – but can you both do something for me?'

'Anything you say,' Katie replied, digging into her bag for a pencil and piece of paper. 'Do I need to make a list?'

'No; but could you let Mr Grant know I'll be off sick for a couple of days, and could you find my keys to the teashop so he can give them to someone else until I'm back? They should be in my coat pocket.'

Flora reached into a locker beside the bed and pulled out Rose's navy wool coat. 'There's nothing in the pockets. Shall I check your handbag?'

Rose nodded and tried to speak after coughing hard. 'I had them in my pocket, but you can check.'

Flora wasn't one for going through people's property, believing that a woman's handbag was private, but she checked all the same. 'Your purse, a handkerchief . . . Oh, and some keys – but they look like house keys,' she said, dangling them from one finger.

'They're the same as mine,' Katie said as she held up her door key to Captain's Cottage. 'The teashop keys will be like these,' she added, holding up the keys she had used to lock up earlier that evening. 'Do you think they were lost during the accident? Perhaps we should go back and look for them?'

'I'll go,' Mildred said. 'I have a torch and can be up there in ten minutes. It's best we find them, before someone picks them up and puts two and two together about you working at the teashop in Margate.'

'But it's pitch black out there. Are you sure?' Lily asked. 'I can come with you, if you like?'

'I'd be grateful. Two hands make lighter work,' Mildred said. 'Will you both wait here until we return?' she asked Flora and Katie. 'I can take you back to Sea View to see everyone, then drop Katie and Lily at the cottage.'

'Be careful,' Rose murmured as they bid their farewells.

'This waiting for news is killing me,' Lady Diana said as she paced the floor of the kitchen. 'Perhaps I should make a call to the hospital?'

'The telephone still isn't working,' Joyce sighed. 'Flora will be home before too long, and then we will know.' As much as she liked and admired Lady Diana, Joyce was becoming exasperated at the woman's restlessness. Her fingers ached and were sore from digging at the rubble trying to rescue Rose. She wanted nothing more than to climb into her bed and sleep. It had been hard to put Pearl to bed, as the young girl had been tearful at having to wait until the morning for news of Rose. Daisy seemed to have picked up on the tension in the house and started to grizzle. Their tears had set off Annabelle and Marina, and soon all the children were fretful. Cocoa and toast, with a little of Flora's precious jam stock spread on top, soon soothed them enough for Joyce to at last settle them down, with promises to let them know how Rose whenever she heard.

Miss Tibbs checked the oven. 'Their dinners are going to dry up completely if they aren't home soon. I'll take the plates out and when Flora and Mildred get home, I will heat them on top of a saucepan of hot water. It's the best I can do,' she muttered, seeing Lady Diana's look of horror.

'Can we not give them something else to eat? After all Flora's been through today she should at least have something better to eat than dried ox liver and mashed potato.'

The old woman put her hands on her hips and glared at Lady Diana. 'I'll have you know there's a war on, my lady. Now, if you can wave your magic wand and provide something tasty, then you go ahead and do it,' she sniffed.

'There is fish and chips if the shop has not run out, and unless there is an air raid – then they close up,' Anya informed them from where she sat studying a map book. 'If you go to the one close to the harbour, it is where Mildred supplies fish and they will know us.'

'I'll not be going out. It's cold and I've had my meal, thank you very much. Jennie too has had her meal.'

The young girl, who had brightened at the mention of fish and chips, glared at Miss Tibbs. 'I'm still hungry,' she mumbled.

'Then you must have worms, young lady. I'll have to see the chemist and ask about a powder for you,' Miss Tibbs said.

'I do not have worms.' The girl sprang to her feet indignantly. 'That's a bloody lie, you silly old woman.'

Lady Diana could see that there would be an unholy row if she didn't step in. 'I'll treat all of us to fish and chips, but I need two people to help me carry them. Anya, you can show me the way. Joyce, would you like to accompany us?'

'If you don't mind, I don't feel up to it,' Joyce said, holding up her red, raw hands. 'I'll stay here and care for Daisy, as it will save us having to push her up and down Madeira Walk in her pram.'

'Oh, my poor dear. They look so painful. Why did you not say something? Let me get you some soothing salve from my first-aid box. I never travel without it,' Lady Diana smiled before hurrying from the room.

'That woman must travel with the kitchen sink in her suitcase,' Miss Tibbs muttered.

'The old woman is raving nuts,' Anya said, shaking her head. 'Who would carry a sink, I ask you?'

'Leave her be, please, Anya,' Joyce sighed. 'We are all very tense at the moment. Shall we have a cup of tea to soothe our nerves?'

'I thought we were going to have fish and chips,' Jennie grumbled.

'You be quiet,' Anya said, pointing her finger at the young girl. 'I have you up to here at work, and now you are living in my home. You are one ungrateful child.'

Jennie started to snivel. 'I just fancied chips, that's all.

I've not had them in a long time, not since . . .' She said no more, and looked alarmed at her own outburst.

'Since when?' Anya shouted. 'Since you were in prison? Since you were walking the streets? Since you were arrested? Spit it out, girl.'

Jennie burst into sobs and Miss Tibbs rushed to comfort her, while Joyce did her best to calm Anya down.

'My, my, whatever is going on here?' Lady Diana asked. 'I leave you alone for a few minutes, and all hell breaks loose. Now tell me, who started this?'

Jennie pointed to Anya. 'She was beastly to me.'

'I simply ask where she comes from. She could murder us all in our beds for all we know.'

'You're a rich one to talk,' Jennie spat back. 'You sound like a German to me. What's to stop you murdering us all in our beds, eh?'

'It'll be me doing the murdering if you both don't stop this childish behaviour and make up. Flora will not want this to deal with when she gets home. Now, I suggest that Anya explains first about how she came to be in Ramsgate. Then you can tell your story, Jennie. No arguing,' Lady Diana added as the girl started to protest.

They sat listening as Anya spoke of how the Germans had invaded her hometown in Poland, killing all her family. She told them how, along with a friend, she had hidden until it was safe to flee the area and, with help, finally arrived in England. She had to pay someone to smuggle her, as she didn't have the right papers.

'I came here to find my husband, Henio, who I found out was in Thanet flying planes to fight the enemy. During my journey, I lost the baby I was carrying. No, please don't pity me,' she said as Lady Diana went to hug her. 'I found my Henio, and now I am with child – but my Henio, he is lost again. This map will show me where I can find where he was based, and ask his comrades of his last days.' She pointed to the map on her lap. 'Now you speak,' she said to Jennie, who had sat wide-eyed listening to Anya's tale of her escape.

'I ran away from the East End during the Blitz. Me mum and dad was killed, and my aunt didn't care about me. I remembered as a kid how we would come to Ramsgate on a charabanc for a holiday, so thought I'd come back again, but it has changed. It's not as nice as it used to be,' she said, looking forlorn.

'How did you get into Thanet?' Lady Diana asked. 'I have connections, and it was hard enough for me.'

'I'm skinny and look young for me age. I hung about the train station until a group from a school was travelling into Thanet, and I tagged along. No one checked us. It was easy. Once I was here I picked up a kitchen job quick enough in Margate, and kipped around the town on benches. I was clever enough to move on so no coppers asked me any questions. It was easy enough, until the weather turned for the worse and I got poorly.'

Joyce tutted. 'You could have died, you poor thing.'

Lady Diana looked at Anya and Jennie. 'You know, you are both very alike. You are both survivors, and that's a good thing in this world at the moment, is it not?'

All the women agreed, although Jennie looked a little sullen. 'You ain't going to kick me out, are you, Lady Diana?'

'And why would I do such a thing? This house is not mine to make rules for, and you seem to be paying your way and pulling your weight. I see nothing to complain about; how old are you, child?'

'I'm fifteen at Christmas. So I'm old enough to work and make my own way.'

'I agree. I too was working at your age.'

Jennie was astounded. 'You went to work? I thought you was proper posh.'

'My dear, Flora will confirm that I was kicking my legs up on the stage along with my three sisters. It was a hard life, but like you I earnt a wage and I paid my way,' Diana said proudly. 'I had fun, too.'

Jennie shook her head in disbelief. 'Blimey – we are a right lot, aren't we?'

'We are women, and we fight to survive,' Anya nodded, holding out her hand to shake Jennie's. 'We are now friends, young Jennie.'

15

'I'd not choose to visit a cemetery in the dark,' Lily said with a shiver as she followed Mildred into the desolate graveyard. 'It's bloody cold,' she added, pulling the collar of her coat up around her neck and tucking the ends of her woolly scarf in securely. 'Have you got that torch? I don't want something jumping out and grabbing me in the dark.' She giggled nervously.

'Don't be daft. And don't you dare do anything funny,' Mildred growled, keeping close behind the younger woman. 'I have my torch in one hand and something to protect us in the other, so if something untoward happens, I'll bash whatever it is before I stop to ask questions. I'd hate to have you end up in the next bed to Rose up at the hospital. Now, let me go first, as I know where the grave is.'

Lily looked over her shoulder, but couldn't see a thing in the pitch black. The hairs on her neck prickled as she hung onto the belt of Mildred's army greatcoat. Mildred had purloined it when it was left on her boat, after she'd helped in the evacuation of the troops from Dunkirk. Flora had called it Mildred's souvenir of the day, and the woman was truly proud of her find.

'Mind yourself. There's a lot of rubble on the path where the wall came down. We can't be far from the grave now,' she said.

'Why are we looking for a particular grave, and how do you remember it?' Lily hissed, afraid to speak to loudly.

'It's the grave marker that protected Rose when the accident happened. I remember it. I'm going to turn on the torch to check where we are and pray to God there's not an ARP warden on duty nearby. Keep your eyes peeled.'

Lily wasn't sure she even wanted to open her eyes, but whispered back that she'd do her best.

Even pointing towards the ground, the bright light illuminated a large expanse of the cemetery. Lily swore as a startled fox was caught in the beam and ran across their path. 'I think I'd rather not have seen that, ta very much,' she said, her heart beating wildly in her chest. 'Do you think we can hurry up and find what we came here for?'

'Look, just over there,' Mildred said, aiming the beam slightly higher, outlining the large headstone. 'That's what saved our Rose from being killed.' She moved closer to the area. 'Start checking the ground. The keys could be anywhere around here, as this is where Rose was checked over before being taken to the hospital.'

'Don't you think someone would have picked them up?'

'Not necessarily. There was an air raid on at the time, so people were more concerned with getting to safety once Rose had been rescued. I suggest we start from where she was trapped and move outwards in a circle. You go that side of the grave, and I'll start here.'

'Can I take the torch?' Lily asked in a wobbly voice.

Mildred laughed, and passed it over to the girl as she felt her way around the grave. 'Keep it aimed low or we could get in trouble,' she hissed, as Lily stumbled and a beam of light shot into the sky. 'You'll have people thinking you're signalling to the enemy.'

'I don't think even the Luftwaffe would be wanting to land down here without a runway,' Lily hissed back, before yelping in pain. 'Ouch – I've knelt on something that hurt.'

'The keys?'

'No such luck; it feels like a stone pierced my knee. Probably ruined my stockings too. Ugh, that's either blood or an insect squashed on my knee.'

'Stop your grumbling and keep looking. Think what Rose must have gone through trapped behind here. She hurt more than her knee!'

Lily shuddered as she ran her fingers through gravel and wet grass. 'It doesn't bear thinking about. I wonder who the inhabitant of this grave is, and what they think about having Rose trapped on top of them.'

'The old bastard would have created merry hell,' Mildred muttered gruffly.

'You knew him?' Lily asked, shining the torch onto the words engraved on the marble. 'Blimey – it's your dad, isn't it? That's a coincidence.'

'You could say that.'

'But you've never said he was buried up here, in all the time Rose has been visiting the General to tend his grave . . .'

'No, I haven't. I had no interest in where he was laid to rest. I didn't even stay to the end of his funeral. He was dead to me after we fell out that last time. The man was a bully and worse. I was glad to see the back of him. He could have pushed me to top myself if I'd not stayed strong. I swear I was close at times,' Mildred said, with a catch in her voice. 'Now let's find these keys and get ourselves out of here, shall we?'

Lily was silent for a while as she searched for the keys. 'We're a right pair, aren't we? Both of us have suffered at the hands of our parents.'

'We came out the other side with our heads held high though, so we are the winners.'

'We are, aren't we?' Lily agreed, although this time she was the one with a catch in her voice. 'You know what – I don't think the keys are here. Do you?'

'No, someone must have picked them up. So much for my big idea,' Mildred said. She stood up, and groaned as she stretched her back. 'Let's run the light from the torch once around the grave quickly to make sure, then make a move. I'm thinking we should speak to that half-sister of Rose's, as they may have seen something.'

Lily flashed the torch before agreeing. 'Come on, there's no better time than the present. I know where they're staying. Crikey, I look a sight,' she grinned, shining the torch down at her dust-covered clothing and quickly turning it off as a voice shouted to them from the street.

'Can you dance, Anya?' Lady Diana asked as they sipped their umpteenth cup of tea.

'Yes, my Henio will tell you I am a very good dancer.

Why do you ask?' Anya said before sadness engulfed her. 'Perhaps he will never again see me dance,' she said.

'Oh, Anya, I do hope he will. I promise that I will make enquiries with my daughter as soon as the telephone is working again.'

'It is of no matter. I will travel to this Biggin Hill and find out for myself.'

'We will do what we can, my dear. You will not have to undertake this by yourself, I promise.'

Anya took a deep breath and smiled. 'Why do you wish to know about my dancing?'

Lady Diana looked down at the notebook she was always scribbling in and placed a tick against a few words she had written earlier. 'It would be wonderful to have Pearl, Annabelle and Marina perform in the show, and as a thank you to our Polish comrades, I wondered if you could teach them a traditional Polish folk dance?'

A smile flooded Anya's usually stern expression. 'I can do that. I was worried that you would want me to sing, and I have a voice like a hog trapped in the barn. My Henio would tell you that too,' she laughed as they all joined in. 'Henio was a good judge of people,' she added.

'Is, Anya. Your Henio is a good judge of people. I don't like to hear you speak of him in the past tense,' Lady Diana said.

Anya brushed away the comment with a wave of her hand. 'That is just my way of speaking. My English is not yet that good.'

'It is much better than our Polish,' Joyce said, as she carefully rubbed the salve Lady Diana had given her into her sore hands. 'You have a beautiful language, and I for one would love to learn a little of it. Would anyone else?'

The women agreed, and Jennie raised her hand. 'Can I dance with the children? When my parents were alive, I had some ballet lessons,' she said, her eyes shining with the memory.

'Perfect, I too learnt to ballet dance. You can learn my country's dance with the little ones,' Anya said. 'We will be friends, yes?'

'I'd like that,' Jennie said with a smile.

'Then tomorrow we start the lessons. No time like the present, eh? We will need music, though . . .'

'I will play for you on the piano,' Lady Diana said.

'I will help with the costumes,' Miss Tibbs put in.

'And I will convince my daughter she will enjoy the experience.' Joyce grimaced, wondering how Pearl would take the news that she would be cavorting on stage dressed as a Polish peasant. 'She's rather shy,' she explained, before anyone thought they did not wish to do their part.

'It will be fine, everything will be wonderful,' Anya said with a grin. 'We need this show to take away the worries of the war. For one evening we will enjoy ourselves and cheer up the people of Ramsgate.'

'Oh listen, that sounds like the telephone. They must have fixed it,' Lady Diana said excitedly. 'Hurry and answer, Jennie, before the person hangs up. It may be Flora calling from the hospital with news of Rose.'

Jennie ran to the hall and they all waited with bated breath to hear who the caller could be. Returning to the kitchen, Jennie looked to Lady Diana. 'It's your son, Ben. He is asking to speak to Rose.'

'Oh dear, the poor love has no idea what has happened. I'd better speak to him,' she said, hurrying to the telephone as fast as she could.

'Ben, darling, it is Mother here, how are you? Where are you?'

'Mother, you know I can't tell you where I am, but believe me, I am well. More than well, as at last Rose and I can book the wedding. As much as I love to talk with you, can you put Rose on the telephone, please?'

'I'm afraid that's not possible at the moment, my love. Rose is unwell.'

There was a short silence as Ben digested the information. 'What do you mean by unwell? Has she taken to her bed? She knew I would try to speak to her this evening. Mother, this is important,' he said, sounding worried.

'Now Ben, I don't want you to get upset, but Rose was hurt when a wall collapsed on top of her. She is not badly hurt,' Diana added quickly, as she hurried to explain how it had happened and Rose's obvious injuries. 'We are waiting to hear news of her at the moment, but the telephone line has only just been repaired. The air raids have been relentless these past few days.'

Ben continued to ask questions until Diana stopped him. 'My love, all the time we tie up this line we will be none the wiser about Rose. May I suggest that you put the phone down, and once I hear something, I will place a call to you – if that is possible?'

Ben gave her a telephone number where he could be reached, and assured his mother he would not leave the telephone until she rang him back. After giving him a firm talking-to about staying positive, she replaced the receiver.

'That was very hard,' she sighed as she explained to the women how distressed Ben had been at the news.

'He really does love Rose,' Joyce said. 'They may have only known each other a short while, but war tends to speed up a romance. Let's hope they will get their wedding before too long. God knows they both deserve it. That's if Rose isn't seriously injured . . .'

Lady Diana agreed. The news of the impending wedding was not hers to pass on. The inhabitants of Sea View knew it would be soon, but she would leave it to the couple to share any further news. 'I hope Ben doesn't throw caution to the wind and come rushing down here. He can be a tad hot-headed at times.'

'Is this it?' Mildred asked as she pulled up at the pavement of a decidedly run-down hotel. 'How do you know this place?'

'I heard Eileen mention the name, and it's somewhere I spent the night once,' Lily answered, not wishing to elaborate that it was where she had stayed with Tom White on the night her daughter was conceived.

Mildred gave her a sideways glance, but knew better than to ask any questions. 'Do you think the pair of them will speak to us?'

'If I get my foot in the door, I'll not leave until they tell me why they ran off without helping our Rose. No one does that, let alone family.'

'I can't say I've taken to them. She's nothing like Rose. They must both take after their mothers,' Mildred huffed as they entered the small foyer of the hotel.

Lily went to the counter and rang the bell. A yawning night porter appeared and told them the room number, which was on the top floor.

'I know where to go,' she replied, guiding Mildred to a lift that carried them to the floor above. 'We have to climb the last flight of stairs,' she said, nodding towards a door. So many emotions were churning through her head as she led the way.

Mildred could see that being in the hotel was causing some distress to Lily, so she took over, stepping in front of her to knock sharply on the door of the room booked by Gerald and Eileen.

'Who is that at this time of night?' Gerald asked as he opened the door, dressed only in his trousers and a yellowing singlet.

'Friends of Rose and Flora,' Mildred said, stepping forward so that he had no choice but to let them into the room. 'We want to speak to you about Rose's accident.'

'We didn't see anything,' Eileen said as she tied the belt of her dressing gown and ran her fingers through her hair.

'You didn't hang around to find out how your half-sister was either, did you?' Lily fired back at her.

'I wasn't feeling so good,' Gerald said, pulling on his shirt. 'It was the shock of what happened,' he added. 'You weren't there, you don't know what it was like.'

'I was there soon after, and I can tell you it got much worse as they tried to rescue Rose,' Mildred said as she gazed at the unmade bed and the partially dressed couple. 'I take it you soon felt better?'

'We've been sleeping,' Eileen replied, giving Mildred

a surly look. 'Does that mean she's dead, if you've come here to see us?'

Lily and Mildred both noticed the hopeful glance Eileen gave her husband. 'If she is, you don't look very upset,' Lily said.

'My wife feared the worst, as did I. That's why we had to leave. Can you give our condolences to Mrs Neville, when you see her? We will be in touch with regards to the will and Eileen's inheritance.'

Mildred's eyes flicked between them before meeting Lily's, with a look that warned her friend not to say anything. She would have expected Gerald and Eileen to be more upset, thinking as they did that Rose had perished in an accident. With Eileen only recently having discovered she had a sister, and then supposedly losing her so soon, Mildred thought there would have been more concern for Rose. 'Why don't you visit Sea View tomorrow and speak to Flora yourself?' she asked.

'No, we have to get back to London. Something's come up that can't be ignored,' Gerald said, reaching for his tie. 'In fact, we should really leave this evening rather than tomorrow, don't you think, my dear?'

'Don't you even want to stay and sort out Eileen's inheritance?' Lily asked.

Eileen looked at her husband. 'They have our address, so any money can be sent there. We don't want the property, so it can be sold. That's right, isn't it, Gerald?'

'Eileen only wants what has been denied her all these years. It's only fair,' he said.

Mildred mulled over what had been said. 'You'd best give me your address. Flora is under a lot of pressure at the moment. At least I can help bring this to an end as quickly as possible.'

'I say, would you really do that? Here's my business card. Anything can reach me there, and do pass on our condolences,' he said, brightening up at once.

Mildred tucked the card into her pocket before looking round the room. 'Condolences?'

'For Rose's death. Why else would we be discussing Eileen's inheritance?'

'Oh, Rose isn't dead. Why would you think that?'

Gerald frowned. 'You came here to see us.'

'To ask if you'd noticed anything about the accident. Rose's keys are missing. But I can see that you must have picked them up,' Mildred said – and before they could react, she swooped to grab a set of keys that had been placed on top of a chest of drawers.

'I think you will find those are mine,' Gerald said, holding out his hand for Mildred to hand them back.

'No – they are the same as these ones,' Lily replied, waving her own set of keys to the teashop so Mildred could compare them.

'Yes, they are both the same. Why do you have them?' Mildred demanded.

Gerald turned red in the face and started to open and close his mouth. 'Why, I must have picked them up in all the confusion. Accidents happen, don't they?'

'Yes, but some of us don't expect to profit from them,' Lily snapped. 'Now listen to me. Rose has given Sea View to her mother. I'm given to believe that the legal documents have been created, but I'd not ask, as it's none of my business. Just as it is none of yours.'

Eileen frowned. 'But General Sykes . . . I mean, my father owned the house. Half should be mine by rights.'

'As I said before, it is none of my business or yours who owns Sea View. I suggest that if you aren't interested in your half-sister's welfare, you should head back to London and remove yourself from her life.'

Gerald opened the door. 'I wish you to leave now but, be warned, this is not the end of the matter. My wife is entitled to her share of the guesthouse.'

Mildred and Lily left, more confused than when they'd arrived. 'I'm not sure about any of this,' Mildred muttered as they walked to the lift.

Rose lay awake, long after her mum had been collected by Mildred and Lily, still drowsy, but more aware now of what was going on around her. The ward was in semi-darkness with just one small light over a desk in the middle, where the night sister was on duty. Apart from the squeak of the nurses' shoes as they carried out their duties, and the gentle snores and mumblings of other patients, it was quiet.

Rose thought about her day, and how brave Lily had been facing up to what had happened between her and Tom White. With the man now gone from Lyons and her not having to see him at work, Lily could become even stronger and look to the future with baby Mary. Rose frowned as she tried to think what had happened next. Suddenly the memory came back with a flash. She recalled being at the cemetery with Joyce and her half-sister and husband – the wall coming down on her, and not being able to move. She shuddered and automatically put out her arms to fight her way out of the tomb of bricks that surrounded her. Sweat broke out on her face as she tossed from side to side, such was the strength of the memory.

'Hey, what's all this?' a familiar voice said as her hands were taken in his before a gentle kiss was placed on her cheek.

'Ben?' she whispered, as the memory of her incarceration faded away and her breath slowed down to normal. 'I'm not dreaming, am I?'

'I'm here, my love,' he said, brushing a few stray hairs from her hot cheeks before sitting down. 'I'm not a dream.'

Rose opened her eyes and focused on his face. 'I've never been so glad to see you in my life. I called out for you when I was trapped,' she said, grabbing tightly to his hand. 'I knew you'd come.' She smiled at him.

Ben did his utmost not to imagine Rose trapped and almost dying in that cemetery. 'I'd have come if I'd known. Right now, I never want to leave your side again,' he whispered close to her ear, so as not to wake those in nearby beds. 'As soon as my mother told me, I got in touch with John Bentley, as he had a vehicle available. We talked our way through roadblocks to be with you. I even have roses for my Rose,' he said, lifting a bunch of red roses that he'd placed at the bottom of her bed.

'They are beautiful, thank you. I'm glad you came, but how did you get past the ward sister?'

Ben looked shamefaced. 'There is one rose missing from your bouquet. I handed it to her and threw myself at her feet, begging her to let me see you for a few minutes as I intended to propose to you. She melted in front of me.'

'Oh Ben, that is such a huge fib,' she smiled, feeling heaps better just knowing he was there beside her. 'But thank you for coming.'

He took her hand and slipped the ring onto her finger. 'Look, I have the ring back from the jeweller and the stones are now properly set – so in a way, I am proposing all over again. If you can talk your vicar into marrying us, let's do it on Christmas Day, when I have a seventy-two-hour leave?'

'I'd love nothing more than to marry you on Christmas Day. But what if your leave is cancelled, or there's an air raid?'

Ben kissed the palm of her hand. 'What if my leave isn't cancelled and there isn't an air raid, and we marry and live happily ever after? We can live our lives wondering what if? Come on, Rose, take a gamble. The odds are in our favour.'

'I would like to marry in Ramsgate. To be honest, a registry office in London, like your mum suggested, isn't really my idea of a wedding – but I'd still have married you there if that was the only choice. Ramsgate amongst my friends would be perfect, and marrying you will be even more perfect,' she said, throwing herself into his arms and enjoying his kiss despite her cuts and bruises protesting.

A polite cough from nearby had Ben leaning back in his seat. 'Mission accomplished, Sister,' he said with a grin. 'This beautiful woman said yes.'

'May I be the first to congratulate you both! Now, this young lady needs her sleep, so she is fighting fit to organize her wedding.'

With a promise to treat the sister to a slap-up meal at

the teashop when he was next in town, Ben kissed Rose and wished both women goodnight. As the sister went back to her desk, he rushed back to Rose's bed for a final goodnight kiss. 'When are they letting you out?'

'It could be as early as tomorrow, once the doctor has seen me. Mum wants me to go back to Sea View to be cared for until I'm fit for work.'

'Then I'll fix it with the old man to stay on for a day, and John Bentley can transport you in luxury to stay with your mum.'

'In his Bentley?' Rose giggled, having been told about the chauffeur owning a rather posh Bentley car.

'Sorry, he only has his Rolls-Royce with him, so you'll have to slum it this time,' Ben said with a smile as the sister returned to shoo him away.

How the other half live, Rose thought to herself. But then, I'll be joining that other half come Christmas Day . . .

It was her last thought as her eyes fluttered closed and she dreamt of wedding dresses and her handsome army captain.

Katie arrived bright and early in order to open up the Margate teashop. She left Lily asleep in her room, as Mary had kept her up part of the night. In her handbag she had a second set of keys that Lily had given her when, along with Mildred, they'd arrived back at the hospital to collect Flora. Lily had explained how they'd found them with Gilbert and Eileen, but she had not said much more. With promises of 'I'll explain later', Lily had taken her daughter from Mrs Nichols and put the child to bed.

Climbing aboard the bus for the short journey into Margate, she thought about returning to work in Ramsgate. Word was that the Ramsgate branch would be up and running very soon after incurring serious bomb damage, so she would be going back to work there. She'd miss working with Rose, Lily and Anya and she wondered who her manager would be. Would Miss Roberts be returning as her boss, or were they bringing on someone from another shop? Perhaps when Rose was back on her feet Katie would ask if she had any news.

As the bus pulled up close to the teashop on the seafront, she joined a couple of other Nippies heading in the same direction.

'Goodness – what's happened here?' Edie said, as they approached the shop and saw a policeman standing at the door.

'Probably waiting for his breakfast,' another Nippy laughed.

Katie frowned. 'It does look as though something has happened,' she said, crossing the road and hurrying through the door, where she nearly bumped into Mr Grant.

'Ah, Mrs Jones. Just the lady I wanted to see. How is Miss Neville? It was good of Mrs Neville to let me know that Rose would not be at work today. Mrs Grant and I were most disturbed to hear of her accident. I would like to speak to you in the office if you could spare me a moment before you prepare for work.'

'I've no news of Rose since last night,' Katie explained as she followed him to Rose's office at the back of the teashop. 'Flora – that is, Mrs Neville – promised to make a telephone call to us when she knows more.'

'Very good,' he said, indicating that she should sit down. 'I will be driving to the Ramsgate branch when I leave here. Would you let me know if you do hear? Apart from Rose being a valued manageress, I have a fondness for her – and she has invited me to give her hand away in marriage.'

'That's splendid news,' Katie beamed. The girls had wondered who Rose would ask. 'May I ask why there is a policeman at the door to the teashop?'

Mr Grant frowned. 'We had an after-hours visitor last night.'

'A burglar?' Katie asked, putting her hand to her mouth in surprise. 'Has the door been damaged?'

'That is what is so strange about the business. Yes, there is some splintering to the wooden door, but it seems a key must have been used to gain entry, as the lock was not broken. Apart from my set, and whoever is on duty holding a set, there just remains the set belonging to Miss Neville . . .'

Katie put her hand into her pocket and pulled out both sets, laying them on the desk. 'Rose's set was lost in the accident. Lily – Miss Douglas – and our friend Mildred Dalrymple went back to the cemetery last night to look for them,' she explained. 'Lily has agreed to let me know the full story when she gets into work later this morning.'

'I will look into this once I've listened to Miss Douglas. Something doesn't seem right.'

'Would you like me to return my keys?' Katie said, concerned that she could be a suspect. 'I'd hate to think . . .'

Mr Grant raised his hands in protest. 'Mrs Jones, not for one moment do we believe you are involved in this burglary. Rest assured that you are one of our most trustworthy employees. I insist that you hold onto one set of keys. I will lock Rose's set in the safe for now . . . Ah! That may be a problem.'

It was only then that Katie took a good look around the room, and what she saw made her gasp. She'd been so intent on explaining why she had two sets of shop keys that she hadn't noticed her surroundings. Now she saw that the filing cabinets had been pulled open and ransacked. The safe, where Rose placed important paperwork as well as the takings until such time as she was able to visit the bank, was wide open, and its contents were spread all over the floor. 'Oh no! This is terrible,' she cried. 'Isn't it bad enough that we are at war, without people stealing from each other?'

'Do not distress yourself, Mrs Jones. I have been reliably informed by my superiors that crime tends to rise during wartime. You and I find this despicable, but many do not. All I can advise at this time is that we stay vigilant – and that you ask yourself who else was about when you locked up the premises and left last night. No doubt the police will wish to speak to you, but you are not a suspect, and neither is Miss Douglas.'

'But Rose's keys?'

'Pure coincidence. Now, I'll leave you to get on with your work. Your pay will be made up to that of temporary manageress while Rose is incapacitated.'

Katie nodded her head and thanked the area manager before hurrying to the staffroom to give the Nippies and kitchen staff their orders for the day. Her head was filled with thoughts of who had burgled the teashop and how much money had been taken – not to mention why they would target the shop, rather than any other business in Margate.

'Blimey, I picked the right day to start a late shift. What's the copper doing out the front?' Lily said as Katie followed her into the staffroom so that she could change into her uniform. 'I take it they've put you in charge while Rose is off work?'

Katie couldn't help but laugh. Lily was always firing off questions without waiting for an answer. 'Yes, I'm a temporary manageress until Rose is back on her feet. To answer your other question, we were burgled last night.'

'Blooming heck. Do you think they hid in here while we locked up?'

'No, we both checked the building together, remember?'

'They could have been in the cellar,' Lily suggested as she checked the seams of her stockings before going to the small mirror on the wall to top up her red lipstick.

'But I locked the door from up here, so anyone down in the cellar would still be locked in. Mr Grant wants to speak to you as soon as you are ready. I'll come in with you,' she said, before quickly updating Lily with what she'd learnt so far. 'I've got a funny feeling about this, but I have no idea why . . . Why are you looking at me like that? You know I get these hunches from time to time.'

'There's no time to tell you now – all I'll say is, we didn't find those keys in the cemetery. Come on, let's go chat to Mr Grant. And don't be nervous, we've done nothing wrong.'

Lily strode through the teashop with Katie trailing behind, just as she'd done in their school days, hurrying to keep up with her two friends: Lily the hot-headed one and Rose the maternal one. Katie had always kept her light under a bushel, although of the three girls she was the most sensible one, thinking first before acting on her decisions.

'Come in, ladies, and take a seat,' Mr Grant said as he wiped his mouth on a napkin. 'Mrs Jones, you must convey my appreciation to your kitchen staff. The Welsh rarebit was delicious.'

'I will, thank you,' she said, daring not look at Lily. Her friend was of the opinion that their area manager was working his way through the Lyons tariff card.

'Miss Douglas, I take it Mrs Jones has explained about our burglary.'

'Just a brief outline while I was putting on my uniform and Mrs Jones inspected me,' Lily said. 'I must say I was shocked. Whoever would want to burgle a teashop? May I ask how much money was taken?'

'You may. Very little money was taken. Rose – that is, Miss Neville – keeps scrupulous records. Notes and coins were bagged and banded and placed at the back of the safe, with the bank deposit book completed. From there, fifty pounds is missing. From the metal drawer where the teashop float is kept, we have lost another ten pounds. If you would be so kind as to check my calculations, Mrs Jones, you will see that the thief left behind over one hundred pounds. Most strange,' he muttered to himself.

They watched while Katie checked the figures. She asked Lily to count the bags of money, and together they confirmed their boss's calculations were correct. 'I agree, sir, it is most strange.'

'Mr Grant,' Lily interrupted, 'may I explain what happened when Miss Dalrymple and I went to look for Rose's keys?'

'There's no need, as I would think whoever picked them up after Rose dropped them threw them back after the robbery,' he said, as if he'd already made his mind up what had happened.

'Can I ask why the door was damaged if the thief, or thieves, had Rose's set of keys?' Katie asked.

'The police are of the impression that the door was damaged to make us believe the thieves did not have a door key. However, they must have done, as the safe door was not damaged in any way. The police wondered if Rose had accidentally left the safe door open, and the thieves took the opportunity to snatch some money.'

Katie looked thoughtful as Lily spoke out. 'Pretty poor thieves not to have taken all the money, eh?'

'Perhaps they were interrupted. Was there an air raid last night?' he asked.

'No, not after we left. But Mr Grant, it was me that locked the safe last night and I checked twice that it was locked properly, just as Rose taught me,' Katie said, close to tears. 'I'd not do anything as stupid as to not check everything was locked up.'

'I believe you, Mrs Jones; please do not distress yourself. I'm going to inform the police that it was an opportunist thief who snatched the keys, and in his haste to return them to the cemetery he didn't take all the cash. The paperwork in the safe, along with Miss Neville's private papers that we allow her to keep there, seem to be intact. So in my mind, it is simply an opportunistic theft.'

Katie and Lily shook their heads. 'Sir, are you sure?' Katie asked, but was ignored.

'Run along, ladies. And Mrs Jones – I'd like to see you before I leave.'

'Sir?'

'It's nothing to be concerned about, Mrs Jones; I simply wish to discuss you taking on the Ramsgate teashop as manageress when it reopens in December. Are you ready for the challenge?'

'Yes, sir – thank you, sir,' Katie beamed. As they left the office, she beckoned to Lily to follow her. Ignoring calls for their attention from the other Nippies, the two girls made their way quickly back to the staffroom and collapsed into chairs. 'I never expected that,' Katie said delightedly.

'Neither did I; the silly old bugger's got it all wrong,' Lily spat out.

'What, you don't think I'm capable of being manageress of the Ramsgate teashop?'

'No, I mean he didn't listen to me. Me and Mildred came across the keys in Eileen and Gerald's hotel room. I reckon they were in here – but it wasn't for the money. They took that money to make it look like a burglary. But what were they really after?'

Katie frowned. 'It must have been something in Rose's papers. She kept her personal bits in there, just in case our house was damaged or caught fire in a raid.'

'Well, we can't bother Rose while she is poorly; and Flora is up to her eyes with work and doesn't need the extra worry right now.'

The girls looked at each other. 'Mildred!'

16

Miss Tibbs raised her eyebrows but said nothing as Flora served tea in her best teapot and cups to John Bentley. She would take her own cup and slip away to give them time alone. It was time Flora had a little romance in her life, rather than constantly looking after the motley crew who lived at Sea View.

'Would you like a biscuit, Miss Tibbs? They are quite fresh; Joyce made a batch yesterday while I was at the hospital visiting Rose.'

'I can recommend them,' John said, taking a second.

'I won't, thank you. Perhaps later. I want to get back to my room and complete an inventory of my sewing threads. I have a feeling we will all be very busy making someone's trousseau before too long,' she smiled. 'I do love a Christmas wedding. I'll bid you goodbye now, Mr Bentley, in case you leave before I come down again.'

John stood up and helped Miss Tibbs with the door. 'What a pleasant lady she is,' he said as he took his seat. 'You seem to have a charming group of guests staying here.'

Flora smiled. 'They drive me up the wall sometimes

when they fall out. Miss Tibbs and Anya can quarrel over nothing at times, but they are good souls. With Lady Diana living here, everyone seems to have mellowed. She can charm the birds from the trees, that one.'

'And remain a formidable woman at the same time. No one would dare cross her. I once found myself driving her all the way to Scotland after her train broke down. Scotland!' he exclaimed good-naturedly.

Flora chuckled. 'I'm pleased she will be my daughter's mother-in-law. Rose will be moving in different circles once the war is over, and I know Diana will guide her and see she does well.'

'Did I hear right that you knew her when you were young girls?'

'That was a lifetime ago, but yes: we both trod the boards, and were on nodding terms. She was top of the bill in the variety halls as one of the Desmond Sisters, while I was in the chorus most of the time. They were happy days, but I'd not do it again for all the tea in China. I'm content with my lot here in Ramsgate.'

'You seem contented,' he said, a fleeting smile crossing his face as he looked at her.

'Goodness, that makes me sound so boring,' Flora said, feeling flustered at being watched so closely.

'There's a lot to be said for contentment. I'd settle for that any day of the week.'

'Rather than rushing about the country chauffeuring people in your posh cars?'

He shrugged his shoulders. 'It's a living.'

Flora sipped her tea as she thought about his job. 'Don't think I'm being nosy, but how do you manage for petrol?'

John reached into the inside pocket of his jacket and pulled out an official-looking card. 'My business has several special clients, Lord McDouglas being just one of them. Occasionally it is possible to do the odd trip for family members of my clients.' He gave her a grin that almost melted her heart. 'Did you think I was on the fiddle?'

'Good grief, of course I didn't. Whatever do you take me for? Gosh, I've never felt so embarrassed in all my life. I'm sorry I even asked.' Flora didn't know where to put her face, such was her mortification. Her feelings were all over the place. Above anything else, she so admired this man; his very presence had her acting like a lovesick young woman. Then to make it sound as though she thought he was on the fiddle . . . Trying to rise above her emotions, she looked him in the eye. 'Be assured I've never taken you to be the type of person who flouts the rationing laws. It is something of which I do not approve.'

'I never thought you did,' he smiled, enjoying her discomfort. 'Do you always turn that shade of pink when you are embarrassed?'

'Why, I . . .' Flora was lost for words, instead putting her hands to her cheeks. They did feel warm.

'It's a very attractive colour,' he said, turning as the kitchen door opened. Mildred bustled into the room carrying a box, which she plonked onto the table.

'I need to leave this and go over to Margate. Lily and Katie want to speak to me. Goodness knows what for. There's some fresh fish in there, and Joe at the pub gave me a bag of loose tea in exchange for some cod. I'd best dash,' she said, giving John a nod and disappearing as quickly as she had come.

Flora and John looked for a moment at the box she had left on the table before glancing at each other, and both began to laugh. Flora wiped her eyes as their laughter subsided. 'Oh dear, I am sorry. We do drink rather a lot of tea in this house.'

John waved off her words. 'And I can always spare some petrol to take a charming lady for a drive. I'm here until tomorrow to pick up Rose and escort her home – Lady Diana's orders,' he explained, as she started to protest. 'Would you like to join me after Rose is settled?'

'That would be delightful. Joyce will be home to care for Daisy, and I'm not on fire-watch duties until the evening. Thank you, John. I'd like that very much.'

Mildred entered the Margate teashop, looking round for Katie and Lily. When she'd dropped the fresh fish in to Captain's Cottage, Mrs Nichols had been most insistent that she should go straight to the teashop and see them as soon as she'd finished her work. It was clearly important – Katie had telephoned and made sure Mrs Nichols wrote the message down in case she forgot.

In her haste to find out what was wrong, Mildred had not even stopped to have a wash at Sea View. Knowing her work clothes would be a tad whiffy, she took herself to the corner of the teashop, away from the late afternoon diners. A Nippy approached, so she ordered cheese sandwiches and tea before asking if the girl would let Katie know she was in the teashop. She'd hardly stirred her tea when Lily arrived and sat down at her table.

'Thanks for coming, Mildred.'

'How could I refuse, after such an intriguing message?' Mildred said, as a plate of sandwiches was placed in front of her. 'What's the mystery?'

'The teashop was broken into some time after me and Katie locked up last night. I tried to explain to Mr Grant that we found the keys, but he didn't listen to me. He couldn't think past someone picking up the keys in the cemetery, and then throwing them back there after they'd burgled the shop.'

'But we found them in the hotel room,' Mildred frowned before biting into her sandwich.

'I know – and try as I might to tell him, he still thought his idea was correct. Surely the thief would have taken all the cash from the safe, rather than the little that was gone?'

'It's possible they were disturbed by someone or something and scarpered,' Mildred said, 'but then that doesn't explain the keys we picked up in the hotel. My gut tells me that Gerald and Eileen, after taking the keys and letting themselves into the teashop, would not have left that cash behind. From what we've seen of them, it's obvious his life revolves around money – look at how he harps on about Eileen having her rightful share of Sea View. He seems fixated on it, and his wife isn't much better. I've not noticed her being excited about meeting Rose, or inviting her to get to know them more. Why, she never even shed a tear when we thought Rose could have died. The relationship – what there is of it – seems to be very one-sided.'

Lily was thoughtful as she watched Mildred eating her sandwiches. 'There's more in this, and I can't quite put my finger on it.'

'Where's Katie?'

'In the office, clearing up. Whoever came into the teashop uninvited made a right mess. I've no idea why, when the money was easy to find.'

'Can we go and take a look?'

Lily nodded. 'Of course, but I can't see why looking at a mess will help.' She nodded to the Nippy serving Mildred's table to indicate that her friend was not legging it without paying, and led Mildred through to the office. Katie was on her hands and knees, sorting through paperwork.

'What a mess,' Mildred said as she bent over to help Katie pile the paperwork onto the desk.

Katie greeted her with a kiss on the cheek. 'Did Lily tell you what has happened?' she said as she piled the last of the loose papers onto the desk.

'Yes, and it is most puzzling. I can confirm that I picked up those keys from the side table in Gerald and Eileen's hotel room. Going by what we interrupted, they would have been there a little while – so it would have been a rushed visit here.'

'That makes sense,' Lily agreed. 'I did notice earlier, when we were in here with Mr Grant, that some of the papers were the property of Rose and not Joe Lyons.'

'Well, we knew Rose had permission to keep some paperwork in the safe as it could have been lost or damaged at home. I just need to put everything in the right piles,' Katie said, 'and then Rose can look at it all when she returns to work.'

'Do you think that's what Gerald and Eileen were after, but they made their visit look more like a break-in?' Mildred asked, looking more closely at the paperwork.

'I've had the same thought,' Lily said. 'What if Rose keeps the legal stuff here for Sea View?'

Mildred nodded. 'They are called the deeds. You girls have a set for Captain's Cottage. Would they be kept here as well?'

'No, those are in a biscuit tin down in the Anderson shelter. We thought they'd be best kept there,' Katie answered.

'A direct hit would destroy them. Perhaps I should have them kept in a safe deposit box at my bank; I could do the same for anything else you don't want to lose? I'd defy Hitler and his chums to destroy anything that's down in the bank's vault.'

'That's decent of you, Mildred. Do you think we should sort out Rose's paperwork and do the same with that? I'd hate to see that pair make a return visit and take anything else – not that they have the keys anymore.' Katie chewed her fingernail as she thought about the situation. 'Perhaps they'd be that desperate they would cause more damage, and not just make a show of damaging the front door to pretend they'd broken in.'

Lily shuddered. 'What a horrid pair – and to think that Rose made them so welcome when they visited.'

'Don't forget, we may be wrong,' Mildred reminded them. 'We need more evidence. Would it be all right to sort through this lot now, or is Mr Grant due back?'

'He's not due back for a couple of days. He told me in my interview,' Katie said with a smile.

Lily slapped her hand to her mouth. 'Sorry, with all this going on I forgot to ask how it went.'

Katie chuckled. 'There's no need to apologize. You are now looking at the next manageress of the Ramsgate teashop,' she grinned. 'Who'd have thought it? I can't wait to write to Jack and let him know.'

Lily screeched with delight, grabbing Katie and swinging her round in the small office. Mildred gave her congratulations by slapping Katie on her back. 'Under the circumstances, you should get yourself out into this teashop and do whatever it is a manageress has to do. Lily and I will sort this lot out for you – we'll see if we can make sense of what Rose left here.'

'All right, I'll do that; but don't you think we should speak to Rose and let her know what has happened?'

Both girls watched Mildred while she thought for a few seconds. 'Am I right that Mr Grant and the police think it was a random burglary – and Mr Grant didn't think it was worth telling them about the spare set of keys?'

'No, he dismissed what I tried to tell him. I've put the keys in Rose's desk drawer for now.'

'Good; then let's not worry Rose. There's no need to alarm her while she is poorly. It's best she gets well and spends her time thinking about that Christmas wedding. Shall we make this our secret while we do our utmost to find the truth behind this new family of hers? If we go pointing the finger and we are wrong, it would cause too much heartbreak at Sea View and we could lose a friend in the process.'

'But we aren't wrong, are we?' Lily asked. 'I'd lay my life on that couple being behind all this.'

'Me too, and we aren't going to let them get away with it,' Katie agreed. Leaving the office to concentrate on running the teashop, she reminded Lily to lock the door behind her so that they could work in peace.

'Where to start?' Lily asked, looking at the papers heaped on the desk.

'I suggest we make three piles. Anything that is obviously related to Lyons, we place in one pile for Katie to go through. Any paperwork that looks like it's Rose's personal business, we can put on this chair to be taken home – and anything we aren't sure of, let's just leave here on the desk for now. We can ask Katie if she recognizes it.'

Lily nodded and set to checking each sheet of paper, envelope and handwritten note. Gradually, two heaps grew, with only a few pieces of paper in the third. Neither spoke as they sorted and sifted.

'I think that's it,' Mildred said as she leant back in her seat. 'Can you put that pile into the safe? Then Katie can lock up when she comes back in. What do you have there?' she added, as Lily held out a smaller piece of paper that looked like a receipt. 'An address in London . . . and something I can't read. What do you make of it?'

'I wonder if this fell out of Gerald's pocket while he was rummaging around,' Lily said. 'It's a landlord's receipt, and most certainly nothing to do with Lyons teashops or Rose's personal business.'

'I'll hold onto it for now,' Mildred decided, slipping it into the pocket of her overalls. 'Now I'll put Rose's bits and bobs in order. I may be able to tell if anything is missing that ought to be there.'

'I'll let Katie know how we're doing, and get you a drink. I don't know what we would do without you, Mildred,' Lily said, giving her friend a kiss on the cheek. 'You are just like a mum to me and Katie,' she grinned as she hurried away.

Mildred had never felt prouder as she started to put Rose's personal papers in some kind of order. These girls were like family to her, and she'd not see a hair on their heads harmed. She'd do anything to keep them safe, legal or not.

'Come on in, Vicar. What a lovely surprise,' Flora exclaimed, as Lady Diana ushered the vicar ahead of her into the kitchen.

'I found him on the doorstep,' Lady Diana said as she removed her coat and said greeted John Bentley, before introducing him to the Reverend Dunlop.

'What must you think of me, greeting visitors in my kitchen!' Flora fussed. 'It won't take me more than a minute or so to light the fire in the front room, and then we can sit and chat more comfortably,' she said.

'No, Mrs Neville, I'd not hear of it,' the vicar said, indicating for them all to sit down. 'I always find the kitchen is the heart of the home. And it's close to the kettle,' he said as Flora hurried to place it back on the hob, giving John a smile as she did so. Thank goodness Mildred had dropped off those extra packets of tea only a few hours earlier.

'It's such a shame that Rose is not yet home from hospital, as she would have loved to talk with you about the wedding. I assume you received Ben's letter?' Flora asked. She knew that Ben couldn't wait to have the vicar pencil them in for a Christmas Day wedding, and had dropped a note through the letterbox of the vicarage after visiting Rose in hospital.

'Most certainly, and it is marked in my diary. Three o'clock on the twenty-fifth of December. I hope the bride-to-be will be fighting fit by then?' he smiled.

'Most certainly she will, Reverend. From what we've been told, she will be released from hospital this very afternoon. John here will be collecting her as soon as Ben rings to let us know.'

'Ah, to have a motor vehicle at one's disposal,' the vicar said. 'My car is now without wheels and up on bricks for the duration, and I have to rely on my trusty bicycle.'

Flora felt embarrassed by the ostentatious vehicle parked in front of Sea View, but it didn't seem to worry Diana, who brushed away his comment with a wave of her hand. 'We cut back as much as we can, Reverend, but my husband's work with the Ministry of Food means he has to travel at such inconvenient hours, we could not be without a vehicle. However, like yours, our own car has been put into storage and we use the excellent services of John Bentley here.' She gave John one of her most charming smiles. 'I take it you will be able to transport the bride on the day of her wedding, John?'

'Oh no, it wouldn't be fair to take John away from his family at Christmas,' Flora cried. 'Oh my – there is so much to plan, and only weeks to do it in. Thank goodness everything is organized for the concert and we have no need to worry about that – apart from hoping all the tickets are sold and everyone remembers their parts.'

'Ah, that was one of my reasons for coming to see you. I'm afraid there is a problem with you using the church hall on that day,' the vicar said, looking rather ashamed.

The kettle started to whistle on the hob, giving time

for Flora to take a few deep breaths to calm herself before she started to ask questions. Whatever had happened to prevent them using the church hall? Filling her larger teapot, she covered it with a knitted tea cosy and carried it to the table, while Diana had laid out clean cups and saucers and found the remaining biscuits. Sitting down, Flora again composed herself and looked the vicar straight in the eye. 'Please tell me what the problem is?' she said.

'It is rather embarrassing,' he said, running a finger around his neck as if his dog collar was too tight. 'One of the ladies who uses the hall has overruled the use of it for –' he looked down at a notebook he held in his hand – 'she has overruled the use of the hall for frivolous entertainment.'

'Frivolous? We are raising funds for local people who are affected by the war. Some of the money will go to the orphanage where our Katie was brought up, so that the kiddies can have some treats from Father Christmas. Please tell me how that is deemed frivolous?' Flora demanded, losing her temper. 'I thought we were all supposed to pull together during wartime, but some busybody is trying to stop us doing something good for our community. I really don't believe it,' she finished, as John reached out and squeezed her hand for support.

'It is Councillor Mould, isn't it?' Lady Diana said.

The vicar nodded. 'I'm sorry, but she wields a lot of power on the council and in this town. If I were a braver man, I'd stand up to her, but I have a position and a family to think of.'

'It's not your fault, Vicar. I dared to stand up to her, and have brought this all upon myself as a result. No doubt this means she has also thwarted my attempts to foster and ultimately adopt Daisy?' Flora said, looking to Diana, who was shaking her head in horror.

'Flora, my dear, I honestly thought we'd put paid to this nasty woman. If my interfering has in any way stopped Daisy becoming part of your family, I can only apologize.'

John took charge of pouring and handing out tea while the ladies composed themselves.

Reverend Dunlop was silent until handed his tea. 'Perhaps I can be of some assistance with your problem,' he said, looking down into his cup rather than at Flora. 'I shouldn't really say, but I too have positions on several committees in this area of Kent. It goes with the job.' He smiled at the ladies. 'I was able to put in a good word for your application to take the child into your family. As you know, it can be a long process, but in our current state of war some things are speeded up. Several days ago, the committee agreed to your application. No doubt there will be a letter delivered to you shortly. Only one committee person disagreed; she was not happy to be overruled. It was the next day that your use of the church hall was questioned and blocked.'

Lady Diana hugged Flora as she sat there letting the news sink in. 'My dear, this is excellent news, thank you,' she said to the vicar, before hurrying round the table and hugging him, much to his surprise.

'I can't believe it,' Flora said, still stunned from the news. 'I feared I had lost the child.'

'And we haven't lost the concert, either. I have an idea which means that *Flora's Follies* will entertain the town and be bigger and better than anything we could have run in a church hall. I just need to make a telephone call. Sorry, Vicar,' Lady Diana said as she spotted the smile slip from his face. 'I meant no offence. I simply can't let that woman beat us.'

'Not at all,' Reverend Dunlop said as he helped himself to a biscuit. 'The church choir is at your disposal, as is my family. Between you and me, my dear wife calls her Councillor Mouldy and won't have her in the vicarage,' he said, giving them a crafty wink.

Flora suppressed a giggle at the vicar's comment, instead trying the change the topic. 'Oh my, it's going to be a wonderful Christmas,' she beamed at John.

'It certainly will, and I'll be here to help make sure everything runs smoothly,' he smiled, raising his cup to toast her. 'To a very happy Christmas.'

As they topped up their cups and chatted about the wedding, Lady Diana slipped away to the hall to use the telephone. In some ways she wished she was at home in London where she could use her own telephone, as it was essential for arranging her appointments and commitments. She made a mental note to compensate Flora for the many times she'd used the instrument. Lifting the receiver, she thanked her lucky stars that there was a tone and started to ring the number listed in the notebook she always kept in her pocket. 'Ah, hello Charles, it is Lady Diana here. I wonder if I could throw myself on your mercy . . .'

As she replaced the receiver and closed her notebook, the front door opened. Standing on the doorstep was her son, with a pale-looking Rose on his arm. 'Darlings, John was going to collect you. Why did you not let us know?'

'There was a taxi-cab dropping off a visitor, so we decided it would be quicker,' Ben explained, helping Rose inside and closing the door. 'Where is everyone?'

'In the kitchen, drinking tea with the vicar. Come on through; we have so much to tell you,' she said, kissing Rose's cheek and helping her off with her coat.

A cheer went up as Rose entered the kitchen. Flora could see how tired her daughter looked, and insisted that once she'd had a cup of tea she would be packed off to bed with a hot-water bottle. They were soon chatting about the wedding. Reverend Dunlop came into his own as he imparted his knowledge of weddings and what was required when organizing such an event – not only at short notice, but also during a time when most people were celebrating Christmas.

'Of course, for the bride the most important decision would be her wedding gown,' he said, looking between Rose and Flora. 'I take it you have matters in hand? I recall my wife thought of nothing else for months when our eldest daughter named the day.'

'I'd not given it much thought, as we've not long known that Ben would have three days' leave for the wedding,' Rose said.

'I'll be arriving on the afternoon of Christmas Eve and must be back the day after Boxing Day,' Ben said. 'We shall have to have our honeymoon another time.'

'The war comes first,' Rose said. 'I'm just so pleased we can fit a wedding in around Ben's work.'

'Why not have a short honeymoon in London? You can use the flat and be alone until Ben rejoins his regiment,' Lady Diana suggested.

'I'll drive you there after the reception and do any running around that's required before the big day,' John Bentley offered.

'That's very kind of you, John,' Flora smiled. 'It won't be a big affair. Just family and a few friends, and of course we include you in the guest list. Will your father be here to join us, Ben?'

'I sincerely hope so,' Diana said before Ben could answer. 'It's not every day one of our children gets married. Ruth will have to fit us in around her social engagements as well,' she said as she started to write in her notebook.

'Heaven knows where I will find room for everyone,' Flora said, knowing that most rooms in the house were now taken by her long-term tenants.

Diana looked up from where she was making notes. 'Do not worry about my family. I will book rooms for us all at a hotel so that we are out of your hair for the few days before the wedding. What about the reception and the bridesmaids?' she asked.

'I was thinking about that while I was lying awake in my hospital bed,' Rose said, finally managing to get a word in. 'I'm going to ask Mr Grant if we can use the Ramsgate teashop for the reception; as long as it doesn't sustain more bomb damage between now and Christmas, that is. The teashop will be closed to the public that day in any case. I might even be able to pay some of the Nippies to work for a few hours – that would take the pressure off Mum doing all the work, as I know she was thinking of inviting everyone back here.'

'It sounds perfect,' Flora beamed.

'I agree,' Lady Diana said. 'It means that after all the excitement of *Flora's Follies* you won't be rushing about arranging a wedding breakfast,' she said.

Flora frowned. 'What do you mean? We no longer have use of the church hall for the performance, and if we found somewhere else that would be weeks before the wedding.'

Amid cries of 'That's a shame!' from Ben and Rose, along with the vicar voicing that he thought Lady Diana understood the situation, she gave a loud cough and requested silence from those present. 'I made a telephone call to a friend just before Rose and Ben arrived. We have use of the Winter Gardens theatre for one evening. There's no cost to us,' she said, seeing Flora about to speak. 'There is just one small problem: we have to change the date.'

'I don't feel we can be ready any sooner – I'm not sure Rose is up to performing at the moment,' Flora said, looking worried.

Diana brushed away her concerns with a gesture. 'We have the venue for December the twenty-third – so there is plenty of time for rehearsals,' she smiled, oblivious to the groans around the table.

Rose tried to object when she saw that she'd been given her mother's bed, but Flora pointed out she was more than comfortable on the small put-you-up in the corner of the room. 'I want you to rest and get your strength back. As you can see I've moved the crib from the corner and Daisy is settled in with Joyce for now. When you are ready you can return to work and living at Captain's

Cottage. Until then, you do as I say,' she reprimanded her, albeit with a smile and a hug. 'When you feel up to it, we can chat about your gown and the bridesmaids. Have you made any decisions?' she couldn't help asking, even though she could see Rose was close to falling asleep.

'The children, I suppose, and also Lily and Katie. It is such a shame my new baby sister will be too young, but I'm so happy she will be staying with us. I know how much it means to you.'

'Oh my goodness,' Flora exclaimed. 'I've just realized that not only will I be a mother to a young child – but soon, with you marrying, I could be a grandmother!'

Two weeks later

'Are we all ready?' Lady Diana asked, ushering Anya, Mildred and Flora out the door of Sea View to where John Bentley was waiting by his Rolls-Royce, resplendent in his chauffeur's uniform. 'Do you have everything you need for the trip?' she added. 'We have so much to do in London – we can't turn around and come back if you've forgotten anything.'

Anya gave a curt nod, and Flora lifted her handbag to show she hadn't forgotten anything. Mildred simply smiled, feeling uncomfortable out of her overalls. She was wearing a tweed suit that had been in mothballs for more years that she cared to remember.

'Flora, would you like to sit in the front with John?'

Flora gave John a quick smile, which he returned. They'd spent several afternoons together since going out for a drive earlier in the month. He'd even spent time on fire-watching duties, and down in the tunnels during a raid. 'If you don't mind, I'll travel with you in the back, Diana? Mildred, why don't you sit with John? You must have lots of questions about this wonderful vehicle. We are so very lucky to be able to travel in such style.'

'Thank goodness,' Anya muttered. 'The mothballs are almost as bad as the fish, and with me in a delicate condition it is not good. I do have paper bags in case I am sick,' she added, checking her bag to be sure.

Flora grinned at Diana as they all climbed aboard, and John started the engine. Joyce, holding Daisy, waved them off from the doorstep.

'How long will it take to reach London?' Anya asked.

'A couple of hours – but we may have to stop if there is an air raid,' John called over his shoulder. 'Let me know if you need to stop at any time, as I can find a public house for you to use their facilities.'

'I would prefer to get to London as soon as possible, to speak to Ruth. You said she may have news for me?' Anya said.

Lady Diana nodded slowly. 'I assume everyone in this car knows not to talk about this at any time – Ruth could get into serious trouble if it becomes known she used her position and contacts to find out about Henio. I would have preferred to go to Biggin Hill, as Anya suggested, and ask directly. I have contacts in high places,' she said, seeing Mildred give her a disparaging look. 'However, with the concert and the wedding to arrange, we are running out of time, and Anya needs to know about her husband. Ruth says that if we meet at my apartment for midday, she may be able to advise you. I have arranged for lunch to be laid on, and then we can all go our own ways to complete our errands. We will meet back at four o'clock to return to Ramsgate. Does this suit everyone?'

'Thank you,' Anya said. 'I need to know what has happened to Henio. Then I can accept my fate and plan for my future with my child.'

They fell quiet until Mildred said, 'I will forgo lunch, thank you very much, as I may be a while looking up an old friend.'

'And I will have to go to my business premises and check everything's been ticking over while I've been away. Lunch would have been nice. Perhaps another time?' John said.

'Then it will be just the three of us. After lunch, perhaps we can leave Anya with Ruth and do some shopping, Flora? I have a few surprises for Rose. There should also be a box that was brought down from our home in Scotland. If you like what you see, we can take it back with us to Ramsgate.'

Flora nodded in agreement. Diana had come up trumps finding outfits for the performers to wear for *Flora's Follies*. Hopefully she'd laid her hands on a few more, as they were short on uniforms from the last war for their own performance.

They travelled in silence for most of the journey, passing mainly army trucks. Only once were they flagged down, as they approached the outer limits of south-east London, for John to show his travel papers.

Mildred studied a map as the route became more built up. 'If you want to drop me along here somewhere, that'll be fine,' she said to John as they reached Tower Bridge Road. 'What I have to do will only take a couple of hours, and I'll get to your place before four so won't hold you up.' Thanking them all for the lift, she climbed out of her comfortable seat.

Watching the car disappear from view, she turned to look at the address written on the receipt she'd found in amongst the paperwork in Rose's office safe.

'Here, can you help me?' she asked a couple of women passing her on the street. 'Do you know where I can find number seventy-four?'

She looked to where one of them pointed, and raised her eyebrows. Mildred was no snob, but this was not what she'd expected: a block of flats over three floors, with many of the windows boarded up and tiles missing from the roof.

'Cheers,' she said as she crossed the road and climbed an external staircase to the second floor, where she could see a glimpse of the Thames – and smell it as well. Not a patch on the sea at her beloved Ramsgate. Wrinkling her nose, she hammered on the door of number seventy-four and waited. After a couple of minutes' wait, she knocked again.

'They're not there, ducks,' called out a woman who was beating a rug over the balcony wall.

'Do you know when they are expected back?' Mildred said, annoyed. If she'd come all this way trussed up in her tweeds not to find who she was looking for, she'd be none too happy.

'Ooh, I doubt they'll be back. She told me in no uncertain terms she was done with this place. If you pop down the George, they may well know where she's gone. If she wasn't doing a shift for them, she was propping up the bar,' the woman said helpfully, turning to go back indoors.

'A barmaid, is she?' Mildred asked, feeling as though all was not lost.

The woman roared with laughter. 'Her a barmaid? No, love. She calls herself a cleaner. But you'd not think so, looking at the state of her own place.'

Mildred made her thanks and headed back across the road in the direction the woman had pointed out. She soon found the pub and, pushing open the door into a cheery atmosphere, was surprised at how many people were there considering it was the middle of the day. In a corner a woman was playing the piano and belting out well-known songs. Mildred pushed her way through the crowd and ordered herself a half pint of mild. She stayed at the bar, rather than moving to the seats at tables that seemed to be occupied by the womenfolk. 'You've got a nice place here,' she said as the landlord put the drink in front of her and slid her change across the bar.

'We like it,' he said, picking up the newspaper he'd put down before serving her. 'I've not seen you in here before?'

'I'm visiting the area, looking up some old friends I'd lost touch with,' she said, not wanting to give too much away.

'What are their names? They may drink in here,' he asked, putting his paper down ready for a chat.

Mildred froze for a moment – had she been told their surname? 'It's been a while, and I knew my friend as a Sykes. I was told she got married, and his name is Gerald, but I'll be blowed if I can remember his surname,' she answered, giving herself a secret thumbs up for thinking on her feet.

'You've most certainly come to the right place. They both worked here until a couple of months ago. He was our pot man, and she cleaned for us.'

'Blimey, that's a bit of luck,' Mildred said, praying that they wouldn't walk in the door anytime soon and catch her out. What would she do if that was the case? 'Where do you think I could find them?'

He scratched his balding head for a moment before calling over to a short woman. 'Here, Doll – what 'appened to Gerry and his missus? This lady is asking after them. Seems she knew her way back and is paying a visit.'

'They had a bit of luck,' the woman said, coming over to join him. 'It seems her half-sister passed away, and she inherited the family guesthouse down in Ramsgate. Told me I could take the kids to visit once she'd settled in. Mind you, from what I've heard, they've had it as bad as we have up here,' she tutted. 'This bloody war is a bugger for folk. I'll be glad when it's over.'

Mildred made the right noises while feeling extremely worried. 'I'm sorry to hear that. Which of her relatives died?'

'Hmm, she did say . . . I know it's a flower. Rose, yes, it was Rose. Seems they hadn't met for years, as the woman's mother was a tyrant who had split up the family.'

'Was this long ago?'

'Now let me think . . . three months, I'd say.'

Mildred had to bite her lip. Instead she finished her drink and gave them a smile. 'Perhaps I'll give her a look up when I'm down that way. Sea View guesthouse, you say? Many thanks,' she nodded, turning away. Behind her she heard the woman say, 'But I never told her the name of the place.'

She hurried from the pub, jumping on the first bus she

saw heading into town in case they followed her outside to question her. She could have kicked herself for being so stupid. However, why were Eileen and Gerald telling people they'd inherited Sea View – and worse still, that Rose had died? She'd keep her discovery from Flora and Rose for the moment; with only a couple of weeks until the wedding, she wouldn't wish to frighten them. The couple had vanished after the teashop burglary, so perhaps they'd been scared off and she'd hear no more from them.

'My, that was a tasty lunch,' Flora said as she dabbed her mouth with a linen napkin. 'You certainly know how to treat us. Anya, dear, you've hardly eaten. Did the car journey upset you that much?'

Anya shook her head and looked to Lady Diana. 'I am sorry, but I cannot eat a thing until I know what your daughter has to tell me about my Henio.'

'It is understandable. She should have been here ten minutes ago. I shall make sure we pack what is left. We can then have a picnic on our way home, if you feel like eating. Tell me, Anya – have you visited a doctor yet about your pregnancy?'

'Yes, there will be a child in May if all is well. You know I lost my last child while fleeing from my homeland after the Germans invaded? I will not let them take another from me. Whatever news your daughter has for me, I will hold onto my baby.'

Flora was unsure what to say. Anya deserved to have her child, and she prayed there would not be bad news.

'I will give her another ten minutes and then make a

call to her office. She should be here by now – she knows how important this is,' Lady Diana said, checking a dainty clock on the nearby sideboard as the hands steadily moved toward two o'clock.

'Perhaps something held her up at work,' Flora said, sticking up for the girl. 'I would think she must hold down an important position.'

'I would not wish the war to suffer because Ruth left her desk to speak to me,' Anya said. 'I can go to this Biggin place and find out for myself.'

'If it comes to that, I will accompany you,' Lady Diana said. 'As I told you before, I do know people who can help me. I'm not sure they will like me appearing in their office, but if I have the position in life to get people to listen, then I'll do it.'

Anya surprised them all by hurrying to Lady Diana and hugging her as tight as she could. There wasn't a dry eye around the table.

'What have I missed?' Ruth said as she entered the room and leant over the table to take a slice of chicken that she quickly demolished. 'I'm starving. We had a problem crop up with an operative going missing out in the field, so I wasn't able to leave any earlier. Sorry, I shouldn't have said that. Forget I spoke. Let's grab a cup of coffee and go into the lounge, shall we?' she said to Anya, who looked paler than usual.

'I'll have some fresh sent in,' Lady Diana said, as the two women left them.

'What do you think?' Flora asked as the door was closed and they were left alone.

'My daughter could play poker for a living. I have no

idea what she will tell Anya. Rather than sit here wondering, I want you to come through to my bedroom and see what I have to show you,' Diana said, holding her hand out for Flora to follow and at the same time asking the maid to send coffee to the other two women.

'I cannot believe you have all this and want to live at Sea View,' Flora remarked as she looked around at the opulence of the room.

'I want to be amongst friends and family. Besides, this means nothing to me,' Diana said, waving her arms around the room. 'Now, I want your opinion on this.' Opening her wardrobe, she pulled out a cream silk wedding gown.

'Oh my, this is gorgeous,' Flora said as she ran her fingers over the detailed embroidery on the bodice and the high, lacy neck. 'Is it yours?'

'Yes, it is just over thirty years old. I have a photograph somewhere,' Diana said, looking on her dressing table until she found an ornate silver-framed photograph. It showed her standing beside a man who looked remarkably like Ben.

'The apple didn't fall far from the tree there,' Flora said.

'I wondered if the apple's fiancée would like to wear the dress at her wedding? I don't want to step on anyone's toes, or force my opinions on what the bride-to-be should wear . . .'

'Why don't we take it to Ramsgate and ask her?' Flora said, knowing that Rose would fall in love with the gown. 'Will Ruth not wish to wear it when she marries?'

'Goodness, no. Ruth is one of those girls who does not stand on tradition; I doubt whether she will ever walk down the aisle. I did ask her, and she said that she would be happy to see Rose wear the gown, as long as she wasn't expected to walk behind the bride carrying flowers alongside Marina and Annabelle. She would rather act as best woman, and make sure her dear brother arrives on time and says "I do" at the right moment.'

Flora laughed. 'I'm sorry, I shouldn't laugh; but our children seem to know their own minds, more than we did at that age. I can see no reason why Rose would not love to wear the gown. What's that saying we keep being told – "Make do and mend"?'

'We shouldn't need to mend the gown, but Miss Tibbs may need to take it in slightly,' Lady Diana said as she looked at the side seams.

'You are a most generous woman,' Flora said as she flung her arms around Diana.

A tap on the door interrupted them. 'I've got to be off now,' Ruth said. 'You may wish to see to Anya. I've left her in a bit of a state. Toodle pip!' She hurried out of the flat.

'He is alive,' Anya sobbed as the two women hurried in to her. 'My Henio is not dead – he is helping with war effort on a project. Ruth would say no more than that. But it is enough. It is more than enough,' she cried, as Flora took her into her arms to soothe her and Lady Diana poured three large brandies to celebrate.

17

December 23rd 1940

'I thought the day would never come,' Flora said as she leant into the mirror in her dressing room and checked her make-up one more time.

'This feels just like it did when we trod the boards for a living.' Lady Diana smiled, joining her to check there wasn't a hair out of place.

'I'm not so sure about that. I wasn't so nervous back then – and I didn't have to worry about so many Thanet dignitaries sitting in the audience, waiting to be impressed.'

'Look at it this way. We've sold every single ticket, and no one is getting a penny back, even if the air-raid sirens go off and we have to take *Flora's Follies* to the tunnels,' Lady Diana grinned.

'You are incorrigible, Diana Desmond. Now, tell me, is everyone ready?'

Diana picked up her clipboard and began to read. 'Miss Tibbs and Joyce are ready with their sewing kits in case we have a wardrobe problem. Joyce is also in charge of the costumes, to make sure we put on the right outfits at the right time. Anya has all the children with her ready for their folk dance. Daisy and Mary are asleep in our dressing room, and Mildred is pulling the curtains up and down and making sure performers don't miss their cues.'

'What about Rose, Lily and Katie? Where are they?' Flora asked, her voice tinged with panic.

'They are by the side of the stage, as they will go on straight after Reverend Dunlop's choir. You ought to see them, Flora, they look the spitting image of the Andrews Sisters. They will go down a storm. All the other acts are backstage waiting to be called. Any other questions, or are you feeling calmer?'

'Does the mayor have the list to introduce the acts?'

'No, he's not doing it,' Diana said, suddenly busy packing her make-up into a bag.

'Then what . . . who . . . ?'

'A rather handsome man of our acquaintance who suddenly appeared wearing a dinner jacket and offered his services.'

'Ben? But he doesn't have leave until Christmas Eve, and that's two days away,' Flora said, shaking her head in disbelief.

'There are more handsome men in Ramsgate than just my son,' Diana laughed. 'Go and take a look from the wings.'

Flora did as she was told, and couldn't believe her eyes when she spotted John Bentley chatting to bandleader Silvano Caprice behind the closed curtain. Looking round, he spotted her and wandered over. 'Well, look at you,' he said, admiring her Edwardian dinner jacket and top hat. 'We look a right pair,' he smiled.

Flora felt herself blush. Why did this man affect her so? 'You ought to see Diana,' she said, forcing herself to look away from his gaze. 'I just wanted to say break a leg.'

'You too, and thank you for what you are doing for the town. Going by the crowd out there, you have raised an amazing amount of money for charity.'

'That's down to Diana. She had the local newspapers run articles on why we are doing this, and who is performing in the show. We sold umpteen tickets after that.'

Behind them, Mildred, who was checking her notes, froze as she overheard what Flora said. Had she heard right? Did that mean Sea View was empty and the world and its neighbour was aware – and Gerald and Eileen might come back to do damage? Ever since she'd removed Rose's paperwork from the Margate teashop, she'd worried that something had been stolen; but so as not to worry the girl over nothing, she'd kept quiet, deciding instead to keep an eye on Rose and to keep her safe. Many evenings she'd been about to give Rose a lift home and stay at Captain's Cottage if the girl was alone. Lily knew of Mildred's worry over the paperwork, but not the details of what she'd found out in London.

Now Mildred wondered who she should confide in, in case there was a problem at Sea View while the house was left empty. Peering through the curtains to look into the audience, she spotted one of the fishermen she worked alongside sitting in the front row of seats. Stepping briskly down the stairs at the side of the stage, she had a quick word. He promised to go at once to use the public telephone box outside the hall and ask his mate, who was on ARP duty, to keep an eye on Sea View, as it was known the house would be empty during the evening. Confident she had done her best to keep everything safe, Mildred went back to her work for the evening.

The show flew past in a blur, with the audience joining in with Christmas carols sung by Reverend Dunlop's choristers followed by Rose, Lily and Katie singing songs made popular by the Andrews Sisters. When Anya appeared with the youngsters dancing Polish polkas and singing a short song in her native tongue – with Marina going terribly wrong – the women in the audience sighed with sympathy, while the men tried hard not to laugh.

After a short interval with tea and biscuits (supplied by Lyons teashops and served by several of the Nippies), it was time for more entertainment. Silvano Caprice had his whole band on stage playing well-known dance music, which had many in the audience up and dancing in the aisles.

Everyone settled back into their seats as Silvano introduced Rose to the stage. This time wearing her best dance frock, with her hair styled by Lily to look like her idol Helen Forrest, Rose started to sing 'You Made Me Love You' as the lights dimmed, giving an intimate atmosphere. After a rousing cheer, she continued with 'Perfidia' and then 'Smoke Gets in Your Eyes'.

As the audience got to their feet to clap the talented singer, Silvano gave her a hug, pulling her close. 'Forget the chap you're marrying, and come away with me. I can make you a star,' he said.

With her back to the audience, she answered: 'But I love him, thanks all the same.'

John came back onto the stage to announce the final

act of the evening: Diana and Flora, with songs from their days in variety. The two women appeared from opposite sides of the stage and burst into song, starting with 'I'm Following in Father's Footsteps' and then 'The Man Who Broke the Bank at Monte Carlo'. Flora then sat down on the edge of the stage while Diana performed a medley of songs she'd made famous along with her siblings, the Desmond Sisters.

Flora moved to the front of the stage and encouraged the audience to join in with a medley of wartime songs, finishing with 'There'll Always Be an England', which was enhanced by the frantic waving of miniature flags that had been left on each seat.

The finale to the show was John calling on each act in turn to take a bow, after which everyone sang Vera Lynn's 'We'll Meet Again' before the audience all stood to join in with the National Anthem.

The curtains opened and closed three times before the audience fell quiet and headed for their homes, being careful not to let their torches alert the enemy to what a wonderful time the town had enjoyed that night.

'What a fantastic evening. And the icing on the cake was when I saw the mayor wagging his finger at Councillor Mould, and her looking quite downcast,' Rose said as she fussed about making sure everyone had a cup of cocoa once they reached Sea View and collapsed into chairs in the living room. Lily and Katie put the two babies into their cots while Joyce and Mildred led Marina, Annabelle and Pearl up to their beds. Jennie too went straight to bed.

'Everyone did so well,' Rose said to Mildred, as they

checked the blackout curtains in the bedrooms and the lower floors of the house. 'No one's going to forget *Flora's Follies* for a long time.'

Mildred nodded as she tugged at the kitchen window, and it flew open. 'This window wasn't shut properly,' she said as she secured the catch.

'But it was,' Joyce said, as she stood at the sink washing the pan they'd used to heat milk. 'I did it myself.'

Mildred frowned. Her worst fears washed over her. 'Can you spare me a minute?' she asked Joyce quietly, as Rose went back to join the others in the living room.

Joyce handed her a mug of cocoa and waved at her to sit down. 'You've had something on your mind for a while now. Spit it out, and I'll help if I can.'

Mildred poured everything out: from what she'd found after the teashop was burgled, to going to Eileen and Gerald's hotel room, and then her discovery in London.

'That fits in with what I overheard Douglas and Eileen muttering in the cemetery, when Rose was still trapped,' Joyce said thoughtfully.

Mildred sighed. 'Until we have proof that the couple are here and up to no good, I really don't want to worry anyone. Calling the police won't help at this stage, when everything is down to us putting two and two together and possibly making five.' She looked up at the clock as the hands ticked past midnight. 'It's Christmas Eve, and we have a wedding tomorrow. Thank goodness the girls are staying here tonight, and Flora is cooking a special meal for everyone's Christmas Eve dinner. That means we can easily keep an eye on Rose so nothing will happen to her.' Setting down her mug, she got to her feet. 'I'm going to check the other bedrooms in case there's been any disturbance. If there has, then we can call the police – but I fear whoever came through this window tonight was very careful. I just wish I knew what Gerald and Eileen were up to.'

Christmas Eve

Everyone was up late the next morning after the exertions of the night before. Rose, Lily and Katie had topped and tailed in Flora's bed, just like they used to as children staying over with Rose. Flora slept in the folding bed, which was still set up from when Rose had been injured, although she had brought Daisy back in with her.

Lily and Anya had to go in to work at the Margate teashop on a late shift, and hurriedly grabbed toast and tea before heading off. Rose wanted to help Katie now that she was manageress of the Ramsgate teashop, as they needed to prepare for the wedding breakfast.

'You're getting married tomorrow. Why not stay home and have a relaxing day?' Katie said. 'I'm perfectly capable of making sure everything is ready for the wedding once we close up. You want to be here when Ben arrives, don't you?'

Rose was torn – she felt she should help her friend, but on the other hand, it seemed like an age since she'd seen Ben. And she really ought to help her mum get the house straight. 'As long as you get word to me if you need help. Promise?' she asked, as Katie assured her she'd be able to cope alone.

Once her friends had set off for work and Lady Diana

had taken the children out for a walk, pushing the large pram which held both Daisy and Mary, Rose set to cleaning the house from top to bottom along with Flora and Joyce. Miss Tibbs polished the furniture in the living room.

'You shouldn't be doing this on the day before your wedding,' Flora said, feeling guilty. 'Why don't you go and have a relaxing bath, and then check that the dresses are all right? I had a dream that your gown was terribly creased and we couldn't get them out. I was following you down the aisle with my iron, would you believe.'

'Mum, I would believe that, as you're such a worrier,' Rose chuckled. 'I will go and have that bath, if you don't mind. I want to look my best for when Ben gets here this evening.'

'Then check those frocks for me, so at least I have some peace of mind. Can you ask Mildred to come in and help me move this settee against the wall? It will make more space for when everyone comes back here after the wedding reception.'

'She popped out for an hour,' Joyce said as she looked up from where she was brushing down the heavy velvet curtains in the window. After much discussion the night before, Joyce had convinced Mildred to visit the police station and have a chat about their concerns. As she explained to Mildred, if the police thought she was worrying over nothing then they'd not lost anything – but if they did think they had cause for concern, it would help if anything happened. 'I'll help you move the settee. We can do it between the three of us.'

Rose enjoyed a soak in the bath, although she was wary of using too much hot water. Just to lie and think of nothing for a while was restful. Climbing out as the water cooled, she scrubbed herself dry and borrowed her mum's dressing gown, rushing into the bedroom, where she thought to put on the one-bar electric heater so she wouldn't freeze while she dressed. Mindful of what Flora had requested, she opened the larger wardrobe and carefully lifted out the beautiful gown lent by Lady Diana. The heavy skirt of the dress hung without a single crease, which made her smile. There were also two matching pale blue crêpe de chine dresses that Miss Tibbs had lovingly made for Lily and Katie, with Lady Diana donating pretty pink dresses for her two granddaughters and Pearl. Giving a deep sigh of happiness, Rose carefully placed them all back and closed the door.

Towelling her hair dry, she brushed it until the curls bounced loosely around her shoulders before getting dressed and hurrying down to the kitchen to help prepare the special meal Flora had planned for her guests. There was already the aroma of roasting chicken in the kitchen, and checking the oven, she could see potatoes browning in the pan. Miss Tibbs had chopped cabbage and sliced carrots, and Rose knew that in the pantry sat a large sherry trifle and a Dundee cake donated by Lady Diana. It was a feast fit for a king, and all to celebrate her marriage to Ben the following day. A thrill ran through Rose as she thought of how soon she would be Ben's wife.

A knock on the door had her hurrying to answer in case Ben had arrived early. However, it was a delivery lad with a gift of three bottles of sherry and a box of chocolates. 'Sent with thanks for last night's show' was all that was written on the card. They would be perfect for after dinner,

Rose thought. As she left them in the living room for later, Mildred came in the front door and gave her a weak smile. 'You look tired,' Rose said. 'Have you been working today?'

'No, I just had to run a few errands. Can you let Joyce know I'm back, and I'll be in my room getting dressed for our meal?' she said, hurrying past Rose without stopping to chat.

Rose shrugged her shoulders and went to find her mum to see if she could help with anything.

'We are just about done here, love. If you could put the kettle on, I reckon everyone would like a nice cup of tea, don't you? Then we can relax until everyone arrives for the meal.'

Rose returned to the kitchen and switched on the wireless. Carols were being broadcast from one of the London churches. As she made the tea and pottered about she joined in with 'Silent Night', her clear voice reaching the high notes along with the choristers. As the carol finished she heard a sound behind her and spun round to see Ben standing there, holding a bouquet of roses and carnations.

'Flowers for the beautiful bride,' he said before setting them down and opening his arms for her to join him, which she did without a second bidding. He quickly sought her lips, his kisses making her feel giddy until she broke free. They could hear footsteps and excited chatter from the children, and suddenly the kitchen was full of people talking non-stop. 'At least we had a few moments together,' he whispered before greeting his mother and daughters.

Distributing slices of the cake and cups of tea while helping Flora finish dinner preparations, Rose found the afternoon had run away with them as darkness fell. Ruth arrived at the same time as Lily and Katie, and the extended family was soon sitting down to the special meal.

'Is this our Christmas dinner?' Annabelle asked, spooning trifle into her mouth.

'I suppose it is, dear, as we are having other celebrations tomorrow,' Lady Diana said as she wiped the child's face with a napkin.

'Does that mean we have presents today, then?'

The adults laughed at her cunning, and her expression when told that Father Christmas would still be arriving in the morning if she was good. 'So you had best go to sleep straight away when you go up to bed,' Lady Diana said, 'or he will fly straight past Sea View and there won't be any presents.'

After the meal Joyce, Miss Tibbs and Mildred ushered everyone into the living room while they washed up, then joined the family. The fire was burning brightly in the grate, and lamps had been lit. Flora opened the sherry and poured out glasses for everyone apart from the children, who were given a chocolate apiece before retiring to their beds.

The warmth and the alcohol soon had everyone feeling sleepy, with many of them dropping off in their seats. Rose saw her mum leave the room and remembered they'd promised to put a carrot by the hearth for Father Christmas's reindeer – and Pearl had yet to post her letter up the chimney. She followed Flora into the hall. After that, when she replayed the evening in her mind, she could remember almost nothing more . . .

*

'Mum, we must have been floating out here for hours,' Rose said as she started to shiver again. 'Come below deck and let's try to warm ourselves.'

'I thought I saw something on the water, but I must have been mistaken,' Flora said, following Rose below deck. 'Gosh it's dark down here.' She held her arms out in front of her to feel the way. 'Where are you?'

'I'm over here. Follow the sound of my voice. I've found some overalls and Mildred's old oilskin jacket. We can snuggle down in them until daylight, then see if we can try to alert someone by waving.'

Flora wasn't so sure that would work – but, chilled to the bone, she knew she would need to warm herself up, otherwise she could die of exposure. If it had just gone midnight, they could be aboard the boat for another six hours at least before the dawn light.

Cuddling together closely, they wrapped the overalls around them and then put the jacket over their shoulders. 'I never thought I'd be so pleased to find Mildred's fishy-smelling jacket,' Rose said between chattering teeth.

'Shh, try to get some sleep,' Flora said, holding her daughter as close as she could.

'Mum, I've been thinking. Everyone back at Sea View seemed pretty groggy. Do you think there was something in that sherry that was delivered this afternoon?'

'I was wondering the same, as I have a strange taste in my mouth. I hope everyone is all right back home.'

The gentle bobbing of the boat sent them drifting off to sleep for a while until something knocked on the side of the boat, causing them to wake suddenly. 'What was that?' Rose whispered, sitting up and trying to listen.

'Something's coming alongside the boat. Could it be the people who kidnapped us?' Flora said, sounding scared.

'They may have a torch and look for us. Let's hide behind the steps, then jump on them when they come down. You never know, we may be able to pinch their boat and escape.'

As quietly as they could, they felt their way back to the steps and huddled down. Hardly daring to breathe, they waited. Soon, footsteps could be heard climbing aboard, along with men's muffled voices.

'Two men – we'll never overpower them,' Flora whispered, discouraged.

'Now!' hissed Rose, ignoring her mum's words. They both threw themselves at the men and fought as best they could, until they found themselves pinned to the deck.

'What the hell's all this noise?' a familiar voice said as light flooded the scene.

'Rose? Flora?'

Both women were released, and as they shielded their eyes from the light they recognized Ben and John, with Mildred shining the torch at them from the steps. Rose threw herself at Ben as John put his arm around a shaking Flora.

'Thank God we found you,' Ben said as the men helped them to their feet. 'Mildred, can you get us back to shore?'

'There's a chain around the wheelhouse. Whoever kidnapped us chained it up to stop us escaping,' Flora explained.

'I've been keeping the wheelhouse secure in case of invasion. Unfortunately, what with all that's been going on, I was in a rush this morning and left the key in the padlock. You can blame me for them bringing the boat outside the harbour and leaving you to the mercy of the sea,' Mildred apologized. 'However, I keep a spare on my bunch of keys,' she explained as she quickly released the chain. She soon started the engine as the men helped Flora and Rose up on deck.

'What happened – how did you know where to find us?' Rose asked as Ben put his army greatcoat around her shoulders.

'It was Mildred who discovered Eileen was out to get Sea View from you. She and Gerald planned to bump you off and claim the house for themselves. But then you scuppered their plans by having signed the house over to your mum,' Ben explained.

'I don't understand. How did they know about me, and the house, and the wedding . . . ?' Rose shook her head in frustration.

Mildred pointed the boat towards the harbour and took over the conversation. 'It was Ben and John who got the truth out of them even before the coppers took the pair away,' she said, looking to Ben, who nodded to her to continue. 'Eileen isn't your relative. She's the daughter of Diana's ne'er-do-well sister, the one who became estranged from her family after being in prison. Eileen is Ben and Ruth's cousin, Beatrice, and a nasty bit of work she is too.'

Flora looked confused. 'How did she know about the General having another daughter? We aren't ones to wash our dirty linen in public,' she said.

'I'm inclined to agree with Mum,' Rose said.

'My love, in our circles everyone knew the General, his wife and his other daughter. And then it was the advertisement in *The Times* about our engagement that revealed your existence too, and she started poking about in your business,' Ben said. 'It didn't take much to find out you lived with your mum in a big house, and there could be money to be had. They are professional thieves. With a sniff of money, both from my family and yours, their greed would have known no bounds. Add to that a jealousy they held for Mother doing so well in life, and nothing would have stopped them getting what they were after.'

Mildred took over. 'When they found out your mother lived in a big house, they assumed General Sykes had left you the property. So Beatrice pretended to be your half-sister Eileen, hoping to claim her share of the inheritance as the eldest child of the General. Flora owning the house put paid to that idea. When she and Gerald decided to try to kill you, they stole your will from the safe at the teashop. They then drew up a forged version and put it in Sea View while we were at the concert,' Mildred said, going on to describe how she'd found an open window on the night of the concert and quietly started to go through the house to see if there was anything untoward. 'I hope you don't mind, but I found Rose's will in your dressing-table drawer, Flora. That forged version leaves everything to Eileen and Gerald.'

Flora waved away Mildred's apology. 'But what made you suspect them?'

'Remember how I brought all Rose's personal paperwork home with me after the teashop was burgled? It had been on my mind that it looked as though it had all been rifled through. It stood to reason something had to be missing.

I kept going over everything in my mind, thinking about what anyone would store away in case of enemy action. It hit me one day when my own solicitor wrote to ask me to visit his office over a business matter. The last time I'd seen him had been to amend my will and the deeds to Captain's Cottage. I then realized that Rose's will would have been with her other personal effects.'

'And you knew that I'd still to transfer the deeds to Sea View over to Mum, as you'd reminded me a while back to get everything up to date in case . . . in case anything happened to me. It meant a special visit to the bank in Canterbury to get the papers from our safe deposit box, so in the meantime I'd updated my will, as our solicitor had an office in town.'

'The crafty pair,' Flora declared. 'I could never be a criminal. I wouldn't have the intelligence to work out how to do such things.'

John took over the conversation. 'I arrived late and when I was driving past the harbour, I spotted Mildred's boat heading out. Even in the blackout I could tell it was hers. I wondered why she was going fishing so late on Christmas Eve, when we had a wedding the next day. When I reached Sea View there were police out the front of the house – and also Mildred. '

'After discovering the fake will, my suspicions were confirmed and I spoke to the coppers this afternoon,' Mildred said. 'They told me to contact them at once if anything should happen, and in the meantime they started checking out your so-called relatives.'

'All hell let loose when we came to hours later, and found the pair of you missing. Mildred knew at once that it must have been Eileen and Gerald behind it all,' Ben said as he took Rose's now shaking hands and squeezed them tight.

'You mean . . . ?'

'They'd put something in the sherry and chocolate,' he said. 'Those were not a gift from your adoring fans.'

'I wanted to wake up some of the boat owners and go after them, but the police said to wait and watch,' Mildred added. 'It was a long wait, I can tell you. We were waiting for Gerald and Eileen when they rowed themselves back into the harbour. They could see straight away there was no escape once they spotted the police. Eileen was in a pretty bad state what with her being seasick, so in a way it was an easy cop,' she grinned.

'We asked to row out to you ourselves rather than wait for the police boat to get here from Margate,' John said as he put his arm around Flora's shoulders.

'I'm glad you did,' Flora replied. 'It will take a while for me to understand all that has happened, but I'm so grateful you came to rescue us.'

'I just want to get home, have a bath, fall into my bed and sleep for a week,' Rose sighed.

Ben laughed before gently kissing her lips. 'I hope you don't mean that, as in a few hours' time I will be nervously waiting for you to walk down the aisle towards me.'

'Oh my gosh, however could I have forgotten our wedding?' Rose said before giving a big yawn. 'Don't worry – I'll be there. Happy wedding day, my darling.'

18

'I have to say, there was a time I thought we'd never see this wedding happen,' Flora said as she stepped back to take in the sight of Rose in her wedding gown after checking the veil was straight.

Rose ran her hands over the full skirts. 'I still feel as though the floor is moving beneath my feet – and I've always thought myself to have sturdy sea legs.'

'I've never been so pleased to see the pair of you. It was hell waiting at Sea View for news. Katie and Jennie must have run back and forth to the harbour for hours trying to see if anything was happening,' Lily said.

'I've got blisters on my heels, as I had my best shoes on and never thought to change into my work ones,' Katie added from where she was sitting on the wall beside the church door.

'Well, you look pretty happy for someone in pain,' Lily said as she joined her.

'That's because I've received a letter from Jack. Mildred found it on the doormat when she popped over to Captain's Cottage this morning to collect the extra cups and saucers Flora asked for. It must have come yesterday.'

'And?'

'What is said between a husband and wife is private, Lily Douglas, but I will tell you that he is all right, and he misses me. He sends his love to you all,' she said to the group of women.

'That is a relief, after all that has happened,' Flora sighed. 'At least we know Jack and Henio are safe. And with Eileen and Gerald being carted back to London to answer to other crimes, we can have a peaceful Christmas.'

'Make the most of it, my dear,' Diana said as she checked her face in a gold compact before snapping it closed. 'There was someone in the audience I'd invited down from London. It seems you and I are in demand to entertain the troops, Flora. Our double act went down a storm.'

'Oh, I don't know about that,' Flora said as the girls all cheered, causing Reverend Dunlop to pop his head out of the door to see what the commotion was all about before begging them to be quiet, as they could be heard inside the church. 'I'm much too old for such things.'

'I wouldn't say that,' John said from behind the vicar. 'From where I was watching, you can kick your legs up with the best of them.'

The girls giggled as Flora's cheeks turned pink. 'This is not the place to talk about such things,' she said, shushing the littler bridesmaids. 'Is it time?' she asked the vicar.

He nodded. 'If you would escort Mrs Neville and Lady Diana to their seats, we just need Mr Grant to walk you down the aisle and you will soon be a married woman,' he said to Rose. 'Now, where is he?'

The women turned to where Mr Grant was smoking

369

a cigarette on the pavement outside the church gates and talking to someone in an RAF uniform. Lily stood up, giving a big sigh of joy. 'Flora, Rose – would it be all right if we invited another guest?'

'It's the pilot who was up the tree in Lily's garden,' young Pearl said excitedly to Annabelle and Marina.

'Go tell him,' Flora said. 'Anyone who can put a smile like that on your face is more than welcome in our house.'

'I agree,' Rose said. 'But please tell them to hurry, as I really do want to get married before anything else happens.'

As Rose never stopped saying for the rest of that day, it was the perfect wedding. The most handsome man in the world was waiting for her as she walked down the aisle on the arm of Mr Grant. In what seemed only a matter of seconds, she took her husband's arm and it felt as if they floated on air out of the church as man and wife.

'My goodness, it's like confetti,' she exclaimed as she held out her hand to the gentle snowflakes falling from the sky.

'I ordered it specially for you,' Ben said as he swept his bride into his arms and kissed her gently. 'Happy Christmas, Mrs Hargreaves.'

Acknowledgements

My thanks must first go to the fabulous team at Pan Macmillan, who are there not only to turn my words into beautiful books but are just an email or telephone call away when I need to ask a question or be reassured about something that has cropped up. Thank you all.

To Bethan and her colleagues at ED PR Ltd for letting the world know I have a new book on the horizon. You do a fabulous job!

Thank you to my lovely literary agent, Caroline Sheldon. You calm me down and are always there in my corner. My moans and queries are always dealt with professionally and with kindness. I'm eternally grateful to have you in my life.

A very big thank you once again to Annie Aldington, who does such a splendid job narrating my books. It is always a joy to listen to Annie reading my stories, even though I know the ending!

Thank you also to Charlotte Duckworth, who has designed, built and maintains my website elaineeverest. com. Charlotte, you have the patience of a saint and do a wonderful job turning my ideas into beautiful pages.

Technology can be so confusing. Everyone should have a Charlotte in their life.

Where would I be without our great libraries? From the lovely librarians who invite me along to chat about my books, to the archive department of Bexley Library, who are able to help with items of local interest that bring my stories alive. You have all been wonderful – thank you.

How about a cup of tea? In Ramsgate, the main setting for the Teashop Girls series, there are so many places of interest connected to my books. The Ramsgate Tunnels, where Flora and the residents of Sea View take shelter, the harbour where Mildred keeps her fishing boat, and of course the site of the 'real' Lyons teashop. However, a trip to Ramsgate would not be complete without a visit to the Home Front Tea Room in King Street to experience what life was like back in the 1940s.

Finally, a big thank you to my husband, Michael. Living with an author whose head is firmly stuck in the 1940s must be difficult at times. For readers who come along to my talks, you will find him being the bookseller giving me time to chat to readers. Thank you also for the lovely flowers on publication day, and being there to cheer me on when I'm unsure of the plot or have lost all confidence to write another book.

A Letter from Elaine

Dear Reader,

The time has flown since my last letter to you and so much has happened. I've been lucky to meet some of you while at signing events and talks and it has been a joy to chat about Woolies, teashops and holiday camps. Some of you have taken trips to Thanet to visit places mentioned in the Teashop series and been kind enough to let me know about your adventures.

Recently, a reader suggested I also run a trip around Erith pointing out the settings for the Woolworths series. Perhaps it is time I purchased a tour bus and we did it in style?

By the time you read this book we will have commemorated the anniversary of the evacuation of Dunkirk at the end of May. Eighty years have passed and still we hold those brave owners of the Little Ships in our hearts. We owe so much to the people of Great Britain for laying their lives on the line for our country during those dark days of the Second World War. We should never forget.

As I write these words, we are in the fourth week of lockdown due to the Covid-19 virus. I pray that when you read this we are back to our normal way of life and your loved ones are safe and well. I do feel that having to follow our Government's guidelines and changing our lifestyle means we have experienced just a little of what our families must have gone through during the war, albeit without bombs and warfare, wondering what each day would bring and if they'd ever see their families again.

Missing the freedom to go where we please, and do as we please, will have been hard for many, but hopefully now we are looking forward to a healthy future.

Do you like to chat? Why not pop along to my 'Elaine Everest Author' page on Facebook, where we often put the world to rights and share a moan or two. I now have a shiny new website where you can read my blog posts, look at the latest book news, and sign up for my newsletter. I will be having special competitions in the newsletter so why not sign up for it by leaving your email address on my website? The address is www.elaineeverest.com. You can also find me on Twitter and Instagram.

I do hope you have enjoyed *Christmas with the Teashop Girls*. Please do let me know your thoughts about the girls from Thanet.

With love and best wishes,

Elaine xxx

The Teashop Girls

~

Three friends, two secrets and a war that will change everything . . .

It is early 1940 and the Second World War is starting to take a hold on the country. Rose Neville works as a Lyons teashop Nippy on the Kent coast alongside her childhood friends, the ambitious Lily and Katie, whose fiancé is about to be posted overseas in the navy. As war creates havoc in Europe, Rose relies on the close friendship of her friends and family.

When Captain Benjamin Hargreaves enters her life, Rose is immediately drawn to him. But as doubts and family secrets cloud her thoughts, she tries to put the handsome officer out of her mind.

In increasingly dark and dangerous times, Rose wonders what her future holds . . .